THE
HUNTERS

ALSO BY TOM YOUNG

FICTION

The Mullah's Storm

Silent Enemy

The Renegades

The Warriors

Sand and Fire

NONFICTION

The Speed of Heat:
An Airlift Wing at War in Iraq and Afghanistan

THE
HUNTERS

TOM YOUNG

G. P. PUTNAM'S SONS | NEW YORK

PUTNAM

G. P. Putnam's Sons
Publishers Since 1838
An imprint of Penguin Random House LLC
375 Hudson Street
New York, New York 10014

Library of Congress Cataloging-in-Publication Data

Young, Thomas W., date.
The hunters / Tom Young.
p.   cm.
ISBN 978-0-399-16689-1
I. Title.
PS3625.O97335H86   2015   2015007428
813'.6—dc23

Printed in the United States of America
1   3   5   7   9   10   8   6   4   2

Book design by Gretchen Achilles

For Kristen

THE
HUNTERS

1.

Hunger. Rage.

Fourteen-year-old Hussein felt little else as he rode in the back of a Nissan pickup truck along a dirt road south of Mogadishu. Five fellow al-Shabaab fighters traveled with him in the truck bed. One manned a Kord 12.7-millimeter machine gun bolted near the tailgate, and the rest brandished AK-47s. Hussein's entire worldly possessions consisted of his AK, his sandals, a dirty cotton shirt and trousers, and the machete hanging from a rope belt in a leather sheath.

For a promised piece of fruit every day, Hussein had become a soldier of God. The older men had yet to give him his daily tangerine; rewards would come later if he and his brothers in jihad performed this mission well. Along with the fruit, he hoped to get a bowl of onion and potato soup. Just like yesterday and the day before that.

His mouth still watered when he remembered that day last week when the men fed him fried goat meat. Such feasts came rarely for the young soldiers of God. Al-Shabaab, or "The Youth," faced many hardships inflicted by the infidels. These *gaalos*, the unbelieving foreigners, brought hunger, the death of parents and friends, and so-called medicine that only made diseases worse.

But today, the unbelievers would feel God's wrath.

The truck slowed and stopped at a crossroads. Dust kicked up by the Nissan's tires rolled in clouds and stung Hussein's eyes. Thorn scrub littered the dunes that stretched from the crossroads to the beach. Beyond the beach, the Indian Ocean sparkled blue to the horizon. Seagulls wheeled over the surf.

The new boss got out of the passenger side of the pickup. Hussein knew him only as "the Sheikh," a man who spoke of many things Hussein did not understand. But the Sheikh led the struggle now, and God gave him his words just as the angels had bidden Mohammed to recite the holy book.

"Out of the truck, my pups," the Sheikh said.

Hussein and four of his comrades scrambled over the tailgate and hopped to the ground. One stayed behind to man the machine gun. The driver got out of the truck and stood beside the Sheikh. Hussein knew the driver as Abdullahi. Abdullahi would beat you for laziness or for grabbing at food. He wore a black kerchief around his head and neck, which left only his eyes visible. The Sheikh wore plain clothes like Hussein, and mirrored sunglasses.

Another al-Shabaab truck arrived, carrying only the driver. The driver remained inside and kept the engine idling.

"A nest of vipers has installed itself in Mogadishu," the Sheikh said. He gestured with his right hand, index finger extended, as he often did during his sermons. "They dare to call themselves a legitimate government, with their sham elections and unclean money from the Americans and the British and the United Nations. The only legitimate government is that of God, of the Islamic Emirate of Somalia."

At the mention of the Islamic emirate, the fighters cheered. Hussein cheered with them, raised his weapon high into the air.

"At any moment," the Sheikh continued, "a vehicle will come this way. It will probably be from Mogadishu. We will stop the vehicle and give the occupants a test. If they pass the test, they may proceed on their way. If they fail, you will administer God's justice. We will stand firm here at this crossroads and test the fidelity of travelers for the rest of the day."

Hussein did not know all of these words. He did not know *administer* or *occupant*. For that matter, he did not know what *emirate* meant. But he knew his duty, and he would carry it out with righteous conviction.

As the Sheikh predicted, in a few minutes a car approached. Two men rode in a Mazda with a dragging tailpipe and rusted-out fenders. As the Mazda neared the gun truck, the other truck pulled across the road behind the car and blocked escape back toward Mogadishu. The boy manning the machine gun fired a burst over the car. The three rapid-fire shots sounded like hammer blows, and the heavy brass casings clanged onto the truck bed as if someone had dropped three wrenches.

"Halt!" the Sheikh shouted, needlessly. The Mazda had already skidded to a stop. The driver and passenger sat frozen. Both looked like men in their thirties. Neither wore a beard.

"Out of the car," the Sheikh ordered.

Slowly, the driver opened his door. Not fast enough for Abdullahi. Abdullahi tore open the car door, grabbed the driver by the shirt, and slammed him against the hood of the car. Another of the al-Shabaab fighters yanked out the passenger.

Hussein trembled with anticipation. These looked like *kafirs*, those who denied God's truth. *Kafir* was a new word for Hussein, one the al-Shabaab men had taught him. *Kafirs* lurked all around, and they deserved no mercy. Hussein would show none.

He would not hesitate to carry out al-Shabaab's bidding. In its ranks he had found belonging and importance. No longer rabble of the streets, now he was a man of weapons. God rewarded his ferocity with tangerines and plums.

Already the *kafirs* begged for their lives.

"Brothers, brothers, who are you?" the passenger asked. "We have done nothing to you."

"We have only a little money," the driver cried. "You can take it. Just let us go."

Abdullahi slapped the driver.

"You came from the direction of Mogadishu," the Sheikh said. "What were you doing there?"

Hussein had seen the Sheikh do this before—toy with his victims the way a cat plays with a mouse. The question made both travelers look even more frightened. The driver glanced at his passenger, then turned to the Sheikh with pleading eyes.

"We are fishermen," the driver said. "We have been repairing our boat."

They didn't look like fishermen. They wore the shirts and slacks of the *gaalos*, and leather shoes instead of sandals.

Abdullahi slapped the man again.

"You lie," Abdullahi said. "You have repaired nothing in these clean clothes. You have worked in the offices of the infidel, stealing from the people."

"No, no," the driver said. "We are good Muslims, just like you, brother."

"We shall see if you are faithful," the Sheikh said. "Tell me of the Prophet's Night Journey, exactly as the Quran tells it."

"What, brother?" the driver asked. "I do not understand."

"Because I am generous and kind," the Sheikh said, "I will give you a hint. Recite for me Surah Seventeen."

"Recite?" the passenger asked. "What?"

"Recite for us," Abdullahi said through gritted teeth, "Surah Seventeen."

"What is this madness?" the driver asked.

The travelers did not know the section of the Quran the Sheikh wanted to hear. Hussein did not know it, either, because he could not read. Nor could most of the al-Shabaab fighters. This did not trouble Hussein. Hunger left little space in his mind for irony.

"Then I will tell you," the Sheikh said. He began to recite from memory.

> *Glory to Allah, who did take His Servant*
> *For a journey by night from the Sacred Mosque to the Farthest*
>   *Mosque,*
> *Whose precincts we did bless—*

In order that we might show him some of our signs: for He is the One Who heareth and seeth all things.

The two *kafirs* must have figured out what lay in store. The driver began to weep. The passenger blubbered, "We have always been good Muslims. I have even made the Hajj."

"You dare to brag of your pilgrimage to Mecca?" Abdullahi said. "That makes your sins all the worse."

The Sheikh stepped back from the men's car. He raised one arm above his head and barked an order:

"Give them justice."

Hussein slung his AK across his shoulder and unsheathed his machete.

2.

In the pilot's seat of an ancient twin-engine DC-3 cargo plane, Michael Parson felt the aircraft yaw. One of the engines had quit. Instinctively, he pressed the left rudder pedal to keep the nose on heading. With his left boot feeding in rudder pressure and his right boot flat on the floor, he knew the right engine was the one that had failed. Dead foot, dead engine. Parson swore under his breath, then called to his copilot.

"Damn it, Frenchie, we got a problem. Feather number two for me, will you?"

"Merde," the copilot said. "I'm on it."

Copilot Alain Chartier usually flew much newer and faster airplanes with the French Armée de l'Air. Parson, a U.S. Air Force colonel, had met Chartier a year ago during a joint counterterrorist operation in North Africa. French Mirage jets, along with American aircraft and U.S. Marines, had put a hurting on some very bad people who attacked civilians with chemical weapons.

Today, at eighty-five hundred feet over Somalia, Parson and Chartier flew as civilians. Both had taken leave from their military jobs to volunteer for a few weeks as pilots for World Relief Airlift. They wore military-style desert flight suits with WRA patches on their right sleeves. On Parson's left sleeve he wore a U.S. flag, while Chartier wore the *drapeau tricolore* of France. Parson had plunked down eighteen thousand dollars of his own money to get a DC-3 type rating—so he could fly a seventy-five-year-old unpressurized airplane over hellholes in the Horn of Africa. He'd done it because he loved to fly. And because he'd do anything for Sophia Gold.

"Can't believe the things I do to spend time with Sophia," Parson muttered.

Engine failure hardly came as a surprise in an airplane this old, and it didn't frighten him. As an experienced military aviator, Parson had seen far worse. Even if the second engine failed, the DC-3 would just become a big glider, and Parson could dead-stick to a survivable touchdown on the flat plain below. Just hold her at the pitch angle to get maximum lift over drag and let her settle to the ground.

The airplane's third crew member was a Somali American flight mechanic who looked as thin as the struts on a Piper Cub. He wore two flags on his left sleeve: the Stars and Stripes on top, and underneath, the banner of Somalia—a field of light blue with a single white star in the middle. His nametag read GEEDI MURSAL, FLT MECH, WORLD RELIEF AIRLIFT. He had just started working full-time for WRA after spending six years as a jet engine mechanic in the U.S. Air Force. Parson had known Geedi for about a month and had flown with him three times: not enough to know him well, but enough to know he was dependable.

"I'll go scan number two," Geedi said.

"Thanks, Geedi," Parson said.

Geedi unbuckled his jump seat harness. He kept on his headset; his interphone cord stretched long enough to keep in contact with the pilots as he disappeared into the cargo compartment.

Parson pushed the left prop lever to set a higher RPM, and he added power with the left throttle. Chartier placed his thumb and forefinger on the knob for the right engine's mixture lever.

"Confirm number two," Chartier said.

"Confirm," Parson said, after looking to make sure Chartier hadn't chosen the wrong control.

Chartier pulled the mixture lever to idle cutoff. He reached overhead and put a finger on the feathering button for the right engine.

"Confirm two," he said.

"Confirm," Parson responded.

Chartier pressed the button, and the right propeller stopped wind-milling. As its blade angle changed, the prop slowed down until it stood motionless in the slipstream.

"Number two standing tall," Geedi called from the back.

"Thanks, Geedi," Parson said. "See anything on that cowling?"

"Leaking some oil."

That told Parson little. If those old Pratt & Whitney radials weren't leaking oil, it meant they didn't have any oil. Some DC-3s had been upgraded with turboprop engines, but this one staggered through the skies on Depression-era technology.

"Everything still tied down good back there?" Parson asked.

"I'm checking now," Geedi said.

"Good man."

The cargo compartment contained pallets of food. One pallet held several hundred pounds of Humanitarian Daily Rations, much like military MREs. Another consisted of hundred-pound bags of rice. Yet another pallet held boxes of cooking oil and bags of flour and beans. Charitable organizations had donated these relief supplies for Somalis returning home from Kenyan refugee camps.

From the start of the civil war in 1991, Somalis had fled their homeland by the thousands. For more than two decades, Somalia had no real central government. Armed clans and Islamic militants ran riot, and Somali pirates threatened maritime shipping. Now, at least, Somalia had a president and a parliament, but the country remained impoverished, unstable, and dangerous.

Adding to the chaos, neighboring Kenya had decided it could no longer host the world's largest refugee camp. The Dadaab camp complex had housed nearly half a million refugees. Now they were heading home, usually on foot, across miles of dust-blown wasteland and thickets prowled by lions and hyenas.

Economic pressures played a role in Kenya's decision, but so did politics. In a 2013 attack on the Westgate shopping mall in Nairobi, terrorists from the Somali Islamist group al-Shabaab killed dozens of people. In 2014, al-Shabaab stopped a bus in northern Kenya, separated Muslim passengers from non-Muslims, and murdered twenty-eight. The terrorists said the attacks were retribution for Kenyan military deployment in Somalia. Now Kenyan leaders wanted to wash their hands of the problems next door.

Cash-strapped governments elsewhere offered little assistance. Bad memories of the 1993 Battle of Mogadishu left American leaders reluctant to commit troops to the region. Many politicians couldn't find Somalia on a map, but all of them knew about the films *Black Hawk Down* and *Captain Phillips*.

If help was coming from anywhere, it was from private donations. A few pallets at a time. In airplanes old enough for museums. Parson and his crew had picked up this load at the international airport in Djibouti. That's as close as some big cargo carriers wanted to get to Somalia. Supplies had to travel the rest of the way in rattletraps flown by pilots with more guts than sense. Over the past year, Parson had made two previous short trips as a volunteer pilot for World Relief Airlift, but this was Chartier's first flight with WRA. Geedi was WRA's only paid staffer on the crew.

Chartier ran through the emergency checklist for a single-engine landing. He turned off the bad engine's fuel valve. Closed the oil shutter. Turned off the failed engine's magnetos.

"Guess we better tell Baidoa we're limping our asses in on one engine," Parson said. Baidoa was Parson's original destination, and it was the closest airport with a fire department.

Chartier pressed his transmit switch mounted on the right yoke. "Baidoa Tower," he called, "World Relief Eight-Two Alpha with an emergency. Right engine failure."

The answer came back in accented but competent English: "World Relief Eight-Two Alpha, Baidoa Tower. We copy your emergency, will have equipment standing by. You are cleared for a straight-in visual approach, Runway Two-Two."

"Cleared for the visual to Two-Two," Chartier said. He released his transmit switch and said to Parson, "I am surprised they have any equipment to put on standby."

"We're lucky they even have a tower," Parson said, "but that guy sounds like he knows what he's doing."

Parson had landed this DC-3 on dirt strips in Somalia with no facilities beyond a wind sock. At least this time he had nearly ten thousand feet of pavement, and personnel to help with an emergency.

A dusty plateau of reddish soil and scattered vegetation stretched below. Acacia trees studded the terrain. The seedpods from acacias made good livestock fodder, and the blooms supported honeybees. But the acacias bristled with thorns. Everything about life came hard and painful in this part of the world.

Baidoa slid into view through the distant haze. Home to more than a hundred thousand, the city had suffered a tortured past. When militias blocked food shipments during a 1992 famine, Baidoa became known as the city of walking skeletons. Starvation killed up to sixty people a day. Aid groups and UN troops helped ease the famine the following year, but the city remained a battleground.

In 2006, the country's Transitional Federal Government attacked Islamists holed up in Baidoa. Somali government troops, aided by Ethiopian forces, routed Islamic Courts Union fighters. Two years later, another terrorist group, al-Shabaab, laid siege to the city, and Baidoa fell temporarily to the militants. Ethiopian and Somali troops eventually retook the city. Somalia's new government now controlled Baidoa—at least for the moment. But terrorists still fought to turn the entire country into an Islamist caliphate under sharia law.

Today, Parson just hoped Baidoa remained stable enough for him to land and get the engine fixed.

"All right," he said, "let's see if we can get this pig on the ground." He throttled back on his one good engine and began to descend.

The airport lay southwest of the city, and Parson approached from the north. The DC-3 glided above the rubble of blasted concrete and cinder-block buildings. Other structures showed glimpses of life within: clotheslines draped with bright fabrics, smoke from cooking fires.

"Mon Dieu," Chartier said, "That is a bleak-looking place. What if you always had to cook over a fire in this heat?"

The outside air-temp gauge read thirty degrees Celsius. Mental math told Parson that meant eighty-six degrees Fahrenheit. Not as hot as the Iraqi desert, which Parson knew well, but plenty warm in a place without the luxury of air-conditioning.

"At least they got something to cook," Parson said.

"Oui."

"Gimme one-quarter flaps, will you?"

Chartier reached down between the pilots' seats and pulled a lever until it clicked into a detent. Parson let some of the airspeed bleed off. The airspeed indicator, old enough to show miles per hour rather than knots, read 120. The luminescent paint on the needle had yellowed and cracked with age. Reminded Parson of the dashboard in an old hand-cranked car.

"Thanks, Frenchie," Parson said. "Put the gear down."

"Yes, sir."

Parson started to tell Chartier not to call him "sir." Their ranks held no relevance in World Relief Airlift. But Parson let the honorific stand. Military courtesy meant more than respect for those of higher ranks. *Sir* implied a respect for the overall institution, a regard for shared experiences, acknowledgment of an ordered brotherhood and sisterhood. Get a group of veterans together who've not worn a uniform in decades, and you'll still hear "sirs" and "ma'ams."

Chartier moved the landing gear lever, on the floor near the flap handle, from NEUTRAL to DOWN. The gear extended and locked, and Parson felt the increased drag slow the plane further. He shoved the throttle for a few more inches of manifold pressure to hold his airspeed.

Geedi returned to the cockpit and buckled into the jump seat.

"Cargo all secure, sir," he said.

"Good," Parson replied.

The tower called again. "World Relief Eight-Two Alpha, you are cleared to land, Two-Two. Altimeter setting three-zero-zero-one."

"Eight-Two Alpha cleared to land," Chartier answered. He dialed the new barometric pressure setting into both altimeters.

The altimeter needles swung through four thousand feet. Baidoa lay at a field elevation of eighteen hundred feet above sea level, so Parson knew he was roughly two thousand feet above the ground. The runway loomed straight ahead, centerline stripes faded nearly to invisibility. Parson saw no traffic on the taxiway, and only three aircraft parked on the ramp. He recognized an Ethiopian Airlines Dash 8 turboprop, along with a UN helicopter, and an Antonov An-24 from who knew where. Maybe bringing in the daily shipment of khat.

"I think we got the field made now," Parson said. "Full flaps."

Chartier moved the flap lever again, and Parson pitched for ninety-five miles per hour. With the power almost back to idle on the operating engine, the old bird floated smoothly down to the pavement. Parson had spent little time in tailwheel airplanes, but he managed a good landing.

For all Parson's grousing about the outdated aircraft, he loved returning to the cockpit. The responsibilities of a full-bird colonel had kept him on the ground for most of the last year. He took it easy on the brakes, let the DC-3 roll along and slow itself to walking speed. In the scrub brush off the runway, two derelict Hawkers lay in the dirt on collapsed landing gear. Artifacts of a defunct Somali air force, the old aircraft were subsonic fighter bombers built by the British in the 1950s.

Parson shook his head. What a sad end for once-magnificent jets. The sight added to the aura of decay and anarchy.

Near the end of the runway, Chartier unlocked the tailwheel. Parson tapped the right brake to begin a turn, and he goosed the left throttle ever so slightly. The plane handled a little differently on the ground with a dead engine, but Parson used differential braking to make up for the loss of differential power. He rolled onto the taxiway while Chartier cleaned up the after-landing checklist.

"Geedi, does any of this look familiar?" Parson asked.

"Not really. My family moved to Minneapolis when I was little."

Parson scanned the temperature gauges so he could watch the good engine cool down in idle before he shut it off. He kept the palm of his hand cupped over the engine's throttle.

"Who the hell are those guys?" Geedi asked, pointing out the windscreen.

"Oh, boy," Chartier said. "What a welcoming committee."

Parson looked up. Four Somali men walked toward the airplane, brandishing automatic weapons. Three of them carried AK-47s, but one wielded a PKM, a belt-fed machine gun. Bandoliers of ammunition dangled from his neck. The armed men strolled casually, and they wore civilian clothes and ratty tennis shoes.

Alarmed, Parson wished he could take off on one engine. But if these guys wanted him to stay on the ground, they could riddle the engine—or the cockpit—before he ever got airborne. Parson pulled the left mixture control to idle cutoff, and the propeller spun down to a stop. Without taking his eyes off the gunmen, Chartier reached overhead and turned off the magnetos.

Underneath his flight suit, in an elastic bellyband holster, Parson wore a Beretta nine millimeter. A lame defense against a PKM, but all he had. He unzipped the suit, drew the weapon, zipped his suit back up. Parson held the pistol low, below the cockpit windows, invisible to the gunmen on the ramp. Clicked off the safety.

"You're armed?" Geedi said. "We're not supposed to be armed."

"Neither are they," Parson said.

3.

Four armed men surrounded Parson's airplane. In one of the world's most lawless countries, he knew anything could happen next. What did happen was the last thing he expected. Sophia Gold came out of the terminal building. Or what passed for a terminal building, with its broken windows, peeling paint, and sagging electrical wires. She wore her ever-present green-and-black Afghan scarf, a green bush shirt, khaki tactical trousers, and desert combat boots. Given her choice of clothing and her straight-postured walk, even a civilian would have pegged her as ex-military. A former U.S. Army sergeant major, Gold now worked for the United Nations. Still, Parson was surprised to find her here. When he'd spoken to her on the phone yesterday, she was in Mogadishu.

Gold talked with the armed men, and she smiled as if greeting cousins. Chatted briefly with the PKM guy, put her hand on his arm for a moment. She looked up at the cockpit and waved to Parson. Parson waved back, still a little dumbstruck.

Parson put his weapon on safe and slid it back into his concealment holster. Wiped sweat from his nose with the sleeve of his flight suit. Now, on the ground in the Somali sun, the DC-3's aluminum hull turned into an oven.

Chartier had also drawn a pistol—the biggest stainless-steel revolver Parson had ever seen. The third big surprise in the space of about a minute.

"Damn, son," Parson said. "What the hell is that?"

"A Smith & Wesson .500 Magnum."

"You planning on shooting elephants or something?"

"If necessary," Chartier said, grinning. "As your southern Americans say, my *maman* didn't raise no clown."

Parson laughed. "You mean fool," he said. "Your mama didn't raise no fool."

"*Oui.* She didn't raise no fool."

"I agree, but put that thing away before we scare Sophia's friends."

"*D'accord.*"

Chartier stowed the big revolver in his flight bag. Geedi smiled and shook his head. Outside, Gold disappeared under the wing as she headed toward the door near the back of the DC-3.

"Well," Parson said, "let's not just sit here. Open the door and let the lady in the airplane."

"Yes, sir," Geedi said.

The flight mechanic unstrapped and headed aft. Parson heard him stepping around the cargo, and then the boarding door squeaked open. Now that Parson no longer worried about getting shot, he turned his thoughts to his other problem. He took off his headset, unbuckled his harness, and looked over at Chartier.

"I wonder why that engine failed," Parson said. "These Pratts are old, but they're usually pretty reliable."

"How much time have they flown since the last overhaul?"

"Less than forty hours."

Chartier shrugged. "Geedi will figure it out."

Parson didn't doubt that; he knew he had a good flight mechanic. He worried more about how long they'd stay stuck in this rat hole of an airport. Had the engine thrown a rod or cracked a piston? What if they had to wait until a newly rebuilt engine could be flown in?

Like any sensible flier, Parson carried an emergency overnight bag. But he didn't relish the idea of sleeping in the terminal on his bedroll. Better to get back to the Sheraton Djibouti Hotel, preferably before happy hour. Get cleaned up and sip an old-fashioned while looking out over the Red Sea. He flew pro bono for WRA, but at least they put him and his crew in decent quarters. Mama didn't raise no fool.

The sound of Gold's voice interrupted Parson's thoughts. She had climbed aboard, and Parson heard her exchanging pleasantries with Geedi. He turned to see her making her way through the cargo compartment toward the cockpit—an uphill walk in this big taildragger. She smiled when she saw him. Parson had last seen her two weeks ago in Djibouti; running into her today was a bonus.

"I see you guys made a dramatic entrance," Gold said. "What's wrong with the engine?"

"We don't know yet," Parson said. "What are you doing here? I thought you were in Mog."

Gold stepped into the cramped flight deck. Parson rose to greet her, but in the cramped cockpit, he managed to stand up only halfway. Gold embraced him and kissed the top of his head. Even in Somalia's heat and dust, she smelled of scented lotion.

"I was, but I had to come out here to arrange for more security guys," Gold said. "You saw them when you taxied in." Gold turned to Chartier, who remained sitting in the copilot's seat. "Hello, Captain Chartier. I'm delighted you could volunteer your time and talent." She took his outstretched hand.

"*Enchanté,*" Chartier said. "Call me Alain."

"Or Frenchie," Parson said. "He answers to that, too. And Froggy Bastard."

"We'll make it Alain," Gold said.

"You see?" Chartier said to Parson. "She does everything with class. Why can't you be more like her?"

Parson smiled. For him, or anyone, to be like Sophia Gold would amount to a tall order. He considered her the smartest—and toughest—person he knew, and Parson knew a lot of military badasses. He had first met her in the worst of circumstances. Years ago, she had boarded his C-130 Hercules at Bagram Air Base, Afghanistan. At the time, she served as an Army interpreter accompanying a high-value Taliban prisoner. Soon after takeoff, a shoulder-fired missile downed the Herk. After the crash, Parson and Gold endured a winter ordeal as they evaded capture and kept the Taliban mullah in custody.

They had shared many missions since then, most recently in North Africa to stop a terrorist group armed with chemical weapons. That's when they'd met Chartier.

Parson loved her dearly, though their relationship defied definition. No strings, but strong ties. Because Gold wanted to save the world, Parson had agreed to spend his military leave hauling relief supplies in an antique airplane.

And getting paid nothing—except time with her.

The humanitarian work did have another appeal: He'd gotten checked out on the DC-3, one of the classic machines of aviation history, and he could write off the expense as charity. He was even considering taking a longer break with a new sabbatical deal the Air Force offered. Under the Career Intermission Pilot Program, he could take off one to three years for charity work, a graduate degree, or whatever struck his fancy—then resume his military career.

"So who are those choirboys out there?" Parson asked. "You got the U.S. and French air forces working for you. Did you manage to recruit al-Shabaab, too?"

"Oh, no," Gold said. Her tone turned serious. "Don't even joke to those guys about that. They *hate* al-Shabaab, like a lot of Somalis."

"Sorry, no offense."

"It's okay. Actually, they're private security. And al-Shabaab is the reason the UN hired them."

"How's that?" Parson asked.

"With all the refugees coming home, Somalia's government wants to show it can handle the situation. Al-Shabaab wants to prove the government can't."

"Bastards," Chartier said.

Parson considered the implications. The terrorists might try anything. Interrupting food shipments—a tried-and-true tactic in Somalia. Attacking government facilities. Assaulting civilian crowds. The African Union Mission in Somalia—AMISOM—provided troops to fight al-Shabaab, but the terrorists remained active and dangerous.

And here we are in the middle of it, Parson thought. With a geriatric airplane and two pistols. Perfect.

He didn't blame Gold for getting him into a risky situation. After decades of anarchy, piracy, civil war, and Black Hawks going down, he hadn't expected a trouble-free Somalia. If Parson had wanted to spend his leave doing something easy, he'd have gone fishing. But he liked to keep moving, to keep facing challenges. Though he loved the solitude of water and woods, those quiet moments gave him too much time to think, invited painful memories.

Clanging noises came from the cargo compartment. Parson glanced back. Geedi was removing cargo straps from an aluminum ladder. The flight mechanic needed the ladder to inspect the bad engine.

"Lemme help you with that, Geedi," Parson called.

"Thanks, sir."

"I see you met our flight mechanic," Chartier said to Gold. "He comes from the Somali American community in Minneapolis."

"He's a good dude," Parson said. "Knows his shit. But I better give him a hand with that ladder before it falls on his skinny ass."

Parson went aft and helped Geedi lift the ladder that had been strapped to the floor. They slid it halfway out the boarding door, and Parson jumped down from the aircraft. He took the ladder by its base, and he and Geedi moved it out of the DC-3 and set it up under the right engine.

Black droplets of leaking oil already spattered the dusty pavement beneath the engine, but that was normal. Geedi climbed the ladder. He wore a Leatherman multi-tool in a sheath attached to the waist strap of his flight suit. The flight mechanic took out the Leatherman, opened a screwdriver blade, and began turning the Dzus fasteners that pinned the cowling panels in place. He worked with a practiced hand, popping open each fastener with a quick leftward flick of his wrist.

Gold and Chartier emerged from the airplane and headed toward the terminal.

"I'll get some people to unload your cargo," Gold called.

"Thanks, Sophia," Parson answered. "Just make sure they don't take our oil and stuff." In addition to the relief supplies, the DC-3's cargo compartment also contained cartons of oil and hydraulic fluid, a spare tire, jacks, spark plugs, and other items Geedi used to maintain the old airplane.

"Will do," Gold said.

Parson waited underneath the wing to see what Geedi might find. He unzipped a chest pocket on his flight suit, took out his aviator sunglasses, and put them on. While Geedi examined the engine, Parson folded his arms and admired the DC-3's lines.

The old girl had style, no doubt about that. The sweep of the wings' leading edges, the rounded nose, the twist of the three-bladed props hinted of 1930s art deco. Built originally as a twin-engine airliner, by modern standards she was small for a passenger plane: She'd have carried twenty-one people. The plush seats had been removed long ago to make way for cargo. A decal on one of the blades read HAMILTON STANDARD PROPELLERS. Reliable enough to survive decades of constant flying, she was a tough plane designed to handle tough conditions and do it with class.

Geedi removed a panel and handed it down to Parson. Parson placed the sheet of aluminum on the tarmac beside the ladder. The flight mechanic dug into one of his leg pockets and produced a mini-flashlight. He shone the light into the engine and looked around.

"See anything?" Parson asked.

"Not really. No obvious damage, anyway."

"Hmm," Parson said. Though he'd experienced most of the problems that caused turboprop and turbojet engines to fail, he had logged little flight time on radial piston engines. Didn't know where to start speculating about the source of the problem. That's why he flew with a flight mechanic.

"Sir," Geedi said, "you don't have to stay out here. This might take a while. You can go inside if you want."

"Thanks, Geedi," Parson said. "Just let me know if you need anything."

"Yes, sir."

Inside, Parson found more activity than he'd expected. About forty people milled about in a room the size of a basketball court. No ticket counters or baggage carousels, just wooden benches along the walls. At an unpainted rough-hewn table, a woman stirred a pot that rested on a grate above a can of burning Sterno. Steam rose from the pot. The smell of something edible filled the air; Parson could not identify the food. Four men stood around Gold as she addressed them in Arabic while Chartier looked on.

"*Hassalan,*" one of the men responded. Parson didn't know the words, but the tone sounded like "okay," "you got it," or "will do." The men wore UN ID tags on chains around their necks. They walked outside, and through a broken window Parson saw them begin to unload the bags of rice and boxes of rations from the airplane. The armed guards, still out on the ramp, seemed more alert during the unloading. They eyed the parking areas, the fences, and the road to the airport. One of them hooked his right thumb over the safety lever of his AK, ready to click it into firing mode.

"How come those guys are so spring-loaded?" Parson asked. "Is my flight mechanic safe out there?"

"He's as safe as we are in here," Gold said. "We don't know of any specific threats."

"But you have general threats," Chartier speculated.

"We do. All the older people remember when warlords hijacked aid shipments to use hunger as a weapon. They wonder if al-Shabaab will take a page from that playbook. Everybody's pretty tense, especially when food comes in."

The woman at the cook pot called out in Arabic, and Gold answered. Then she turned back to Parson and Chartier.

"Lunch is ready for the staff," Gold said. "Do you want to eat something?"

A question Parson hadn't anticipated. He gave Gold a puzzled look.

"Not if food for these folks is an issue. I can wait till I get back to Djibouti."

"Don't worry about it," Gold said. "You just brought us tons of food. I think we can feed you lunch."

Several Somalis, presumably on the UN payroll, lined up at the food table. The cook began spooning something into paper bowls. The Somalis ate with relish, though not as if they were starving. Parson and Chartier followed Gold into the line, and when Parson's turn came, he received a bowl of rice cooked in goat's milk. He dipped a plastic spoon into the bowl and began eating.

"Not bad," he said, though he thought the rice could use some pepper.

"Bon appétit," Chartier said.

"Can I take a bowl to Geedi?" Parson asked Gold.

"Of course."

"You won't have to," Chartier said. "He's coming inside."

Parson looked out the window and saw the flight mechanic heading for the terminal, wiping his hands with a red rag. When Geedi came in, Parson said, "Take a break and get some lunch. What did you find?"

"Thank you, sir," Geedi said. "I didn't find anything. I think it was just water in the fuel. I drained several cups from the main tank sump on that side. Drained some out of the carb bowl, too."

Parson frowned. "Didn't you check the sumps before we took off?" he asked.

"I did, and I found a little water then. I think more of it settled out of the fuel later on."

Entirely possible, Parson knew. They'd filled up at Djibouti, and heaven only knew the quality of fuel storage there. Water could have contaminated the airport's storage tanks. It seemed the worst of the watery fuel had gone into the DC-3's right main tank, and not all the water droplets had settled around the sump drain when Geedi first checked it. The water, heavier than gasoline, eventually pooled at the bottom of the tank. In flight, when Parson switched from the aux tank to the mains, the right engine apparently ingested a big slug of water. When flying in this environment, Parson realized, you couldn't take anything for granted. Hell, you couldn't even count on your fuel to burn.

"So, do you think we're good to go?" Parson asked.

"I'd like to run the engine," Geedi said. "If it fires up and stays running, I don't know what else to check."

"You the man."

Geedi dug into a pocket and found a wet wipe in a paper pouch. He tore open the pouch, unfolded the wipe, and washed his hands as best he could. The flight mechanic stood in line for a bowl of the rice and milk, and he chatted pleasantly in Somali with other people in the line. After he received his bowl, he stood next to Parson and dipped a plastic spoon into the food.

As Geedi ate, Parson asked, "Is this a typical meal around here?"

"It is if they're lucky enough to have rice and milk at the same time," Geedi said.

Gold moved to the other side of the room and made a call on her satellite phone. Checking with the UN office in New York, Parson assumed. She looked like a woman in her element—chatting easily with local hires one moment, and in the next moment parlaying with high officials across oceans. Whatever she did, she made it look natural: from holding her own in a firefight—which Parson had seen more than once—to negotiating the bureaucracy of the UN.

The call lasted about ten minutes. When that call ended, Gold punched in another number and made another call, then another. Parson couldn't hear the conversations, but he guessed something was up. Eventually, she turned off the phone and returned to Parson and his crew.

"Can I ask a favor?" Gold said. "Could I hitch a ride back to Djibouti with you guys?"

"Of course," Parson said. "You know you can fly with me any day. What's happening?"

"We're getting a special guest. Carolyn Stewart is coming to shoot a documentary. They want us to meet her in Djibouti and escort her around Somalia."

Parson knew the name. An A-list actress, Carolyn Stewart had appeared in several top-grossing films over the past few years. In *Arlington*, she'd played the wife of a soldier killed in Iraq. In *With Extreme Prejudice*, she'd played an Air Force drone sensor operator torn by conflicting emotions about her job. Reasonably hot, by Parson's reckoning. Mid-thirties, long red hair, nice figure.

Though Parson couldn't remember the details, he knew Stewart also had a second career as a documentary filmmaker. Maybe a bit like Kevin Bacon's side project as a musician, or Angelina Jolie's deal as a UN special envoy. Stewart was a bit too liberal for Parson's taste, though. She had a thing about animal rights and vegetarianism. But if she wanted to draw attention to the plight of Somalis, Parson couldn't fault her for that. To him, it made a lot more sense to worry about human beings than calves destined for veal.

"*Très bien,*" Chartier said. "My girlfriend will be jealous."

"You mean your girlfriends, plural?" Parson said.

"*Oui.*"

Gold shook her head and smiled. "Do you think you guys can concentrate on flying, with her in the airplane?"

"Nope," Parson said.

"Absolutely not," Chartier said.

"No way," Geedi added.

"All right," Gold said. "Try to inspire a little more confidence when she gets on board."

All in all, Parson thought, an interesting twist for this mission. He hadn't met many celebrities, and it could be fun to fly one around for a few days. He'd just avoid talking politics—usually a good policy with anybody, let alone a VIP.

But the mood turned serious when Gold told her Somali coworkers about Stewart's visit. She spoke in English and Arabic, and then the Somalis talked to one another in their own language. They didn't seem happy about meeting an American movie star. Parson kept hearing one word over and over: *khatar*.

"What's *khatar*?" Parson asked.

"Dangerous," Geedi said.

4.

Once again, Hussein found himself riding in the gun truck, or "technical truck," as the men called it. As always, the Sheikh and Abdullahi rode in the cab, and the young soldiers of God occupied the back. The pickup bed offered even less room than usual for Hussein and the five other boys. Next to the Kord machine gun, a heavy green box rattled with every rut and hole in the unpaved road. About five feet long and several inches thick, the box looked like a case for some special weapon. Metal latches held the plastic box closed.

"Do not sit on it," the Sheikh had ordered. "Do not open it. Do not touch it."

The boys had received no instructions to man the gun or to stay alert. We control this part of the country, Hussein guessed, though the older men never told him such things.

Hussein had no idea where he was. He could no longer see the ocean; the truck had driven inland. Coastal sand dunes gave way to choking dust, and scrubby vegetation clung to life in the dry soil. The truck rolled past a few cultivated fields. Some farmer had tilled the soil with a hoe to prepare for seed, just the way Hussein's father used to do. But no one worked the fields today.

Women were not supposed to be in the fields on any day. The Sheikh and other men had taught Hussein that women should not show themselves outside the home. Violations would be punished: anything from flogging to amputation to stoning, depending on what the woman was doing outside.

But it seemed strange to see no men, either. Yes, Hussein thought, al-Shabaab does control this area. The sinful fear us, as they should. These farmers must have sinned.

The truck bounced through a deep gulley, and each sway of the suspension deepened the pangs in Hussein's stomach. Each boy had received an orange that morning before setting out on the journey. Hussein had already eaten the juicy sections of fruit, but the peels remained in his pocket, saved for later.

He decided he could no longer wait. Hussein shifted his AK-47 from his right hand to his left and dug into his trouser pocket. He pulled out a handful of orange peels.

The pickup hit another rut, and the impact knocked two pieces from his hand. The other boys lunged for the peels. Hussein's instincts took over.

"That's mine!" Hussein shouted.

He grabbed at the nearest boy who'd snatched a fragment of rind. All of Hussein's orange peels went flying, and the other boys fought for them. Fists and elbows flew. Hussein punched a boy in the face. Blood spurted from the boy's nose. The boy raised his rifle with both hands as if to smash Hussein with the stock.

The Sheikh stuck his head out of the window and shouted, "Silence! Or I will have Abdullahi flog you all."

The fight ended immediately. The boys settled back into their places. Hussein found himself with only one piece of rind no bigger than a ten-*senti* coin. Dirt from the pickup bed covered the rind, but he popped it into his mouth anyway. Felt the grit grinding in his teeth as he chewed.

He turned his face into the rushing wind as the truck raced along. Hussein hoped the air would dry the water welling in his eyes. He would not let the other boys see him cry. He was just as strong as they were. He was a soldier of God.

Hussein swallowed the dirty remnant of his orange. One boy smirked at him, but the gloating went no further. At one point or another, they had all felt the back of Abdullahi's hand or the sting of his lash. The older men must be obeyed, for they were the leaders of the soldiers of God.

"They are taking us for training," one of the boys supposed.

Orange peels forgotten now, everyone's attention returned to the box and whatever it contained. *Training* could mean anything.

Training could mean target practice. Several times since the older men had found Hussein hungry in the streets of Mogadishu, they had let him shoot his beloved AK, his symbol of manhood. The first time, a rusting oil drum on the beach served as a target. Abdullahi showed him how to load the Kalashnikov and how the lever on the right side of the weapon worked.

The weapon would not fire with the lever all the way up. With the lever in the middle, the weapon would shoot all the bullets at one burst.

With the lever clicked all the way down, Hussein had to pull the trigger each time he fired. "Usually you will use it this way," Abdullahi told him.

Hussein held the rifle at his waist when he fired at the oil drum. He missed, and the bullet slashed into the surf. A jet of foam shot upward from the impact. The sense of power Hussein felt from the bang left him immediately when the other boys laughed.

Then Abdullahi showed Hussein how to hold the Kalashnikov to his shoulder, to line up the front and the rear sights. What magic, to put the sights on the target and make the bullet go there. Hussein pulled the trigger and hit the center of the drum.

"Again," Abdullahi said.

Hussein fired again. Another hole appeared in the drum, less than a finger's length from the first.

"Very good," Abdullahi said.

Hussein shot six more times, and all the bullets struck in a space the size of his fist. The men gave him two tangerines that day.

Training could also mean a long talk by the Sheikh. He might preach the glories of sharia law, how you could find your place in heaven by enforcing God's law. For example, he declared music *haraam*. Forbidden.

Hussein saw the Sheikh enforce sharia one day in a market, in the town of Jowhar. The Sheikh and his soldiers were patrolling the market, ensuring women remained indoors. Ensuring no youths played with soccer balls, and no music defiled the air. *Kafirs* and infidels sought always to spread the devil's music, alcohol, and sins of the flesh. The soldiers of God had to remain vigilant.

Everything seemed in order. Carrying a pole flying the black banner of jihad, Hussein followed the Sheikh and some of the other al-Shabaab men. No one in the market showed any signs of infidelity—until a man's mobile phone chimed. Not a monotone buzz, but three descending notes of a tune Hussein did not know.

"Where is that?" the Sheikh demanded. "Get him."

The phone chimed once more, and the soldiers of God found the offender. The man looked terrified when Abdullahi grabbed him. The man had good reason for terror—*kafirs* and infidels must die. It was written.

But the Sheikh must have been in a good mood that day. Abdullahi and two other fighters dragged the offender before the Sheikh.

"Give me your mobile," the Sheikh demanded.

Trembling, the man handed over the flip-open phone. The Sheikh opened the device, cracked it backward against its hinge, and broke it in two. He dropped one half of the phone, and from the other he extracted some sort of metal chip.

"You know music is forbidden," the Sheikh said.

"I know, brother," the man said. "I play no music. I keep God's law."

"You lie," the Sheikh said. "Your mobile just sounded forbidden notes."

"I did not—"

"Silence. Because I am merciful I will give you one chance to redeem yourself."

"Anything, brother. Anything."

The Sheikh held out the little chip.

"Eat the SIM card," the Sheikh demanded.

"What?"

Abdullahi slapped the offender. Grabbed him by the front of his shirt.

"Are you deaf?" Abdullahi said. "You heard the Sheikh."

With shaking hands, the man took the card and put it in his mouth. Crunched as if eating a nut. Swallowed hard, once, twice, three times. Abdullahi pushed the offender so hard that the man fell to the ground.

Hussein felt proud of his small role in keeping God's law. And yet he wondered how one could always know what God wanted. If Hussein had owned a mobile phone, would he have realized its ring could be sinful? An unimportant question; he could no more own a phone than own the sky.

People blessed with such wealth should know, he decided. Hussein was but a simple fighter.

His mind returned to the present when the technical truck finally stopped by the side of the road. Was something wrong? No buildings, no villages, no one in sight. What could the Sheikh have in mind?

Abdullahi turned off the engine. He and the Sheikh got out of the cab.

"Drop the tailgate and pull the box onto it," the Sheikh said.

One boy opened the back of the pickup, and Hussein and another boy dragged the box by handles on both ends. They left it on the tailgate.

"Today we will show you a demonstration," the Sheikh continued. "Infidel nations such as America and Britain are sending unclean food to Somalia. With this food they hope to bribe us away from the true path and make our souls impure to God. This *haraam* food comes on airplanes. Sometimes the airplanes going to and from Baidoa pass over this spot."

Abdullahi opened the box. Inside lay some sort of metal tube.

"Is that a grenade launcher?" one boy asked.

Looked like one to Hussein. He had never fired such a weapon, but all good fighters knew rocket-propelled grenades had taken down American helicopters in Mogadishu. Maalintii Rangers, they called it. Day of the Rangers.

"No, it is not," the Sheikh said.

Abdullahi hefted the weapon so the boys could see it better. Now, the thing appeared longer than a grenade launcher. It had a pistol grip like Hussein's AK, but the sights looked different from those of a rifle.

"This is an SA-7 Grail," the Sheikh explained. "A shoulder-fired heat-seeking antiaircraft missile."

5.

In the DC-3 cockpit, Parson and Chartier strapped into their seats, and Geedi sat behind them in the jump seat. Gold stood in the flight deck doorway. Her duffel bag lay in the cargo compartment, secured by a cargo strap. If the test run works, Parson had told everyone, we'll just start the other engine, finish the checklist, and get out of here. The fuel truck pulled away; Geedi had topped off the tanks and double-checked the sumps for water contamination. So far, the fuel checked good.

Parson donned his headset, reached up and turned on the battery master switches and the avionics master. The interphone came alive, and static fried in his headset.

"All right," he said, "here goes nothing. Let's see if she'll crank."

"*Ouais*," Chartier said. He'd used that expression often enough for Parson to realize it meant "yeah."

Chartier turned on the right fuel boost pump. By 1930s standards, the electric boost pump was a modern convenience. In the DC-3's original configuration, Chartier would have had to operate a wobble pump by hand. All surviving DC-3s had received modifications over the years, with new avionics, GPS screens, even weather radar. Now no two looked alike.

When the fuel pressure on the right side showed ten PSI, Chartier pressed the right starter switch. The prop began turning, and he counted as the blades passed the twelve-o'clock position.

"*Un, deux, trois, quatre*," Chartier muttered to himself.

When he'd counted ten blades, he moved the right mixture control to AUTO RICH, and he placed the right engine's magneto switch to BOTH.

The Pratt & Whitney coughed, sputtered, belched blue smoke, and fired up.

"*Très bien,*" Chartier said. "Geedi, you really know your airplane."

"Cool," Parson said. He glanced back at Gold and said, "Looks like you're going to Djibouti. And you say I never take you anywhere."

"That's the last thing I'd say about you," Gold said.

Chartier let the engine idle as the oil pressure needle came alive. When the oil temperature rose, he bumped up the throttle to one thousand RPM and began the checklist for the left engine.

The left engine started normally, and Parson steered the airplane to the end of the taxiway. Geedi scanned the instruments and looked outside at the right engine. Gold strapped into a seat at the front of the cargo compartment, wearing a spare headset with an interphone cord running from the cockpit. Parson ran up the engines and tested the propeller controls. Checked the magnetos and scanned the gauges one more time. Shoved the prop levers full forward and said to Chartier, "Let's tell 'em we're ready to go."

Chartier pressed his transmit switch and said, "Baidoa Tower, World Relief Eight-Two Alpha ready for departure."

"Eight-Two Alpha," came the answer, "you are cleared for takeoff, Runway Two-Two."

"Cleared for takeoff," Chartier responded.

Parson advanced the throttles and taxied onto the runway. Chartier locked the tailwheel and began to make snorting noises.

"Oh, I ain't believing this," Parson said. He glanced back at Geedi in the jump seat. "He's calling me a stick hog. Can you believe this froggy bastard is calling me a stick hog?"

Geedi chuckled. Chartier snorted again.

"Okay, you truffle-eating son of a bitch," Parson said. "Your takeoff."

Chartier grinned, and he placed one hand on the throttles and the other on the right yoke. He eased the power up to forty-eight inches of manifold pressure on both engines, and the aircraft began to accelerate. As the weight of the airplane transferred from the wheels to the wings, the tail came off the ground. A few seconds later, the DC-3 lifted into the air.

Parson eyed the instruments, with special attention to the right side's engine gauges. Everything looked normal, and he brought up the landing gear on Chartier's call. The DC-3 climbed above arid terrain on a northerly heading that would take it over Ethiopia's Ogaden Desert before reaching Djibouti. When the radio traffic quieted, Gold spoke up on the interphone from her seat in the cargo compartment.

"Michael," she said, "I didn't know you were a stick hog."

"Me neither," Geedi said.

"Oh, hell," Parson said. "Now I got a mutiny by the whole crew."

Chartier laughed as he tweaked the throttles to adjust climb power. He leveled off at seventy-five hundred feet, a low cruising altitude by modern standards. In the unpressurized aircraft, Parson swallowed to equalize the pressure in his sinuses, and he felt his ears pop.

"Mind if I come up to the flight deck?" Gold asked.

"Not at all," Parson said. "The view's a lot better up here."

A few seconds later Gold appeared in the flight deck entrance. Her untied blond hair spilled over her scarf. She put her hand on Parson's shoulder and stood over the cockpit in a way that made him think of a guardian angel—if guardian angels wore David Clark headsets and Ray-Bans.

Maybe Gold possessed no powers of divine intervention, but with her, Parson had survived many dangers. As his interpreter during his time as an adviser to the Afghan air force, she'd helped him take down a tyrant who forced kids to become child soldiers. On another mission, she'd given him the encouragement and strength he needed to land a crippled C-5 Galaxy, despite serious injuries and one hell of a lot of pain. Her knowledge of languages and cultures awed him, as did her compassion for people in need.

The aircraft droned over dirt roads, sparse trees, and villages made of cardboard and scrap sheet metal. The six-hundred-mile flight would take about three hours.

"Looks pretty bleak down there," Chartier said.

"You got that right," Parson said.

Parson recalled a story he'd heard about a well-intentioned but clueless pilot back during the 1990s relief effort in Somalia. In a crowd of Somalis outside the Mogadishu airport, the dumbass held up a carton of canned beef stew.

One carton.

The crowd surged at him, knocked him down, and broke open the carton. Cans of beef stew rolled across the ground. Fights broke out over each can. Somalis suffered split lips, broken noses. The pilot got trampled but somehow escaped serious injury. A UN official with a British accent yanked him to his feet and said, "You bloody idiot. Don't you ever, ever fucking do that again."

Overwhelmed and shocked, the young pilot stammered, "I paid for that myself. I just wanted to give somebody something that tasted better than all these emergency rations."

Reared in American suburbia, the guy could not comprehend need on a Somali scale. To him, hunger meant the way you felt after missing one meal. He had no concept of true hunger, the desperation that stripped away everything but the basest animal survival instinct. The knowledge that you must eat something, anything, *now*, because in a day or two your body will pass a point of no return, too weak to digest food.

As Parson considered that incident, somewhere in the back of his mind a warning light came on. A vague note of caution. Something he saw in the corner of his eye kicked in his combat instincts. He looked down and to the left.

A white smoke trail lifted from the ground. Corkscrewed for an instant. Traced a path straight toward the DC-3.

"My airplane," Parson called. "Missile, ten o'clock."

Parson grabbed the yoke with his left hand. With his right, he snatched both throttles back to idle to cut his heat signature. Rolled hard and kicked full left rudder. Stood the DC-3 on its wingtip. The horizon tilted to nearly vertical.

Gold lost her balance and tumbled against the folding seats on the side of the cargo compartment. Parson kept his eyes on the white smoke burning right at him.

With no countermeasures or missile warning system, nothing protected the old airplane except eyeballs and reflexes. G-forces pressed Parson into his seat as he held the steep turn. His arms grew heavy, and he even felt his cheeks sag.

In a military aircraft, his crew would have punched flares as defensive countermeasures; a sky suddenly full of hot things might confuse a heat-seeking missile. Over Iraq and Afghanistan, Parson had seen heat-seekers chase flares in crazy directions, much to the relief of aviators. He had also seen countermeasures fail.

But right now Parson had no options except maneuvering: The missile's seeker head expected to intercept the airplane at point X. Parson hoped to put the plane anywhere but there. The missile scorched closer, seemed headed right between his eyes. Parson held the turn.

The threat reduced life and death to geometry. Rate of turn. Radius of a circle. Vector of a missile. Angle of intercept.

The warhead shot across the nose of the airplane like a smoking dagger. So close that Parson saw the flame of burning rocket fuel.

"You made it," Chartier called.

Parson rolled out of the turn. Pushed the nose over and dived toward the ground. The noise of the rushing slipstream rose as speed increased. He glanced at the unwinding altimeter and kept his airspeed just shy of the two-hundred-and-twenty-mile-an-hour redline.

"They might have another missile, Frenchie," Parson said. "Let's get low and fast."

"Absolument."

Fast was a relative term in a DC-3. Parson knew he could not climb out of missile range quickly enough. He could only dive, fly as low as he dared, and hope his angular velocity across the ground would make him a difficult target. Wouldn't hurt to blend the heat of his engines with that of the warm land, either.

Parson pulled up a hundred feet off the deck. At that altitude, two hundred felt like blinding speed. The parched fields, scrub brush, and wasteland melted into swells on an earthen sea.

"Sophia, are you all right?" Parson called on interphone. Hadn't she been right behind him?

No answer. Geedi looked back into the cargo compartment.

"I think she hit her head," the flight mechanic said. He started to get out of his seat to help Gold get up.

"I'm all right," Gold said.

A moment later she appeared in the flight deck entrance. With a bloody handkerchief, she dabbed at a cut on her temple. Parson glanced up at her for a second, then returned his eyes to the horizon and his instruments.

"Damn, Sophia," he said. "I'm sorry."

"No, you did what you had to do."

"Let's hope we don't have to do it again," Parson said. "Frenchie, sorry to jerk the plane away from you like that."

"Do not apologize, *mon colonel.* I think you saved our lives."

In the jump seat, Geedi placed his hand against the frame of the cockpit entrance to steady himself.

"Nobody ever tried to blow me up before," Geedi said.

"I think we're all right now," Parson said. "Frenchie, tell ATC we just got shot at."

Chartier reported the missile to air traffic control, but the radio call seemed a hollow gesture. What could ATC do? On a military mission, the report would go to an AWACS bird, which would immediately relay the information to a Quick Reaction Force. The QRF, likely in the form of Apache attack helicopters, would go hunting with missiles of their own. *Give your soul to Allah, 'cause your ass is mine.*

Not today, though. Parson felt impotent in this defenseless old crate.

Once he felt he'd put more than enough distance between the airplane and whoever fired the missile, he climbed back up to seventy-five hundred feet. They flew on in silence except for radio calls. Parson had seen that reaction before; people in an airplane got quiet after a close brush with death.

He let Chartier take control of the airplane again. With his hands now off the yoke, Parson noticed his palms were sweating. A shoulder-fired missile had come up at him in Afghanistan the first time he ever flew with Gold. That time, the missile connected. He forced himself to keep his mind on the DC-3's flight.

Eventually, ATC cleared World Relief Eight-Two Alpha for descent to Djibouti-Ambouli International Airport. Djibouti, a tiny republic with a capital city of the same name, stood in the Horn of Africa where the Red Sea met the Gulf of Aden. Parson had flown to Djibouti many times in C-130s and C-5s. The U.S. military's Combined Joint Task Force–Horn of Africa maintained a base there, sharing a runway with the civilian airport. The base, dubbed Camp Lemonnier by the French who built it, had once hosted Marine Corps helicopters, Air Force C-130s and Pave Hawk choppers, Navy P-3 Orions, and from time to time, various special ops forces such as SEALs and Green Berets. But now, the American presence was dwindling because of budget cuts and the demands of other hotspots.

When approach control handed the DC-3 over to Djibouti Tower, the routine of procedure began to settle Parson's nerves.

"World Relief Eight-Two Alpha," the tower said. "Descend and maintain three thousand feet. Expect visual approach to Runway Two-Seven."

"Eight-Two Alpha down to three thousand," Parson responded, "looking for the visual to Two-Seven."

Chartier pulled back the throttles to begin the descent. Gold buckled into a seat in the cargo compartment. Parson checked to make sure the tailwheel was locked, flipped on the landing lights, and completed the rest of the approach checklist. The sapphire waters of the Gulf of Tadjoura glittered in the distance, and the glitter spread into the larger Gulf of Aden at the southern end of the Red Sea. The city of Djibouti lay on the southern coast of the Gulf of Tadjoura. A couple miles off-shore, a warship cut a wake across the water's surface. As an Air Force guy, Parson didn't know a cruiser from a destroyer. However, the vessel's guns and multiple antennas, as well as the shape of its superstructure, made clear its military purpose.

"Looks like somebody's on pirate patrol," Parson said.

"Ça, c'est sûr," Chartier said.

The DC-3 glided over the coastline and banked onto final approach. The turn put the aircraft over the sea and on a westerly heading, with the Somali border and coastline to Parson's left. In that direction, just off the beach, a civilian freighter lay aground, rusting in shallow water. The wreck listed at some forty-five degrees, corroded chains dangling from the deck.

Parson cocked his thumb toward the shipwreck.

"Bet Lloyd's of London wrote that off as a total loss," he said.

"I wonder what ransom the owners paid for the crew," Chartier said.

"No telling."

"Gear down, s'il vous plaît."

"Gear down," Parson said. He moved the landing gear handle. After the green light came on, he locked the safety latch lever to the floor. Glanced out the window at the left landing gear strut. "Down and latched, good visual check on the left," he added.

Chartier looked out his window and said, "Good check right. Half flaps, please."

"Half flaps." Parson moved the flap handle and said, "All right, good configuration, and you're cleared to land."

A direct headwind made for a slow groundspeed on final approach, and Chartier touched down on the main wheels with hardly a bump. He let the airplane decelerate on its own, saving wear on the brakes. As the plane slowed, the tail settled to the runway.

"Nice landing, Frenchie," Parson said. His voice conveyed more of an upbeat attitude than he really felt.

"*Merci.*"

"By the way, who was Camp Lemonnier named for?" Parson asked. "I assume it's a French dude."

"*Oui,*" Chartier answered. "Général Émile René Lemonnier. The Japanese beheaded him in Indochina in 1945."

Chartier taxied to the civilian side of the field and shut down on the cargo apron. He parked beside a beat-up Dornier 328 turboprop. Ground crewmen were unloading its cargo of pasteboard boxes. Another khat shipment, Parson suspected. The drug was popular everywhere in the Horn of Africa.

An hour later, Parson joined Gold, Chartier, and Geedi in the bar at the Sheraton. Freshly showered and in civilian clothes, he could hardly believe he sat just a few miles from Somalia and all its danger and desperation. Illuminated rows of bottles stood on mirrored liquor shelves. Arab and African businessmen conferred over cocktails and hors d'oeuvres. A pianist in a coat and tie played "The Girl from Ipanema." Was it even possible that someone had tried to kill Parson and his crew just a few hours ago?

Gold wore a short-sleeved blue dress that extended below her knees. The dark dress contrasted with her blond hair, which fell unfettered around her shoulders. She seemed to take today's close call in stride. Except for a small adhesive bandage on her temple, Gold looked like a fit, attractive, forty-something businesswoman.

"I don't know about you guys," Parson said, "but I could really use a drink. I got the first round."

He found a waiter and ordered cognac for Chartier, wine for Gold, and Johnnie Walker Black for himself. Geedi, a devout Sufi Muslim, drank tea. Sitting with this crew, all the things Parson had refused to think about in the airplane came flooding back. He could still see the faces of the crew he'd lost in Afghanistan. They were his brothers.

Not one of them survived. Parson raised his glass, thought about those crewmates. He recalled pouring a shot of Scotch into the grass near Arlington National Cemetery in their honor. They should be here now, not cold in the ground.

Parson placed his nose near the glass in his hand, inhaled the aroma of Scotch. He swirled the Johnnie Walker with the ice, but he did not take a sip. Decided he didn't want the whisky after all.

Gold's voice brought him into the present.

"Sorry, Sophia," Parson said. "What did you say?"

"Carolyn Stewart gets here tomorrow," Gold said. "She wants to go right into Somalia."

Tomorrow? Parson rotated his Scotch glass between his fingers. The ice had started to cool the liquor, and the glass began to sweat with condensation. Why did the actress have to get into the country so soon?

"Do you really think that's a good idea?" Parson asked. "I mean, especially after what happened today. This is practically a combat zone."

"I called her from my room and filled her in on what happened. She's still bound and determined to go," Gold said, "and the UN did grant her access to its operations in Somalia."

"Yeah, but nobody granted her access to my airplane."

Gold shrugged. "That's between you and World Relief Airlift," she said.

At least Gold understood the prerogative of a pilot-in-command. Parson appreciated that. Some other UN types, with no military experience, might have considered him just a well-trained taxi driver. He'd have set them straight in half a second.

"You say she's shooting a documentary?" Parson asked. "She's not just dropping in for a photo op?"

"She is," Gold said. "She's produced docs before, and I think she's pretty serious. She took a break from her acting career to get an MFA in documentary film from Stanford."

Parson put down his glass, laced his fingers together, and thought about that for a moment. At least it sounded better than taking a break from acting to go into rehab.

"All right, fine with me," Parson said finally. "As long as she understands what she's getting into."

Gold kept glancing toward the television over the bar. Parson wondered what had caught her attention, so he turned to look.

The set was turned to BBC World News. The screen showed a wide shot of the Dadaab refugee camp in Kenya. In the foreground, Somalis in colorful but ragged sarongs walked through an opening in a chain-link fence topped with razor wire. In the background, rows of white tents extended through the camera's entire depth of focus.

The Sheraton's bartender saw that the broadcast interested his patrons, so he picked up a remote and turned up the volume. An anchor spoke with a crisp British accent:

Months ago, Kenya's interior minister ordered the closure of all refugee camps in the country, and Somalis have begun streaming home to an uncertain fate. Conditions in their nation have not stabilized much since these refugees left. Some have stayed away for more than two decades. An international relief effort may help Somalia prepare for the influx of returnees.

The screen changed to a shot of the World Relief Airlift DC-3 on the ramp at Djibouti.

"Hey, we're famous," Geedi said.

However, an al-Shabaab leader says acceptance of Western aid is haraam, *or religiously forbidden. Gutaale Yasin, known by his followers as the Sheikh, warns that Somali returnees must swear allegiance to his Islamic government. Yasin vows to enforce sharia law across all of Somalia. He appears to have risen to leadership in the power vacuum that followed the 2014 U.S. air strike that killed al-Shabaab leader Ahmed Godane.*

The broadcast cut to video of a man standing atop a pickup with a crew-served machine gun mounted in the bed. Crates of ammunition surrounded the weapon, and the Sheikh stood with his foot on one of the crates. He looked stockier than most Somalis; apparently he ate better than most of them. The terrorist did not quite grin, but his lips parted enough to reveal gold in his front teeth. He wore a collared blue shirt and brown trousers like an everyday shopkeeper. The men behind him wore an assortment of militaria: Camo fatigues of American, British, Russian, and German origin. Tactical vests, holsters, slings, and web gear. Some of the fighters were not men, but boys. Three or four looked to be in their early teens.

None smiled. All brandished AKs, M16s, or sawed-off shotguns. A couple of them also waved machetes.

"Wonder if that's who shot at us today," Parson said.

Geedi shifted in his chair. His face took on an expression of undiluted disgust. That surprised Parson; he had never seen the young flight mechanic show that kind of emotion. Geedi pointed at the screen, eyes flinted with anger.

"That is why my people starve," he said.

6.

The dhow pitched and rolled as it chugged through the ink-black Gulf of Aden. Hussein leaned against the gunwale, miserably seasick, clutching his AK-47. Though he had often dreamed of joining a band of pirates—*badaadinta badah*, or "saviors of the sea," as they called themselves—Hussein had never before taken a boat ride. And he vowed to Allah that after this mission, he would never take another.

Tonight's voyage had nothing to do with piracy. Though this dhow and its crew had likely preyed on many infidel ships, now the vessel served as a taxi. Hussein and his fellow soldiers of God had proved themselves well enough to embark on a special project. They would strike at a high-ranking *kafir* in Djibouti, a den of infidelity on Somalia's border. The al-Shabaab fighters would infiltrate by sea, carry out the attack, and escape the same way they'd arrived.

Yesterday's attempt to down an airplane had failed, but the Sheikh said it did not matter; the missile firing was merely a demonstration. However, weeks of planning had gone into the operation at hand. For many days, the Sheikh and Abdullahi had been preparing Hussein and the other boys for the roles each fighter would play.

Abdullahi sat in the vessel's prow, talking with some of the older men. He led this mission; the Sheikh remained on land. Starlight silhouetted Abdullahi, his AK across his shoulders. Overhead, the clear night glistened black and silver.

Hussein recalled that the sky had looked this way the night his father died. He did not know how many years had passed since then;

he knew only that it seemed long ago, when he was little. And that it happened during the *Burburki*, or "the Destruction," as Somalis called their civil war.

Drought had forced Hussein and his dad to move from a rural section of Bay province to Mogadishu. Until then, Hussein's father, a grain farmer, had managed to scratch a living from the unforgiving Somali soil. Even after disease had taken Hussein's mother and sister, his widowed dad toiled on in the fields. But when the sorghum withered and died, Father sought refuge with relatives in the capital. Hussein and his dad lived with extended family in a two-room cinder-block hovel near the Bakaara Market. In a shop constructed of discarded tin and burlap, his father sold canned goods, knives, pens, jars, and whatever else he could scrounge.

Some days, Hussein and his cousins ate. Some days, they didn't. When they did eat, the meal might consist of bony scraps of fish and a handful of rice. A round of spongy *lahoh* bread, perhaps. Shredded camel meat on rare occasions.

Nearly every day, booms and pops sounded in the distance. One night, as Hussein and his dad were closing the shop, the booms sounded closer and closer. Shouts and screams echoed in the darkness. The fighting ebbed and flowed like a tide through Hussein's new neighborhood, and on that night the blood tide reached a high mark.

Hussein and his father ran for home. The streets swarmed with running figures—some unarmed and fleeing, others carrying weapons and firing every which way. Muzzle flashes illuminated corners and alleyways. Hussein sprinted through the darkness to keep up with his father. Odors marked their progress along the street: Rotting garbage. A whiff of gunpowder. Charcoal. A days-old corpse.

A band of armed men appeared at an intersection, and Hussein and his father darted down a side street. Bad choice. A chain-link fence strung across the street created a dead end.

They turned to retrace their steps, but three gunmen blocked their escape. The men wore an assortment of camouflage clothing, with patterned kerchiefs over their faces. All three dripped with belts and pouches of ammunition. Bullets seemed the only thing plentiful in Somalia.

"*Yaa tahay?*" one of them demanded. What clan are you?

Hussein's father stood with his palms outstretched, gaping at the men as if he didn't understand the question.

"*Yaa tahay?*" a gunman repeated.

"We are of the Rahanweyn," Hussein's father answered, truthfully. "From Bay."

Wrong answer.

One of the men fired a burst on full automatic. Four rounds slammed into Hussein's father. The flashes lit up the alley. The scene remained in Hussein's mind like a series of nightmare images: His father wide-eyed as the rounds struck. A leering shooter. Expended cartridges in the air. Spatters of blood.

Hussein turned and ran toward the fence. He climbed the chain-link like a cat and flung himself over the top. Barbed wire cut his hand. Gunfire ripped behind him but no bullets struck him. Hussein ran as hard as he could. He hid inside an overturned, burned car.

He stifled his sobs to keep silent. Ran his hands over his limbs to see where he was hurt. He bled only from the gouge on his palm. The blood on his face and chest had come from his father.

Hussein cowered all night inside the burned-out vehicle. Most of the time, he looked up at the dusting of stars overhead. He did not know how far away the stars were or why they looked different on different evenings; he had never attended school. He passed that awful night in a befogged state, trying to get his mind around his new existence: He had just become a blood-spattered orphan. In Somalia, that meant his life would end badly and soon unless he kept his wits and built his strength.

A change in the tone of the dhow's engine brought Hussein back to the present. The diesel grumbled down to idle, and the vessel slowed. The rocking motion grew worse, and once more Hussein leaned over the side and vomited. One of the crewmen laughed at him, and Hussein glared.

From the dhow's oil-slicked deck, crewmen lowered a motorized skiff. On the back of the skiff, an outboard engine bore letters that meant nothing to Hussein: Y-A-M-A-H-A. Someone threw a rope ladder from the deck down into the skiff, and Abdullahi barked, "Into the boat."

Five al-Shabaab fighters clambered down the ladder, and Hussein followed, his AK slung across his back. Abdullahi boarded last. The skiff pitched and rocked even more than the dhow. Hussein heaved, but nothing remained in his stomach.

"Weakling," one of the other boys muttered.

Hussein flung himself on the boy and began pounding with his fists. The boy kicked back, tried to strike Hussein in the groin. Hussein started to draw his machete. No one had called him weak when he hacked that *kafir* to death the other day.

"Enough!" Abdullahi shouted. "Save your strength for killing infidels. If any of you cause more trouble, I will feed you to the sharks."

Hussein believed him. Al-Shabaab showed no mercy to its enemies and found little for its own members. Hussein took a seat in the skiff. Seawater sloshed at his feet, making him even more uncomfortable. Abdullahi started the outboard. Crewmen aboard the dhow pulled up the rope ladder, and the skiff motored away from its mother ship.

The lights of Djibouti glowed along the shore. Wealthy infidels with their whores and their alcohol. A bad clan always out to rob and enslave the believers. They would soon know God's wrath.

"Remember your instructions," Abdullahi yelled over the clatter of the engine. "This is an important operation. If you have any questions, ask them now. Tomorrow there will be no time. And on the beach, you must stay quiet."

Hussein had no questions. Because he could shoot with accuracy, he would carry out a particular task. There would be a car, he was told. When the time comes, shoot at the car in a special way. Pick one spot, as we have described to you. Concentrate your fire on that one spot. Keep firing and reloading until Abdullahi tells you to stop.

7.

Carolyn Stewart arrived in Djibouti on an Air France flight from New York via Paris. She came down the air stairs by herself. That gave Parson a good first impression; he'd expected an entourage.

The actress wore Dior sunglasses and an Orvis shirt with the sleeves secured by roll-up tabs. In contrast with the four-hundred-dollar eyewear, she'd tied her red hair back with a rubber band. Stewart carried a khaki-colored backpack by one strap over her shoulder. Gold and Parson greeted her in the terminal. Parson carried no illicit weapon today. They'd had to go through airport security to meet their guest at the gate.

"Ms. Stewart," Gold called out.

Stewart turned, and Parson thought he saw a hint of annoyance. An instinct brought on by years of harassment by paparazzi, he guessed. The actress's expression softened when she saw no photographers.

"Are you Ms. Gold?" Stewart asked.

"Yes, ma'am, and this is my partner, Colonel Parson."

Stewart shifted the bag on her shoulder, extended her arm. Gold shook her hand.

"Please, call me Carolyn," Stewart said. She turned to shake hands with Parson. "Nice to meet you, Colonel."

Parson noticed her cold-cream complexion and hint of perfume. "On this mission, it's just Michael," he said.

At the baggage carousel, Stewart picked up one piece of luggage— a rolling duffel bag with shoulder straps. Parson took it from her and carried it to the Land Rover. The actress sat in the front passenger seat while Gold drove, with Parson in the back.

"How was the flight?" Gold asked.

"Not too bad," Stewart said. "I bought two first-class tickets so nobody in the next seat would wake me up, and I popped an Ambien when we took off. Slept most of the way."

"Well," Parson said, "that's one way to fight jet lag."

Stewart dug a Nikon camera from her backpack and snapped photos.

"I never can get used to sights like that," the actress said as she took a shot of roadside hovels.

"It gets a lot worse where you're going," Parson said. He thought to himself: You're gonna think that Ambien sleep has put you in a very bad dream.

"Oh, I know. I think the worst place I've seen is Darfur. Went there a few years ago with George Clooney."

"Oh, yeah?" Parson said. "What's he like?"

"Perfect gentleman. Very committed."

Parson nodded. He really didn't care what George Clooney was like; Parson was just making conversation. Sometimes these A-listers and their causes seemed like just a lot of grandstanding. But, he conceded, if they used their star power to bring this stuff to people's attention, that was better than throwing tantrums in nightclubs and wrecking Alfa Romeos.

"We understand you'd like to get into Somalia as soon as possible," Gold said.

"I would," Stewart said. "In fact, I hope to set up a meeting with the president."

Oh, hell, Parson thought. Since the missile attack yesterday, his sense of unease had grown. He felt vaguely that Stewart's visit, however well intentioned, pulled things out of alignment. Stirred up forces best left alone. The Somalis at Baidoa certainly seemed to think so.

Nah, Parson told himself. You're getting superstitious, like the old-time sailors who got caught in storms and blamed it on the stranger who'd booked passage. He chided himself for getting spooked. Just because the bad guys put a shot across your bow—literally—didn't mean you had to lose your nerve. He had seen worse.

"Glad to have you with us," Parson lied. "But the World Relief Airlift operations center in London runs the show. Everything depends on where the cargo needs to fly."

He really meant: *All right, lady, you're cute and all, and it's kinda cool hanging out with a movie star. But I'm not your taxi driver, and I won't waste WRA money flying you around in an empty airplane.* Diplomacy, never Parson's strong suit, came with effort.

"Oh, I realize that," Stewart said. "Moving that food is a lot more important than anything I'm doing. In fact, I'd like to shoot some video of you while I'm here. I'm making a documentary."

"Yeah, we heard," Parson said. "I was surprised you didn't have a film crew with you."

"Well, it usually makes my life easier to have a real cinematographer do the shooting, and a sound man, too. But when you deal with people who aren't used to media, like the Somalis, the smaller your footprint, the better. You make a more authentic picture that way."

"Sounds like you've put some thought into it," Parson said. "Sophia told me you took a break from acting to learn about making documentaries."

"I did," Stewart said. "Master's program at Stanford. After I finished my undergrad degree, I planned to go into TV news. Then the acting career took off. After a while I realized I had the freedom to go do other things, too. I really appreciate you letting me fly with you. I understand you have a vintage airplane, and that will add some great visuals."

Parson wasn't sure he liked that idea. A famous actress taking pictures of his airplane? Let's just paint a big arrow on the DC-3 that reads AIM HERE, he thought. Maybe they won't miss next time.

He almost wished one of those old radial engines would break down hard, so he and the crew could drink in the bar until Carolyn Stewart decided to go the hell away. Then he thought, No, publicity would probably boost donations to WRA. With more money, the organization could buy more airplanes and do more good.

So quit complaining, Parson told himself. This mission—just like a military mission—has its risks and its rewards. You volunteered for it.

A loud boom stopped Parson's thoughts.

Black smoke boiled upward from something on the road up ahead. The car in front of their Land Rover—maybe fifty yards away—slid to a stop. Gold slammed on the brakes.

"Ambush," she said.

No panic in her voice; she didn't even shout. Just stated a fact.

"Oh my God," Stewart said.

"Get down," Parson told Stewart. She didn't move fast enough for him. He reached over the seat, grabbed her by the back of her shirt collar, and pushed her down below the dashboard.

Gold shifted into reverse. Checked the mirrors. Two other cars stopped behind her, but not at an angle to block the road. No signs of gunmen. She backed up a few yards, shifted into drive, stomped the gas, turned the wheel.

She's on it, Parson thought. In the Army, Gold had learned to drive a vehicle as tactically as he could fly a plane. He knew what she was thinking: Keep moving or die.

The Land Rover's tires threw grit as Gold executed a 180-degree turn back toward the airport. That worked for Parson. Unarmed and in a thin-skinned SUV, he wanted to get away from trouble as quickly as possible.

Four hundred yards behind them, figures darted among the stopped traffic. Men with guns. They fired at something; Parson could not see the target.

The gunfire spat intermittently. Five or six shots, then a pause. Then another five or six rounds on semiauto. Sounded almost like a training drill.

An ambush, all right. Just not against this Land Rover. Not yet, anyway.

Gold drove for about two miles. Parson wondered whether multiple attacks would come, but he saw no more signs of trouble. Finally, Gold pulled over beside a dirt soccer field. At the far end of the field, shreds of netting hung from a rusted goal frame. The area looked safe enough—no cars or buildings within a few hundred yards, so no one could get close to the Land Rover unobserved.

"You guys okay?" Gold asked. She sat with her foot on the brake, transmission still in drive, ready to move fast if she had to.

"I'm good," Parson said.

Stewart sat up in the front seat. She adjusted her blouse, retrieved her Dior sunglasses from the floor. She looked pale but not terrified. Wisps of her red hair, loosed from the rubber band, lay across her cheek.

"Good driving," she said. Stewart braced herself against the dashboard. She let out a long breath as if struggling to keep her composure.

Parson still didn't know what to make of this woman, but he gave her credit for not screaming and freaking out.

"Sorry to grab you by the scruff of the neck," he said.

"No, it's okay," the actress said.

Parson wished he had his weapon with him. He made a mental note not to go without it again; he'd just avoid walking through the civilian passenger terminal.

"What do you think that was all about?" Gold asked.

"Not something random," Parson said. "Sounded like they took their sweet time firing into one particular car. If they'd wanted to kill just *anybody*, they'd have sprayed full auto on *everybody*."

"Lucky for us, maybe," Stewart said.

"Yeah," Parson said, "but somebody else just had a real bad day."

Though he had no confirmation of a fatality, and he'd not seen much of the attack, he'd heard plenty. The sounds carried echoes of a well-planned and well-executed hit. In Parson's long travels he had witnessed all manner of death and injury—so much that he'd learned the patterns of violence, its varied natures, much the way he could hear an airplane and tell fighter from transport, turboprop from turbojet.

Twenty minutes passed with no more booms or gunfire.

"Whatever happened," Parson said, "it's probably over. Might as well get back to the hotel."

Gold drummed her fingers on the steering wheel, thinking.

"Yeah," she said. "Even if that was one of those double attacks that target first responders after the initial blast, the secondary strike would have happened by now."

"I don't think that's what it was."

"Me neither."

Gold turned the wheel to move back into the street.

"What do you think is the safest route?" Parson asked.

"Let's go back the way we came," Gold said. "If the shooters fled on foot and are still running around, I don't want to bump into them. That's less likely if we stay on the road they ran away from."

Made sense to Parson. If the police blocked off the attack site, Gold could just detour where necessary. You could overthink these things and still get killed.

Gold made a U-turn and headed back toward the Sheraton. Sure enough, the traffic slowed where a police car blocked the road, blue lights flashing. A Djiboutian officer dressed in olive fatigues with blue epaulets diverted traffic down a side street.

"Seems safe enough now," Parson said. "Let's see if we can find out what happened."

As Gold pulled up near the police vehicle, Parson dug his wallet from his pocket and pulled out his military ID. Rolled down his window.

"We're with the United Nations," he said. Not entirely the truth, but Gold was UN, at least. "Is it all right if we observe?"

Parson planned to keep his distance, but he wanted to know more about the threat. He handed over his ID. The officer read it, handed it back.

"You may, Colonel," the man said in accented English. "But please do not cross the yellow tape."

Gold parked the Land Rover along the side of the street. Crime scene tape marked off an entire intersection. The tape carried script in both of Djibouti's official languages, French and Arabic. The French wording read SCÈNE DE CRIME, NE PAS ENTRER. Parson, Gold, and Stewart got out of the vehicle.

The smoking carcass of an armored Toyota SUV sat in the middle of the intersection. Two police officers worked around the wreckage, pointing and snapping photos. The driver's door hung open. A covered body lay slumped on the ground beside the vehicle. Blood soaked the front seat, and more blood stained the door and the pavement beneath.

"That's horrible," whispered Stewart. She raised her camera, adjusted the zoom, and took a picture.

Parson and Gold moved as close as the crime tape allowed. From a distance of about forty yards, Parson tried to discern the story told by the evidence. An explosion had clearly struck the Toyota, but not ripped it apart. That was interesting; some IEDs, especially EFPs, or explosively formed penetrators, could rip right through armor. Parson had seen those used in Iraq; the blast formed a slug of copper that could turn an up-armored Humvee into a tangle of scrap metal. This explosion, however, had inflicted only enough damage to stop the vehicle.

Brass cartridge casings lay scattered all around. Rounds had gouged white pocks in the Toyota's bullet-resistant glass. Most of the bullets had hit near the top of the back window. There, concentrated fire had opened a baseball-sized hole in the glass.

Son of a bitch, Parson thought. Yeah, they did take their time—and aimed at the seam between the glass and the metal. The weakest point.

No such thing as bullet*proof* glass, he knew. Bullet-resistant glass only bought you time. In this case, not enough.

Gold went to the officer directing traffic and asked, "Who was the victim?"

"His identification said Dr. Maurice Kalinga," the officer said.

Gold's mouth dropped open slightly, and she closed her eyes for a moment.

"Was anyone else with him?" Gold asked.

"No, ma'am. A terrible crime, I must tell you. We found him beheaded. They took the head."

Gold closed her eyes again. Stewart shuddered.

"Al-Shabaab?" Parson asked.

"Unknown," the officer said, "but that is a fair guess."

Wouldn't be the first time al-Shabaab had struck outside of Somalia, Parson knew. They stormed that mall in Kenya in 2013, and in 2010 they bombed bars and restaurants in Kampala, Uganda, on the night of the World Cup Final. The Uganda attacks killed more than sixty.

"Sophia," Parson said, "you look like you recognize the victim's name."

"I do," Gold said. "Dr. Kalinga is—was—the police training director of the African Union Mission in Somalia."

"Oh, hell."

"Bastards," Stewart said.

"Did you know him?" Parson asked.

"No," Stewart said, "but I knew of him. Good man, from what I've read." As she spoke, the actress wiped her eyes.

So, what had actually happened here? The bad guys would have used a bigger IED if they'd just wanted Kalinga dead, Parson figured. They stopped his car, then drilled through the glass with rifle fire, only to kill him with a knife? That didn't make sense.

"A botched kidnapping," Gold said.

"You're reading my mind," Parson said.

Yeah, Parson thought, they'd shot through the glass and ordered him to open the door. But some of the bullets had probably hit him. Maybe they saw he was mortally wounded. No point abducting somebody who has about ten minutes to live. So instead of putting a living Dr. Kalinga on camera as a hostage, they did what they'd consider the next best thing: take his head and put that on video. Dear God.

"I want the world to know what they did to him," Stewart said. "Do you mind if we stay a few more minutes?"

Parson shrugged. Stewart put away her still camera and retrieved a video recorder from her backpack. She aimed the camcorder and began shooting. She panned along the street, adjusted the zoom, took a long shot of the wrecked SUV.

"Based on initial reports," she said as she continued recording, "this is the murder scene of an official with the African Union Mission in Somalia. Dr. Maurice Kalinga worked with an organization trying to bring order to chaos, to help some of the most victimized people on this continent. And he paid with his life."

Stewart turned the video camera toward Parson and Gold.

"These are my hosts, Sophia Gold and Michael Parson," the actress narrated. "Both are highly decorated veterans of the war in Afghanistan, now using their skills to fight a different kind of war. But, sadly, today looks all too similar to the sort of conflict they've seen before."

At the moment, Stewart sounded more like a TV reporter doing a standup than an actress making a movie. Maybe she was serious about shooting the documentary she mentioned. Parson just wished he didn't have to star in it.

"Carolyn," Gold said, "go ahead and take all the video you need. But don't post anything online while we're still in Africa."

Stewart stopped the camera and nodded. Then she took more footage of the murder scene. People began to emerge from nearby buildings; workers at a Mobil station across the street went about their tasks. A man walked past, leading a donkey burdened with crates of fruits and vegetables. Static crackled through the air, and the amplified words of a muezzin called the faithful to pray.

8.

In a Djibouti slum, Hussein and the other soldiers of God hid and waited for darkness. They huddled in a makeshift home built of discarded cinder blocks and tarps. Apparently, heaven had blessed their mission, just as the Sheikh had promised. None of them had died or suffered an injury; Hussein and the five other boys, commanded by Abdullahi, had stolen away to this safe house. A brother in jihad had scouted the abandoned dwelling days before.

The orange tarp that made up part of the roof gave a copper glow to the room as the sunlight filtered through. Hussein thought the glow looked like firelight without a fire. The dirt floor felt cool. A dead rat lay in a corner, and the rat smelled bad.

"I wish we could have taken him alive," Abdullahi said. "But we took him, all right."

Abdullahi hefted a bloody canvas bag. It contained the head of the *kafir* the al-Shabaab squad had come to capture. One of the boys giggled.

"Quiet," Abdullahi hissed.

The boy put his hand over his mouth but continued to snicker. The weird laughter went on for so long Hussein wondered if something was wrong with the boy. Hussein found this mission glorious, to be sure, but not funny. Worth a lot of fruit, he hoped, and maybe even some meat later on. Too bad that rat was too rotted to cook. Hussein had eaten rats before.

At the very least, he felt the satisfaction of having done his job well. As instructed, he'd taken a position at the rear of the infidel's vehicle.

He'd chosen a spot where the back glass touched the metal. Aimed carefully and fired.

The first bullet gouged a white hole and ricocheted off the glass. The next shot dug its own little trench and sang off into the distance. So did the third and fourth rounds.

Other boys fired at other spots. They peppered the vehicle, scalloped the windows and pricked the metal. Chips flew with each bullet strike to the glass. But no one else could manage to put two shots close together. In their excitement, the other boys seemed to forget the special way to shoot.

Not Hussein. He could follow simple instructions.

In the safe house, he remembered how he'd moved a little closer to the vehicle and pulled the trigger a fifth time. The fifth bullet hit near enough where another bullet had struck that it deepened the furrow in the glass. White flakes flew. Hussein fired again and again until he opened a hole in the supposedly bulletproof rear window. Nothing could stop holy bullets. He widened the hole with more shots.

"Out of the car," Abdullahi had shouted to the *kafir*.

The man inside did not obey. Abdullahi motioned for Hussein to keep shooting. One of the bullets hit the man inside. The *kafir* cried out in pain.

"Open the door or we will shoot you again," Abdullahi screamed.

The infidel opened the door and slumped halfway out of the car. Abdullahi ran over, grabbed him by the collar, and held him up to examine him. Hussein could not see what damage his bullet had done, but apparently the infidel was too wounded to take hostage. Abdullahi unsheathed his machete.

The victim screamed for only a few seconds, but the bleeding went on forever. More blood than when Hussein used his machete on the *kafirs* at the crossroads. Worse than slaughtering a goat. He almost wished Abdullahi would stop. But now Hussein felt ashamed of that thought. Wasn't this Allah's work? Who was he to think it should stop?

When Abdullahi finished sawing, he picked up the head by the ear. The *kafir's* eyes remained open, oddly calm. Despite the calm appearance, surely the man was in hell by then.

Hussein thought in silence until distant sirens and shouts brought him to the present.

"The police are looking for us," Hussein said.

"As we said they would," Abdullahi said. "Everyone stay quiet. They will not find us. But if they do, you will all fire your rifles until you have achieved martyrdom."

Hussein sat with his back to the wall, AK-47 at the ready. He still had half a magazine of bullets. The weapon smelled of burned gunpowder. The weapon made him a man.

His service for al-Shabaab gave him new purpose. Earlier, in his sinful life outside the ways of God, he had not expected to live long. He had seen so many other children die in so many ways: His playmate Fatima, part of her head blown off by a stray bullet. His friend Kaahiye, torn nearly in half by a speeding truck. Seven-year-old Saad, drowned after falling off a fishing boat.

But now Hussein thought of the future. As he grew older, what great things might he do? He might even learn to read. Then he could read the Quran. He could read for himself the passages the older men had told him about. The words that said kill all the infidels. That said women must remain hidden and must not seek learning. That said girls must be cut a certain way or they will become harlots. All these words were in the book; the older men said so.

The sound of sirens faded away. The hand of God must be pushing the police to look in the wrong places, Hussein thought.

Abdullahi crept around the house until he found a plastic water bottle. He opened it and drank, then handed it to one of the boys.

"Drink and pass it around," Abdullahi ordered. "Save some for everyone else."

When Hussein's turn came, he took two swallows and passed the bottle back to Abdullahi. At that moment, footsteps sounded outside.

Had the police arrived? Hussein clicked the lever to make his rifle shoot one bullet at a time.

"Shhhh," Abdullahi said.

Hussein held his breath. Everyone remained silent. All the boys raised their weapons. The giggler put his hand over his mouth to stifle more laughter. What was wrong with that boy? Hussein tried to remember the strange boy's name. Dawo. Yes, Dawo the giggler.

Voices sounded from outside. Not those of police.

"Who lives here?" a female voice said in Somali.

"No one," a male voice answered.

"Come on, there's nothing any good in there."

"I found some khat leaves once. They were too wilted, though."

The footsteps sounded closer.

"We will get in trouble," the girl said.

"No, we won't. Nobody lives here."

Abdullahi put down his rifle and crouched near the canvas flap that served as an entrance. He motioned for Dawo, who was one of the bigger boys, to join him.

"If they come in," Abdullahi whispered, "everybody help me grab them. Do not let them cry out. Do not fire a weapon."

"Do we hack them?" Dawo asked.

"No. They might scream. Just keep them quiet."

The footsteps sounded closer.

Go away, Hussein thought. You will make us get caught. Go away.

A shadow fell across the canvas flap. A sandaled foot appeared beneath it. Dawo's eyes grew wide. A hand moved the flap aside.

Abdullahi and Dawo sprang. Abdullahi grabbed the figure at the flap entrance. Turned out to be a thin teenage boy about Hussein's age. Dawo seized the girl, another teenager.

The girl tried to scream, but Dawo put a hand over her mouth. Abdullahi wrestled the boy to the ground, and they dragged both of them inside. The boy kicked and struggled. He made a grunting sound when Abdullahi punched him in the stomach. Hussein grabbed his feet to help hold him down. Another of the al-Shabaab fighters put a hand over the boy's mouth.

"Quiet," Abdullahi said. "If you speak above a whisper, we will kill you."

The captives' eyes darted around at the soldiers of God. To Hussein, their eyes looked like those of a pigeon he once captured, right before he wrung its neck to pluck and cook it. Abdullahi drew his machete, held it up, and said to the male captive, "Listen. Are you listening to me? Nod your head if you are paying attention."

The boy nodded.

"We only want you to be quiet. We will tie gags in your mouths. If you scream, you will die. If you stay quiet, you will live. Do you understand?"

The boy nodded.

"And you?" Abdullahi pointed his machete at the girl.

She nodded.

"Gag them," Abdullahi ordered. "Use rags. Tear your shirts if you have to. Find something."

Hussein looked around the hovel. He found remnants of a dirty sheet, and with his machete, cut two strips. Handed them to Abdullahi, who forced the captives to open their mouths and let him tie the cloth strips as gags.

"Cut more of that cloth," Abdullahi said.

Hussein did as ordered, and Abdullahi used the strips to tie the captives' hands and feet. When he finished, the two looked like goats trussed for market. Dawo laughed at them, and Abdullahi slapped him and told him to keep quiet.

Never before had Hussein handled prisoners. He had killed with fury, because the men told him those he killed were enemies of God. But never had he taken hostages like a pirate.

"Are we going to sell them for money?" Hussein whispered.

"No, idiot," Abdullahi hissed. "They are worthless."

The insult stung, but Hussein knew Abdullahi was right. The pirates took crewmen from foreign ships. Rich infidels working for rich countries. Probably no one would or could pay ransom for two poor teenagers. Just as no one would pay ransom for Hussein.

Abdullahi sat back and looked at the prisoners. He had a worried look on his face. Sometimes the older men appeared worried and even fought among themselves. These things troubled Hussein. The older men were supposed to lead the jihad, to know all things.

"When we try to go back to the boat in the dark," one of the boys said, "they will tell on us."

"We must kill them," Dawo said.

Through the gags, the young prisoners made pleading sounds. The girl shook her head from side to side. Tears streamed from her eyes.

A fine punishment, Hussein thought, for *kafirs* to sit and listen to their fates decided. But were these *kafirs*? They had mistakenly wandered to the hiding place of the soldiers of God.

"But if someone hears us killing them, we will still get caught," another boy said.

"Silence," Abdullahi said. "I will decide."

The girl kept looking around, crying through her gag. She looked at Hussein.

Hussein looked away. He looked at the dead rat. When he looked back up, the girl was still staring at him.

Hussein looked away again. The girl might have been his sister, though Hussein could not remember his sister's face clearly.

"What if they are faithful?" Hussein said. "Then they will help us."

"Faithful?" Abdullahi said. "This girl is walking around uncovered with a male. She is a whore, and the boy consorts with whores."

"But—"

"Did I not call for silence?" Abdullahi said.

"Maybe if we leave them tied—"

Abdullahi's face flashed with anger. He got to his knees—he could not stand erect without ruffling the tarp roof—and leaned toward Hussein. Clamped his fingers over Hussein's cheeks so that his mouth twisted into a foolish-looking shape. Hussein pressed his lips closed to look more like a man.

"I said *quiet*," Abdullahi said. Spit flew from his mouth.

Hussein wanted to hit Abdullahi with his rifle. He wanted to shoot Abdullahi with his rifle. Yet he could not. Abdullahi was a leader of the jihad.

Abdullahi let him go, sat down again across from the prisoners. Hussein rubbed the back of his hand over his mouth and glared at Abdullahi.

When I lead the jihad, Hussein thought, I will say you are a *kafir*.

Hussein wanted to leave the captives tied. Maybe they were good Muslims, despite what Abdullahi had said about the girl. Hussein's mother had been a good woman; he knew that for sure, and she did not always cover her head. Even if the boy and girl were infidels, they could not untie themselves before the soldiers of God reached the boat at nightfall. If the prisoners were good, God would send someone by morning to untie them.

Mercy did not enter Hussein's thinking. No one had ever shown him any mercy. The best thing, the quietest thing, he believed, would be to leave the prisoners tied. We are lions of jihad, Hussein thought, but a lion does not kill everything it sees. A lion kills only when it must.

As a man who would someday read the Quran and lead the jihad, Hussein knew he must think about such things. The aim here was to keep them quiet. The giggling fool Dawo did not think about things.

The sun began to set. Hussein watched the copper glow under the orange tarp darken to bronze. Soon the al-Shabaab fighters would make their dash for the sea and get back home.

Abdullahi stared at the prisoners. Then he announced, "We will silence them for good."

The boy and the girl started their muffled wailing again. This time they wailed louder. Maybe their gags had worked loose.

"Let me do the girl," Dawo said. "Let me do the girl."

Abdullahi nodded, and Dawo grabbed at the girl. Held her down on the dirt floor. The girl kicked, and he hit her on the head. Then he began to choke her.

Dawo started giggling like a mad jinn. Abdullahi slapped him. Dawo let go of the girl's throat long enough for her to let out a dampened shriek. Dawo stopped giggling but kept his wild grin. Put his hands back onto the girl's neck and choked harder. The girl flailed and struggled.

The boy sat trembling and silent. Abdullahi put away his machete and drew his other knife. A fearsome thing, with a blade as long as a dog's front leg. Notches along the top of the blade for sawing. Hussein had seen this knife take the hand off a thief.

"Hold him still," Abdullahi ordered.

Two of the other al-Shabaab boys pulled him down.

Hussein did not help. His idea would have been better, he knew. He sat and glared with his arms folded.

The girl stopped struggling. Dawo let go of her. He breathed in and out hard. The girl's dead eyes stared up at him.

"She thinks I am handsome," Dawo said.

Hussein picked up the dead rat and threw it at Dawo. Missed. The rat thudded against the cinder-block wall. No one else saw Hussein throw the rat. They were all looking at the other captive.

"Hold his mouth closed," Abdullahi ordered.

One fighter put two hands over the boy prisoner's mouth. Another clamped a hand under the prisoner's jaw.

Abdullahi kneeled over the prisoner. The boys holding the captive's mouth closed had to fight him. Their shoulders shook as they forced his head down.

With a sawing motion, Abdullahi stroked the blade across the boy's throat. Hussein heard a popping sound, like when a man cleaning a fish cuts open the air bladder. The boy bled for a long time. He bled until it was dark outside.

9.

The atmosphere in the Sheraton Djibouti Hotel felt like a siege. American military personnel had received orders to stay inside after the terrorist strike in the city. The State Department urged civilians to sit tight, too. In his current role, Parson wasn't sure which status applied to him, but it didn't matter. He wasn't going anywhere tonight. Parson, Chartier, Gold, Geedi, and Carolyn Stewart had little choice but to eat at the Sheraton.

At the hotel restaurant, some of the diners looked frightened, some looked annoyed, and some looked unconcerned. At Parson's table, the conversation went on as if no danger existed. The actress chatted amiably with the whole crew, but she seemed most taken with Geedi. In his flowered Hawaiian short-sleeved shirt, the flight mechanic resembled a college student on spring break more than an aircrew member on a mission. The white tablecloths, the potted ficus, the well-presented seafood made it hard to believe terrorists lurked outside and starvation loomed nearby.

"So, what made you join the Air Force?" Stewart asked.

She took a sip of wine as she waited for Geedi's answer. Left red lipstick on the glass.

"I wanted to give back to the country that took in my family."

"Fascinating," Stewart said. "And after the Air Force, you went to World Relief Airlift to give back to your home country?"

"Yes, ma'am."

Parson forked a chunk of Lobster Thermidor as he followed the conversation. He was paying for his own meals during this mission; in fact, he'd told the waiter to bring him the bill for the whole table. It still felt a little strange to eat gourmet food in the hunger-ravaged Horn of Africa. Gold sat beside him. She spooned an oyster from her Oysters Rockefeller and placed it on Parson's plate.

"When did your family leave Somalia?" Stewart asked.

Geedi looked around the restaurant. Hesitated before speaking.

"Ah, I don't mean to be rude. But I'd rather not discuss it here."

"Forgive me," Stewart said. "I was the rude one, asking a personal question like that."

"Not at all," Geedi said. "I don't mind telling you, just not in public."

Stewart regarded him for a moment. Took a bite of her shrimp salad.

"In that case, would you mind if I interviewed you on camera? In a more private setting, of course."

Geedi looked over at Parson.

"You're a civilian now, dude," Parson said. "Colonels can't tell you what to do anymore."

"In that case," Geedi said, "I don't see the harm in it."

After dinner, the crew gathered in Stewart's hotel room. An open laptop computer rested on the room's steel desk. Notepads, Stewart's Nikon, and pens surrounded the laptop. The actress invited Geedi to sit in one of two leather chairs. Chartier leaned across the bed. Parson and Gold sat cross-legged on the floor. Gold placed her hand on Parson's back, a small gesture of affection now entirely proper. No longer a member of the active-duty military, she did not have to conceal their relationship—such as it was. However, they still refrained from more obvious displays. Old habits died hard.

Stewart took the second leather chair, and as she fiddled with adjustments on her video camera, she said to Geedi, "When you answer the questions, talk to your friends instead of the camera. That'll look more natural."

Geedi sat up straight and grinned sheepishly at his crewmates. He wore a lavalier microphone clipped to his shirt collar. To Parson, the flight mechanic looked like a nervous schoolkid called on by the teacher. But when Geedi began answering questions, he surprised Parson with his grave tone and with a story Parson had never heard before.

"When the civil war began in Somalia in 1991," Geedi said, "my uncle worked for Radio Mogadishu. The station got shut down, and my uncle found himself without a job. I don't remember much of this myself, but my parents often spoke about it."

Geedi explained how his uncle somehow scrounged a low-wattage AM transmitter and put together his own private radio station. The station amounted to little but the transmitter, an antenna mounted on top of an abandoned clinic, a four-channel audio board, and one microphone. Such makeshift radio stations were not new; some warlords used unlicensed radio to beam propaganda to a population that was sixty percent illiterate.

But Geedi's uncle served no warlord, nor did he try to make money with the station. In Mogadishu, who would have bought advertising? The uncle merely wanted people to know what was going on.

"He was a broadcaster," Geedi said. "I guess that means, by nature, he couldn't keep his mouth shut. And he felt he was helping the best way he could during a crisis."

The famine became the uncle's top story. He told of the bodies sewn up in cheesecloth, left by the side of the streets for pickup like daily garbage. The children with limbs like sticks and the distended bellies of kwashiorkor, a swelling of the gut caused by extreme protein deficiency. And the attacks on food convoys and distribution centers, by warlords who hijacked the supplies and sold them for arms.

"Mohammed Farrah Aidid's men warned him to stop," Geedi said, "or he and all his family would be killed."

One day the radio station fell silent. Relatives went to check. The uncle's bullet-riddled body lay slumped over the audio board.

"They had cut out his tongue and draped it across the microphone," Geedi said. "The rest of the family knew we had to leave."

Geedi's father spent his last shillings to buy a rust-bucket Fiat for the escape to Kenya. The Ethiopian border was closer, but Geedi's dad had fought Ethiopians in the Ogaden War and did not want to travel in that direction. Somewhere in the Middle Jubba administrative region of Somalia, the Fiat broke down. Geedi, his parents, and an aunt and a cousin made the rest of the journey on foot.

"That part, I remember," Geedi said. "I remember that my parents were very scared, and that scared me. They tell me I cried all the time. Some of the time, my father carried me. Some of the time, I walked. They tell me I lived up to my name."

"How is that?" Stewart asked.

"Geedi means 'traveler.'"

Geedi said the family skulked through the landscape like fugitives. In those desperate days, anybody might attack you for money, food, or perhaps your clothes and shoes to trade for food. Rumors spread that the starving even resorted to cannibalism, though Geedi recalled no hard evidence of that. More than likely, he said, the strictures of Islam prevented that particular horror.

The little food they'd carried with them did not last long because they had packed for a car trip, not days of hiking. When the tinned fish, crackers, and bottled water ran out, the group turned to scavenging.

"We came upon a cornfield," Geedi said. "At first we thought Allah had answered our prayers. But of course, with such a famine going on, all the ears of corn were gone."

So they ate leaves and stalks. The dried corn leaves carried the texture and taste of old paper and probably about the same nutritional value. Geedi's parents saved for him the most edible parts—the core of the stalks, which still retained a little moisture. His dad whittled sections of the stalks with a folding knife and cut bite-sized portions for little Geedi.

Parson listened to the story in amazement. Now and then he and Gold glanced at each other. Geedi's tale reminded him of their trek through the Afghan mountains years ago, though the weather and terrain had been vastly different. But he and Gold had faced that ordeal as well-trained, well-armed adults. Parson could hardly imagine going through something like that as a child—or as a civilian with the responsibility of protecting that child. He had no idea he'd been flying alongside someone with such a harrowing background, and he wanted to comment and ask questions. But he didn't want to interrupt the recording, so he kept quiet and listened.

"We took to moving mainly at night," Geedi said, "and we avoided the main roads."

One evening as they began the night's trek—right around sunset—they came upon a tamarind tree heavy with vultures. Geedi's mom wanted to avoid the tree and the ill-omened birds, but his father knew the tamarind pods might provide a little sustenance.

As the group approached the tree, Geedi eyed the great birds, their bald heads like the skin of old men. The vultures flapped off the branches and formed a black cloud circling the tamarind. Beneath the tree lay three skeletons, nearly all the flesh and viscera picked away. From the remnants of clothing hanging on the ribs and clavicles, Geedi discerned a mother, a father, and a child. Much like his own family.

Carolyn Stewart kept recording, holding the camera to her eye.

"Did that frighten you?" she asked.

"You bet it did," Geedi said. "That could have been us any day."

Parson continued listening in rapt silence. Strange to hear such a tale told by someone who spoke with an American accent, using American slang.

Geedi and his family eventually came to the Jubba River. Not a creek you could step over, but a wide artery that drained the basin of southern Somalia and spilled into the Indian Ocean. There was no bridge where the family came to the shoreline. Seeing no other option, Geedi's father took a chance and approached a man fishing from a wooden boat.

The man wanted payment to ferry the family across the river. Geedi's dad had nothing to offer but his pistol. He handed the revolver to the boatman. The boatman stuck the weapon in his waistband and motioned for everyone to come aboard.

The crossing frightened Geedi. The river flowed fast and muddy. Eddies swirled and foamed. Crocodiles sunned themselves on a sandbar.

As the boatman rowed, he kept staring at Geedi's cousin, a pretty girl of thirteen. When the boat grated into the wet sand on the other riverbank, the man pulled the revolver.

"The girl stays with me," he said.

Geedi's dad pulled an oar out of an oarlock. Held the oar like a rifle with a bayonet affixed.

"I don't think so," Geedi's father said.

The boatman pulled the trigger. Click. Tried to fire again. The hammer dropped on six empty chambers.

Geedi's dad lunged with the oar, rammed the narrow end into the boatman's stomach. The man dropped the pistol into the boat as he tumbled into the water. Geedi's father picked up the gun. The crocodiles slid off the sandbar. They began swimming toward the would-be kidnapper and rapist as he splashed around and struggled to stay afloat.

"Our barter did not include ammunition," Geedi's dad said. "You assumed."

"Please help me out of the water," the man shouted.

Geedi's father considered for a moment. He pocketed the pistol, extended an arm, and helped the miscreant back into the boat. The man collapsed into the hull, soaked. Geedi's aunt fell on him with punches and kicks. So did his mother. The crocodiles swam around the boat, disappointed.

When the crocs finally lost interest and swam away, the family stepped out of the boat and onto shore. They left the boatman sitting in his vessel, next to the bank. He bled from his lip and nose. Geedi's father began loading his pistol.

"Are you going to kill me?" the man asked.

"No."

Geedi's dad cocked the revolver. Fired into the boat. The blast lifted a heron from the shallows, and the bird glided toward the other side of the river. Geedi's father shot two more holes through the boat's bottom, and water seeped in. The boatman scrambled onto shore and watched his boat sink.

More nights of walking followed. Days of exhaustion, hunger, and thirst. The family finally made it across the border and into a refugee camp.

"We didn't stay there long," Geedi said. "We had relations on my mother's side in Nairobi. They took us in."

"How did you get to the U.S.?" Stewart asked, still recording.

"Completely legally." Geedi laughed. "My dad worked in Nairobi until he had enough money for plane tickets. He knew some people who had already moved to Minneapolis, and we left as soon as we got visas. We got refugee status."

"And then you became an American kid?"

"Well, not that easily. Minneapolis was so cold. You know, up there in Minne-snow-ta. And at first I didn't speak any English. Neither did my mom. When you get thrown into a new culture, though, you learn fast. We found a mosque where the imam kept the young people away from the wrong crowd."

"And then you joined the Air Force."

"I did. A high school buddy who was a grade ahead of me went in, and he e-mailed me about all the things he was doing. Sounded good to me, and I didn't have many other prospects, so I signed up. By the time I got out, I was a U.S. citizen."

"Wow," Stewart said. "The American dream."

"Big time. Now I just want to see the Vikings get back to the Super Bowl."

Parson chuckled. Gold smiled. Chartier looked puzzled.

Stewart spoke for the camera: "We've been talking with Geedi Mursal, a Somali American flight mechanic with World Relief Airlift. He chatted with us at the Sheraton Hotel, in Djibouti, East Africa."

Geedi unclipped his microphone and handed it to the actress.

"Thank you so much, Geedi," Stewart said.

Parson started to say something to Geedi. A faint noise interrupted him. In the distance, he heard a shot.

10.

The soldiers of God ran through the Djibouti slum. Hussein saw that darkness brought no cover; this city had far more lights than Mogadishu.

All hope of slipping back to sea quietly was gone. When Abdullahi had led the fighters out of the safe house a few minutes ago, they'd found the infidel police still on patrol. Police cars and military vehicles crisscrossed the neighborhoods. Checkpoints clogged intersections.

None of that would have mattered. The al-Shabaab soldiers could have scurried a block here, taken cover there, avoided traffic and crowds. They'd have had all night to go just the distance a cat might wander from its house. Before joining the jihad, Hussein had survived many a night like that, stealing food and looking for places to sleep. But that fool Dawo had to go and fire a shot at a policeman.

It was like kicking a termite mound. Dawo missed, and the policeman, stooge of the Jews and Crusaders, returned fire and struck Dawo in the shoulder. Then the stooge made a radio call. Now sirens screamed. A helicopter pounded overhead. Hussein sprinted, AK-47 across his chest, to keep up with Abdullahi and the others.

Behind Hussein, two more shots echoed through the streets. More police gunfire, probably. Hussein did not turn to look. Someone screamed. Hussein still did not turn to look. A voice, amplified by some kind of device, called out in a language he did not understand. Telling him to give up, he supposed. Telling him to halt. Never.

Hussein caught up with Abdullahi, Dawo, and two of the other boys. They crouched beside a car and looked around for the rest of their fighters. Dawo bled so much that his shirt became soaked, and the blood dripped to the pavement. Abdullahi panted, ducked low when a military truck rolled through a nearby intersection. He raised his rifle. Smashed the butt into the side of Dawo's head. Dawo crumpled to the ground.

"Idiot," Abdullahi hissed. "You alerted the police, and now you cannot keep up with us."

Dawo did not move or speak. He lay like someone asleep.

The sirens grew louder. The helicopter thudded closer. A shaft of light, brighter than any Hussein had ever seen, beamed down from the flying machine. The forces of *Shaytan*, the evil one, had many powerful things. The Youth had God.

But the Youth did not have much time. The beam of light swept close. Abdullahi looked around for the rest of his young soldiers. The original team had consisted of seven, including Hussein and Abdullahi. Two were missing.

"We cannot drag this moron," Abdullahi said, pointing to Dawo. "And we cannot allow him to talk."

Abdullahi pulled out his knife. With the heel of his boot, he kicked Dawo over so that the boy lay on his back. Dawo's eyes remained shut; the blow from the rifle stock had knocked him out cold. Abdullahi gripped the knife in his fist. Plunged it through Dawo's breastbone. The bone made a cracking sound, like when you step on a dead bird that has dried up by the side of the road. Abdullahi pressed his hand on Dawo's chest, pulled out the blade. Wiped it on Dawo's pants.

"Let this be a lesson to all of you," Abdullahi said.

Hussein gaped. He did not like Dawo, and he knew from experience to expect swift and hard punishment from Abdullahi. Yet he never expected anything like this. Which one was the sinner? Had Dawo angered God by making a bad mistake on an important mission? Or had Abdullahi lost the true path? Maybe he liked too much to draw a blade or pull a trigger. Maybe he really was a *kafir*.

No time to think about such things now. Hussein knew if the police caught him, they would put him to death or lock him up for life. Worse, they might turn him over to the Americans. The Americans would take him to a place called Gwan-tahn-moh. There, they would do terrible things to him until he renounced the Prophet and bowed to the false gods of the Crusaders. The Americans would boil him in oil, skin him alive, take needles and put diseases in his body. Grind up the Quran and make him eat it. These things were true; the Sheikh and the other older men had told him so.

The helicopter noise grew fainter. That was good. The soldiers of God needed to reach the shoreline. Maybe the flying machine had turned farther back over the land. A light wind touched Hussein's face. Abdullahi pointed into the breeze.

"The sea is that way," Abdullahi said. "Spread out. Run in the way we have taught you. Meet me at the boat. I will not wait for you long."

Hussein clutched his rifle. Checked again that he'd set the lever to make the weapon fire one shot at a time. Looked toward the ocean.

He could not see the water—only a street, a car park, and a darkened storefront. He did not need to see the water yet. The men had taught him to pick a place to run to—one you can reach in the time it takes to say to yourself, *Run like a cheetah, hide like a snake.* Stop there, hide, look around, find another place.

A child or a weakling would panic in battle, but a man could still think. Hussein remembered the things he'd learned. He darted from behind the car.

Run like a cheetah. . . .

His sandals slapped the pavement as he sprinted for the storefront. He heard the footsteps of other boys but did not look to see his fellow fighters. Ducked behind a row of trash cans at the side of the store.

He smelled the food inside the store. Some sort of cooked meat. He spotted stacks of cans and cartons through the window. Hussein had never seen so much food in one place in his life. How could these infidels be so blessed? What thievery was this?

On another night he would have broken a window and taken some of the food. His mouth watered, and he felt *Shaytan* tempting him. But Allah needed him to escape, to reach the boat.

More sirens screeched. The helicopter grew louder. Hussein saw the flying machine turn again, still shining that shaft of light so bright it hurt his eyes. Dust and trash swirled underneath the machine as it approached the street Hussein had just crossed. He had run like a cheetah, and now he was hiding like a snake, and the men in the machine would not see him.

One of the other boys charged out into the street. A bad time to move, Hussein thought.

Sure enough, the light from the helicopter caught the boy. A loud voice came down from the helicopter, more words Hussein did not know. The helicopter stopped moving. It remained in one place and shone the light down. The boy raised his rifle and fired up at the machine.

Stupid, Hussein thought. There will come a day when we shall bring down such a machine for Allah. Tonight, however, we must escape.

A police car roared down the street, toward the boy under the helicopter. The boy tried to run. Two shots sounded from the police car, and the boy fell. The light swept over him again. Now he lay motionless, sprawled on his stomach, AK beside him.

Hussein wanted to flee, but they would see him if he ran. He kept as still as he could, as still as a tortoise drawn up in its shell. Now, if he moved at all, he must move slowly and quietly.

A man got out of the police car. Examined the boy shot in the street. The helicopter began moving again, circling and searching. When it flew farther from Hussein's hiding place, he crept away from the store. He crouched in the darkness behind the store and eased down an alley that led to sand. Hussein could not see the sand very well, but he felt the way it ground beneath his sandals. He began to hear the ocean. Because he could think like a man, he would make his escape and not die like a dog.

Footsteps padded near him. He raised his rifle, froze. Saw no one. Maybe it was another of the al-Shabaab fighters making his way to the beach.

More gunfire chattered from the direction of the city. Hussein stalked across the sand, hoping to find a clear path to the water. Instead of a clear path, he came to a wire fence too high to climb. There had been no fence where he and the others first sneaked into Djibouti. Perhaps he had returned to the beach down a different street. He crept along the fence, looking for an opening.

He found no opening, but he came to a culvert running under the fence. The cement pipe yawned wide enough for Hussein's shoulders. He wriggled into the culvert on his back, holding his rifle above him. The inside of the culvert smelled like a dead animal, and the water trickling through it soaked his shirt and made him shiver. No matter; he had hidden in filthier places. He propelled himself by pushing with his feet and rocking his shoulders from side to side. Tried not to think about what sewage or carrion he might be crawling through. Hussein felt as if he were worming into the earth itself.

Wet grit scraped his elbows. Despite the stench and discomfort, he decided he'd found a good path to the beach. No one could see him here.

A whiff of fresh air told Hussein he was nearing the other end of the culvert. Once again he heard the ocean. When his head poked out and he saw the stars overhead, he took in a long breath. Now, where was the boat?

He put his rifle down beside him and turned over on his stomach. Peered out toward the surf. Saw nothing but waves foaming in the moonlight. Had someone stolen the boat? Had Abdullahi already left him?

Hussein fought the urge to leap from the culvert and run up and down the beach calling for help. He would stay inside this good hiding place until he figured out what to do.

The sirens sounded fainter now, but the helicopter noise grew louder. The flying machine swung out over the water, its beam still searching. The light revealed a crumbling dock, a half-sunk scow. Where was al-Shabaab's skiff?

There.

The beam swept across the boat, beached above the high-tide mark. Praise be to Allah, Hussein thought. The infidels had shown him what he needed to find. The helicopter turned back toward the city.

Hussein saw no one in or near the boat. A good thing for now, or else the police in the flying machine might have opened fire. But where was everyone else?

Something thudded into the sand, off to Hussein's right. He looked and spied movement. Little more than a stirring in the darkness. On another night he might have thought he saw a jinn. Everyone knew jinns prowled the beaches after sundown, and mortal men could catch only glimpses of them. Best to stay away from such spirits. You never knew if they were good or bad, and nothing could kill them but a stone flung from a sling.

But tonight, more than likely, this movement in the blackness was a fellow fighter. Hussein squinted, forced his eyes to focus. Yes, a solid form crouched in the sand. Rifle over one shoulder. The figure rose, trotted toward the skiff. Hussein saw that the person also carried a bag. Abdullahi, with the head of the *kafir*.

Abdullahi reached the boat. Placed the bag inside, at the back near the motor. Paused and looked around.

"Get out of that pipe," Abdullahi said. "Come and help me."

Hussein had thought he was invisible. He crept through the end of the culvert and dropped to the wet sand underneath. He stumbled to his knees but kept his weapon raised so that the muzzle did not get clogged with sand. Just as he'd been taught. Picked himself up and jogged to the boat.

"Help me move it to the water," Abdullahi said.

"Where is everyone else?" Hussein asked.

"Dead or arrested unless they get here soon."

Dawo was dead, all right, and Hussein had seen another boy shot. And two had been missing earlier.

Hussein slung his weapon across his back, and he and Abdullahi dragged the skiff down to the surf. The boat did not feel heavy; Hussein was strong. The water felt warm as it curled over his toes. The surf took the weight of the boat, and Abdullahi held on to the transom.

"Get ready to shoot if you see the police," Abdullahi ordered. "Those stooges saw some of us running toward the beach."

Hussein pulled his AK off his shoulder and knelt where the wet sand touched the dry sand. He moved his eyes all around, watched closely. Darkness would make it hard to tell the difference between a policeman, a fellow fighter, or someone passing by. Hussein knew he must not shoot a fellow fighter. But do not worry about passersby, he had been told. If he killed someone by accident while shooting at an infidel or a *kafir*, that person—if a Muslim—would go to paradise as a martyr. If not a Muslim, then the person deserved to die anyway.

A shot sounded close by. Shouts in some strange language. Pounding of running feet. Roar of a car engine.

A boy appeared on the beach near the old dock. Hussein could not tell where or how the boy had cleared the fence. The boy scrabbled toward the water. Two figures ran behind him. When one of the figures called out in that strange language, Hussein knew they were police. He aimed as best he could in the darkness, and he fired.

One of the policemen fell and lay still. The other dropped to the sand and pointed a pistol.

"Over here," Abdullahi called to the boy.

Abdullahi lowered the boat motor and started it. The policeman with the pistol began shooting. The boy kept running toward the boat. Hussein pointed his rifle toward the policeman and squeezed off four shots.

The policeman did not fire back. The boy clambered into the boat.

"We have to go," Abdullahi said.

Hussein waded to the boat, now in waist-deep water. He put his rifle across one of the thwarts, then pulled himself, dripping, over the gunwale. Abdullahi gunned the motor, and the skiff plowed through the waves. The flying machine hovered over the city, still searching with its beam, searching in the wrong place.

We started with seven, Hussein thought as he watched the coastline fade away. Now we are three.

Would Abdullahi kill or abandon him so easily if he made a mistake like Dawo? Hussein wanted to belong to something, to join something like the family lost to him. Al-Shabaab was that family, he wanted to believe, a family of the soldiers of God. But the family tolerated no errors. Hussein knew if he'd been less crafty, less fleet of foot, he would be dead in Djibouti. Or soon to be dead, cornered in some alleyway like a rat.

Abdullahi kept one hand on the motor handle. With the other he raised the bloody bag with the head of the *kafir*. The crescent moon hung high, a symbol for the faithful. Allah had granted success.

Still, Hussein pondered his questions. He decided he must not ask questions. He must fight and follow orders. Perhaps then Allah would grant him understanding.

11.

Two days after the al-Shabaab assassination, Parson got the green light to fly again. A C-17 Globemaster from Britain's Royal Air Force dropped off several tons of supplies at Djibouti. Two pallets carried a manifest for Mogadishu, and ground crewmen transferred them to his DC-3. At the same time, Carolyn Stewart contacted the Somali government and requested a meeting that day with President Hassan Sheikh Mohamud. To Parson's surprise, Mohamud's staff granted the last-minute request.

The DC-3 lifted off from the Djibouti airport with Chartier at the controls, Parson handling the radios, and Geedi in the cockpit jump seat. Once Parson brought the gear up, he let Stewart come to the cockpit to enjoy the view. Geedi found a headset for the actress, and Gold showed her how to use the interphone switch to talk to the crew. The Gulf of Aden shimmered below while Chartier pitched for a gentle five-hundred-foot-per-minute climb.

"How do you say 'stick hog' in French?" Parson asked.

"Very funny," Chartier said, smiling as he tweaked the throttles.

"What's a stick hog?" Stewart asked.

"Long story," Parson said.

As usual, getting airborne put Parson in a better mood. Outside air ducted from the ventilation system flowed across his face and kept him pleasantly cool. He reached across the center console to fine-tune the prop levers. The engines made a rhythmic thrumming sound until he found the sweet spot and had both propellers synced to a harmonic RPM. The two Pratt engines purred as if new.

"Bravo, maestro," Chartier said.

Before Parson could respond, a radio call demanded his attention.

"World Relief Eight-Two Bravo, Djibouti Departure," the controller said. "Turn right heading one-seven-zero. Traffic is an MQ-1 entering the downwind. Should pass beneath you."

"One-seven-zero for Eight-Two Bravo," Parson said. "Looking for the traffic."

As Chartier rolled into the turn, Parson scanned outside but saw nothing. That didn't surprise him. Something as small as an MQ-1 Predator could be hard to spot, especially over hazy water. Parson checked the screen for the traffic collision avoidance system, an upgrade installed long after the DC-3 rolled off the assembly line. A white blip showed the Predator's location.

"Got him on TCAS," Parson radioed. "Negative contact visually."

"He'll pass a couple thousand feet below you," the controller answered.

"Anything wrong?" Stewart asked.

Just as the actress spoke, Parson spotted the Predator. The aircraft looked like a big insect flitting across a pond.

"Eight-Two Bravo has the traffic," Parson transmitted. Then he answered Stewart on interphone: "Nope. Just a drone passing beneath us."

"A drone?"

Stewart's face fell to an expression of great seriousness. She leaned to look out the window. By then the Predator had flown under the DC-3 and disappeared.

"What's a drone doing here?" she asked.

"Hard to guess," Parson said. "Predators were based here for a long time, and then they were transferred somewhere else. That's not an armed model, so it's just doing surveillance for somebody."

A truthful enough answer, but one Parson kept deliberately vague. Stewart's nose wrinkled as if she smelled some foul odor. From the actress's manner, Parson figured she had a hang-up about drones. Why did these lefties—as well as some wingnuts on the far right—get so excited about one particular piece of technology? Drones seemed to figure in every wackadoodle conspiracy theory: Secret misdoings, nefarious intent. Blood for oil.

To Parson's thinking, drones—or, more correctly, remotely piloted aircraft—were just tools. They did nothing that hadn't been done before with manned aircraft. Except RPAs put no crews at risk and saved the expense of life support systems such as pressurization and oxygen. No drone had the payload capacity to carry all the symbolism heaped on it by people with political axes to grind. Would it make people happier, Parson wondered, if a pilot died every time a drone hit a target?

He kept those thoughts to himself as Chartier held the aircraft on a southerly course toward Mogadishu. But the Predator did raise questions in his mind. Yeah, what *was* that thing doing here? Presumably the United States was feeding imagery to AMISOM commanders fighting al-Shabaab. Why now? Had things in Somalia taken a turn for the worse?

Not Parson's business, at least not officially. As far as the Air Force was concerned, he was on vacation.

The airplane's new heading put it over turquoise shallows, and then the DC-3 crossed the beach. Camels grazed on sparse grasses among sand dunes.

"Are we over Somalia already?" Stewart asked.

"Yep," Parson said.

"Somaliland, more specifically," Geedi said.

"Like a province?" Parson asked. His charts showed airways and navaids, not state lines.

"Sort of," Geedi said. "It's an autonomous region. Back before the civil war, the dictator Siad Barre killed a lot of people there. The region declared independence in 1991, but other countries haven't recognized it."

"Sounds like they're holding this country together with baling twine and chewing gum," Parson said. "Kinda like this old airplane." Parson patted the control yoke.

"I'd like to disagree with you, sir," Geedi said, "but you speak the truth. The Somali language wasn't even written in a standard way until 1972."

Over land again, Parson included the ground in his scan, just as carefully as he watched the flight instruments and the GPS receiver. He half expected to see another smoke trail come up at him from the tormented land below. Today, however, the parched terrain scrolled underneath his wings with no hint of threat.

For a moment, Parson imagined himself as a pioneering flier in the youth of aviation—and the youth of this particular airplane. What was it like to cross oceans and deserts aided by little more than a whiskey compass and a sextant? In those days, Parson knew, just the sight of an airplane caused people to look up in wonder. And what was it like to fly those missions in peace, plotting routes for airlines or surveying virgin territory for mapmakers?

This Somalia trip, he figured, represented the closest thing in his experience to a sepia-toned 1930s expedition. Especially with Gold on board. In another era, she would have been the flaxen-haired adventurer, versed in languages and culture, waking up beside him in a bed shrouded with mosquito netting, wooden blades of a ceiling fan twirling overhead.

It sounded romantic, but the rational part of Parson's mind knew there was no romance in slamming into a befogged, uncharted peak. Or getting lost because cloud cover kept your navigator from taking a celestial shot. Or just vanishing, like Amelia Earhart.

A request from Carolyn Stewart broke into Parson's thoughts about the bad old days. "May I shoot some video?" she asked.

"No problem," Parson said.

Geedi unstrapped and rose from his jump seat. "You can sit here for a few minutes," he said.

"Thank you so much," Stewart said.

The actress traded places with Geedi, settled into his seat. She raised her video camera and began shooting through the windscreen.

"Oh, this will be so cool," she said.

Parson caught a whiff of Stewart's perfume. Looked to his right, saw the blinking green light on her camera. She panned toward his face, then across the instrument panel.

"If you had to choose," Chartier asked her, "would you stick with acting or become the next—what's his name, the documentary guy?"

Without taking her eyes from the viewfinder, Stewart said, "Ken Burns. Yeah, today, I'd say I want his job. Don't get me wrong; I know I'm living a dream. But when I come out and do this, there are no paparazzi, no egos, no attitudes. I get to be a normal person."

"No paparazzi," Parson said. "Just shoulder-fired missiles."

"Gimme the missiles any day," Stewart said.

"I thought you were smart until you said that," Parson said. Stewart chuckled, still shooting video.

As the aircraft droned south, the radio traffic on the VHF air-traffic-control frequencies grew sparse. Parson continued to monitor the VHF radios, and he also fiddled with the HF radio. Fliers normally used HF radios for long-range communication over oceans. The HF sets could also tune in shortwave broadcasts from the Voice of America and other news services.

"I got the BBC World Service," Parson said. "Anybody want to hear the news?"

"Yes, please," Stewart said.

"Sure," Gold said. She spoke on interphone from her seat in the cargo compartment.

Parson adjusted the comm boxes, and the voice of a British-accented broadcaster flowed into the headsets:

. . . has claimed responsibility for the murder of an African Union official in Djibouti. Dr. Maurice Kalinga directed police training for AMISOM, the African Union Mission in Somalia. Kalinga

died in what officials call a botched abduction. Attackers severed his head and posted gruesome video on jihadist websites. AMISOM commanders, as well as Somali government leaders, vow to bring the killers to justice. An al-Shabaab militant who goes by the nom de guerre of "the Sheikh" says he has taken up the mantle of Mohammed Abdullah Hassan, a Somali fighter who led a revolt against the British a century ago.

"Lovely," Stewart said. She stopped recording and stood up to let Geedi return to his place in the cockpit.

Parson turned down the HF volume, twisted his face into a look that combined disgust with puzzlement. "Taken up the mantle of who?" he asked.

"Mohammed Abdullah Hassan," Geedi said, strapping back into his seat. "The Mad Mullah."

Parson rolled his eyes. "These guys and their egos and their nicknames. They're like professional wrestlers. The Sheikh. The Mad Mullah. The Undertaker. It would be funny if it weren't so damned sick."

"Roger that, sir," Geedi said.

"Actually," Gold said, "al-Shabaab really does have a lot in common with the Mad Mullah and his insurgents."

"How so?" Chartier asked.

"Just like al-Shabaab," Gold said, "the Mad Mullah claimed to fight on behalf of Islam."

Gold described how Mohammed Abdullah Hassan massacred thousands of Somalis. The Mad Mullah ordered people skinned alive if he even suspected them of cooperating with the British. And, like Osama bin Laden, he fancied himself a poet.

"Winston Churchill deployed the brand-new RAF to bomb the Mad Mullah's forts," Geedi said. "Churchill was minister of war at the time."

"Good for Winston," Parson said. Sounded like the trouble here had gone on forever. How could Parson possibly make a dent with one outdated airplane, a handful of friends, and a hitchhiking actress?

He thought about a story he once read on a greeting card from an old girlfriend. A little kid walks along the beach with Grandma. A bunch of starfish have washed up on the beach. Kid starts throwing some of them back in the water. Grandma says, "Little Portnoy, you can't make a difference, with all these hundreds of starfish washed up." Little Portnoy throws back one more and says, "But Grandma, I made a difference to that one."

Good thing I wasn't there, Parson thought. I'd have said: Once you've flown around the world and fought a couple wars, you stupid little brat, you'll realize your starfish will just wash up again in an hour.

He kept that bit of cynicism to himself; Gold wouldn't like it, and he wanted to stay on his best behavior with Carolyn Stewart on board. Air traffic control handed him off to Mogadishu Approach, and Parson changed frequencies to check in.

"Mogadishu Approach," Parson radioed, "World Relief Eight-Two Bravo is with you, level nine thousand feet."

Though he had flown some of his Somalia missions under visual flight rules, he'd filed a flight plan under instrument flight rules today. The controllers would watch the DC-3 more closely. They'd know exactly where to find the wreckage if the aircraft got shot down.

"World Relief Eight-Two Bravo, Mogadishu Approach," the controller answered. "Radar contact, expect visual approach to Runway Two-Three."

"We'll look for the visual to Two-Three," Parson said.

Parson had not flown to Mogadishu in a very long time. As a young C-130 navigator in the 1990s, he had brought in loads of Unimix—a combination of mainly corn flour and soybeans. The stuff didn't look very appetizing, but dangerously malnourished people could eat a porridge made from Unimix and not throw it up. In time, their bodies could tolerate more substantial food.

Didn't look like the area had changed much. Acacia trees dotted an otherwise featureless expanse of brown, marked by a single road. Off to Parson's left, a blue line appeared at the horizon. The blue line glowed and expanded as the airplane flew south—the Indian Ocean coming into view.

Eventually, approach cleared World Relief Eight-Two Bravo for descent, and Chartier knuckled back the throttles. Mud huts and tin shacks clustered along the outskirts of the city. The water loomed close now, with flocks of gulls riding the sea breezes. Those same breezes rocked the DC-3 with turbulence.

"Merde," Chartier said when a hard jolt hit the aircraft. "At least I have an excuse for a rough landing today."

"Never," Parson said. He glanced back to make sure Gold and Stewart were buckled in.

Approach handed off the flight to Mogadishu Tower. When Parson tuned the frequency, he had to wait to make his call because another conversation was going on.

"Mercy Four-Two, Mogadishu Tower," the controller said in Somali-accented English. "You are cleared for landing, Runway Two-Three."

Funny call sign, Parson thought. Who are they?

When Parson finally checked in, the controller cleared him for approach and said, "You're number two for landing behind a Kenyan Air Force Dash Eight."

"Cleared for the visual, looking for traffic," Parson said. He squinted, adjusted his sunglasses, and saw a twin-engine de Havilland turboprop turning from base leg to final approach. The civilian version of the Dash 8 served as an airliner. Parson wondered what this one was up to with a call sign like "Mercy."

"I guess those guys are flying some kind of mission for AMISOM," Parson said on interphone.

The suburban slums gave way to the mosques and multistory buildings of central Mogadishu, a few still bearing blast marks. Cars crawled along some of the streets, and in the distance, Parson spotted the runway. The airport's new spire of a control tower looked out of place next to the destruction and decay of the city. Parson lowered the flaps and gear on Chartier's call. By the time Chartier banked onto final, the Dash 8 had landed and taxied off the runway.

"World Relief Eight-Two Bravo cleared for landing," the tower called.

"Eight-Two Bravo cleared for landing, Two-Three," Parson said. Then he added, on interphone, "All right, Frenchie. Lemme see you plant it on centerline."

"*Pas de problème.*"

To the left of the runway, Parson saw the pulsating visual approach slope indicator. The device consisted of a single light module and served as a low-budget visual aid. A pulsing white light meant a high approach. Steady white meant on glide path. Steady red meant low. Pulsing red meant dangerously low. Parson remembered an old flier's saying: *Flashing white, up all night. Flashing red, your ass is dead.*

The light pulsed white twice and then went steady.

"You're looking good on PLASI," Parson said.

"*Bon.*"

Parson double-checked items on the landing checklist: gear down and locked, tailwheel locked, cowl flaps in the trail position, fuel crossfeed off.

"Configuration rechecks," Parson said.

Chartier flew down final with the aircraft in a crabbed position. The maneuver corrected for the crosswind coming in from the ocean. Just before touchdown, he kicked the rudder pedals to straighten the nose, and he dipped a wing into the crosswind. The left main wheel contacted the runway first, and when the right wheel settled to the pavement, the DC-3 straddled the white stripes in the center of the runway. The tail settled to the ground, and Chartier let the airplane roll along at idle power.

"Well, Frenchie," Parson said, "you might be a froggy bastard, but you can fly an airplane."

"Merci."

Chartier turned onto a taxiway and headed for the parking apron. Ahead, a sign on the terminal building read ADEN ADDE INTERNA- TIONAL AIRPORT. Shrubbery thrashed in the wind.

An odd mix of aircraft populated the ramp. An Emirates Airbus. A Ugandan L-39 Albatros attack jet. A Cessna Caravan. Parson remembered when C-130s and C-141s crowded this tarmac during Operation Restore Hope.

By the time Chartier rolled into a parking spot, the Kenyan Dash 8 had shut down its engines. An unusual amount of activity surrounded the Dash 8. A military staff car pulled up, followed by two red-and-white ambulances. Three more ambulances stopped behind the aircraft. Uniformed figures ran from the ambulances to the airplane.

Gold unbuckled her seat belt, stood behind Geedi's jump seat, and looked out the window.

"What's going on over there?" she asked.

"Looks like a medevac flight," Parson said.

Medics began unloading patients from the Dash 8. The patients lay on litters, all black men in uniform. AMISOM troops, evidently. Some wore bandages on their heads or arms; others suffered from wounds Parson could not see. He counted the injured soldiers coming off the airplane: three, four, six, eight. More followed. For some, medics held IV bottles above them as stretcher-bearers carried them to the ambulances.

Parson stopped counting at twenty.

12.

Hussein had no idea that his al-Shabaab brothers numbered so many. He and six other boys had ridden all night long in the back of a pickup truck. At daybreak they found themselves in greener country; one of the boys said the truck must have driven south. After stopping the vehicle along a remote dirt path, the Sheikh and Abdullahi led a march into a wooded area. Along the way, they passed other parked trucks, all empty.

The march ended at a clearing, where the soldiers of God gathered for a council of war. Hussein could not remember what number came after twenty-nine, but he could count twenty-nine soldiers four times and never count the same one twice. A few of them were much younger than him, perhaps ten years old. In all his time with the Youth—a dry season and a wet season—he had never seen such a large gathering.

From the white, sandy ground underneath his sandals, he judged he was near the coast, though he could see no water. Cases of ammunition and weapons lay at the foot of a wild date palm. The Sheikh stepped atop one of the cases. He wore dark sunglasses and a green field jacket, and he brandished a Kalashnikov. He spoke in a loud voice so the great number of fighters could hear him.

"My pups," the Sheikh said, "we have brought you here to help brothers already waging jihad in an important place. For those of you who do not know, you are near the town of Ras Kamboni, near the border with Kenya. Our former neighbors who fled to Kenya are coming home now, and we have no quarrel with them if they are faithful.

Yet they must know they are returning to an Islamic emirate under sharia law."

The soldiers of God cheered, and Hussein cheered with them. He did not yet know his role here, but Allah and the Sheikh would give him knowledge.

"Al-Shabaab once ruled this region," the Sheikh continued, "but the enemies of God drove us out. The stooges of the African Union have made themselves slaves to the Crusaders. We will take this land back and make it the heart of our emirate. We have already killed and wounded many of the stooges in this new operation."

More cheers. Hussein raised his rifle and shouted the only words he knew in Arabic, the language of the Prophet: *"Allahu akbar!"*

"There is something else you should know," the Sheikh said. "We have learned that some new Americans are in Somalia, no doubt engaged in errands for *Shaytan*. One of them is famous. We do not know where they are. If you see these *gaalos*, you must try to capture at least one of them. If you cannot capture, you must kill."

"Allahu akbar!" Hussein shouted, along with many others.

"I know most of you are unschooled," the Sheikh went on, "and that is of no concern. Only your courage and your piety matter. But I wish you to know about your country's greatest warrior and poet, Mohammed Abdullah Hassan. Some call him the Mad Mullah."

Some of the fighters cheered at the name. The Sheikh continued.

"Many years ago Mohammed Abdullah Hassan waged jihad against the British," the Sheikh said. "As he looked on the severed head of a British officer named Corfield, he wrote these lines."

From memory, the Sheikh recited a poem that told of this Corfield on the road to hell, and the things Corfield should tell those he met on his way. The Sheikh raised his voice when he came to certain verses:

Say, "The beasts of the wild devoured my body and dragged away the carcass."
Say, "The hyena chewed and swallowed morsels of my flesh."

The soldiers of God cheered. The Sheikh let the cheers fade, and then he went on:

Say, "The bones and tendons were left for the crows."
Say, "My kin and my army were defeated."

"You will kill new Corfields," the Sheikh said. "You will write new poems. Show them no mercy."

When the final cheers and war cries died down, Abdullahi and some of the other older men opened the cases and began passing out ammunition. Some of the boys received launchers for rocket-propelled grenades. When Hussein's turn came, he received three full magazines for his AK-47, along with one hand grenade. He placed the magazines in the special pockets of his combat vest.

"I have not used this before," Hussein said as he held the grenade. He did not know the man who gave it to him.

"It is simple," the man said. "You squeeze this lever and pull the pin. After you let go of the lever, you must throw it quickly. You must throw it far. Do not waste it."

That Hussein could do. He could throw stones far. He had hunted pigeons with stones. This weapon was merely an exploding stone.

He took his grenade and ammunition and waited for his orders. While he waited, the man who had given him the grenade handed out bullets to some of the youngest boys. To one boy, the man also gave a necklace of cowrie shells.

"Allah has granted you protection," the man said. "With this necklace, the infidels' guns cannot pierce your invisible armor."

Hussein had never heard such a thing. No invisible armor had protected his fellow fighters during the mission in Djibouti. Was this man a special sheikh with special powers? If magical necklaces existed, why wouldn't all the soldiers of God have them? Hussein's puzzling over the matter ended with a shouted order from Abdullahi.

"You," Abdullahi said, "come with me. I need six of you who can shoot." Abdullahi pointed to a fighter with a grenade launcher. "And you. I need someone with an RPG."

Hussein joined the squad gathering around Abdullahi. He did not like Abdullahi, but his job was to fight for Allah, not make friends. The boy with the cowrie-shell necklace stood beside Hussein, fingering the shells with one hand, holding his Kalashnikov with another.

"My name is Ibn," the boy said. "What is yours?'

"Hussein."

"I am from Beledwyene. Where are you from?"

Why did this boy need to talk so much? Maybe he was nervous. Hussein remembered the fear he felt when he first joined the jihad.

"Mogadishu," Hussein said. Not the whole truth, but enough of an answer. "How old are you?"

The boy pressed his lips together as if pondering a hard question. "I think I am nine," he said.

That did not necessarily mean the boy was weak in the head. Not everyone recorded birth dates.

"Are you scared?" Hussein asked.

The boy's face brightened, and he held up the necklace.

"Not anymore."

"Listen," Abdullahi barked to the squad. "Most of our brothers are going to fight the main force of infidels. But we will stop the stooges from getting reinforcements. There is a road nearby. We will take up positions on either side of the road. When a vehicle full of the stooges comes along, we will destroy it. This tactic has already proved very successful in this operation."

As Abdullahi spoke, gunfire popped in the distance. Two shots, then a rip of automatic fire. Most of the older men ignored the shooting. Abdullahi glanced toward the sound of battle, but he did not look concerned. Under a nearby tree, the Sheikh huddled with some of the men and looked at a map.

Hussein and the rest of Abdullahi's squad set out on foot. At the same time, other groups of fighters broke away from the main group and headed in other directions. Hussein walked for a long time, Ibn beside him each step of the way.

"Have you ever killed an infidel or a Crusader?" Ibn asked.

"Yes," Hussein said. "But you must be quiet now. You do not want the enemy to hear you."

The soldiers of God kept walking. Hussein did not know how far, but it seemed a long way, farther than the distance a gull flies if it flaps up at your feet and then lands so far down the beach you can barely see it. They came to a road of broken pavement, more dirt than hard surface. Berms of sand rose on either side of the road and thorny brush grew in the sand.

Abdullahi chose a hiding spot next to a sharp bend in the road. The reason became apparent to Hussein immediately. Though Hussein could not drive, he had ridden in enough trucks to see that for a driver, this was a blind curve. With the berms and vegetation, nearly anywhere along this road would have made a good ambush site. The curve, however, provided a perfect location. Any vehicle traveling this way would slow almost to a stop to get around the curve. Allah's justice would be waiting on the other side.

Abdullahi, Hussein, Ibn, and the boy with the RPG tube hid in vegetation atop a berm. Four other al-Shabaab fighters scrambled across the road and took similar positions on the other side.

"Do not fire your rifles before the tube fires the grenade," Abdullahi ordered. "We will not shoot the first car that passes. We will wait for a truck full of stooges."

For a moment, Hussein felt like a hunter, a lion hiding in tall grass, flicking its tail and waiting for prey. Allah had chosen him to exact vengeance. But what about this boy Ibn? Did Allah really need one so young? And what about this magical protection from a necklace of shells?

These things were confusing, but Hussein's job was simple: Wait for the grenade launcher, then fire and fire.

Dust rose from beyond the curve; a vehicle was coming. Hussein felt his heart beat faster. He lay in a prone position among the scrub brush, placed his cheek to the stock of his rifle. Pointed the barrel toward the bend in the road. The sound of a sputtering engine grew louder.

"Remember," Abdullahi said, "hold your fire until the RPG shoots."

Abdullahi bent low next to the boy with the grenade launcher.

The vehicle rounded the curve no faster than a man could trot. Not a military truck full of *gaalos*, but a civilian car. Dented bumper, white hood, doors painted only with gray primer. Dangling exhaust pipe. Three people inside, probably going home to Ras Kamboni. The soldiers of God let the car pass.

The sun beat down. Hussein wiped his face on his sleeve. Distant gunfire popped again, this time so far away that it sounded like the cracking of sticks. A helicopter throbbed in the background, but Hussein could not see the aircraft.

While he waited, he reached into a pocket and found one of the food packets the Sheikh had passed out to the boys yesterday. Hussein could not read the label, but the men called the food "Plumpy." As the Sheikh had explained, the infidels were trying to tempt the people away from Islam by bribing them with food. This food had been diverted from that purpose and would now feed the soldiers of God.

Hussein tore open the foil pouch and squeezed some of the contents into his mouth. The Plumpy felt like mud and tasted like peanuts. Very good, actually. Not as good as an orange peel, but close. Hussein finished the Plumpy and dropped the empty pouch. Breeze caught the foil, and the foil sailed with the wind until it became what people called a "Somali rose," one more scrap of trash caught on a thornbush.

An hour passed with no traffic on the road. Hussein grew thirstier, and he wished he'd brought water. Maybe the men would reward him with water after the mission. To keep his mind off his thirst, he thought back to his few weeks at the al-Shabaab training camp.

Many of the trainees were boys like himself, but others were men in their twenties. When the brother with the video camera came, he took pictures of only the men. They marched with their weapons, wearing their camouflage and head scarves. The younger boys, with their tattered assortment of clothing, would not appear in the pictures. Hussein resented being deemed unworthy of a picture, but he knew he must not question the ways of Allah.

Of all the trainees, al-Shabaab most revered the martyr corps, those selected for suicide bombings. The men said only the smartest and purest could join the martyr corps. Hussein did not ask to join them. Not because he feared death; for Hussein, death was a constant companion, a thing coming soon regardless of his actions. Nor did he doubt his ability. But for now at least, he thought he could best serve Allah as a regular foot soldier. From experience, Hussein knew life was short, hard, and cheap. Yet it was the only life he had.

The rumble of an approaching vehicle brought him back to the present. Sounded like something heavy. Hussein clicked the lever on his rifle to make the weapon ready to fire. He saw Ibn and the others in the bushes across the road raise their AKs.

"Wait," Abdullahi said to the boy with the RPG. "Wait."

Dust rose from the far side of the curve. The vehicle slowed, and when it appeared, Hussein saw it was military. Antennas swayed from a truck painted the color of sand. Two symbols, A and U, had been painted on the hood. At least four men inside and one stooge on top, swiveling a big gun.

"Now," Abdullahi shouted.

The boy raised the launch tube and fired.

Backblast from the tube threw sand into Hussein's eyes. He felt a wave of heat. The bang of the launch and the explosion on impact came close together—*ka-KOOM!* A black cloud of smoke filled the roadway and boiled over the berms on either side.

Gunfire followed immediately. The soldiers of God opened up on the stooges. Hussein started firing late because he had to wipe his eyes.

When he finally aimed, he saw that the RPG had blown the stooge gunner apart. The truck veered into the ditch on Hussein's side of the road and came to a dead stop.

His sights on the windshield in front of the driver, Hussein pulled his trigger. The round punched through the glass. Hussein thought he hit the driver, but he couldn't be sure. All the men in the truck were moving around. Hussein kept shooting. Each shot punctured glass. The men inside must have been stunned or wounded; they didn't return fire.

Hussein concentrated so hard on his shooting that he did not notice the second truck. Only when Abdullahi shouted, "Another one," did Hussein look up.

The truck came around the bend with its turret gun blazing. Bullets slammed into the berm on Hussein's side of the road. One hit the boy with the RPG launcher as he tried to reload. The boy collapsed beside Abdullahi.

Hussein expected the machine-gun fire to stitch right through him. But the stooge gunner shifted his aim.

Ibn stood squarely in the middle of the road. He held his AK-47 to his shoulder and began to fire the way one might shoot at a can or a piece of paper. No effort to use cover. Absolute faith in his cowrie shells.

Fire from the heavy machine gun cut Ibn nearly in half. His rifle flew from his hands and tumbled away amid red splatter. The truck veered past the first vehicle and sped through the kill zone. Crushed what remained of Ibn. Hussein lined up his sights and shot the gunner. The man slumped behind his weapon as the truck grew smaller in the swirling dust.

For a moment, the al-Shabaab fighters held their positions. After all the gunfire and explosions, a strange silence took hold. Hussein's ears rang. After a few minutes, moaning came from inside the wrecked truck.

"Everybody stay where you are," Abdullahi ordered.

Abdullahi rose from his hiding place, rifle in hand. He picked his way down the berm, through the brush. Stopped to free his sleeve from a thorn.

He walked over to the truck. Smoke still rose from the vehicle, and fluid leaked underneath.

Abdullahi pried open the driver's door. Peered inside for a moment. Raised his AK to his hip, one-handed. He spoke words Hussein could not hear. Fired two shots. The empty casings flipped through the air like two brass butterflies.

"Get ready to move," Abdullahi shouted. "Pick up weapons left by the dead."

Hussein looked down at the torn body of Ibn. The sight made him think of a melon dropped into the street and run over by cars. If the boy had not been told such foolishness about the cowrie shells, he might have stayed concealed and lived to fight another day.

When Allah commands us to die, we must die, Hussein thought, but Allah gave us brains for a reason. Hussein began moving down the side of the berm. He cursed at the thorns that pricked him as he went.

13.

After Gold and Carolyn Stewart had left for their meeting, Parson, Chartier, and Geedi waited at the Mogadishu airport. Parson watched the activity on the ramp. After the medics finished loading the most seriously injured patients onto trucks and ambulances, the walking wounded limped and shambled to the nearest hangar. They wore an assortment of bloody bandages across foreheads, over eyes, around arms. When all the wounded departed, men carried three long boxes off the Dash 8 and set them down on the tarmac one by one, working quietly and with solemn gestures. The scene reminded Parson of evac missions he'd flown in Iraq and Afghanistan; you didn't like to transport wounded in the same aircraft with the dead, but sometimes it couldn't be helped.

Having seen enough, Parson stepped away from the DC-3 and found a restroom inside a cargo hangar. He relieved himself at a filthy urinal, then zipped up his flight suit over the bellyband that held his pistol. When he washed his hands, he noticed the old faucets were labeled C and F. Back at the airplane, in the shade of the wing, Geedi explained when Parson asked about those letters.

"This part of the country used to be Italian Somaliland," Geedi said. "C and F are for *Caldo* and *Freddo*."

"Fair enough," Parson said.

He checked his watch. The DC-3 had been on the ground for more than two hours, and he expected Gold and Stewart back any minute. Geedi had refueled the DC-3 for the flight back to Djibouti, and

Chartier had just returned from the freight operations building, where he'd checked the weather. Parson wanted to get ready to start engines—kick the tires and light the fires—and get out of Somalia.

A Somali government van entered the airport ramp. That didn't surprise Parson; the same van had picked up Gold and Stewart to take them to the actress's meeting with the president. What surprised Parson was the van's flashing red light and the way the vehicle sped across the tarmac. What was wrong?

Parson looked at the van closely. Both women sat in the back, and they seemed safe enough.

The van stopped in front of the aircraft, and Gold and Stewart climbed out carrying their backpacks. Gold pulled her Afghan scarf from around her neck and wiped her face.

"You guys know how to make an entrance," Parson said.

"Michael," Gold said. "Those wounded Somali and AMISOM troops came from new fighting that's flared up down south. More than thirty wounded, three dead, and those numbers are probably going to rise. Al-Shabaab is making a big push into an area they used to control. The president himself asked if we could help."

"You're kidding," Parson said. "I know you told them we can't carry military cargo."

"They want us to fly medical supplies down to Ras Kamboni. No weapons or troops, just medical stuff. They're short of helicopters, and they need something that can land in the dirt."

Parson saw that he and Gold had a tough choice to make. The good guys needed supplies by the quickest means possible, and Somalia had precious little combat airlift capability. The DC-3 sat fueled and ready. But it belonged in a museum, not a combat zone.

"I don't know, Sophia," Parson said. "If al-Shabaab's in the area, it'll be pretty damned dangerous."

"Remember Major Ongondo?" Gold asked. "He's the African Union officer we met in North Africa."

"Of course I remember," Parson said. Ongondo had been with Gold when terrorists ambushed the two of them in North Africa. They were gathering important intel for Parson at the time. You didn't forget something like that. "What about him?"

"He's the commander down there," Gold said. "A lieutenant colonel now."

"Hell, why didn't you say so?"

Now all of Parson's instincts said go. Despite the Somali president's unusual request—and the downright recklessness of taking an antique plane into a combat zone—Parson thought mainly of a friend in need. The crew dog in him strained at the leash; this was what tactical airlift was all about. And it had been a long time since he'd landed on a dirt strip to help fellow troops. Earlier in his career, as a C-130 navigator, he'd flown with crews that landed on "unimproved" runways in Afghanistan. Unimproved sometimes meant no runway at all, just dirt and rocks.

Parson turned to Chartier and said, "Frenchie, what do you think? Ongondo needs our help."

"*Absolument*, we help him," Chartier said, "but what do we do about our VIP?"

"Oh, I'm not a VIP," Stewart said. "Think of me as an embedded reporter. Well, filmmaker. And I feel safer staying with you, Alain. And with Colonel Parson and Ms. Gold."

Then you don't know our luck very well, Parson thought. He found it brave of her to want to go, and Parson respected courage—even if it was what fliers called "Kodak courage," the urge to do something stupid for good photos. But you couldn't let Kodak courage make your decisions.

"I appreciate your confidence, Carolyn," Parson said. "But for a combat mission like this, the protocol is minimum crew." So you kill the least number of people if something goes wrong, Parson thought. Minimum crew didn't include documentary-shooting VIP actresses. Minimum crew didn't even include Gold.

"Michael," Gold said, "I'd rather not leave her anywhere in Somalia without security. If we do this, let's do it together."

Gold really wanted this mission to go; Parson could see that clearly. Did she miss the action, too? Or could she just not turn her back on someone in need?

"Sounds like you're growing fangs, Sophia," Parson said. An old Air Force expression. It meant you'd become so focused on the mission that you'd abandoned prudent caution. Officially discouraged—but not always looked down upon.

"This isn't necessarily a combat mission," Gold said. "AMISOM should have cleared the area if they're calling for resupply. Technically, the flight's still a humanitarian mission."

And that made it legal under the WRA charter, Parson knew. WRA didn't take orders from the Somali government—or any government. The president had made a request, not a directive. Parson would have to check with flight ops in London, but as pilot-in-command, he had final authority. He felt his own fangs growing a little sharper.

"So are we all on board with this?" Parson asked Chartier and Geedi.

"You bet," Geedi said.

"*Oui.*"

"All right, then," Parson said. "It's okay with me if it's okay with the operations desk." Stewart clapped like an excited schoolgirl. Parson turned to Gold. "Can I use your sat phone? I'll call home to mom."

"Sure."

She gave that half smile he loved so well. Yep, Parson realized, she got her way again. And made it look like it was his idea.

Gold dug the phone from her backpack, and Parson dialed the number for World Relief Airlift. At the ops desk in London, a kindred spirit answered the phone: a retired group captain who had flown C-130s in Britain's Royal Air Force.

"Hey, Simon," Parson said. "I'm on the ramp in Mogadishu. You ain't gonna believe what they want me to do."

"What's that, mate?"

Parson explained the situation.

"Wow," Simon said. "Are you game?"

"I've landed bigger planes in smaller places."

"Sounds like a personal problem, mate, but if you think you can manage, I think it's legal. Just make sure all the cargo is medical. Not one round of ammunition. You don't have any ammunition, do you?"

"Uh, no."

"Good. And you're sure the old bird can handle it?"

"Oh, yeah. She was built for this stuff." So was I, Parson thought.

Parson terminated the call, then took Gold's phone into the airplane. He sat down in the pilot's seat and opened a cockpit window to let in some breeze. Reached into his flight bag and pulled out a tablet computer. He kept most of his charts and flight publications digitally now. Saved a lot of weight and paper.

When the tablet booted up, he opened a VFR chart that included southern Somalia. He noted the land elevations around Ras Kamboni. Close to sea level, naturally. No real obstacles—certainly no big buildings, not even any power lines or antennas. No hills and valleys that would require fancy gear like terrain-following radar. As tactical airlift went, this looked easy.

Except for the presence of al-Shabaab.

Parson leaned out the cockpit window and called, "Hey, Sophia. Did they give you Ongondo's sat-phone number?"

"I'll bring it to you."

While he waited, Parson felt his pulse quicken. He hated like hell to hear the good guys were getting chewed up, but he felt excitement at a chance to help. The situation demanded his greatest strengths—and robbed him of his best tools. The prospect of an assault landing with a DC-3 made him feel like an expert modern sniper sent into battle with a Kentucky long rifle.

Even his emergency equipment came from another era. A survival vest hung from the back of his pilot's seat, but not one as well stocked as the Air Force would have issued. This vest Parson had put together himself. From an online supplier, he'd bought a sage-green mesh-type vest from the Vietnam War. It had arrived with empty pouches. He'd filled the pouches with odds and ends ordered from U.S. Cavalry and Brigade Quartermaster: camo face paint, a signal mirror, a lensatic compass, a pocket first-aid kit, water purification tablets, and other items. A handheld GPS receiver had set him back five hundred bucks—and he hoped never to use it. The unit was made for land navigation, which Parson would need only if shot down. He'd special-ordered topographical data for Somalia and loaded it into the GPS with an SD card.

Did I really need all this stuff? Parson asked himself. Chartier had shown up with nothing except an overnight bag and a big gun. But Parson was an old navigator, and he had a navigator's love of gadgets.

Among all the other gear, almost as an afterthought, he'd picked up a bracelet made of braided parachute cord, which he wore on his right wrist. In a pinch, he could unbraid the cord for ten feet of emergency line.

In addition to his first-aid kit, he'd also bought a more complete medical bag—a small rucksack filled with bandages, tourniquets, and other gear. He kept the medical ruck stowed behind the pilot's seat.

Parson couldn't get his hands on a state-of-the-art military survival radio, so he'd substituted a handheld pilot's nav/com radio ordered from Sporty's Pilot Shop. If necessary, he'd use that radio to speak with other aircraft and perhaps to military units. In a lower leg pocket of his flight suit, he had another radio, as well—a little Midland civilian radio used by hikers and hunters for short-range communication. He'd given Chartier an identical radio in case something happened and they got separated on the ground.

Parson's survival vest also carried a folding knife and a multi-tool, and—as always—he wore his boot knife on his left boot, a finely crafted weapon made from Damascus steel. He'd put together all this gear in case an emergency forced him to the ground: "Dress to egress," as they said in the Air Force.

Gold entered the cockpit and sat down beside Parson in the copilot's seat. She handed him a scrap of paper from a waterproof field notebook. The specially treated paper felt rougher than regular writing paper, and it had a number written on it.

Parson had always felt he owed his friend Ongondo a case of beer, at a minimum. Looked like the debt might get paid with a case of blood plasma instead. Parson dialed the number. The phone rang several times before anyone answered.

"Ongondo here," a voice finally said.

Parson thought he heard gunfire in the background. Hadn't the area been cleared? Didn't matter. An old friend was on the phone, and Parson had made his decision.

"Lieutenant Colonel," Parson said, "this is Michael Parson. Remember me?"

Ongondo paused. Then he said, "Yes, sir, I do. To what do I owe this honor?"

"No 'sirs' today, buddy. I'm working as a civilian at the moment. I know you got your hands full, so I'll be brief. I'm flying an old DC-3 for an NGO. I'm in Mogadishu, and they tell me you need a rush delivery."

"I certainly do, sir. I have many wounded."

"You got a landing zone set up?"

"I do." Ongondo read off the coordinates.

"What you got for comms?"

"Can you call me on UHF, frequency two-four-three?"

"Negative. Civilian airplane. All I got is VHF."

Parson heard Ongondo put his hand over the receiver and confer with some of his men. When Ongondo came back on the line, he said, "We can talk to you on one-two-one-point-five. We have smoke flares, too. We'll give you green for a good LZ, red if anything goes wrong. My call sign is Spear Alpha."

"That'll work. I'll see you this afternoon."

"Bless you, Colonel."

"Forget it. I still owe you."

As Parson terminated the phone call, he hoped he wasn't letting loyalty supersede his judgment. But he found it hard to say no to a friend in trouble. There were worse reasons to get yourself killed.

14.

Before takeoff, Parson tried to think of anything he could do to improve the odds of success. Ideally, an op like this would involve hours of mission planning. With people bleeding in the field, however, he didn't have the luxury of time. He leaned out the cockpit window and called to Chartier and Geedi.

"Hey, guys," Parson said. "Can you see if you can scrounge some body armor for us? Maybe there's some lying around these military hangars."

"You got it, sir," Geedi said.

"If you can't find any in about fifteen minutes, don't worry about it."

"Okay," Chartier said.

Gold took back her phone and called her contacts with the Somali government. When she told them the mission was a go, a flatbed truck rolled out to the DC-3. The truck carried Igloo coolers containing blood and blood plasma. Cardboard boxes and wooden cartons of bandages and dressings. QuikClot and morphine. Cases of bottled water. None of the cargo had been palletized or packaged for air shipment. Parson, Gold, and Stewart—along with the Somali truck driver—began loading the boxes directly onto the floor of the aircraft. For once, Stewart wasn't taking photos; there was too much else to do.

"Let's put the heavier stuff toward the front of the cargo compartment," Parson said. "Geedi will check the weight and balance when he gets back."

"What does that mean?" Stewart asked.

Parson explained to the actress that you couldn't put cargo just anywhere in an airplane. The load had to balance. He knew she wouldn't understand tech talk like "leading edge of mean aerodynamic chord," so he kept his explanation simple.

"Imagine if you tape a lead weight to the tail of a toy glider," Parson said. "If you throw that glider, it won't go anywhere but down. But if you tape the weight to the right spot in the middle of the glider, it'll fly just fine."

"I had no idea," Stewart said as she put down a cooler of blood plasma. She took her smartphone from her pocket. "Hey, can you take a picture of me helping?" Passed the phone to him.

Parson had to check himself to keep from rolling his eyes. Loading boxes hadn't kept her busy for long, after all. He aimed the phone, eager to get the silly task out of the way. Without worrying about framing the shot, he tapped with his finger to snap the photo. Caught an image of Carolyn Stewart standing amid the medical supplies, untied red hair spilling over the shoulders of her safari jacket. A little blurry. Stewart stood motionless, apparently expecting Parson to take more pictures, but he ignored her. Passed the camera back to her. Stewart helped load a few more boxes, then took video of Parson and Gold at work.

On Parson's last trip down the steps to load cargo, he saw Chartier and Geedi return with body armor. Geedi carried two sets, and Chartier had three. Not the newer lightweight flak jackets the Air Force issued, but the Ranger Body Armor vests from the 1990s. With the ceramic plates installed, those things weighed about twenty-five pounds. Not very comfortable, especially in this climate, but a hell of a lot better than nothing.

"Excellent," Parson said. "Who gave you those?"

"Uh, we found them at the back of a hangar," Geedi said. "We couldn't find anybody to ask, so we just sort of liberated them."

Parson chuckled. Too bad to borrow without permission, but he'd bring back the vests in a matter of hours. "That'll work," he said. "Hey, we just put all the cargo on board. We tried not to dork up your weight and balance too bad."

"I'll check it and strap everything down, sir."

"Good man."

Chartier filed a new flight plan, and twenty minutes later Parson eased back on the yoke to lift the DC-3 into a bright East African sky. Below, combers rolled in from the ocean and sprayed white spume across rocks and coral. Parson intended to follow the coastline down to Ras Kamboni on a VFR flight plan. No established IFR airway could take him to his destination; airways went to real airports. Gold sat in the cargo compartment. Stewart stood behind Geedi's jump seat, wearing a headset and peering outside through her Dior sunglasses.

"A little more than you bargained for?" Parson asked her on interphone.

"Oh, this is terrific," the actress said.

Brave or stupid, one or the other, Parson thought. Or both. At least she didn't mind a little manual labor when the airplane needed loading.

Once Parson leveled the plane at altitude and put it on autopilot, he considered how he could graft his old combat procedures onto this weird, half-civilian, half-military mission. As he neared Ras Kamboni, he'd have everybody put on body armor, just as if he were running a combat entry checklist. He'd stay high until he flew over the landing zone, and then he'd do a random steep approach: put down the gear and flaps, chop the power, and spiral down over the LZ. That would keep the airplane over a supposedly secure area during descent.

Just like dropping a C-130 into Baghdad or Kandahar. Except a C-130 would have armor, a missile warning system, and defensive countermeasures. Parson had none of that now. Just a defenseless piston-driven airplane full of highly explosive aviation gasoline, avgas, instead of relatively stable jet fuel.

The terrain scrolling beneath the aircraft gave little indication of renewed combat. Parson knew that could be deceptive. Sometimes battles on the ground made themselves obvious: smoke rising, fires raging, tracers flashing. At other times, battles hid themselves—at least from aviators. You could glide down final approach thinking everybody on the ground was singing "Kumbaya," then get out of the airplane and find bullet holes in the tail.

Sparse traffic moved along a coastal highway. The few cars and trucks looked fairly normal. In addition, two military personnel carriers, probably belonging to AMISOM, sped south. But that could happen on any day in Somalia.

About a hundred miles from Ras Kamboni, Parson decided to run his makeshift combat entry checks, such as they were. He asked Chartier to switch the fuel selectors from the aux tank to the mains. That meant fuel flowing through shorter plumbing, with less chance of gasoline meeting a high-velocity round. He also switched off the external lights, mainly out of habit from flying night missions in war zones. He knew bad guys couldn't miss a shiny DC-3 flying overhead in daytime, lights on or off. Finally, he told everyone to put on their body armor.

Parson unbuckled his harness, unzipped his flight suit, and removed the Beretta and its bellyband holster. He zipped the suit up again, hoisted his body armor, and donned it. Closed the fasteners on the front of the armor and put on his survival vest over it. Removed the Beretta from the bellyband and secured it in the holster sewn into the survival vest. Now anyone could see he was armed, but he didn't care.

From the corner of his eye, Parson saw Gold in the cargo compartment, helping Stewart don her vest. Gold glanced toward the cockpit, frowned, and said on interphone, "Michael, we're not supposed to be armed."

"We're not supposed to be doing tactical approaches into hostile fire zones, either," Parson said. He smiled at Gold and raised his eyebrows, just to take the edge off his retort.

Parson figured she couldn't really be surprised to see him with a gun. If he bent the rules under military authority, he sure wouldn't hesitate to break them as a civilian. What would World Relief Airlift do about it? Fire him from a job that paid nothing? Send him to Somalia?

After twenty more minutes of flying, Parson began to make out the anvil-shaped peninsula of Ras Kamboni. From the airplane's GPS moving map display, he could see that Ongondo had given him co-ordinates not for the peninsula itself but for a landing zone a mile or two inland. That suited Parson. The LZ lay well outside the town, in open country.

"Hey, Frenchie," Parson said. "Let's give 'em a call and see if their invitation still stands. You got the comm info I gave you?"

Chartier nodded and dialed in 121.5, the emergency frequency, on the VHF radio. Pressed his transmit switch and said, "Spear Alpha, World Relief Eight-Niner inbound your position." He checked the GPS screen. "We're about fifteen minutes out."

Ongondo answered immediately. "World Relief, Spear Alpha," he said. "Have you five by five. The LZ is cold. We will pop smoke when we have you in sight."

Chartier looked over at Parson, and Parson gave a thumbs-up.

"Ah, that sounds good, Spear Alpha," Chartier transmitted. "We'll see you in a few minutes."

"Cool," Parson said to Chartier on interphone. "You ever do a random steep in a transport plane?"

"*Non,*" Chartier said. "But I have seen the C-130s do it in Afghanistan."

"All right, then you got the concept. Just call my altitudes off the radar altimeter and watch my descent rate. Don't let me drop faster than about two thousand feet per minute."

"*D'accord.*"

"Sounds scary," Stewart said.

"You'll think you're on a roller-coaster," Geedi said.

"Just make sure you guys are buckled in tight," Parson said.

"We are," Gold answered.

Minutes later, Parson flew over the LZ at eighty-five hundred feet. The AMISOM troops on the ground looked like ants. The LZ appeared as an open patch of dirt, surrounded by scattered patches of trees. A much larger field stretched to the north, but Parson could see why Ongondo had not chosen that one for an LZ: Thick grass covered the bigger field. Hard to tell from this altitude, but the grass and weeds looked to be waist high or better.

Green smoke began flowing across the LZ; that meant good conditions for landing. Parson noted that the wind blew from a direction of about zero-seven-zero. With just an open patch of dirt for a runway, he could land in any direction he wanted. He wanted to land directly into the wind.

"You ready?" Parson asked.

"Toujours," Chartier said.

"Huh?"

"Always."

Parson throttled back to get below flap limit speed. When the airspeed needle dropped below 110 miles per hour, he said, "Gear down, and gimme full flaps."

Chartier moved the gear lever, pointed to the green light on the panel, looked outside. "Gear down," he said. "Good visual check right."

Parson looked to see the gear strut extended on his side and said, "Good check left."

Chartier lowered full flaps, and Parson pressed forward on the yoke to fight the resulting burble of lift. When the airplane settled down, Parson said, "Okay, folks, this elevator's going to the first floor."

He rolled into a sixty-degree bank. The horizon tilted in the windscreen. The DC-3's nose dropped below the line where Africa met the sky.

"Woo-hoo," Stewart cried from the back, off interphone.

The airplane began spiraling. Parson held just enough back pressure on the yoke to control the rate of descent. Unlike his hard level turn to avoid the missile the other day, this maneuver actually put little stress on the airplane.

"Eight thousand," Chartier said. "Coming down two thousand feet a minute."

Parson looked down to see the streamer of green smoke getting larger. The DC-3 seemed to orbit around the point marked by the smoke. Parson held the bank angle steady and let the plane spiral around twice more.

"Six thousand," Chartier said. "Bringing back memories?"

"Oh, yeah," Parson said. "She's handling pretty good, too. Who says you can't teach an old bird new tricks?"

Parson kept his scan going: airspeed 110, descent rate good, bank angle sixty degrees. He felt like a young lieutenant, confident in his new flying skills. The ground rotated closer; the ants looked like people now. Parson smiled as he listened to the conversation in the back.

"Wow," Stewart said. "He acts like this is nothing."

"He can do this in his sleep," Gold said.

"Four thousand," Chartier said. "Down two thousand feet a minute."

Parson let the airplane continue spiraling. He heard a click in his headset, as if someone on the radio frequency keyed a mike but said nothing. What was up?

Parson didn't worry about it; radios could do weird things. He rolled out of the bank a few hundred feet off the ground, nose pointed into the wind. Pulled back on the yoke to arrest the descent rate.

"Welcome to Ras Kamboni, folks," he said.

The green smoke flare guttered out. The DC-3 settled toward the LZ.

An AMISOM soldier ran toward the middle of the landing zone.

"What's that fool doing?" Parson said. The airplane was now float-ing just feet above the LZ.

The soldier yanked the pull tab on a flare. Threw the flare hard. The thing tumbled end over end, bounced onto the ground.

The flare spewed red smoke: *closed LZ*. But it was too late.

15.

The al-Shabaab ambush team melted away from the bend in the road. Abdullahi ordered Hussein and the other soldiers of God to move inland, where they would join the main assault force attacking the infidel stooges. Hussein used cover as best he could. He crouched below a thornbush here, ran forward to an acacia tree there, slipping ever closer to the sound of gunfire.

Although hiding and moving across the ground concerned him most, Hussein did notice two odd things in the sky. One was a silver airplane, not like the big machines he'd seen flying into Mogadishu, but something a bit smaller. In the distance, the thing turned round and round as it fell from the sky. Maybe someone skilled with big weapons had shot down the flying machine. Praise be to Allah if that turned out true. Yet the silver airplane trailed no fire or smoke. A very strange sight for Hussein's young eyes.

The other thing he understood better. A *huur*, a marabou stork, flapped across the battle zone with a calmness Hussein envied. What glory to glide across the land so free and untroubled. To float on the wind, to find food whenever needed. But perhaps the stork flew so tranquilly *because* of all the bleeding and fighting below it, and not in spite of the violence.

For the stork was a messenger of death. The old women used to tell how the stork could see the angel of death come to take souls away. Abdullahi would say the stork flew for the infidels. Hussein wondered if the stork flew for him—or for Ibn.

Maybe the stork flies for all of us, Hussein thought.

He turned his eyes from the bird, looked back down to the ground and to the situation around him. Unlike Ibn, Hussein was not yet a martyr; he still had things he must do. And though he did not like Abdullahi, Abdullahi's instructions had made clear the task before the soldiers of God. The orders had come straight from the Sheikh.

A large group of infidel stooges, slaves to the Crusaders, had moved into territory only recently retaken by al-Shabaab. They had come in greater numbers and had set up lines around the town of Ras Kamboni. This would not stand. To beat back these stooges, the soldiers of God would not take them on all at once. Instead, the soldiers would concentrate their attack on one point in the stooge line. Some of the boys did not grasp all of Abdullahi's words, but Hussein understood: Shoot again and again at the same spot. Just the way he had opened a hole in that armored vehicle in Djibouti. Once the hole opened, rush into the opening and press the attack. Fire on the flanks of an enemy thrown into panic. Even one without learning could see how this worked. One needed only to think. Hussein did not know why, for some, these things required so much explaining.

Ahead, Hussein saw the staging point for the attack, a collection of four wattle-and-daub houses on the outskirts of Ras Kamboni. One thatch roof had caught fire. Maybe a tracer round or sparks from a rocket-propelled grenade had ignited the dry thatch. Wind whipped the flames into a crackling fury, and gray smoke billowed into the air. The burning thatch smelled like the dry kindling a woman might use to start a cooking fire.

One of the older men lay on the ground to the left of the burning home. In a prone position, he aimed his AK-47 toward trees behind the little village. A slight rise in the terrain in front of him offered some protection from infidel bullets. The man looked behind him. He motioned for fellow fighters to join him.

Hussein broke from behind an acacia and ran, hunched low, toward the swale where the man lay. Hussein's sheathed machete bounced on his hip, and the grenade in his vest pocket dug at his side.

Gunfire barked from everywhere—one or two shots at a time, then a sizzle of automatic fire. To Hussein's right, another boy ran forward as well. Something hit the boy, and he tumbled to the ground. The boy came to rest sprawled on his back with his rifle sling tangled around his arm. He did not move. Hussein reached the swale and dived into it. Struck the dirt in a way that jammed his extra magazines against his breastbone. That hurt, but he said nothing.

"What happened on the road?" the man asked. The man wore a black shemagh and a green tunic, with a vest laden with pouches for magazines, grenades, and a radio. Hussein had seen him before but did not know his name. One of the Sheikh's lieutenants, probably equal in rank to Abdullahi.

"We killed a truck full of stooges," Hussein said. "Another truck came along and it got away, but I shot a man on that truck, too."

"Very good," the man said. He raised his arm and pointed. "There are stooges in the woods there behind the village."

More al-Shabaab men gathered nearby. Three took cover behind an overturned drinking trough near the houses. Two others found concealment in a dry gully. All five started firing toward trees beyond the village. Hussein could not see their targets.

A voice came from the radio, and the man next to Hussein rolled onto his side. "Qibla, Qibla, Qibla," the voice called. A code name for this man, Hussein supposed. When praying, Qibla was the direction one faced toward Mecca.

The man pulled out the radio and spoke into it. "Qibla here," he said.

"Sheikh here," the man on the other end said. Hussein recognized the voice. "Did you see the airplane circle down?" the Sheikh asked.

"I did," Qibla said. "What of it?"

"Make sure it does not leave. Destroy it. Shoot the pilot. Do whatever you must."

"Understood," Qibla said.

"The famous American has been flying around Somalia. This may be the plane. I want these people captured or dead."

"Praise be to Allah."

"Sheikh out."

Hussein looked toward the wooded area that concealed the infidel troops. He saw a man with a rifle get up, run a few yards, and take cover again. These stooges from Kenya or Ethiopia or wherever should have stayed home, Hussein thought. The Sheikh and the other men said the stooges had no right to oppose the will of God.

The enemy soldier began firing. Smoke from his rifle gave away his position. Hussein took careful aim. Squeezed off two shots. The stooge dropped and fired no more.

"Did you hear the Sheikh's orders?" Qibla asked.

"About the airplane?" Hussein said.

"Yes."

"I do not see it now," Hussein said. "Where did it land?"

"Beyond those trees," Qibla answered.

"Is there an airport here?"

"No. It just landed in a field."

Very strange. Hussein did not know airplanes could do that. No matter. He just needed to get within firing range of it. Or better yet, get close enough to use his grenade.

"What is the best way to cripple an airplane?" Hussein asked.

"If you see the pilots sitting in the front, shoot through the glass. If you do not see the pilots, shoot at the engines."

"I can do that."

More and more al-Shabaab fighters converged on the village. Three men with belts of ammunition draped around their shoulders came from the direction of the road. One carried a large machine gun; Hussein did not know the exact type. They took up a position beside one of the burning wattle-and-daub homes and low-crawled into some weeds. The man with the machine gun extended metal legs from the barrel and rested the weapon on the ground. The other two men took off their belts of bullets and fed one of the belts into the machine gun. The gunner began to fire, and the weapon spewed ammunition at such a rate that the noise sounded like the long roar of a lion. Yes, Hussein thought, we are lions of jihad.

The stooges fired back. Frustration burned in Hussein's chest; he could not see where the enemy hid.

But he could see where their bullets struck. Dirt flew into the air all around him. Rounds slammed so close that grit stung his eyes. No bullets hit him, though. At least not yet. Lucky—or perhaps a blessing from Allah—that he had joined Qibla at this low place in the ground. Hussein wondered if he could count on any sort of luck or protection. Nothing had protected that poor, simple Ibn, despite the faith he had placed in those cowrie shells. A soldier must have faith, to be sure. But he must also think.

More soldiers of God made it to the rally point. A squad of five men and boys ran into the village. Two of them carried grenade launchers.

The plan was working. In his excitement, Hussein forgot his bitterness about Ibn's wasteful death. He forgot his resentment that Abdullahi gave out so much punishment and so little food. He forgot everything but the urge to bring battle to the enemy.

He rose to charge forward. Qibla grabbed his arm.

"Wait," Qibla ordered. "Let them put down more suppressing fire first."

Very well. Hussein could wait. No sense wasting whatever short life he had left. And if important Americans lurked nearby, he wanted to live long enough to see them. And take them prisoner. And kill them.

The fighters with launcher tubes readied their weapons. Two of them fired, and their rocket-propelled grenades whooshed toward the infidels. Explosions rocked the enemy lines. The noise of battle rose all around Hussein. He had never seen such fierce combat; al-Shabaab usually set up ambushes or surprise attacks on unarmed *gaalos* or *kaf-*

irs. Hussein had seen army battles like this only in old movies projected onto bedsheets in the alleyways of Mogadishu.

He felt no great fear. He remained calm enough to think, to know Qibla gave good advice to wait. If Abdullahi would beat him for merely losing a magazine full of bullets or misplacing a machete, then surely Allah would punish Hussein for losing his life before the proper time.

Hussein saw movement behind the trees. More stooges in their camouflage-patterned uniforms. He raised his weapon and fired. One of the stooges fell. Hussein continued firing one shot at a time until the rifle emptied. He could not tell if he hit anyone else. He pulled a fresh magazine from his vest and slapped it against the release lever to knock away the empty. Clicked in the new mag. Cycled the bolt. Scanned for more targets. Qibla raised himself for a better view as well.

There. A stooge aimed over a pile of sandbags.

Hussein lined up the notch and post of his sights. Just before he pressed the trigger, flames spat from the stooge's muzzle.

Despite gunfire cackling all around him, Hussein heard the bullets strike Qibla. The impacts sounded like a halal butcher whacking a blade into the ribs of a goat. Something warm spattered Hussein's cheek. He ducked, turned to see Qibla collapsed, facedown and bleeding. Exit wounds between his shoulder blades and the back of his neck.

Nothing in Hussein's sparse training told him how to help someone badly hurt. Whether the wounded lived or died depended on the will of Allah. And when Hussein turned Qibla over, he could see his lack of knowledge did not matter. Though Hussein knew nothing of medicine, he knew dead, extinguished eyes when he saw them. He also knew that sound of a final breath, a rattling sigh.

Hussein looked away from the body and crouched low in the swale. In his mind, the situation around him began to form itself the way one begins to see the landscape as the sun comes up. Hussein could not set a word to this concept; he knew only that if he observed and thought, he could grasp things more clearly. A soldier of God must trust the mind that God gave him.

What he saw was this: At the point where al-Shabaab meant to pierce the enemy's line, the enemy was weakening. Hussein had killed at least one of the stooges himself. The enemy's fire came in short spasms now. In a few minutes, the al-Shabaab fighters could probably move forward and then attack to either side. He could not see where the infidel airplane had landed, but the thing had to be beyond the trees somewhere.

Hussein drew in a deep breath, readied himself to move forward. Breeze lifted dust into the air. Clouds scudded fast overhead, as if they wanted to withhold rain and fly out of Somalia as quickly as possible. Judging from the dust and dry vegetation, the clouds must have withheld for many days.

One of the al-Shabaab men fired another rocket grenade. The projectile seared into the stooges' line. Exploded in a tangle of thorn scrub and sandbags. A storm of smoke, sparks, grit, splinters, and metal shards boiled from the point of impact. The concussion stunned Hussein for a moment. A ringing sounded in his ears, and little points of silver swam in his eyes. His mind went all muddy, but he blinked and shook his head, and his thoughts came together again.

Gunfire no longer pocked the ground around him. The firefight continued to swirl to either side, but in front of Hussein, the line had opened. From somewhere along the battle line to the left, Abdullahi reappeared with two other fighters. They ran bent over with their heads ducked low like men caught in a monsoon downpour.

"Go!" Abdullahi shouted. "Move up!"

Hussein sprang from the swale. He did not look back at Qibla, or whatever the man's real name was. Hussein ran forward with his AK pointed in front of him, legs pumping, lungs burning. The weapon's sling dug into his shoulder. Sweat ran into his eyes. Smoke salted the air he inhaled. He sprinted past the burning house and up to what remained of the stooges' sandbagged position.

One of the enemy soldiers lay dead from a bullet wound to the chest. Probably the man Hussein had shot. Another body—or maybe two others—spilled across the ground. The explosion from the rocket grenade had torn them up so badly Hussein could not tell which parts belonged where. He wondered if the hand grenade in his pocket could do equal damage.

A bullet sang past Hussein's head. He dived behind the sandbags. Checked his magazine and fire selector: still plenty of rounds, still set for single shots. A bead of his sweat splashed onto the AK's receiver. Hussein wiped his brow with his torn sleeve.

He came up firing at enemy troops running from the breach in their line. No time to align his front and rear sights; Hussein simply brought the weapon to his shoulder and fired instinctively. The recoil felt good as it jolted his cheek. Two of the stooges fell to his rounds. Hussein bobbed beneath the sandbags again. Good of the dead infidels to leave him such fine cover.

Smoke drifted across his position—but not the smoke of rifle fire and grenades. This smoke was red, and it smelled of burning chalk. The smoke came from a clearing behind the stooges' former perimeter. Hussein looked in that direction, and he saw something that made him forget the strange smoke.

There it was. The airplane. Sure enough, it had not crashed but had somehow landed intact, here in the middle of nowhere. Allah's will has brought me to this place, Hussein thought, for this very moment in the jihad.

Gaalos scurried around the airplane, along with a couple of stooge soldiers in their camouflage. Some of them were unloading things from a door in the back of the airplane, and some were standing guard.

Hussein raised his weapon. Rested it across his left forearm. Aimed at one of the *gaalos*.

He chose not to fire. The range was a little too long. He knew he would get only one chance at this, and he needed to make it count. A soldier of God must not waste such an opportunity. Hussein took the grenade from his vest and held it with the thumb and first two fingers of his left hand. The effort felt much like hefting a rock to throw at an unclean stray dog.

Holding the grenade's lever down tight, Hussein pulled the pin with his teeth. Spat out the pin. Set himself to run like a cheetah.

16.

When Parson saw the red smoke, he had only a second to make a decision: stay or go. Shove the throttles to the stops and try to climb away, or touch down and deal with whatever lurked on the ground.

He elected to stay.

With much of the LZ already behind him and trees in front of him, Parson judged it safer to let the DC-3 settle into the dirt. Hardly the first time he'd landed in a hot LZ for troops needing emergency resupply. He just hoped Ongondo's men could keep al-Shabaab at bay long enough to offload the cargo.

Parson closed the throttles and made a three-point landing: He let the tailwheel and the main gear contact the ground at the same time. That made for a shorter landing roll. He hit the brakes with the toes of his boots and let the airplane bounce and rattle through the dust until it rumbled to a stop.

For a few seconds, he peered out the windscreen as the props spun at idle power. No one came near the airplane. The soldiers he could see stayed in their defensive positions in fighting holes and behind piles of sandbags. Where were the troops to handle the cargo?

"Uh, hello?" Parson said, voicing his frustration over the interphone. "A little help here?"

Surely Ongondo and his men would realize Parson wanted to keep his engines running for a quick offload and an immediate takeoff.

"I think they're too busy holding off the enemy," Chartier said.

Parson leaned forward as far as the inertial reel for his harness would allow. He scanned outside and still saw no help coming. Fingered his transmit switch. "Spear Alpha," he called, "we need to offload and get out."

No answer. But apparently Ongondo heard him and sent the only men he could spare. Two AMISOM soldiers emerged from the tree line. At one point both of them raised their rifles and fired at something Parson could not see. They approached the airplane walking backward, facing the firefight. Watching for the enemy. And not watching the spinning propellers.

"They're going to come too close," Chartier said. As he spoke, the men were twenty yards from the left engine and moving closer.

Parson did not want to shut down. Restarting the engines would eat up precious seconds. He slid open his window.

"Hey," he shouted. "The props! Walk around them!"

Amid the gunfire and engine noise, the men did not hear him.

"Stupid sons of bitches," Parson muttered.

He knew they weren't really stupid sons of bitches. They were just not used to working around airplanes—and they were trained to focus on the enemy.

"Damn it to hell," Parson hissed. He yanked the mixture levers to idle cutoff.

The engines died, and the props spun down to a stop. Perfect, Parson thought. Now we're fucked.

Nothing he could do about it, though, except get everybody moving to kick the cargo off the aircraft as quickly as possible.

He popped the buckle on his harness, removed his headset, and pulled himself out of the pilot's seat. Geedi rose from his jump seat to get out of the way.

"All right, people," Parson called, "help those guys get the stuff off this old bird. You, too, Carolyn. No pictures right now. I want to take off five minutes ago. Let's move, move, move."

Geedi and Chartier followed Parson. Gold was already opening the boarding door. She jumped to the ground, stuck her head back inside the airplane, and said, "Pass the boxes to Carolyn and me. Alain can help stand guard."

"*Ouais,*" Chartier said. He and Carolyn Stewart hopped out of the DC-3. Chartier drew his Smith & Wesson revolver and held it with both hands. The pistol seemed pitifully inadequate.

One of the AMISOM troops also stood guard, while the other slung his rifle over his shoulder and helped with the cargo. Parson and Geedi worked in the cargo compartment, handing boxes, coolers, and cartons outside to Gold. Stewart and the AMISOM soldier took each item from Gold and stacked the supplies on the ground.

Gunfire crackled all around the LZ. Rocket-propelled grenades exploded within four hundred yards of the airplane.

"Something's wrong out there," Chartier called.

Of course something's wrong, Parson thought. We came down in the middle of a damned firefight. Couldn't the AMISOM troops beat back a bunch of half-trained jihadists?

He heaved the last item, a crate of bottled water, over to Gold.

"I think they've broken through the perimeter," Gold said.

Parson looked toward a patch of woods. He had to squint and observe closely to believe what he saw. Men fired from sandbagged fighting positions, but not the same men as before. They wore a ragged collection of tunics, field jackets, and head wraps. Other al-Shabaab fighters ran among the trees and scrub, crouching, shooting, moving on. AMISOM troops had pulled back from an opening in their line and were firing at the terrorists from either side of it. Shouts, screams, and gunshots echoed across the field. The two soldiers who'd helped with the offload ran to the aid of their comrades.

"Get in the plane," Parson shouted. "Everybody. Now."

Gold and Stewart clambered aboard. Stewart began buckling herself into a cargo compartment seat. Parson pulled the Beretta out of its holster on his survival vest. Handed the weapon to Gold.

"Frenchie and I will start engines," Parson said. "You watch through the door back here. If any bad guys get near the airplane, light 'em up."

"You got it."

Gold certainly wasn't objecting to having weapons on board now, Parson noted. Old Army instincts kicking in.

Chartier climbed aboard, still holding his Magnum pistol. He followed Parson into the cockpit. Placed the weapon on the floor between the seats. Both pilots put on their headsets. Didn't bother with their harnesses. Neither picked up a checklist. Geedi took his place in the flight mechanic's jump seat.

Chartier reached overhead and popped on both battery switches. Checked the fuel tank selectors, flipped on the boost pumps. Shoved the mixture levers to AUTO RICH. Set the carb air temp controls to COLD.

"I'm gonna gang-start these bitches," Parson said.

In the C-130 and the C-5, his crews had practiced emergency bug-out, screw-the-checklist, simultaneous engine starts. In the Herk, you could start one engine to get bleed air flowing, then gang-start the other three as long as you had a good pneumatic system. The DC-3 had electric starters—and two engines instead of four. Similar concept, though. Parson could save critical seconds and crank both engines at once. If he had strong battery power.

He cracked open the throttles a quarter inch. Set the magneto switches.

"Hold the brakes for me, will you?" Parson said.

Chartier pressed his boots on the pedals while Parson reached up with both hands. Using four fingers, Parson moved the safety switches and starter switches for the engines.

"They're coming," Gold shouted from the cargo compartment.

Over his left arm, Parson looked out the windscreen. Five or six al-Shabaab fighters were running across the field toward the airplane.

The propellers began to turn. The engines coughed, smoked, backfired. Parson almost let go of the starter switches. Then he realized the backfiring was actually Gold firing the Beretta. One of the al-Shabaab men stumbled and dropped.

More shooting. Rounds smacked into the aluminum skin of the DC-3. Parson wanted badly to look behind him to see if anyone was hurt, but he kept his hands on the panel. The left engine caught, sputtered, and its prop began spinning. Then the right engine spun up.

"Everybody all right?" Parson shouted. Took his fingers off the overhead panel.

Chartier turned in his seat, looked, and said, "They're okay."

Seven or eight AMISOM troops sprinted through the field. One of them fell. Two fired from the hip. The firefight seemed to ebb and flow through the very path Parson needed for takeoff. He grabbed the throttles and put his feet on the rudder pedals.

"I got the plane, Frenchie," Parson said.

"D'accord."

The battle intensified, practically under Parson's wings. AMISOM and al-Shabaab fighters kept trading fire throughout the landing zone. Single pops of aimed shots followed long sprays on full auto. Parson figured the only reason the terrorists hadn't emptied a full ammo belt into the cockpit was the AMISOM guys were holding them back. For the moment.

Parson shoved the throttles and began to roll. He wanted to swing the tail around close to the trees to get as long a takeoff run as possible. Launching from this patch of dirt would have been tricky in the best of conditions, let alone in the middle of a damned gun battle. The DC-3 bounced over the uneven ground. The whole airframe vibrated with the power of the engines. The smell of exhaust fumes wafted through the cockpit. The fumes came into the airplane through the door in back, which Gold kept open as she scanned for threats.

The aircraft lumbered to the edge of the LZ. Parson pressed on the top of the right rudder pedal to hold the brake, and he nudged up the left throttle. The DC-3 swung around to the right, with maybe three thousand feet of open dirt in front of it now. The props kicked up plumes of dust.

"All right, Frenchie," Parson said. "Call my airspeeds."

"*Bien sûr.*"

Parson checked the prop levers full forward and placed the heel of his hand on the throttles. He wanted to time his takeoff roll to avoid hitting any of the AMISOM or al-Shabaab fighters. He didn't care if he killed a terrorist, but a jihadist's head going through a prop wouldn't do the airplane much good.

But every time he thought he saw a clear path, more gunmen ran or stumbled through his field of vision. Some were AMISOM; some were terrorists.

"Get the fuck out of the way," Parson muttered.

Three more terrorists came out of the trees. AMISOM soldiers fired on them, and two of them fell. One kept running. Straight at the airplane.

The jihadist wielded an AK-47 in his right hand, and he held something small in his left. A short guy—he looked like just a boy.

"What's that kid doing?" Chartier said.

Parson realized he would never get his clear path. And he couldn't just sit there and let a gunman pump bullets into the cockpit.

"Sucks to be you," Parson said.

He released the brakes and jammed the throttles. The Pratts roared, and the DC-3 began rolling.

The boy terrorist stood defiantly in the takeoff path. He cocked back his arm to throw something. Parson saw the baleful look in the boy's eye as the airplane accelerated past him. Then the boy disappeared behind the left wing.

A fleeting thought entered Parson's mind as he watched the airspeed needle come off the peg: That little fucker's got a grenade.

"Thirty," Chartier said.

"Power's good," Geedi said.

Parson held the throttles forward; they had a way of creeping back if you didn't guard them. The throttles, the instruments, and the chaos outside occupied so much of his mind that for an instant he took in more information than he could process. A sharp thump sounded somewhere behind the DC-3. The airplane jolted slightly.

At the same time, something peppered the left wing. Sounded like gravel slung against the underside of a car.

In Parson's task-saturated state, he did not connect the thump with the boy's grenade. For a second he thought: We just ran over somebody.

The aircraft began to vibrate. The motion came from somewhere on the left side. The left main gear seemed to dig into mud, though the field was dry and dusty.

The DC-3 began to swerve to the left. Parson stomped right rudder. Made no difference at all.

What the fuck's wrong with this airplane? Parson wondered.

"Reject," Chartier called.

All of Parson's instincts screamed for him to continue the takeoff. A firefight swirled around him. The wrong side was winning. Getting airborne was the only escape.

But the DC-3 wasn't getting airborne. The plane was no longer accelerating. The trees on the other side of the field loomed closer, and the Pratts roared at full power, but the airspeed needle hung at forty. Parson couldn't even keep the aircraft tracking a straight line.

Chartier was right. Continuing the takeoff roll amounted to suicide. The airplane would never get off the ground—just rip an exploding, flaming, smoking hole in the trees ahead.

Stopping looked like a death wish, too. The DC-3—and its occupants—would become a stationary bullet magnet. Their only hope lay in getting out and away from the airplane.

Parson yanked the throttles to idle. Stood on the brakes. With his harness unbuckled, the rapid deceleration nearly slid him out of his seat. He braced himself against the instrument panel with his right hand, clutched the yoke with his left.

Chartier ripped the mixture levers back to idle cutoff. Smacked the feathering buttons with the heel of his hand. Slapped the battery switches to OFF. The roar of the Pratts died away, and the aircraft lurched to a stop. With the engines now silent, spatters of gunfire sounded as if the shooters aimed from practically under the wings.

"Get out and find cover!" Parson shouted. As he spoke, Gold fired two rounds through the open door.

Geedi plucked the headset from his ears, stood, and folded his jump seat out of the way. Scrambled aft toward the door. Chartier untangled himself from his harness straps and interphone cord and followed Geedi. Parson left the cockpit last. He didn't have to fumble for his survival vest because he still wore it over his flak jacket. But he nearly forgot about the medical bag; he turned around and grabbed it on the way out.

Gold still aimed Parson's Beretta through the doorway. She fired three more rounds. Parson could not see the target. A bullet from outside tore through the aircraft. Two bright holes of daylight appeared on either side of the cargo compartment.

Sweeping around with the pistol, Gold scanned outside. Apparently she saw no more threats. She jumped from the airplane. Geedi grabbed Stewart and pulled her through the exit. Chartier leaped out behind them, revolver in hand. Standing near the door, Parson confirmed that everyone but him had gotten out of the aircraft; they gathered near the left wing.

"There's a copse of trees to the north," Gold said. "I don't see any bad guys in that direction."

Parson looked where Gold was pointing. About two football fields away stood four or five acacia trees at the edge of the expanse of tall grass he'd seen from the air. Probably as good a place as any to take cover and rally up. Parson leaped from the DC-3.

As soon as his boots hit the ground, he saw what had happened to the plane. Something had shredded the tire. The little fucker with the grenade had thrown the damned thing and it must have detonated right next to the tire.

Grenade shrapnel had also punctured the wing. Fuel from the aux tank trickled from at least three holes. Chartier moved to crouch near the left main gear. He raised his pistol.

"Don't shoot, Frenchie!" Parson yelled. "You got gas all around you."

"Merde," Chartier said. Lowered the weapon.

"Run," Gold shouted.

Chartier ducked around the rivulets of fuel and ran for the copse of trees. When he got well away from the aircraft, he raised his Smith & Wesson and fired at something. The slam of the .500 Magnum sounded more like a shotgun than a pistol.

Geedi sprinted behind Chartier. Parson grabbed the back of Stewart's jacket, and he and Gold ran with her. The gunfire between al-Shabaab and AMISOM came in convulsions. Parson had little idea what to do except flee. Nothing prepared him for rejecting a takeoff at a field the enemy had overrun. Where were Ongondo's men? Where was the enemy? The firefight had devolved into battling mobs. The copse that Gold saw offered the nearest cover. Parson, Gold, Stewart, and Geedi caught up with Chartier under the acacias. Slugs zinged through the branches just overhead. Splinters and twigs sprinkled down from the limbs.

"Get down," Gold said. We're back in *her* territory, Parson realized. Ground combat.

Parson pushed Stewart flat to the dirt. Gold and Geedi dropped to prone positions. Tall grass beneath the trees offered some concealment, but zero protection from gunfire. Gold lay with the Beretta in her hands, pointing the weapon back toward the landing zone. Chartier crouched low, and he poised to fire, the hammer cocked on his revolver.

From two hundred yards, Parson eyed his airplane. The DC-3 listed to the left, and the left wing still leaked fuel. He expected a tracer round or an RPG to ignite the avgas at any moment and turn the plane into a burning hunk of twisted aluminum. But gunfire held the al-Shabaab fighters back, at least for the moment.

No sign of the kid who'd lobbed the grenade, either. Parson wished he could take the little bastard's AK-47 away, grab the barrel, and beat him to death with the stock.

Think, Parson told himself. For all intents and purposes, you just got shot down. What's the first thing you do after bailing out? Disappear.

"We need to hide somewhere before those jackasses start looking for us," Parson said.

"The sooner the better," Gold said.

"D'accord," Chartier said.

But where to hide? Parson wanted to find a deep ditch, a cave, an abandoned building, anything that provided shielding from gunfire. He decided to scout around for a place to hole up. Use the firefight to his advantage. Those al-Shabaab assholes might be too busy to look for him and his crew now, but that could change at any minute.

Parson unzipped a pouch on his survival vest. Took out what looked like a woman's makeup compact, except it was olive drab. He opened the container of camo face paint and started dabbing green and black stripes across his cheeks and forehead. When he finished, he wiped his hands on the legs of his flight suit and put away the face paint. Then he dug for his handheld GPS. He kept his eyes on his surroundings and found the GPS by feel alone; its stubby little quad helix antenna gave the Garmin receiver a distinctive shape.

He pressed the power button on the GPS and waited for the unit to initialize. A status page told him he was receiving a good signal from ten satellites. More than enough. No buildings out here to screw with reception.

To record the location of the airplane, Parson pressed MARK. The GPS displayed the coordinates and field elevation of the spot where Parson stood. He pressed ENTER, and the receiver stored the location as Waypoint One.

"I'm going to look for better cover," Parson said.

"Here," Gold said. "Take this."

She flicked the safety lever on the Beretta to decock it. Then she flicked the lever again, taking the weapon's safety off to make it ready to fire once more. With the hammer no longer set to strike on a hair trigger, she could safely hand the pistol to Parson.

"No, you keep it," Parson said.

"Negative, Michael," Gold said. "If you find cover and don't make it back, you haven't done us any good."

Parson couldn't argue with that; this was no time for his protective feelings toward her to sway his judgment. He took the weapon. After she let go of the pistol, she placed her fingers around his wrist and gave it a brief squeeze.

"All right," Parson said. "You guys stay as low and small as possible. I'll try to find a better place to hide. Frenchie, you got that little radio I gave you?"

"*Oui.*" Chartier patted a leg pocket on his flight suit.

"Good. Turn it on and keep it on channel ten. I'll call you when I find something."

Parson left the medical bag with Chartier and prepared to set out on his own. He hated to leave the crew, but he knew if he led a gaggle of four other people, not knowing where he was going, the group would become a target too big to miss. Better to find a hideout and come back for them. A lame-ass plan, he realized. As lame as his mail-order survival gear and little pissant civilian radios.

He felt a twinge of irony in his nearly hopeless circumstances. During the Iraq War, he had a chance to get out of the Air Force and make big bucks flying in Iraq for a civilian contractor. *Big* bucks. Piloting a twin-engine turboprop on night-vision goggles, carrying ex-military badasses for Blackwater, Triple Canopy, and other companies. But he didn't take the job. He worried that if he got into trouble, he might not have all the resources of the Air Force to come help him. Now he found himself in that very situation.

But not for big bucks.

For nothing. Zilch. Nada. For charity.

I just created a whole new level of stupid that didn't even fucking exist before now, Parson told himself.

He held the Beretta in one hand, and he began to snake through the grass on his knees and elbows. Had no idea where he was going except farther from the airplane. Sweat darkened by face paint dripped from his nose. From time to time he heard the supersonic crack of a bullet passing overhead, a reminder to stay as low as possible. Perfect, Parson thought. If a stray round doesn't get me, I'll probably come eye to eye with a spitting cobra.

Pebbles and grit ground through his clothing. Blades of grass scratched at his face. The gear in his survival vest dug into his ribs and stomach. After fifteen minutes of miserable, slow progress, Parson came to a dry creek bed. The creek bed dipped four feet lower than the surrounding landscape; in heavy rains it probably channeled torrents that cut deeper each season. For now, though, it offered a slight margin of safety.

Parson let himself roll into the creek bed. He checked the GPS for a bearing back to the landing zone. After catching his breath, he'd go back and lead the others here. First, however, he decided to try calling Ongondo. Maybe the AMISOM commander could spare a squad to protect Parson and his crew.

From a vest pocket, Parson took his flier's nav/com radio. He knew of no method to contact Ongondo except what he'd used in the air: the VHF emergency frequency. He turned on the radio and punched in 121.5. Static fried as he adjusted the squelch. He pressed the transmit button.

"Spear Alpha," Parson called, "World Relief Airlift."

No answer.

"Spear Alpha," Parson transmitted, "this is Parson. Are you up on freq?"

No reply except static and the rips of distant gunfire.

17.

Surely Allah had guided Hussein's hand. The infidels' flying machine had passed so near he felt the blast of its spinning blades. Then he'd thrown the grenade as hard as he could.

Hussein aimed ahead of the airplane. No one had trained him for this, but common sense told him that when aiming at a moving target, one must allow for the forward motion. The grenade bounced in front of the wing. It exploded just as the tire rolled by.

And then, praise be to Allah, the airplane shuddered and stopped. Hussein fired at it, hoping to cut down the infidels as they ran out of the machine like unbelieving rats.

But the stooges organized themselves enough to fight back as they retreated. Their bullets came close enough to make the soil dance at Hussein's feet. So once more, Hussein ran like a cheetah.

He felt Allah had given him three great gifts: a clear mind for thinking, good eyes for shooting and throwing, and fast legs for running. And in this matter of the airplane, he had used all three in less time than it takes to stone a man to death.

Hussein knew that measure of time from experience.

He had seen Allah's justice delivered in this way. *Rajam*, it was called. Described and ordered by the Prophet, according to the Sheikh. It had happened early in Hussein's training, a few weeks after al-Shabaab picked him up, starving, off the streets of Mogadishu.

In the village of El Bon, the Sheikh had declared a man guilty of adultery. At a field outside the village, some of the older men dug a hole three feet deep. A group of locals sat on bleachers assembled for the occasion. The villagers waited silently. Hussein wondered if they were eager to see this rare form of entertainment or if they wished not to be there at all.

Their wishes did not matter. One of the soldiers of God stood beside the bleachers with a rifle, forbidding anyone to leave.

Four al-Shabaab fighters stood next to a pickup truck. Two held rifles; two were unarmed. Hussein and four other young recruits watched the proceedings from the shade of a mirimiri tree.

When the men finished digging the hole, the Sheikh barked an order: "Bring the condemned."

Two men at the pickup opened the tailgate and grabbed at something Hussein could not see. Then he realized the sinner lay in the bed of the truck, hidden until now. The men dragged him out by his ankles.

The sinner's feet were bound, but his hands remained untied. He wore a dirty light blue shirt with buttons down the front and plain gray trousers. Probably the clothes he'd worn the day he was arrested. No shoes. The man's head was shaved, and his arms looked as thin as matchsticks. The skin stretched tight around his skull; he looked like the face of death even in life.

The two unarmed al-Shabaab men took the condemned by the elbows, and they pulled him toward the hole. The sinner's bare feet left drag marks in the dry red dirt like the hooves of a dead goat dragged by a lion.

"Be merciful, my brothers," the sinner moaned.

Hussein wondered what the man meant by that. Did he mean let him go? Why would the soldiers of God let a sinner go? Hussein supposed one might beg for one's life no matter how hopeless the circumstances. Or did the sinner mean just kill him quickly? Perhaps so.

The al-Shabaab soldiers dumped the man feetfirst into the hole. The fighters who had dug the hole began scooping dirt and refilling the hole around the sinner. One tossed a shovel full of dirt into the sinner's face, and the men laughed. The condemned man brushed dirt from his eyes and head as the men buried him up to his waist. He looked weak and pitiful, like a bird with a broken wing.

"I have harmed no one," the man pleaded. Then he cried out in a singsong voice, appealing to Allah for mercy, for justice.

"Silence," the Sheikh shouted. "You shall have justice." The Sheikh turned and ordered, "Bring the stones."

Four al-Shabaab men returned to the pickup. Two of them climbed into the bed. They lifted a wooden crate. The two grunted and strained as they worked, and they handed the crate to the men on the ground. Then all four carried the crate, and they dumped the stones a car's length from the sinner. At the sight of the stones, the condemned man began to wail.

"Townspeople," the Sheikh called out in a loud voice, "some of you may think this punishment harsh. However, showing mercy to a sinner is itself a sin. Allah demands strength and steadfastness from His people. Today, the Youth will school you in such strength and steadfastness."

The Sheikh pointed to Hussein and the four other new boys. He motioned for them to come forward.

"You five will begin the execution," the Sheikh said. "You must learn to strike hard for Allah, to serve as His arm and sword."

Three of the boys ran to the pile of rocks. Each of them grabbed a stone and began to prance and bob, eager for the order to throw. Hussein and another boy walked more slowly. Hussein sensed the eyes of the crowd on him; his fingertips buzzed with nervousness.

He felt honored, frightened, and confused at the same time. He had never killed anyone. Did Allah really want him to do this? The sinner, buried up to his waist, looked like a small child playing in the dirt. The Sheikh apparently saw Hussein's reluctance.

"Go on," the Sheikh said. "Pick up a stone." He spoke in an almost fatherly voice, as if teaching a son to build a house with rocks.

Hussein chose a rock. A white one, large enough that he could not wrap his fingers all the way around. Holes and facets marked the stone; perhaps it was ancient coral eroded from coastal ground. Hussein hefted the rock, and he looked at his target.

The sinner made no sound now, but tears streamed muddy tracks down his face. His eyes looked as big as the shells of clams, and with them he seemed to beg for release. When Hussein was little, he once saw older boys stone a puppy, and the animal's eyes looked the same way before it died.

Hussein's anxiety came from more than drawing blood for the first time. At first his thoughts flowed cloudy; he could not set words to what bothered him. Then a memory gave form to his troubles: Before his time with al-Shabaab, he had met a girl. Another hungry orphan, scrounging for food. One night on the seashore they kissed.

If the al-Shabaab men knew, would they stone him, too?

The Sheikh's next command gave Hussein no time for thought, no room for doubts.

"If you are ready to be men," the Sheikh said, "if you are ready to serve as soldiers of God, carry out the sentence."

One of the prancing boys threw the first stone. It missed wide, sailed over the sinner's head. The condemned man watched the rock pass as if it had no connection with his fate whatsoever.

The miss infuriated the boy who threw it. He grabbed rocks in both hands. With his right, he flung another stone. That one missed, too. He transferred the other rock from his left hand to his right, and he let fly again.

That rock hit the sinner in the chest. The man let out a grunt like when you step on a dead puffer fish. Then he began to scream.

Hussein threw his rock. Struck the man in the side of the head hard enough to silence the screams. The sinner swayed as if his powers of balance had left him. Blood poured from his temple, stained his shirt, and dripped into the freshly turned soil around him.

The man covered his head with his arms, and he leaned face-forward onto the ground. Now Hussein understood the reason for leaving his arms untied. The sinner would instinctively cover himself. And that would prolong his agony. More than likely, killing blows would not crush his skull until his arms were too broken to hold up and protect him.

"*Joogso,*" the sinner moaned. "*Joogso, joogso.*" Stop, stop, stop.

One of the boys laughed. Some of the older men joined the boys at the rock pile. Now stones flew like storm-driven hail. The ones that missed the man bounced and rolled all around him.

The condemned raised himself. One of his arms hung limp, twisted, and bloody. The other covered his eyes. A stone cracked into the elbow of the upheld arm, and that arm dropped, too. Another rock hit the man's face so hard that dust flew from his head. His left eye dangled from its socket. The next stone tore away the eye.

Hussein did not pick up another stone. He gaped in silence, paralyzed by a mixture of fear, excitement, and power. Yes, power. He had delivered the first damaging blow to this sinner.

Perhaps for that reason the Sheikh did not berate Hussein for not flinging more rocks. When someone else's well-thrown rock cracked the sinner's skull and exposed his brain, Hussein felt only horror.

Did Allah really demand so much blood? Hussein was glad the Sheikh and the other men could not know his thoughts.

The condemned man slumped as stones continued to pulverize him. He fell back at a contorted angle, almost surely dead by now. Yet the Sheikh did not stop the stoning. Rocks pounded the man's face to a flat, bleeding pulp. The boy who had thrown the first stone began slinging more rocks sidearm, one after another as fast as he could. They struck the ground or the man's torso, then bounced away, spinning.

By the time the rocks stopped flying, only the red-stained clothing gave any sign that the dead thing had been a man. The wind rose, died away, and gusted again. It seemed to Hussein that the land itself was breathing. If Allah meant this as some kind of sign, Hussein could not decipher it.

The stone-throwing men and boys milled around with an unnatural wildness in their eyes. They looked like people who had chewed too much khat and could not stand still.

Such memories came to Hussein without his willing them, both in times of calm and in times of action. Now, in this time of action, he forced his mind to think about the fight at hand. A soldier of God must focus.

Hussein hid in a clump of tiger bush and clutched his rifle. He could see neither Abdullahi nor the Sheikh. Al-Shabaab men ran among the tiger bush, grass, and acacia trees, but not with any organization that Hussein could see. Rifle shots snapped in twos and threes; Hussein couldn't spot any of the shooters.

He'd been waiting for a chance to approach the airplane again. Maybe spray its motors with gunfire. But the Sheikh had seemed more interested in the people from the flying machine than in the machine itself. Was one of those people the famous person the Sheikh had mentioned? If I can kill or capture this person so revered by the infidels, Hussein thought, I can win glory.

He gazed across the field. He did not see any of the *gaalos* now, but he knew the direction they'd fled. Preparing himself for another cheetahlike dash, he felt his bones and tendons contract. His limbs, muscles, and connective tissues collected themselves into a coiled spring. At this moment, he did not feel tired at all.

Hussein waited and watched, hoping the stooges' gunfire would die down and give him a chance to hunt his prey. He would not run foolishly into the arms of death, but neither would he shirk his duty. The thought of dying did not frighten him; he did not care why the *huur* had flown overhead. Its ways remained mysterious; Hussein did not recall seeing a *huur* on the day of the stoning.

Today, however, that awful bird had come for a reason. No doubt about that. And no matter what the bird's purpose, Hussein had a mission to complete.

A plan formed in his mind: He would sprint to the airplane and hide under it for a moment. In the time he would need to cover that distance, only the most expert infidel shooter could bring up a weapon, center his sights, and fire. Behind the shield of the airplane's tire, perhaps, he would catch his breath. Then he would choose another goal— a tree, a clump of grass, a destroyed vehicle, any point that brought him closer to the *gaalos*.

He would chase them wherever they went. If necessary, he would chase them all the way to Mogadishu. He would chase them to the sea or to the desert. Surely they had strong weapons and expensive training. Hussein had his AK, his quick feet, and the blessings of Allah.

For maximum speed, he kicked off his sandals. Hussein liked the feel of grit flicking from beneath his feet when he dashed as hard as he could. He considered it a sign of Allah's infinite wisdom that one could run fastest without shoes. Man could not improve on Allah's work.

In an instant, Hussein uncoiled himself and sprinted. Only his toes and the balls of his feet touched the ground.

18.

Low-crawling through the grass, heading back toward the landing zone, Parson cursed the very ground, the entire country of Somalia. Cursed himself as well. Pain radiated from his knees and elbows with every foot of slow progress toward his crew. Dust choked him. The landscape seemed in a perpetual aftermath of plague—pestilence, drought, insects.

Especially insects. Damned bugs swarmed around him. Something bit him on the side of his jaw.

"Son of a bitch," Parson hissed. He swatted at the bug that tormented him. Looked at his hand to see a smashed ant. The kind with wings.

The fucking ants can fly here, Parson thought, but my ass gets stuck on the ground.

He flicked the dead ant away, squirmed another aching yard. He wanted to get back to his crew and lead them—by the same painful means—to the relative safety of the creek bed. Parson hadn't low-crawled this far since his ROTC days. He recalled the sand pit, the barbed wire, the machine gun firing blanks. The red-faced sergeant shouting, "Get your ass flat to the ground, Cadet! You just got killed four times there, college boy. Move, move, move!"

Low-crawling sucked then, when he was twenty. And it sucked worse now, at more than twice that age. With real bullets this time. He stopped for a moment to check his slow progress on his GPS.

Every muscle in his legs and arms screamed for him to just get up and run. Parson knew that could amount to suicide. Rounds snapped overhead at irregular intervals. He could not tell their direction. The cracks and zings of their close passage seemed out of sync with the more distant pops of muzzle reports.

Parson startled when one shot boomed from only yards ahead of him. He recognized the weapon: Chartier's Magnum pistol. The monster revolver spoke with a heavy voice that put Parson in mind of a thousand-pound chunk of iron thudding from the sky.

What the hell was Frenchie shooting at?

Parson needed all his willpower to stay low and not get up to look. He gripped his Beretta in one hand and crawled as quickly as he could. He heard no more pistol rounds; maybe Chartier had just fired a quick potshot to make one of those jihadist bastards keep down.

But you couldn't put out much suppressing fire with a revolver. Chances are, Parson realized, the terrorists he's shooting at have a lot more firepower. Gotta get everybody the hell away from the threat.

Parson rolled onto his side and pulled the Midland radio from a pocket of his survival vest. Checked to make sure the radio was tuned to channel ten. Turned the volume down low. Pressed the talk button and said, "Hey, Frenchie. You up?"

Lame-ass radio procedure, Parson thought. Lame-ass situation. No call signs, no AWACS to talk to, no backup.

And no answer from Chartier. Parson tried again. The radio hissed and popped. Then Chartier's voice came over the tiny speaker:

"*Oui?* Colonel, where are you?"

"Hey, Frenchie. I'm about thirty yards away from you. I found a creek bed that leads away from here. We gotta low-crawl to it, though."

"Good. It's getting a bit hot here."

"What did you just shoot at?"

"One of the al-Shabaab ran over to our airplane. Then he started toward us, quick like a deer. I fired to hold him off."

"Where is he now?"

"Still at the airplane. He fired some rounds in our general direction, but I don't think he sees us."

"All right. I'll be there in a few minutes. Don't blow my head off with that hand cannon of yours."

Parson hated to think what further damage might be happening to the DC-3, but he could do nothing about that now. Probably didn't matter, anyway. With the flat tire, the plane was unflyable. Geedi had a spare, but then there were the holes in the aux tank—plus whatever else was wrong. Parson doubted the airplane would ever move again. He'd seen derelict airplanes rusting at remote strips and LZs all over the world, mute monuments to some past disaster. Now he'd left one of his own—and that was the least of his problems.

He jammed the radio back into his vest and resumed his crawl. Nearer the trees, where Chartier and the others had taken cover, the grass grew taller. That offered enough concealment for Parson to get up on his hands and knees and crawl faster. He found Chartier, Geedi, Gold, and Stewart hunkered in the grass.

The actress lay sprawled on the ground, her video recorder in one hand. She pointed it at Parson as he scrabbled, gripping his Beretta, into their hide site.

"Put that away for now," Parson said. Tried to keep his voice even and not sound angry. He couldn't blame Stewart for wanting to capture the action; that was why she was here. At the moment, however, he didn't want sunlight glinting off a camera lens. Stewart turned off the camera and placed it in her pack.

"You found a way to a safe spot?" the actress asked.

"I don't know about that," Parson said. "But I found a way out of here."

"That's a start," Gold said.

Parson handed Chartier the face paint.

"Put this stuff on, pass it around," Parson said. "Do anything you can to blend in with the weeds. Do it fast and follow me."

Gold pulled her Afghan scarf from around her neck. She wrapped it over her head, left a slit for her eyes, and let the ends of it dangle down her back. That made sense; the scarf broke up the outline of her head and shoulders. The scarf's green and black color blended somewhat with the vegetation.

Chartier and Stewart smeared on a few streaks of face paint. Not the actress's usual experience with makeup, Parson imagined. He watched her apply the camouflage, and he thought how nothing in her background prepared her for this situation. Even trained people made mistakes under fire; what error or breakdown might she introduce? Nothing Parson could do about it now, though. And, ultimately, he bore responsibility for anything she did because he'd let her come along.

Geedi didn't bother with the face paint, but he removed his silver-banded watch and placed it in a pocket of his flight suit.

"I'll take back that medical ruck if it's heavy," Parson told Chartier.

"Non," Chartier said. "It is light. I will carry it."

Before retreating, Parson couldn't resist one last look at the airplane. He peeked through the grass. Sure enough, an al-Shabaab gunman, barefoot and skinny, kneeled behind the right main landing gear.

Get the hell away from my aircraft, Parson thought. Might have been the same kid who'd thrown the grenade; he couldn't be sure. Parson would have given a month's Air Force pay for an M-40 rifle with a noise suppressor. Put the crosshairs on that little shit and make the world a safer place. Wouldn't be the first time a terrorist had fallen to Parson's marksmanship. But his pistol lacked the necessary range, and a shot would give away his position to all the little shit's friends. Parson could only turn away and slink through the grass.

"Follow me," he said. "Stay low and quiet."

Inching along once more, Parson doubted he could keep everybody alive. Evading capture in enemy territory presented a challenge even for a well-trained person traveling alone. For a group of five— one with no training at all—the situation seemed hopeless. Why the hell had he let Carolyn Stewart come along? He wasn't angry with her; he was angry with himself.

Another flying ant bit him. Parson slapped and cursed. He looked behind him to see Gold moving elbow over elbow, right on his heels. His face and limbs grew damp with sweat. The last time he and Gold had faced anything like this, the climate had been different. Back then, cold sapped their strength and will. Now heat and humidity did the same.

"How are they doing back there?" Parson whispered.

"Geedi's behind me," Gold said. She rolled onto her side and looked back. "I don't see Alain and Carolyn now."

Parson supposed Chartier was having to remind the actress to stay flat to the ground. Low-crawling did not come naturally to anyone.

The situation reminded Parson of another scenario from his training. Back during survival school, in that other world before 9/11, he'd led a team of three other trainees. In the thick underbrush of the Colville National Forest, he could see only the guy behind him. The others could see only the man in front and the man in back. Somehow, the last guy got lost. Parson, a natural navigator, couldn't imagine how you could get lost if you had a compass and a map. The guy stayed missing the rest of the day. Never made it to the checkpoint. Dumbass hiked to a road and thumbed a ride on a logging truck. Parson got bawled out for losing a man.

He couldn't let that happen today. Anyone who got lost would almost surely get killed. Parson paused, rolled onto his side.

"Sophia," he whispered, "ask Geedi if he can see Frenchie and Carolyn. I don't want to get too far ahead of them."

"All right," Gold answered. She twisted to look behind her. Parson heard murmurs, then a long pause. Eventually Gold said, "They're right in back of us."

"Good."

After what felt like hours, though it was probably less than twenty minutes, they reached the creek bed. Parson let himself tumble into the serpentine depression. He reentered the creek bed near where he'd been before; he saw his old boot prints. He could not tell when water had last flowed here, but it must have been quite a while. Even at its deepest point, the channel showed no hint of moisture—just grainy pebbles and sand that had washed along during the last monsoon.

Gold pulled herself through the grass to the lip of the creek bed, and she, too, rolled into the channel. She sat up, brushed dust from her trousers, and shook grass and debris from her scarf. Over her shoulder, she carried her old Army backpack. The backpack bore a faded patch: the purple dragon of the 18th Airborne Corps. She looked at Parson, and despite the tension, she gave that half smile of hers.

Yeah, I know, Parson thought. Here we go again.

A moment later, Parson heard Geedi sliding through the grass. Geedi emerged on the creek bank, his face beaded with sweat, flight suit stained with dirt and smeared vegetation. The flight mechanic met Parson's eyes, shook his head, and scraped his way down the embankment. Geedi sat up, wiped his forehead with his sleeve.

"Those Wahhabi sons of bitches broke my airplane," he muttered.

Parson had never before heard Geedi curse. He liked the direction of the man's anger; instead of worrying about his own hide, Geedi worried about the job. Too bad his skill as a flight mechanic could do no good now.

"I'm sorry, man," Parson said. "We came so close to making it out of here."

"You did your best, sir. Al-Shabaab just got lucky."

Parson felt a flash of anger that a bunch of ignorant terrorists had endangered his friends and cut off his escape—by simply chucking one damned grenade. He should be droning back to Mogadishu now. He and his crew could have topped off the tanks there and flown back to Djibouti before nightfall. Hit the bar to celebrate pulling off a glorious tactical mission with next to nothing for equipment and support.

Now they had to survive with next to nothing.

Chartier and Carolyn Stewart pulled themselves to the creek bed. The Frenchman held his Smith & Wesson in his right hand, and he kept his left on Stewart's back. He carried the medical ruck slung over one shoulder. Sweat matted his hair, and a hole had ripped open at the elbow of one of his sleeves. Stewart looked a mess—hair tangled, jacket torn and dirty, a bloody scratch across the bridge of her nose. When she and Chartier dropped into the creek bed, Parson saw that the actress had tied the strap of her backpack to her belt. Snipers sometimes carried drag bags that way as they crawled to within firing distance of a target.

"Hey, that was smart," Parson whispered, pointing at the backpack.

"Alain suggested it," Stewart said.

"Good move, Frenchie."

Chartier paid no attention to the compliment. He held his weapon upraised, hammer cocked, like some Western gunslinger.

"I thought I heard footsteps a minute ago," Chartier said.

Parson had hoped nobody saw him and his crew escape to the creek bed. No such luck, apparently.

"You guys stay down," Parson said.

He raised his pistol and peered above the top of the embankment. He saw nothing but grass blades rustling in the breeze, dry from weeks without rain. Chartier kneeled beside him with the revolver. Despite the reliability of Parson's Beretta and the large caliber of Chartier's Smith & Wesson, both weapons were woefully inadequate against terrorists with AKs.

Parson could think of no better plan than to stay in the creek bed and travel along its length. He had no idea whether that would take his crew closer to Ongondo's AMISOM troops, but any place seemed better than here. Stray rounds still zipped overhead. Sooner or later the al-Shabaab fighters would catch up and cut down everybody with a burst of fire. No choice but to keep moving.

"Follow me," Parson said.

He stepped around Chartier to lead the way down the creek bed. The dry channel ran roughly west to east. Parson decided to evade in an easterly direction. That would take them nearer to Ras Kamboni. Maybe the AMISOM troops had moved into the village to protect locals.

As he turned, Parson caught a flicker of movement above the creek bank. Chartier fired twice. The booms sounded so close that it hurt. Ears ringing, Parson pointed his weapon and scanned in the direction where Chartier had aimed.

"What did you see, Frenchie?" Parson asked.

"That kid who shot at us. He got up out of the grass and came running."

"Did you hit him?"

"*Non.* He dropped, but not like he was hurt. He's really fast."

Great, Parson thought. In a better world, that damned kid would be captain of the school track team instead of a pain in my ass. Welcome to fucking Somalia.

And he's a smart little son of a bitch, Parson noted. The boy knew enough to make a brief dash and then get down again. The average jihadist moron would have kept running, firing wildly, and caught Frenchie's half-inch slug in the chest.

"Can you cover us while I reload?" Chartier asked.

"You got it," Parson said. He kept scanning, holding his Beretta with both hands.

Chartier had fired three rounds from his five-shot revolver. When he pressed the release latch, the heavy cylinder dropped open like a lead ingot on a hinge. Chartier extracted the empty brass and reached into his pocket for more ammo.

The .500 Magnum cartridges, topped with seven-hundred-grain bullets, put Parson in mind of the bolts on the landing gear of big airplanes. He had killed elk with bullets a quarter of that size. The Frenchman had chosen to arm himself with one of the most powerful handguns commercially available. A hunter could use it as a backup weapon to stop a charge by a Cape buffalo.

Chartier dropped in three fresh rounds and slammed the cylinder closed. He looked over the edge of the creek bank and raised the weapon once more. Propped himself against the creek bank. He let his elbows dig into the soil to brace his arms for holding the big handgun.

At that same moment, Parson thought he saw movement in the grass. Not weeds swaying in the breeze, either. Something else.

Carolyn Stewart started to raise herself for a better view.

"Stay down," Gold whispered.

Parson touched the first joint of his index finger to the trigger of his Beretta. Kept both eyes open as he scanned over the barrel. He swept right to left, pointing the weapon where he looked, ready to squeeze off a snap shot. Or two, or three, or ten.

There.

Among the blades of grass and stems of wilted weeds, Parson made out the unmistakable front sight post of an AK-47.

Parson aimed into the grass and fired double-action. Shooting the pistol in that condition made for a longer trigger pull; with one motion he cycled the hammer to its cocked position and fired. The effort pulled his aim off a bit: The muzzle dipped down and to the right.

The bullet burned a path through the grass. Parson could not see if his round struck anything except vegetation. Just when he felt the pistol's recoil, the AK-47 sight post disappeared.

Chartier held his fire. Wise move by Frenchie, Parson thought. You don't blast through your ammo, firing for effect, when you have only five shots at a time.

Parson waited, watched, waited. Where was that little fucker?

Time stopped. To Parson, the moment felt like an aircraft simulator put on freeze: instruments still showing speed and altitude, but no forward movement. The breeze still rustled, though the world froze on its axis.

Now that Parson had fired, his weapon's hammer remained poised in the cocked position. His next shot would require a much lighter trigger pull, and he could fire more accurately. He felt like a hunter expecting a wounded lion to charge out of the grass. No use in running; you could only stand fast and keep firing.

But instead of a lion's charge, what came was a fusillade of lead. From an unseen position, the boy terrorist opened up on full auto.

The 7.62-millimeter bullets tore over Parson's head. They slammed into the opposite creek bank and churned the soil like an invisible harrow. The passage of that much kinetic energy so near felt like the close strike of lightning bolts, power in its purest expression, raw and formless. The air itself seemed to rip and burn.

Gold grabbed Stewart's shirt collar to keep her head low. Geedi stayed hunkered to the ground.

Parson pumped three rounds in the general direction of the shooter; Chartier fired once: *pop, pop pop, WHAM.*

One of the shots must have connected; the storm of bullets from the AK-47 stopped. Parson snapped two more shots toward an enemy he still couldn't see.

"Let's move," he said. "Now."

Bent low, Parson led his crew eastward down the creek bed.

19.

Pain.

Pain like Hussein had never known surged from his right foot. He felt as if an invisible jinn had hacked off his toes with an ax. In fact, for all he knew, a jinn really had brought him this bad luck. Jinns were the descendants of an angel who had defied Allah. Entirely possible that one would try to rob Hussein of his moment of triumph.

Hussein rolled onto his side amid crushed blades of grass and hot, expended cartridges. He did not scream. He ground his teeth and let a moaning whine escape his lips as he exhaled. But he made no other sound. It would take more than an infidel bullet to make him cry. Hussein was a soldier of God.

His foot hurt so much he forgot his hunger. He wanted to look at the wound, but he kept enough of his wits to avoid sitting up. Surely the *gaalos* would see him and get off a better shot next time. They had hit him purely by luck. By the will of Allah, maybe he had hit one of them the same way. No way to find out now.

Keeping his head low, he shifted his weight to his elbow and glanced down toward his feet.

Blood already stained the grass stems, and flies and flying ants began investigating the blood. The sight reminded Hussein of places where hyenas had torn their kill. Even the thought of moving the foot brought more pain. Hussein drew in a long breath. He held the air in his chest, then let it come out hissing from between clenched teeth. He rotated his ankle to look at his toes.

Or what was left of his toes. A bullet, maybe something even bigger than the rounds fired by his AK, had torn off his big toe and the one beside it. A third toe hung by a tendon. Blood streamed down his foot. The blood pumped out with each beat of his heart.

Hussein squeezed his eyes shut tightly. Opened them again. He did not know whether to curse the jinns for causing this wound or curse them for not letting the big bullet strike his head. He could be in paradise by now, a martyr whose work was done.

But that was not Allah's plan. Hussein remained on earth and in pain.

And *such* pain. He had heard fighters say bullet wounds don't always hurt much at first. Something about shock and the will of Allah and the heat of the bullet dulling the pain.

Those people were fools or liars. Nothing dulled this pain. Hussein's foot felt as if someone were sawing it off, crushing it, and burning it at the same time.

"Allah, give me strength," he whispered to himself.

He wondered if he would bleed to death. Could someone die from a foot wound? Hussein had no idea. Al-Shabaab had given him no first-aid training and no first-aid equipment, except a rag he kept in one of his vest pouches.

Twisting to his left, Hussein opened the pouch and pulled out the rag. The movement caused him to turn his foot just enough to brush the wound against the stalk of a weed, and that sent even more fire shooting up his leg. He clenched his teeth and squeezed his eyes shut until the pain subsided from a raging blaze to a steady boil.

When Hussein was little, he'd suffered a toothache, and an aunt had pulled out the bad tooth with pliers. From that experience, he thought he knew pain, but that was nothing compared to what he felt now.

With his good foot, he beat down some of the grass. He hoped creating a clear spot would let him move around without repeating the mistake that had just caused him so much agony. Hussein bent his right knee and brought his foot within reach.

He gripped the foot with his right hand and felt warm blood flowing over his fingers. If he tied the rag around his foot tightly enough, perhaps the bleeding would stop or at least slow down.

Hussein shook out the rag. Someone had cut it from a dirty bedsheet, to about the size of a man's shirt. The sheet must have belonged to a woman: Pink flowers decorated one corner of the fabric. Not a fitting bandage for a fighter. Hussein did not care. In a minute or two, that frilly flower would be covered with the blood of jihad.

He folded the rag in half lengthwise. Then he folded it again. Hussein raised his mangled, dripping foot as high as he dared. He placed the rag under the arch of his foot, then tied an overhand knot across the top of his foot. He pulled the knot tight.

Oh, the pain.

The knot squeezed the broken bones and torn muscles. The pain made Hussein's eyes fill with water, but he uttered no sound. He sucked air in hard and held it. Underneath the roar of pain, Hussein felt pops and cracks where solid bones should have been.

By now, blood covered his foot and ankle and had spattered all over Hussein's trousers. Splintered toe bones jutted from torn meat in a way that reminded him of a slaughtered chicken.

Now, to cover the wound. That third toe, dangling, presented a problem. No way to save it; the mangled toe could only get in the way.

Hussein knew what he must do. He unsnapped his machete from its sheath, withdrew the long blade. He turned his ankle this way and that, trying to place the machete's cutting edge on the toe's remaining tendon without slicing anything else. Each time the toe flopped, the weight of it pulled at the tendon and sent jolts of pain.

Finally, Hussein contorted himself to rest his bad foot flat on the ground. Holding the machete in his right hand, he touched the tip of the blade to the bloody tendon. The tendon lay across matted, blood-soaked grass.

Hussein gripped the machete handle in his fist and thought to himself: *Allahu akbar.* God is great. He pushed the blade with a stab-bing motion.

Perhaps the blade needed sharpening. Perhaps Hussein did not push hard enough. Instead of making a clean cut, the blade pulled the tendon until it snapped.

Hussein's agony soared to new heights. He would have thought one had to go to hell to feel this much pain. He stifled a cry. His eyes streamed. But his mangled toe was gone.

He lay on his back, still gripping the machete. Breathed in, out, in, out. A dome of blue sky wheeled above him. A cloud in the shape of an angel—a good one, he hoped—drifted with the wind. Hussein won-dered if that was an omen, or if the pain was bending his mind.

If you are an angel, he thought, if you came from Allah, then give me strength and wisdom.

For a moment, Hussein let his body rest and deal with the shock. The pain rolled back some, like a wave breaking on shore and then sliding away into the ocean.

He hadn't imagined this much hurt was possible. No one should have to feel such pain. Not even an unclean animal like a dog. Not even an infidel. Not even a sinner like the one he'd helped stone. The next time I kill an infidel or a *kafir*, Hussein thought, I will try to do it quickly.

Time passed in a way Hussein could not track. Maybe he'd passed out; he had no measure of how long he had lain looking up at the sky. But there came a moment when he felt strong enough to finish tying the rag around his wound.

The ground felt tacky underneath his foot; perhaps the blood had begun to clot and dry. When Hussein raised his foot, grass and leaves stuck to the bottom of it. The severed toe lay in the weeds. Ants crawled around it, their feelers twitching.

Hussein shifted his hips and bent his knee. Now he could reach the ends of the bloody cloth. He wrapped one end over the wound, carefully, carefully. He let the cloth touch the torn flesh and . . . it hurt. Yes, it hurt, but not like before. Maybe he would actually live through this.

I'll never run like I used to, Hussein thought, and that is a curse. I was so fast on my feet.

But he could still walk. He'd seen people with worse injuries hobbling through the streets of Mogadishu.

Hussein wrapped an end of the rag around his ankle, then over the wound once more. He did the same with the opposite end of the rag, and by the time he finished, four layers of cloth covered the injury. He tied the ends together in a final knot around his heel.

The sounds of battle came from farther away now. The booms, pops, and stutters of gunfire gave no indication of who was winning and where Hussein should go. He wanted to rejoin his al-Shabaab brothers. They would help him if they could, but that depended on many things. If we must move quickly and you are wounded, he'd been told, we will give you the gift of a mercy bullet.

Hussein did not want that kind of mercy. He hoped to go to paradise, just not today. If Allah had wanted to bring him home, the bullet that had just crippled Hussein would have killed him.

I have been spared for a reason, he concluded. I will fight on and learn that reason. I cannot run but I can still shoot. I can still kill those *gaalos*.

What glory he could earn if he caught or killed them now. All the al-Shabaab brothers would honor him. Even the hateful Abdullahi would have to respect him.

Hussein thought of a traditional children's tale his mother had told him and his sister when he was little. He used to love hearing the story at bedtime. It was one of the few things he could remember about his mother.

There once was a fine prince from the city of Harar. Tricksters and deceivers within his father's court caused the prince to be cast out from the palace. He fended for himself through travels across Somalia, fording rivers and crossing deserts. He always treated animals with kindness, and the animals returned his goodwill.

One day, the prince saved a mouse from some boys who were chasing it. He threw his coat over the mouse, and when the boys came running up, he told them the mouse had disappeared down a hole. You might as well find something else for amusement, the prince said.

When the boys left, the mouse squeaked in gratitude. She told the prince she would return the favor if ever she got the chance. The prince doubted that a mouse could do him any good, but he thanked the mouse for her courtesy and went on his way.

Later in his travels the prince came across a magnificent mansion with golden gates and windows of crystal. Surely such a wealthy household will give me shelter, the prince thought, so he called at the gate.

The gatekeeper tried to warn the prince away. My mistress is the most beautiful woman in the world, the gatekeeper said, but evil magic has possessed her. Every man who sees her wants to marry her. She says she will agree if the man passes a test. But she kills the man if he fails. The tests are always impossible.

Intrigued, the prince ignored the warning. When he saw the woman, he realized she was indeed the most beautiful woman in the world. He accepted her challenge as the gatekeeper shook his head sadly.

The woman gave the prince this test: He must hide from her for three days. She would use her magic to try to find him, and if she found him, he would die. She would give him a one-day head start.

The prince set out from the mansion, running as fast as he could. He found no safe place to hide, and he realized he would soon lose his life for being so foolish.

His friend the mouse found him in distress. The mouse had an idea to save him, though it would require great courage. She could lead him through a hole in the ground to the throne of the King of the Jinns. The woman, even though possessed by evil, would never think to look for him in such a scary place.

The plan worked. When the third day passed and the beautiful woman had never found the prince, the evil spell was broken and kindness returned to her heart. The woman and the prince married and lived happily ever after.

Hussein knew very well there was no such thing as happily ever after. Still, he thought some of the story's lessons applied: Think for yourself and do brave things—things no one else would do—and you may find reward. He could not run, but maybe he could walk.

Only one way to find out. Hussein raised his shoulders off the ground. He rolled to his left and put most of his weight on the side of his hipbone. The motion jarred his wounded foot, and it hurt. Hussein winced, but he found he could bear the pain.

He propped himself with the heel of his left hand. Rested for a moment. Shifted his right knee, slowly, slowly. Rotated himself until he crouched on his hands and knees. The new position of his legs brought a new kind of hurt. Now the wound throbbed like the beat of Bantu drummers.

Hussein felt queasy. He paused to let his mind clear. Spat into the grass.

He knew he was about to face tests of his courage and strength like never before, and the first test involved merely raising his head. Would an infidel bullet blow his brains out?

The danger did not matter. To walk, he had to get up. He shifted his eyes from the ground and the ants to the tops of the grass and the sky. Extended his elbows so he could see above the grass.

No shot came. The field of dry grass waved like swells on the ocean, moving to a breeze that caressed Hussein's face. Smoke drifted above a distant tree line. Someone's thatch-roofed house was burning. The firefight had died down enough for Hussein to hear the rumble of a truck engine. He had no idea whose truck, and he saw no other person. Hussein knew Abdullahi may have gathered unwounded al-Shabaab survivors and left him to fend for himself.

Now his next test. Hussein reached for his machete and slid it into his sheath. Snapped the sheath closed. He grabbed his AK-47 and stood it with the heel of the stock to the ground.

Hussein used the weapon as a crutch. He placed his good foot flat on the ground. Inch by inch, he raised himself nearly to a standing position. His left leg supported most of his weight, and the rifle took the rest. Hussein picked up his wounded foot and put the heel to the ground.

Experimentally, he shifted a little of his weight to that heel. Now the Bantu drummers drummed loudly. He lifted the rifle and stood straight. Still, no bullet came his way.

Hussein took in a deep breath, picked up his wounded foot, and set it down in front of his good foot. He tightened the muscles of his face. Once again, he whispered, "Allah, give me strength."

He took a step. Oh, yes, it hurt. All the angels and all the jinns knew it hurt. But Hussein was standing, rifle in his hands.

He took another step.

Hussein was walking.

Hussein was a soldier of God.

20.

The dry creek bed led to a collection of huts on the outskirts of Ras Kamboni. Parson stooped low, moving ahead of his crew. He listened to the scattered cracks of rifle fire, trying to discern order, finding none. Though the banks of the creek bed had provided good cover for a mile or so, the channel now shallowed to form little more than a slight depression in the ground. Parson needed a new plan because his group could no longer move and remain hidden.

Geedi and Chartier kneeled beside him. Dirt streaked their flight suits, especially along the forearms and at the knees. The Frenchman's face flushed red with exertion. Grit flecked Geedi's close-cropped hair; Parson wondered if the grit came from low-crawling or from dirt kicked up by bullets.

Body armor weighed down on Parson's shoulders and made him sweat all the more. He longed to take off his armor, and he knew everyone else did, too. But he'd heard too many stories about people removing their armor because they were tired—and then getting killed.

During the pause, Carolyn Stewart took out her camera and, again, began recording. She panned from Gold to Parson to Chartier, paused on Chartier's pistol. The actress had tied her tangled red hair in a knot, and though sweat dampened her face, she seemed no more exhausted than anyone else. Probably the result of a high-dollar personal trainer, Parson figured. At least she could keep up.

Stray strands of blond escaped from Gold's ponytail and fell across

her eyes and cheeks. She seemed the least tired. That didn't surprise
Parson; he knew she kept herself Army fit even out of the Army.

And she was giving him that look—the same one she'd given him
while on the run in Afghanistan. Watching with a detached calmness,
waiting for his next move.

"Are you thinking about taking shelter in one of those houses?"
Gold asked.

"Yeah," Parson said. "I don't see a lot of options right now."

"Let me go see if I can talk to somebody," Geedi said.

Parson considered that for a moment. He hated to put Geedi out
ahead of him; he felt protective of the young flight mechanic. However, a good officer deployed his resources as needed—and nobody
else spoke Somali.

"Do you think it's safe for you?" Parson asked.

"I only know what I read and heard back in Minneapolis," Geedi
said, "but I don't think these people have fond memories of living
under al-Shabaab."

Parson looked at Gold. She nodded.

"All right, dude," Parson said. "Be careful." He decocked his Beretta and offered it to Geedi. The mechanic did not take it.

"Sir," he said, "I think I'll be better off without it."

"You sure?"

"If the people in those huts are friendly, I won't need it. If they're
al-Shabaab, they'll cut me down before I get to the door."

And if that happens, Parson thought, I'll put every round I got left
into the asshole who did it. The situation reminded him of the times
when Gold had contacted locals in Afghanistan. She had an instinct
for knowing whom to trust. Parson hoped Geedi's intuition worked as
well as hers.

As a military officer, Parson had learned you couldn't become an
expert in everything. You had to trust the people under you. A crew's
interdependence reminded him of the aspen groves of his beloved

West. Each tree shared a common root system, living as a single organism.

"Okay, go ahead," Parson said. "If anything happens to you, I'll kick your ass."

Geedi smiled. "I'll be fine," he said.

"Bon courage," Chartier said.

"Thanks," Geedi said.

Parson thumbed the hammer on his Beretta to cock the weapon.

"I'll cover him toward the houses," Parson told Chartier. "You watch for anything sneaking down the creek bed."

"D'accord," Chartier said. He pointed his Smith & Wesson back the way they'd come. The bore of the big pistol looked uncommonly large, practically like a scaled-down grenade launcher. But though the weapon boasted plenty of knockdown power, it offered a pathetic rate of fire. And Parson's nine millimeter ranked as a peashooter compared to an AK-47. They were covering Geedi more in principle than in fact.

"Well," Geedi said, "here goes."

Without hesitating or looking back, Geedi stood up and started walking toward the wattle-and-daub huts. Their thatch roofs appeared cut from the same kind of grass Parson and his group had crawled through earlier. Around the dwellings, the earth looked almost polished—a sheen left by generations of feet and hooves. The firm soil reminded Parson of packed clay runways at forward bases in Afghanistan.

Geedi knocked on a wooden door that hung on a single broken hinge. The door did not open at first; cautious words came from behind it. Parson, of course, understood none of the conversation. The tone sounded matter-of-fact—no one inside seemed to panic or to threaten Geedi. Gold listened closely, too. She spoke no Somali that Parson knew of, but he supposed she judged the tone just as he did. Except, with her experience as an interpreter, she could make a more expert evaluation. She looked interested but not worried.

As Geedi negotiated, begged, or whatever he was doing, Parson recognized a classic blood chit moment. Blood chits were squares of cloth carried by military aviators. The chits bore the image of a U.S. flag, and they carried a message in local languages: *I am an American aviator. Misfortune forces me to seek your assistance. I will not harm you, and in return for your aid, my government may try to repay you.* During World War II, some fliers sewed silk blood chits into the linings of their flight jackets. You couldn't do that anymore; nowadays blood chits were made of Tyvek and treated as a controlled item—issued before each military mission and collected upon return. And on this civilian mission, a blood chit was just one more damned thing Parson didn't have.

Turned out he didn't need one. The door swung open to reveal a thin old man.

"As-salaamu alaikum," Geedi said.

"Wa alaikum as-salaam," the man replied.

With a sweeping gesture, Geedi motioned for Parson and the rest to come to the hut. Parson looked around for signs of the enemy, then stood up and trotted. He kept his Beretta angled toward the ground, finger across the trigger guard. Gold and Stewart followed, with Chartier bringing up the rear, medical ruck still over his shoulder. The old man hastened everyone inside, and Geedi closed the door.

For a few seconds, the hut seemed dark except for slivers of sunlight cutting through cracks in the daubing. When Parson's eyes adjusted, he found himself in a one-room dwelling. The hut looked much like those he'd seen all over the Third World, whether made of tin, cinder blocks, or mud. Blankets covered a thin mattress on a warped timber floor. The floor creaked whenever anyone took a step, but Parson supposed a floor of anything other than dirt qualified as a luxury. The furniture consisted of two mismatched chairs: a wooden chair with broken slats and a folding camp chair with rusty metal framing. Parson saw no means for cooking, but the place smelled of bread; maybe the residents cooked on a hearth outside.

The old man wore canvas trousers frayed at the cuffs. His purple shirt was untucked but buttoned all the way to his neck. His short, thick hair had turned white, and his arms looked thin enough to break at a touch. An elderly woman, presumably his wife, stood in a corner. She wore a loose-fitting garment, like a sarong. Her multicolored wrap and her limbs—as thin as her husband's—put Parson in mind of a frightened tropical bird.

Stewart reached into her pack for her video camera. Gold shook her head. The actress nodded and left the camera alone.

Geedi spoke with the old couple in hushed tones. The language had a pleasant patter to it; Parson's years of working with Gold had helped him notice such things. As the old man talked, he seemed not to emphasize particular syllables like an English speaker. The words flowed in a more even pace, with a pause every now and then as the man assembled his thoughts. Geedi folded his arms, nodded, uttered short comments and questions. Finally, Geedi said something Parson understood.

"He says the fighting has gone on here for two days," Geedi said, "and he has no idea who is winning."

"I couldn't raise Ongondo on the radio," Parson said, "so that sure as hell ain't a good sign for our side."

"Is it safe for him to take us in?" Gold asked.

Parson liked the way she posed the question. Typical Sophia Gold, more concerned with the old couple's safety than with her own.

"I'll ask," Geedi said.

While the conversation continued in Somali, Chartier holstered his pistol in his survival vest and put down the medical bag. Parson decocked his Beretta and holstered it as well. Took out his GPS receiver and pressed MARK to store the location of the hut as Waypoint Two. He noted that Waypoint Two was more than two miles from Waypoint One, near the airplane. A damned long way to low-crawl through grass and evade down a creek bed. With his position stored, Parson powered down the GPS to save the batteries.

"He says he doesn't care if it's safe," Geedi said. "If al-Shabaab takes over again, he doesn't want to live. He says he will help us or die trying."

"Tell him we're grateful," Parson said. "And we're sorry to drop in on him like this. What's his name?"

"I did. And his name is Nadif."

"Mr. and Mrs. Nadif?" Parson asked.

"No, sir. It doesn't work like that. For a Somali's full name, you use a given name, his father's name, and his grandfather's name. You don't have a surname that the wife takes."

Nadif began speaking again, in long sentences and grave tones. Geedi nodded, spoke short replies, listened with his index finger over his lips. When the man finished talking, Geedi translated a tale that explained why the old couple so quickly offered refuge to foreigners on the run from al-Shabaab.

Sometime before the terrorist group first took control of the region around Ras Kamboni, a relief organization dug a well in the village. The well house hummed with electrical power. Villagers did not need to pump water by hand; they had only to flip a switch to activate an electric pump. The motor pushed the water through a cleansing filter; Nadif said he'd never seen or tasted water so pure. Deaths from cholera—especially deaths of children—plummeted.

"Life here was still hard," Geedi translated, "but at least people weren't dying that awful vomiting and shitting death."

Sometime in 2010, when al-Shabaab controlled most of southern Somalia, the group declared the well unclean. Because infidels had built it, the terrorists declared, Muslims could not use it.

At the time, Nadif's son and daughter-in-law had just had a baby. The grandchild—a boy—was the light of Nadif's life. The family hoped to send the boy to school when he grew old enough; maybe he'd become something other than a trash collector like his father and grandfather.

When the villagers abandoned the new well and began using water that was truly unclean, cholera came roaring back to Ras Kamboni. Infants and children began to die. Nadif's son determined he would not let that happen to his child. So he began sneaking to the well at night to collect drinking water in a pail.

The noise of the electric pump gave him away. Naturally, al-Shabaab had posted guards in the trees nearby, and the terrorists grabbed him and held him for a show trial.

According to Nadif, the "judge" had no more training in Islamic studies than in brain surgery; he presided over a sharia court nonetheless. To show the mercy of sharia law and the leniency of al-Shabaab, the judge decreed Nadif's son would not face the death penalty.

He would only lose his right hand.

The judge ordered dozens of villagers to watch as three thugs held Nadif's son to the ground. They pressed his arm over a board the way one might place a fish on a piece of wood before cleaning it. A fourth terrorist wielded a hacksaw. With nothing to kill the pain, they sawed off the arm below the elbow.

"He says they took their time about it, too," Geedi said. Nadif said he could hear the echoes of screams even now. He could still see the arm lying on the ground, the blood gushing from the stump.

Al-Shabaab allowed no doctor to examine Nadif's son. They only covered the stump with a bandage and tied a tourniquet to stop the bleeding. The son's wound became infected. And without clean water, the little grandson became sick.

"His son died of tetanus," Geedi said, "and his grandson died of cholera. His daughter-in-law took her own life. He did not say how."

"No wonder he hates al-Shabaab," Stewart said.

"Nothing more dangerous than a man who has nothing to lose," Chartier said.

"Please give him our condolences," Gold said, "for what little that's worth."

"Yes, ma'am," Geedi said. He spoke again in Somali, and Nadif replied with quick words and waves of his hands.

"What is he saying?" Chartier asked.

"He says he will give us food, shelter, anything we want," Geedi said.

"Very generous," Gold said, "but I hate to put this household in danger." For the first time today, she looked anxious.

Parson knew why. Years ago in Afghanistan a family had sheltered him and Gold, and the family paid for it with their lives. He sure as hell didn't want more deaths like that on his conscience. At the same time, he had a crew and a passenger to protect. He hooked his thumbs into pouches of his survival vest and looked over the old couple.

"They might be all right if nobody saw us come in this direction," Parson said, "and I doubt anyone did. I hope we hit that little bastard who was shooting at us. Even if we didn't, I don't think he followed us."

The bad guys, Parson figured, would probably assume he and his crew had left with the AMISOM troops. In fact, that's exactly what Parson would have done if he'd had the chance. As it was, he had no idea where the AMISOM troops were. Things must have gotten pretty hot for Lieutenant Colonel Ongondo not even to answer the radio.

"Fair enough," Gold said. "But let's tell him to let us know if he gets any hint that al-Shabaab is searching houses."

"Agreed," Parson said. "And, Geedi, please give him our thanks again."

"Yes, sir."

Geedi spoke just a few words in Somali, and Nadif replied in longer sentences. Finally, Geedi translated.

"He says the stars turn in their courses and we in ours," Geedi said, "and that we're welcome to stay."

"Very poetic," Chartier said.

"I think he means whatever happens, happens," Geedi said.

Parson could understand why a man who'd lost so much would take a fatalistic view of things. Maybe the old guy even had a death wish. If he did, Parson had no intention of helping him fulfill that wish. We'll hide here as long as it's safe—for everybody, Parson thought, and we'll move if we have to. With some luck, maybe Ongondo and his AMISOM guys will get reinforcements and sweep back through this area.

"All right, then," Parson said, "we'll take turns keeping watch. I'll take the first couple hours."

Parson settled himself underneath the hut's single window. It offered a limited view, which made "keeping watch" a relative phrase. He'd just have to make do. He reminded himself to listen carefully as well. Perhaps he could hear threats he could not see.

"Can we take off the body armor now?" Carolyn Stewart asked.

Parson sighed, thought for a moment. He really wanted to shed the weight and heat of the armor, but this mud hut offered zero protection from bullets.

"Nah," Parson said. "We better keep it on—as much as I don't want to."

Geedi, Chartier, Gold, and Stewart sat cross-legged on the floor. Parson could see from their movements that the armor allowed them no position that was comfortable. Nadif spoke to his wife, and the wife went outside.

"I think they're going to feed us," Geedi said.

"Good," Parson said.

"I hate to take anything from these people when they're already so poor," Gold said.

"I know what you mean," Parson said. "But you know the drill in a survival situation: Eat as much as you can when you can, because you don't know when you'll get food again."

Gold nodded, acknowledging the truth of Parson's words even though she didn't like it.

"Sir," Geedi said, "you can't see very much from there, can you?"

Parson looked outside. Though the enemy could come from 360 degrees around him, Parson could scan only about 60 degrees. He saw nothing but bare dirt that led to a grassy field and two acacia trees.

"I can't see shit."

"I have an idea. If Nadif will let me borrow some clothes, I'll get out of this flight suit and go outside to look around from time to time. I can blend in the way you white folks can't."

Parson chuckled. "Thanks, Geedi," he said, "but I don't want you taking crazy chances."

"It's not crazy, sir. I'm not much bigger than Nadif, so his clothes will fit me. If I don't speak English, no one will have any idea I'm not from around here."

"You got a set of brass balls, Geedi. I'll give you that."

"Thanks, sir. Just think about it."

"I will."

Parson gazed out at what little he could see. Considered how best to keep his crew and passenger safe, without needlessly endangering Nadif and his wife. For all intents and purposes, Parson had just become responsible for two more lives. And, all too often, Somali lives got swept away as easily as smoke from their cooking fires.

21.

God willing, perhaps Hussein had killed some of the infidels who inflicted such pain upon him. He had fired wildly in their direction. As someone who took pride in marksmanship, he almost never sprayed rounds like that. Better to aim and kill with one shot than to miss with many. But maybe Allah had directed his unaimed bullets to their target.

Hussein wanted to find out. If he'd missed, he wanted to keep hunting his enemies despite his injury. He had managed to get to his feet, and he continued hobbling toward where he had last seen the infidels.

They were either gone or dead; that much Hussein knew already. Now that he stood in plain view, they'd have shot him down if they could have. He moved his right foot forward and took another step.

The throbbing agony turned his vision gray and fuzzy. Hussein took a deep breath, and the signal from his eyes to his brain cleared.

As his vision refocused, he made out a dip in the terrain in front of him. A creek bed or a swale. So, that's where those infidels had hidden.

God willing, Hussein thought, I will find them. And I will find glory.

He took another step. Ground his teeth and looked skyward to fight the pain. The angel shape that had drifted above him earlier was gone now, replaced by mere rags of clouds torn by the wind. The heavens themselves seemed to reflect his suffering.

Allah, Hussein prayed, please help your poor soldier.

He checked the fire selector on his AK-47, set for single shots. No more wasted bullets. He would find his skill and strength again. And as he took more steps, he found he could think through the misery, master his pain the way he'd mastered his fear.

A short, halting walk brought him to the edge of the creek bed. In the dry channel, he saw boot prints and expended brass, but no bodies. Perhaps *Shaytan* had guided those *gaalos* to use the earth itself as cover from his bullets.

Hussein placed the stock of his rifle to the ground and lowered himself to a sitting position. With legs dangling over the dry creek bank, he wiped sweat from his eyebrows and glanced at his right foot. It still bled, but not too badly. Four red drops fell from his makeshift bandage and spattered into the parched soil.

He saw no blood in that dirt other than his own. Not a single stain. Apparently he had failed to wound even one infidel. How could he have missed with every round? Maybe Allah would forgive his poor shooting if he kept up the pursuit.

"I will get them," Hussein whispered to himself. "God willing, I will get them."

He slid down the bank to the center of the creek bed. As he moved, he kept his wounded right foot off the ground and used his left as a brake. Digging his good heel into the soil, he controlled his descent down the embankment until he reached the bottom. Hussein sat leaning on his rifle, panting.

They were right here in this spot, he thought. Just a short time ago my enemies lay in this very place. If I could have gotten closer I might have killed them all.

Hussein did not allow himself to waste time worrying about missed chances. Time lost, like water spilled on the ground, was never coming back, and one could only move ahead.

What to do now? Track them, he decided. They could not have gone far. They were weakling *gaalos*, not toughened Somalis accustomed to a harsh land. They did not know the terrain, and they did not speak the language.

Even wounded, Hussein thought, I can find them. To those pampered white hunters who visit Africa, a lion becomes most dangerous when injured.

The same held true for a lion of jihad.

With the eyes of a wounded lion, he studied the ground around him. The infidels' boots had trampled the soft dirt, and all the footprints led in one direction. He hadn't noticed exactly how many people escaped from the airplane. But from the looks of the footprints, Hussein was following four people, maybe five. These *gaalos* would be as easy to track as a herd of rhinos.

Again Hussein used his AK-47 as a crutch; he placed the butt to the ground, gripped the fore-end with both hands, and pushed himself up. He shifted most of his weight from the rifle to his left foot, while the injured foot touched the ground lightly. He began to limp along the dry creek bed, following the infidels' tracks. Hussein left tracks of his own—the print of one bare foot, along with another less distinct print. The dirty bandage obscured the mark of his wounded foot, leaving little but a heel print. The trail left by his right foot looked more like the marks of a bleeding hoof.

I must remember this for later, Hussein told himself. If ever I need to throw off someone tracking me, I will take off my shoes and wrap rags around my feet.

A corner of his mind recognized his own spark of intelligence. Another boy, especially in such painful circumstances, would not have observed his own tracks and learned something useful for the future. Perhaps when he grew older he could study in an Islamic school and discover more things he could use. Hussein felt frustrated that he could not read and that he had so much yet to learn.

Did Allah mean for him to know so little? Or did men arrange it so? A mind without knowledge was like a bullet without a target, using all its speed and power in a path toward nothing.

No matter. Soon enough Hussein would gain knowledge. Through acts of strength and glory, like the one he now undertook, he would gain respect. Then no one—not even the leaders of al-Shabaab, not even Abdullahi—could deny him the right to learn.

The more he knew, the more powerful a jihadi he would become. Someday all would know him as a proud warlord, maybe even a leader of Somalis after the war ended. He would pray for wise counsel. He would kill the deserving, but show mercy to the innocent and forgiveness to the penitent. He would wear fine clothes, and on a sash around his waist he would carry a *tooray*, a traditional Somali dagger with a curved blade. A blacksmith would fashion the ceremonial weapon for him, forming the handle from the horn of a rhino or a Cape buffalo. The smith would inlay gold, silver, and jewels around the handle, and everyone would see that Hussein had been a warrior. These thoughts helped keep his mind off pain, hunger, and thirst as he trudged along the stream channel.

Hussein could take only a few steps at a time before needing to rest for a few minutes. The wound began bleeding a little faster; he could feel the rag grow soggy around his remaining toes. Now those vague tracks left by his right foot carried a spot of blood. He began to feel woozy, but he would not let weakness rob him. He had already won a great victory by stopping the infidels' airplane. If he could kill or capture them now, especially if one of them was famous, his glory would become all the greater.

"Do not let me pass out," Hussein whispered. "Let me fight on."

He took deep breaths, sucked the warm air down into his lungs. A buzzing sounded in his ears, much like the ringing that had stayed with him after shooting many training rounds from his rifle. The ground began to spin beneath Hussein's feet. He leaned on his weapon and lowered himself onto his left knee. In the process, he twisted his wounded foot just enough to press it harder into the ground—and damn all infidels, the pain flared like kerosene poured on a fire. Hussein clenched his teeth and hissed through them, and he felt sweat stream from his face.

These awful sensations came new and strange. Despite the danger and death that had surrounded Hussein all his short life, he had never before suffered a serious injury. He would have expected the wound to hurt, but not to bring these feelings of sickness.

He resolved to deal with that, too. Though he wanted to pursue his quarry with all the speed he could muster, he would take his time. Sometimes even a lion slowly stalked his prey instead of immediately running it down. If Hussein stopped when he felt sick, he could keep his head clear and still think like a soldier.

In his soldier's clear mind, Hussein knew he needed a plan. Once he caught up to the infidels, how would he attack? That depended on a lot of things. If he found them in the open, he'd get low to the ground and start shooting. But what if they'd hidden somewhere? Hussein thought a village lay in this direction. Would someone turn *kafir* and take them in? Hussein doubted that. Why would any Muslim commit such a sin? Still, Hussein decided he should prepare for this unlikely possibility.

If someone hid the infidels, he thought, this hunt would turn into something like the hiding game he used to play with other children in Mogadishu. Except this time, the loser would pay with his life. Maybe several someones, God willing.

If I come to a village and I cannot find them, Hussein told himself, I will check every hut. I will ask the people who live there if they've seen *gaalos*. If they are lying, their eyes will give them away. And I will execute the *gaalos* and anyone who protects them.

During Hussein's childhood days—what few that he had—no one could beat him at the hiding game. He would cover his eyes for a few moments and let the other children run away. Then he used different tactics on different playmates.

Mohammed—the laughing boy with one arm—always got nervous. He might disappear down an alleyway and remain perfectly invisible among the trash and rubble. Hussein knew he had only to walk down the alleyway slowly and make noise with his footsteps. No need to look for Mohammed at all. Eventually, Mohammed would get nervous and start to giggle, and give himself away.

Ali—poor dumb Ali—fell for the simplest ruses. If Hussein thought Ali might be anywhere within the sound of his voice, he would just call out, "I see you," and Ali would come out.

Little Fatima could be the toughest to find. She could curl up under the smallest scrap of tarp and vanish. That was her habit; she liked to get under tarps or the remnants of plastic sheeting. Hussein learned to ignore every other hiding place when looking for her and just lift up each tarp. He won by thinking one step ahead.

And he would win that way now. He would use his wits to make up for his injury. Hussein rested on his knee for a few minutes until his head stopped spinning. The rest cleared his mind but stiffened his wound. The pain in his right foot doubled as he pushed himself back to his feet. More sweat ran down his brow, and this time the sweat was cold. He held his rifle with his right hand and propped the fore-end in the crook of his left elbow. Took another look at the infidels' tracks, and pressed on.

22.

Nadif's wife lit a fire in some sort of hearth or cooking pit outside. Parson could not see the hearth from the window, but the scent of wood smoke soon gave way to the aroma of searing meat. He hadn't realized how hungry he was until he smelled the food, and his mouth began to water.

"Something smells good," Geedi said.

"It does," Chartier said.

"Remember," Parson said, "you guys eat even if you don't feel like it. God only knows when we can eat again and what you'll need your strength for before this is over."

Gold nodded. Carolyn Stewart seemed to pay attention to Parson's words, but she made little eye contact with anybody and said nothing. Parson wondered why she'd become distracted. Perhaps now that she had time to think, she understood the danger around her.

When Nadif's wife spread a multicolored mat on the floor of the hut, Parson assumed it was a prayer rug. Geedi set him straight.

"Traditionally, we eat sitting on the floor," Geedi said. "And don't expect a fork."

"Thanks for the info," Gold said. "Don't let us do anything rude."

"They'll probably put all the food in common platters," Geedi said. "Somalis usually eat with their hands, maybe with a knife for chunks of meat. Take all the food with your right hand."

"Good thing we got you as a cruise director, Geedi," Parson said.

Geedi smiled, and Parson figured his attempt at humor might have done at least a little good. Let people see the commander's still in control. The remark did nothing for Stewart, though. She did not look up, and Parson realized he'd need to keep a closer eye on her.

He also needed to make contact with somebody on the outside. Parson had kept his radios off to save the batteries, but he decided to try again while waiting to eat.

"Hey, Frenchie," Parson said. "Can you take the watch while I make a radio call?"

"Oui."

Chartier rose and took Parson's place at the window. Parson removed the nav/com radio from his survival vest and tuned it again to the VHF emergency freq. Dug out the earpiece and plugged it into the set, just to make sure no one outside heard the crackle of transmitted English words. Pressed the talk button.

"Spear Alpha," Parson whispered. "World Relief Airlift."

The radio hissed and popped, but no answer came.

"Spear Alpha," Parson repeated. "World Relief Airlift."

The voice of Lieutenant Colonel Ongondo came back weak but readable.

"World Relief Airlift, Spear Alpha," Ongondo said. "Very good to hear you. What is your status?"

The sound of a familiar voice boosted Parson's morale. He pumped his fist into the air. Everyone else, unable to hear the conversation, looked at him with curiosity. Although the radio contact improved his mood, he knew he and his crew were still in a hell of a lot of trouble. Ongondo didn't sound anywhere close.

"Spear Alpha," Parson said, "my aircraft is damaged and unflyable. I'm at a location—"

Parson paused. Better be careful about giving away my position on a nonsecure radio, he thought. No point in transmitting that unless Ongondo could get friendly troops to him quickly.

In Parson's present circumstances, even asking for help got complicated. On a military mission, he could report his position over nonsecure radios as much as he wanted—because he'd describe that position relative to a SARDOT: a random, fixed, and classified position some-where in the region. For example, he could say he was two nautical miles from the SARDOT on a bearing of one-six-zero.

Once again, on this civilian mission of mercy, that was one more thing he didn't have. He felt deprived of his most basic implements, a sailor without sailcloth. The situation reminded him of an ancient tale in which the young champion swordsman must pass a final test by defeating a lion—without his sword.

Except Parson didn't feel much like a champion. And he sure as hell didn't feel young.

"Ah, Spear Alpha," Parson continued. "I'm at a hide site for now. My personnel are accounted for and uninjured."

The radio hissed for several seconds. Parson could imagine On-gondo taking in that information, considering how it affected the battle space. No doubt, the Kenyan officer didn't need any more com-plications.

"You should stay hidden," Ongondo said. "The situation is fluid right now. We will send help when we can."

Sounded like he was choosing his words carefully, too, for the same reasons of security. Over the radio, two shots echoed in the back-ground. Parson couldn't tell whether the rounds were incoming or outgoing.

"By the way," Parson asked, "were you able to pick up the supplies we brought?"

"We got most of it," Ongondo said. "Then we had to move."

"Glad to hear it," Parson said. "And we'll stay out of sight. World Relief Airlift out."

Parson removed the earpiece from his ear and turned off the radio. Gold looked at him and raised her eyebrows.

"What did you find out?" she asked.

"The good news is Ongondo is still out there," Parson said, "and he hasn't forgotten us. He got the medical stuff we offloaded, too, so at least we didn't do this for nothing. The bad news is that he's tied down somewhere. He couldn't say where on an open channel. While I was on the radio, did anyone hear two shots?"

"*Non,*" Chartier said. Everyone else shook their heads.

Parson explained how that told him something: He'd heard the shots over the radio. If no one else heard them, that meant Ongondo's unit was so far away that even rifle fire was out of hearing range.

"What about air support from Djibouti?" Gold asked. "Can they send a helo to pick us up?"

"I was just thinking that," Parson said. "You got your sat phone with you?"

"Got it right here."

Gold opened her backpack and rummaged around. Retrieved her satellite phone and pressed the power button.

"Thanks, Sophia," Parson said. "Lemme know when it initializes." The phone would need a few moments to connect with a satellite.

"You think Djibouti will have an aircraft to send for us?" Geedi asked.

"I sure hope so," Parson said. "But this whole goat rope came down unexpectedly, and I don't know what aircraft they'll have available."

He kept all these things on his mind as Nadif and his wife finished preparing the meal. They brought in a plate of round, flat pieces of bread that looked a lot like the naan bread Parson had seen in Afghanistan.

"That looks good," Parson said.

"It is," Geedi said. "We call it *sabayaad.* I'll show you how to eat with it when the time comes."

"Thanks."

In a better situation, Parson would have seen this dinner as an interesting cultural experience. Gold had taught him to appreciate the customs and habits of people he met on missions around the world. But now he worried mainly about keeping his crew and benefactors safe—and not offending his benefactors in the process.

A few minutes later, the wife entered the hut, carrying a clay pot covered by a metal lid. She set the pot on the floor beside the bread and removed the lid. Steam rose from the food, and Parson saw the pot contained rice with chunks of meat. He smelled a light seasoning he didn't recognize.

While Gold waited for her satellite phone to connect, she tried to bring Stewart out of her funk. Apparently, Parson wasn't the only one to notice the actress needed watching.

"Carolyn," Gold said, "as I recall, this won't be your first documentary."

Stewart brushed the hair from her eyes and glanced up. "Ah, no," she said. "I went to Rwanda in 2014 to interview survivors of the genocide there."

"Your film was called *Truth and Scars*, right?"

"Yes. Nominated for an Academy Award," Stewart said. "Close, but no cigar."

Parson didn't know the film, but he knew a little about the subject. In 1994, members of Rwanda's Hutu majority killed some eight hundred thousand people in only a hundred days. Good on Stewart for not letting people forget, Parson thought. But visiting Rwanda twenty years later was one thing; keeping your shit together in an active combat zone was quite another. Given the mess they now faced, Parson kicked himself for letting her come along. He looked over at Gold and asked, "Is that phone awake yet?"

Gold checked the screen. "Still searching," she said. Parson nodded, tried not to show impatience. If there was any way possible, he wanted to get a helicopter en route immediately.

Geedi spoke in polite tones with the Somali couple, then translated.

"That's goat meat in the rice," he said. "She's poured ghee over it. That's melted butter with sorghum meal and a touch of myrtle."

"Smells wonderful," Gold said.

"They don't eat like this all the time," Geedi said. "I can assure you of that."

Geedi's remark reminded Parson of an admonition he'd heard back in survival school. If you're shot down somewhere and people take you in and feed you, the instructors said, don't dare complain about the food. Whatever it is, they're probably giving you the best they have.

The memory made Parson feel even more guilty. By letting the old couple take in his crew and passenger, he'd not only put them in danger; he'd also given them several mouths to feed—a burden they could hardly afford. Parson resolved to relieve them of this burden as soon as possible, by getting out.

He also wondered if he could repay them in some way. He had no cash in his wallet. They'd probably have little use for anything in his survival vest, and he might need those items for himself. Nothing in his flight suit pockets seemed worthwhile as a gift: a dirty handkerchief, two pens, a pocketknife, the folded pages of an outdated weather forecast, keys to his car and truck back in the States.

But then there was the medical bag. Chartier had lugged it all the way from the airplane. What was in that thing?

"Frenchie," Parson said, "can you hand me the med ruck?"

Chartier lifted the medical bag—essentially a tactical backpack filled with first-aid supplies. Parson took it, placed it on the floor, and unzipped it.

He had ordered the bag online, and he'd not looked closely at its contents before. Parson saw it contained more than first-aid supplies; this thing had stuff a trained combat medic might use. He found scissors, a stethoscope, burn dressing, a fluid pack of Lactated Ringer's solution and an IV needle, forceps, adhesive bandages, splints, latex gloves, and antiseptic cream. No wonder the damned thing had cost more than two hundred bucks.

Parson fished out the scissors, some Band-Aids, two bottles of Advil, and a tube of antibiotic ointment. "Tell them these are a gift," he told Geedi. "Tell them that medicine is for pain, and we wish we could repay them better."

"I will," Geedi said.

Geedi translated, and as Nadif listened, he placed both of his hands together and bowed.

"Alhamdu Lilaahi," Nadif said.

Geedi smiled.

"What does that mean?" Parson asked.

"Literally," Geedi said, "it means gratitude to Allah. It's a way of saying thank you while acknowledging that all blessings ultimately come from Allah."

"That's a whole lot of meaning in a couple words," Parson said.

"Sure is," Gold said. She glanced down at her phone, frowned, picked it up. "Sat phone's initialized," she said. Held out the phone for Parson.

"What's wrong?" he asked as he took the device.

"I got a low-battery light, but that doesn't make sense. I charged this thing before we left."

Parson examined the phone. Sure enough, a tiny red light indicated a weak battery. For a moment, he considered taking the batteries from his radios. Then he remembered the phone took a specially made battery. He ground his teeth and fought the urge to curse.

"Perfect time for the battery to go tango uniform," he said. "Maybe it's got enough juice for one call."

Parson dialed the number for the operations desk at Camp Lemonnier in Djibouti. He knew the number by heart from his tour at U.S. Africa Command. The phone rang four times, then someone picked up. Parson felt excitement swell inside his chest; this might work after all.

"Combined Joint Task Force–Horn of Africa," a voice said. "Lieutenant Wilkerson, nonsecure line."

Though the line wasn't secure, Parson doubted al-Shabaab had the capability to hack into sat-phone comms. He started to explain what he wanted.

"Wilkerson, this Colonel Michael Parson. You don't know me, but I used to be your boss's boss. I need—"

The phone beeped three times, then went dead.

"Son of a bitch," Parson spat. He let his right hand, holding the phone, drop into his lap. Disappointment hit him like sudden nausea. He realized he was as cut off from help as he'd been during that storm in Afghanistan.

"Oh, I'm sorry," Gold said. She wore a look that showed as much disappointment as Parson felt. Parson tried to tamp down his own feelings. You don't get to throw a tantrum, he told himself. You got a crew to lead.

"It's not your fault, Sophia," Parson said. "Batteries don't have unlimited life."

"I'd have brought a spare, but we were just hopping down to Mogadishu for the day."

Parson had faced life-threatening situations often enough to know he could not afford self-recrimination—from himself or anyone else. He wanted everyone to focus solely on surviving. When you got back—if you got back—there would be plenty of time for Monday-morning quarterbacking.

"Don't worry about it," he said. "We'd have done a lot of things differently if we'd known we were going to fly a tactical arrival to a hot LZ. When they asked us to give Ongondo an emergency resupply, the answer was either yes or no. It's not like we had time to fly all the way back to Djibouti to gear up for a no-shit combat mission."

Gold gave him a look that showed she appreciated his words—but she still appeared unhappy with herself. Nadif and his wife talked quietly with each other; Parson guessed they realized something else had gone wrong. But they finished setting out the meal just the same. Nadif placed a bowl of soapy water and a towel on the floor near the food.

"That's for everyone to wash their hands," Geedi said. He took the bowl, washed his hands, and dried them with the cloth. The flight mechanic passed the bowl and towel to Parson. Parson washed his hands, saw the water turn browner from all the dirt, and passed the bowl on to Gold.

From a large kettle, the wife poured tea into small porcelain cups. The coppery liquid steamed as it flowed from the spout, and it gave off a sweet aroma. With a motion of her hand, the woman bade Parson and the others to drink. He lifted his cup, nodded thanks to the couple, and sipped.

The tea carried hints of ginger and cloves; Parson said he had never tasted anything quite like it. Geedi carried a cup to Chartier, who remained on watch by the window. The Frenchman accepted the cup and took a sip.

"Merci," Chartier said. "This is very good."

Geedi translated both the French thanks and the English comment. He broke off a piece of bread and used it as a makeshift spoon to dip into the rice and goat meat. Parson followed Geedi's example and bit into a section of bread rolled around the rice.

The stuff tasted so good Parson had to force himself to stop and take some of the food over to Chartier. Parson had eaten nothing since leaving Djibouti that morning and he was starving. Judging from the way everyone else got quiet and concentrated on eating, they were hungry too.

When the meal ended, Parson felt especially grateful—and especially guilty for taking from the very people he'd come to help. And he admired the couple's eagerness to help, here in this place where catastrophes came and went like seasons.

Gold, sitting beside Parson, remained quiet after she finished eating. Parson supposed she was still berating herself about the sat-phone battery. He leaned over, put his arm around her, pressed his lips into her hair for just a moment. Perhaps that helped; she gave that little half smile of hers.

"I want you guys to know how brave this girl is," Parson said. "Last fall, when everybody was losing their minds about Ebola, she went to Liberia with the UN to help out. Of course, I tried to talk her out of it, but she wouldn't listen to me."

"*C'est admirable*," Chartier said. "She obviously survived. Sophia, did you work closely with patients?"

"No," Gold said. "I just helped counsel people who had lost loved ones. Michael's too kind; my job was easy. The brave ones were the doctors and nurses."

"You all were," Parson said. He shifted his arm from her shoulder and stroked her back. "I don't think I'd have the guts to face down a killer I couldn't see. Give me a bad guy with a gun any day."

As the old couple cleared away the cups and platters, Geedi said, "Colonel Parson, I'd like to ask Nadif for one more favor. I want to borrow some clothes and go have a look around, like we talked about before."

Not no, Parson thought, but *hell* no. All his instincts told him to protect his crew, to minimize risks. But he needed information, and he had damned little of it now. Were al-Shabaab gunmen lurking in the area? Were friendly forces nearby?

If he didn't let Geedi find out, Parson realized, he'd have to ask Nadif to do it. And Nadif had already done more than enough.

"Damn it, Geedi," Parson said. "I don't like it one bit. But I don't have any better ideas. You be careful, though. And take my gun."

"I don't think I'll need a gun."

"You will take my gun. That's an order."

On this civilian relief mission, Parson's military rank carried no more authority than Geedi decided to give it. However, Parson knew that once a person put on a uniform, he never completely took it off. Geedi had worn the uniform, and maybe he'd listen. Parson didn't want to boss him around; he just wanted him to stay safe.

"Yes, sir," Geedi said.

"Good man, Geedi. Thank you."

Parson checked to make sure his Beretta was on safe, and he

handed it to his flight mechanic. Geedi took the weapon and spoke in Somali to Nadif.

Nadif's reaction required no translation. He shook his head, waved his hands. Geedi insisted. Nadif spoke in the tones of a father trying to talk a son out of something dangerous. Geedi would have none of it. Finally, the old man relented. He went to a trunk at one end of the room, opened it, and after a few seconds produced a plain brown pullover shirt and trousers. He handed the clothing to Geedi with a look of regret. Nadif then spoke to his wife, who covered her eyes with her hand.

Geedi sat down, placed the pistol beside him on the floor, and untied his flight boots. He slid the boots off his feet, stood up, unfastened his body armor, and unzipped his flight suit.

"Pardon me, folks," he said. "I guess this isn't a time for modesty."

He pulled off the armor and flight suit, revealing his t-shirt and boxer shorts. Parson hated for him to go outside without armor, but the whole point was to look like a local. Geedi dressed in Nadif's clothing.

"In those pants and shirt," Gold said, "you do look like a Somali villager."

"Well, I am," Geedi said. "Except my village is Minneapolis."

The flight mechanic slid Parson's Beretta into his waistband, then let the shirt drape over it. No one would know Geedi was armed.

"All right," Geedi said, "guess I'll go for a walk."

He glanced through the window, said a few quick words to Nadif, went to the door, and stepped outside.

23.

Hussein felt weak and sick. He wanted to move on, to close with the enemy again. But his foot pulsed with pain, his head swam, and the flies and flying ants tormented him. In his dizziness, heaven and earth seemed to circle each other.

Each step along the creek bed became an agonizing chore. His right foot left ever-larger splotches of blood in the dust, and his weapon grew heavier and heavier. The sun hung low in the sky; the orange orb shimmered just above the horizon. A trio of seagulls flapped across the sun, dark images against the bright backdrop. At this moment, Hussein saw nothing that thrived except those gulls, who fed on things that washed up dead.

Night would fall soon, making it that much harder for him to find the infidels. Every impulse in his fighter's spirit wanted to pursue, but every cell in his body needed rest. And water. And food.

"Allah, forgive my weakness," Hussein muttered.

He closed his eyes, held out his arm for balance. As he lowered himself to a sitting position, it seemed each muscle and bone in his body connected to a tendon that pulled painfully on his wounded foot. Hussein leaned back until his shoulders rested against the creek bank.

It would feel so good just to sleep for a while, Hussein thought. Only his mission kept him going. Who were these *gaalos*, especially the famous one? A noted soccer player, maybe? Perhaps an American warlord. Did Americans have warlords? Hussein knew only a few ways someone might earn fame.

And one way was to kill and capture infidels, especially important ones. Soon he would earn his own fame. And those *gaalos* would learn they should have stayed home.

Despite Hussein's best efforts to stay awake, he drifted into a netherworld between sleep and loss of consciousness from dehydration and shock. He dreamed of—or perhaps he merely recalled—his father's stories about how Somalia was once a great and prosperous nation.

People still called a northern section of the country Puntland. At one time, the ancient Land of Punt drew traders from across the known world. Egyptians came for gold, myrrh, fine hardwoods, and ivory. Queens and pharaohs made pets of Punt's exotic animals such as baboons and leopards. The people of Punt, Hussein's father had told him, were the business partners and equals of the greatest civilizations of the time. Allah had blessed the nation that eventually would be named for Samale: according to folklore, the ancestor of all the tribes of Somalia.

How had Somalis fallen so far, to where they could not govern or even feed themselves? Hussein's father never offered any opinion, but the leaders of al-Shabaab did. It was the fault of the infidels, and of the *kafirs* who became the infidels' stooges. Because the descendants of Samale had turned away from the true path, Allah had withdrawn his blessings.

Only by driving out the infidels and punishing the *kafirs* could Somalis restore their former glory. The Youth, the soldiers of God, would punish by bullet, blade, and stone. Blood would redeem the nation.

As thoughts of jihad turned over in Hussein's mind, he felt a strange presence. Something woke him from his sleep. Not a sound, not a touch. Just a feeling. When he opened his eyes, he did not know if he'd really awakened, or if through pain and exhaustion he had begun to see visions.

Across from him, atop the creek bank, crouched a lion. An enormous beast; its tail alone appeared longer than Hussein was tall. The big cat looked ready to pounce, to spring through the air and shred Hussein in a fury of teeth and claws. But the creature's presence was impossible. Any wild animal, even one as fearsome as a lion, would have long fled the din of battle.

Yet there it was, tawny fur the color of melted butter, with darker streaks in its mane. Hussein's eyes widened with fright. He feared no human, but the speed and power of the wild cat terrified him. This animal could take down the strongest man before he could even scream. The creature possessed strength enough to rip open a zebra's rib cage with one effortless swipe of its claws.

How had the lion found him? The smell of blood, Hussein presumed. He had certainly left an easy trail to follow. Hussein had remained so intent on tracking his prey that he'd forgotten he could become prey himself. The hunter could become the hunted.

The lion's yellow eyes burned at him. Such beautiful eyes for a killer. The mouth, slightly open, revealed a long pink tongue that lolled with each breath. And those fangs—as big as the nails a butcher uses to hang a carcass.

Every impulse screamed for Hussein to run. But he knew even if he could run, he'd take only a step or two before the cat clawed his throat.

His right hand rested on his AK-47. The rifle lay on the ground, pointing down the creek bed, away from the lion. Could he bring up the weapon, bring its muzzle to bear on the cat, and fire in time?

No, Hussein decided. Probably not even if he were unhurt, well fed, and well rested. Certainly not in his weakened state. And a sudden move might trigger the predator to leap.

The animal flicked its tail. The tuft at the end of its tail carried a mark unusual for a lion, a white blotch in the middle of the black tip. Are you some special sort of lion? Hussein wondered. Have you come to take me out of this world, to bring me unto Allah?

The answer came in a soft growl as the cat breathed in and out. If that answer had any meaning, Hussein could not divine it.

So, what could he do? How could he save himself?

Though he could not bring up his rifle quickly, he could do it slowly. Maybe Hussein could swing the muzzle gradually to aim at the cat. If he got that far, he could probably squeeze the trigger as fast as the animal could attack. He'd get only one shot. Maybe two or three, if he set the lever so the rifle kept firing with one pull of the trigger. If he missed, the cat would be on him.

Hussein raised the weapon just inches off the ground. With his elbow fully extended, the rifle felt terribly heavy. The wound had weakened him even more than he'd realized.

The cat cut his eyes to the rifle. The white whiskers twitched.

Anh-anh, the lion seemed to say. Do not make me angry, my boy.

If the whiskers carried a warning, Hussein ignored it. He moved the barrel through a languid arc. The muscles of his upper arm burned with the weight. He would have found it so much easier to swing the weapon all at once and let it rest on his knee.

The cat did not pounce. The whiskers twitched, the tail flicked, and the animal seemed to show every confidence that it could leap before Hussein could aim and fire.

Finally, Hussein brought the AK's fore-end to his knee. From there, he angled the rifle so that the rear sight, the front post, and the cat's throat all lined up. He checked the lever on the side of the rifle—set to shoot only one bullet at a time.

Just as well, Hussein thought. One bullet will do the job if it connects. Two or three more won't help if they miss.

Hussein tightened his finger across the trigger. He knew the weapon well, and he remembered the play in the trigger, the wear in its parts. He felt all of those parts tighten and collect to within an instant of firing.

But he did not shoot.

If I fire, he thought, I will alert the *gaalos*. I still stalk my prey as you do yours, my friend. I am a hunter like you.

The lion's whiskers twitched again.

What are you trying to tell me? Hussein wondered. Am I dreaming or are you real? And why have you shown me such mercy?

Hussein knew he could break the tension with one shot. Kill the lion, give up on the *gaalos*, sneak back the way he had come. Show off his wound, tell of the face-off with the cat, receive honor as a fighter who had done his job.

But that would mean settling for a lesser prize. And it would mean death for this magnificent animal, which had, for reasons of its own, allowed Hussein to live—for now, anyway.

We have reached an understanding, my friend, Hussein thought. I will not hurt you if you will not hurt me.

Surely this animal brought a message from Allah. But what could it be? Hussein thought if his faith were stronger, he'd understand the meaning of this. Once again, he felt frustrated at knowing so little.

The lion tired of Hussein. Or maybe the cat felt it had conveyed its message. Whatever the reason, it backed away from the creek bank just as slowly as Hussein had moved his rifle. The claws remained sheathed. With a final low growl, more a word of parting than a threat, the creature turned and melted into the grass. The last of the lion that Hussein saw was the black-and-white tip of its tail, floating above the vegetation. The rustling blades of dry grass closed behind the animal like waves in the ocean.

Hussein gave the lion time to get well away, and then he tried to stand. The rest had done him no good. He felt a mere husk of himself, famished and parched, wounded and sore. Once again he used the rifle as a crutch; without it, he would never have gotten to his feet.

He struggled along the creek bed, more unsure than ever of his fate.

24.

The sky had grown dark by the time Geedi returned to the hut. He slipped in without knocking and closed the door as quietly as he could. Nadif's oil lamp lit the single room with an orange glow; in the dim light Parson could see no sign that Geedi had been hurt. Parson had spent the last hour worrying and listening for gunfire.

"Where have you been?" Parson asked. His attempt to whisper sounded like an angry hiss, though he didn't mean for it to come out that way. Gold, Chartier, and Carolyn Stewart looked as anxious as he did.

"Looking and listening, sir, just like we said."

"And?"

"The good news is I saw no sign of al-Shabaab. The bad news is they'll probably be back. Everybody knows we came in on a plane and that plane is still here. And the locals say al-Shabaab is looking for a famous American."

Geedi lifted his shirt, pulled the Beretta from his waistband, and gave it back to Parson. Parson took the weapon and looked over at Stewart.

"I think that means you," Parson said.

"How would they know?" Chartier asked.

Parson wondered the same thing. A stricken look came over the actress's face. The dim light from the oil lamp made her auburn hair appear a burgundy color. Strands hung out of place across her cheek, untied from the knot at the back of her head.

"I'm so sorry," she said.

Parson gazed at her, puzzled.

"Sorry for what?" he asked.

"I, I tweeted that I was flying in Somalia on a mission of mercy. Just to keep the fans interested. I didn't think—"

"You're damn right you didn't think," Parson interrupted. "Didn't we tell you not to post anything online while you're here?"

Parson felt that old anger burning in his chest. His crew now faced greater danger. Because someone had screwed up, disobeyed an order.

"Yes, but it was only—"

"But, nothing," Parson said. "We've gone around our ass to accommodate you, and we asked you just one thing: Stay off the net. You couldn't even do that for us."

"Michael," Gold said, "take it easy. She's not military. She doesn't have our training."

"Does she have fucking common sense? Can she understand English? Does she not know who's in charge here?"

Stewart placed her head in her hands and began to weep silently. Nadif and his wife looked on in utter confusion.

Parson had never before felt this much anger toward a woman. A strange brand of rage, one he did not know how to channel. He felt no urge to strike her; he was no bully. But neither did he feel any urge to hold back the harsh words he'd have for a crew member who made such an inexcusable error.

"Lady," Parson continued, "do you think this is some kind of movie? Do you think if my flight mechanic got his ass shot out there, some cokehead director would call 'cut,' and he'd get up and dust himself off?"

"Michael," Gold said.

Parson ignored her.

"Please tell me what the fuck you were thinking," he said.

"Michael," Gold said. Her sergeant major command voice. "Stop it. Now."

Stewart raised her head. Tears streamed from her eyes, glinting in the flame of the lamp.

"This place just seemed so far from my fans back home. I couldn't understand why you didn't want me to put anything on the Internet."

Parson wanted to launch into her again, but Gold spoke up first.

"If you didn't understand, you should have asked," she said. "And Michael, just drop it."

He knew Gold was right; this was not the time for a verbal court-martial. Stewart had made a bad mistake, and she knew it. She couldn't undo it any more than she could call back a bullet.

When someone endangered Parson's crew, whether through malevolence, incompetence, or thoughtlessness, he got very, very angry. That was the one thing that caged his gyros, that let his emotions trump his judgment. Gold recognized that tendency more quickly than he did, and she had a way of pulling him back from the brink.

"I'm so sorry," Stewart said.

Parson let her apology hang in the air. Though he shouldn't have gone off on her as if she were an errant recruit, the fact remained she'd screwed up and should have known better. Terrorist leaders might not have NSA satellites and decrypting technology, but they sure as hell had laptops. And they could sure as hell find stuff out from the open Internet.

"Did you learn anything else?" Parson asked Geedi.

"Not really. Saw some lion tracks. Big guy."

"Did you see the cat itself?" Parson said.

"No."

"So, what do we do now?" Chartier asked.

Parson thought for a moment, and he looked up at Nadif and his wife. He didn't want them to wind up like the family who had given him refuge in Afghanistan. And he couldn't count on AMISOM troops to keep the bulk of the al-Shabaab fighters tied down indefinitely. Sooner or later, the bastards would come looking through Nadif's village.

"We need a better place to hide," Parson said.

"Like where?" Geedi asked.

"I don't know. See if Nadif has any ideas."

Parson didn't like saying those first three words. A commander always should know. If he didn't know, he should know how to find out. But now, grounded and on the run, he had almost no options. Gold, Chartier, and Geedi were experienced military people. No point bullshitting them.

Geedi spoke in Somali with the old couple. After two or three minutes of conversation, Geedi said, "They want to put us in their cellar."

"Where's that?" Parson asked.

"The entrance is out back, outside the house."

Not an ideal solution, Parson knew. If al-Shabaab came through here in a hurry, they might just check the houses and leave. If they did a thorough search, however, they'd surely look in cellars and outbuildings.

"They can't think of anyplace else?" Parson said.

More chatter in Somali. Nadif shook his head, waved his hands.

"Nothing nearby," Geedi said. "He says this area is pretty remote, even for Somalia. And it's too dangerous to take us into the town of Ras Kamboni itself."

Parson considered the bad news. "Yeah," he said. "I suppose he's right. Sophia, Frenchie—any thoughts?"

"If he feels safer with us in the cellar," Gold said, "I think we should go there until we think of something better."

"D'accord," Chartier said. "I don't like it, either. But it is either that or go out into the field."

Sneaking around outside aimlessly held no appeal for Parson. That just increased the chance of running into the wrong people.

"Once we get everybody squared away in the cellar," Geedi said, "I can do some more scouting and see what turns up." Geedi found his flight suit on the floor. He opened one of the pockets, dug out his watch, and buckled it onto his wrist. Dropped the filthy flight suit.

"I don't know if I'm letting you go out there again," Parson said. "But for now, we better hole up as best we can."

"Yes, sir," Geedi said. He spoke again to Nadif and his wife. Nadif responded with a few short syllables in Somali, then stepped out of the hut. After several minutes, he came back and made a beckoning motion with his hand.

Parson and the others collected their backpacks and medical ruck, weapons, and dead sat phone, and followed Nadif. Outside, a canopy of stars lit the sky, an infinity of silver dust. No headlights or street lamps intruded to dim the galaxies. Night insects trilled in the trees and grass. The evening exuded a false peace that Parson found almost heartbreaking.

Nadif led the group around to the back of the hut. In the starlight, Parson watched him pull a sheet of plastic from over a wooden door frame built into the ground. Nadif unlatched a metal hasp and pulled open the door on squeaking hinges. He pointed through the doorway, into a hole of such deep black it might have led to Hades.

In a leg pocket of his flight suit, Parson found a penlight. Clicked it on with his thumb. He shoved his hand down into the darkness, well below the doorway, and let the light shine into the cellar.

The beam illuminated a room not much bigger than the cockpit of a C-5. Rotting wooden steps led down to a dirt floor; warped boards lined the walls. Parson guessed Nadif had dug the cellar with nothing more than a shovel and shored it up with scrap wood.

Shelves built from lumber placed across stacked bricks held an assortment of jars and boxes. The jars contained filmy liquid that apparently preserved whatever food was inside. Baskets on the floor brimmed with yams covered by a dusting of lime. Five people sitting among the baskets would barely fit. Before Parson even entered the cellar, he knew this was only a short-term solution, and a poor one at that. He steadied himself by taking hold of the door frame with his free hand, placed his foot on the first step, and lowered himself into the cellar. The place gave off a dank smell of root vegetables and soil.

When he felt his boots on the floor, Parson turned around and reached up to help Gold descend the steps. She took his hand and climbed down. She gave his fingers a brief squeeze before she released his hand. Parson took that as a gesture of forgiveness, or maybe reassurance and encouragement.

Once again, he thought, my guardian angel keeps me from making an ass of myself. Or at least she keeps me from making *more* of an ass of myself.

Stewart came down behind Gold; Parson offered the actress his hand, as well, and she did not reject it. He pointed with his flashlight to a clear spot on the floor where she could sit. Chartier climbed down next, and Geedi came last. Geedi stood on the steps and exchanged whispers with Nadif. Nadif started to close the door.

"Wait a minute," Parson said.

Geedi spoke in Somali, and Nadif paused.

"Tell him whenever he comes to open that door, cough twice," Parson said. "We're going to take turns keeping watch. Anybody we don't know who opens that door just might get shot."

"Good plan," Geedi said. "I'll tell him." Geedi spoke again in Somali, and Nadif nodded.

Parson knew it was not a good plan. In fact, it sucked. If al-Shabaab came calling, he might get the first one or two bad guys. But a grenade tossed into the cellar would wipe out everybody inside. A two-second spray of automatic rifle fire would accomplish the same thing. The cellar made for a terribly vulnerable hiding place.

It seemed even more vulnerable when Nadif closed the door and blotted out the stars. Nadif had the good sense to leave the hasp unlatched, so Parson and the others could escape if necessary. Yet the cellar felt like a grave, especially when Parson heard the rumble of Nadif pulling the plastic tarp over the door. The situation reminded Parson of those horror stories about people getting abducted and buried alive. His penlight cut only a small slit of light in the cellar's gloom.

"I hope Nadif is a brave man," Chartier whispered.

"Me, too," Gold said.

Parson understood what they meant. If Nadif lost his nerve or got greedy, he could betray them to al-Shabaab and claim whatever reward the terrorists might offer. Seemed unlikely, given Nadif's family history. But you never knew about these things. Put a man in a place with no law except force, and give him an opportunity for short-term gain—or at least short-term safety—and what would he do?

"You guys try to get some sleep," Parson said. "I'll stand guard for a couple hours. You can take off the body armor now."

Parson's crew groaned with relief as they shed the armor. Down in this hole, he knew, flying bullets at ground level wouldn't hit them. Might as well let everyone sleep a little more comfortably.

He slid his own armor off his shoulders, along with the survival vest. Pulled his handgun from the survival vest, checked to make sure the weapon's magazine was seated and the safety was off. Though the Air Force taught airmen to carry the Beretta M9 that way, Parson usually preferred to keep the safety on. But right now he didn't want to risk fumbling in the dark if he needed to fire quickly. He kept his finger out of the trigger guard, with the muzzle pointed in a safe direction.

When he clicked off his penlight, the dark became complete. In the modern electrified world, true darkness was a rare experience. In all of Parson's travels to the most far-flung parts of the globe, he had experienced such blackness only two or three times.

He sat on the cellar steps, robbed entirely of sight but with his hearing finely tuned. Above, the night insects continued their song. A dog barked once. Parson listened most closely for human sounds: excited voices, engines, gunfire. He heard none of those.

At his feet, his crew and passenger settled down to rest. No one spoke, and eventually their breathing grew regular and slow; presumably at least some of them had managed to fall asleep. Parson hoped so. They might need to move quickly and think fast at any moment, so they needed to catch up on sleep if at all possible.

As an aviator, Parson felt entirely out of his element. A man of the sky, hiding in a hole in the ground. His aircraft out of reach—and wrecked. But as an officer, the predicament seemed almost . . . natural: leading a group of people trying to do the right thing, cut off from command and control, teammates looking to him for guidance. Throughout his career, his teammates had always seemed to trust him—even the ones who didn't necessarily like him.

After a time, Chartier whispered, his voice disembodied by the darkness.

"Mon colonel," he said, "can I relieve you for a while?"

Parson checked his watch. The luminescent hands appeared as only a ghostly suggestion of a timepiece. They told him he'd been on guard for about two hours. He wanted to stay up longer and give Frenchie more time to sleep, but he'd already felt himself drowsing. Falling asleep on watch could be disastrous; that's why they used to shoot people for it.

"Yeah, Frenchie," Parson said. "Thanks. Here, take my weapon."

Parson fished into a leg pocket and found his penlight again. He turned on the light and handed the Beretta to Chartier. Told him the safety was off but the hammer was down.

"Not as powerful as that hand cannon of yours," Parson whispered, "but it'll give you a lot more rounds. Magazine's full."

"Merci."

Parson chuckled to himself. Even in the direst circumstances, Chartier managed courtesy. Not one of Parson's strong suits, but he recognized politeness as a good leadership technique. Maintaining social graces reminded everybody you were in control of the situation and of yourself. As an officer, Parson had other ways of inspiring confidence—just not that one. Gotta work on it, he thought.

Chartier followed the beam of the penlight to take his place on the steps. As he moved, he took care not to bump Geedi, Gold, or Stewart. The amber glow revealed Geedi snoozing with his mouth open. Stewart was awake. She looked at Parson, and Parson nodded as a kind of truce gesture. Gold slept with her hands clasped over her knees, as if in prayer.

Parson gave Chartier the penlight and moved to sit next to Gold. The Frenchman turned off the light. In the darkness, Parson considered how the meager store of food in this hole probably represented everything Nadif and his wife owned. Back home, Parson had a nice condo, a healthy balance in the Thrift Savings Plan, and a Chevy Silverado that still smelled new. He was even thinking about buying his own aircraft—maybe getting an old Stearman biplane to restore.

And I'm no more deserving than Nadif, he thought. I just won the lottery in terms of opportunities.

He hoped his group could get out of here without causing the old couple any more grief and loss than they'd already suffered. To live with such grinding poverty was bad enough, but they also had to contend with constant threats of violence. Parson wished you could remove people's capacity for destruction the way you could slide a component out of an airplane's avionics bay—just pop the latches, twist loose the cannon plugs, and it's gone.

That was his last conscious thought before slipping into a deep and dreamless sleep. The next thing he knew, Geedi was shaking his arm; evidently Geedi had relieved Frenchie on watch.

Parson blinked his eyes and squinted. At that moment, the penlight in Geedi's fist glared bright as the landing lights on a C-5.

"Sorry to wake you, sir," Geedi whispered. "Something's going on in Nadif's house."

25.

Hussein did not remember falling down. He certainly did not remember passing out again. He knew only he'd reached a spot where the creek bed passed near a collection of thatched-roof huts, just as darkness fell. The huts seemed a likely spot to look for the *gaalos*, so he'd forced himself to keep moving, to search the homes. But climbing out of the creek bed had proved too much for his wounded and tired body.

He awoke inside a hut, lying on his back on a rug or blanket. A single lamp cast looming shadows against the wall. An old man and an old woman bent over him. The woman wiped his face with a wet rag.

"Thank you, grandmother," Hussein said. He was not hallucinating; he knew very well this woman was not his real grandmother. In fact, he had never met either of his grandmothers; both had died before he was born. But he used the term as a courtesy. These people were helping him in his moment of weakness; perhaps that meant they were good Muslims.

Though Hussein's body had failed him, his mind remained alert. Where were his rifle and machete? The blade no longer hung on his belt, and he did not see his AK-47. The old couple must have taken his weapons when they found him outside. Maybe they had put his rifle and blade aside for safekeeping. Of course, the weapons would have made clear to anyone he was a jihadi.

The cool water on the rag made Hussein feel better, and he tried to sit up. He raised himself up onto his elbows . . . and the hut began to spin.

Bad idea.

He felt a little sick, almost like the seasickness he'd experienced on that boat to Djibouti. Hussein let himself slump back down onto the blanket.

"Rest, my son," the woman said.

Hussein wanted to ask if she'd seen any *gaalos* in the area, anyone who looked foreign. But he decided to bide his time, to wait before letting the couple know anything more about himself or his holy mission.

The woman put a clay cup to his lips. He raised his head and sipped lukewarm water. When he finished the water, the woman went into the shadows with her husband on the far side of the hut. They discussed something in hushed tones; Hussein could not make out the words. Eventually the woman raised her voice, and Hussein clearly heard, "No, we mustn't do that."

"True," the man said. "He is only a child."

"If he were a man it would be different."

I *am* a man, Hussein thought. And what mustn't you do?

Now he began to worry. Why the whispering? Were these people *kafirs*? Were they unfaithful? If they had wanted to kill him they could have done so already.

"He needs a doctor," the woman said.

"There are no doctors among them," the man said.

Doctors among who? What were these people talking about?

Hussein wanted his rifle. Maybe the old couple were faithful; he did not know enough to judge. But he did not like the sound of this conversation.

He sat up. Caught a glimpse of his AK lying on the floor, just a few feet away. Hussein tried to stand and reach for the weapon—and he collapsed. The woman came back with the wet rag.

"Stop, my child," the woman said. "You are hurt."

"Why were you alone?" the man asked. "Were there others with you?"

"I do not know where they went," Hussein said. Then he cursed himself. He should not have answered the question without knowing more about these people.

"As my wife says," the man continued, "you are hurt. You are only a boy, and they should not have made you fight. There are people here with a bag of medicine, and they may be able to help you. You must stay quiet and still."

Now Hussein really worried.

"I am not a boy," Hussein said. "I am a man, and I am a fighter. You know nothing. I have killed *kafirs* and infidels."

"For your own sake," the man said, "you must rest, keep your voice down, and do what we tell you."

Such talk angered Hussein. Got the better of his judgment. Made him forget his resolve to tell these people nothing.

"I am a jihadi," he hissed. "You must do as *I* say."

He tried to get up again, but the man kneeled beside him and pushed him back down. On any other day, Hussein could have over-powered the old man, driven a blade through his throat. But Hussein had no strength to resist. The man held him to the floor with one arm.

"Tie his hands," the man said. "And find something for a gag. He has decided to make himself a nuisance."

Hussein struggled, pointlessly. He could do nothing except wear himself out. In a few seconds, the old couple bound his wrists together in front of him and tied a rag over his mouth—the same wet rag that had brought him such relief minutes ago.

"I will kill you," Hussein tried to growl. The gag garbled his words.

"You are lucky we haven't killed you," the man said, "after what your kind has done to my family. But I cannot murder a child."

If you have felt Allah's justice, Hussein thought, then you deserved it. Hussein lacked the strength to fight his bonds. He lay back sweating, breathing hard.

The old couple spoke to each other again. This time they made no effort to keep Hussein from hearing.

"Shall we show them?" the woman asked.

"I do not think it matters," the man said. "Perhaps they can help him in some way. If they cannot, and if the boy must be killed, then none of this will make any difference."

They? Who was they?

Realization came over Hussein like the exhaustion and shock that had turned his muscles to jelly. He had tracked and found his infidels, all right. Except now he was at their mercy.

Parson heard footsteps approaching the cellar. Now everyone was awake. Parson and Chartier stood with their pistols ready, and Geedi shone the penlight up at the closed door.

Was an al-Shabaab terrorist marching Nadif at gunpoint to the hiding place? Entirely possible. Parson thumbed back the hammer on his Beretta. He could have fired it easily enough with the hammer down, but by cocking the weapon, he placed it in a configuration that required a much shorter trigger pull. That translated to a more accurate shot. And he knew he might get only one, if that.

Two coughs sounded from above. That was the arranged signal, and Parson relaxed just a bit. But he took no chances, and he kept his weapon upraised.

He heard Nadif—or someone—pulling the tarp from over the door. The person seemed to work without urgency. Maybe this was just old Nadif by himself.

"Look before you shoot," Parson whispered, "but be ready."

"Absolument," Chartier whispered in the darkness.

The door hinges groaned with a rasp of rusted metal. Someone lifted the door and revealed the glittering cosmos above.

A shadow in the shape of a man blocked out the stars. The shadow carried no weapon and stood alone.

Geedi moved the penlight, and the beam showed the worried face of Nadif. The two Somalis spoke in their own language. Judging from the tone of Geedi's voice, he seemed not to believe what Nadif was telling him.

"What's going on?" Parson asked.

"They found an al-Shabaab guy passed out right in front of their house," Geedi said. "He's shot in the foot."

"Oh, hell," Parson said. "Where is he now?"

"Inside. They tied him up."

"Mon Dieu," Chartier said.

"What the fuck did they take him inside for?" Parson said. "Are they nuts?"

Geedi spoke in Somali again. The tone implied a pointed question. Nadif gave a long answer and shrugged.

"He is just a boy," Geedi translated. "They could not bring themselves to kill him. But they didn't want him to be seen, either, and maybe cause more al-Shabaab to come here."

"The guy who hit our plane with a grenade and tried to kill us was just a boy, too," Parson said. "Maybe the same one."

"Nadif says the child is in very bad shape. He wants to know if we can help him."

Parson gaped at Geedi, his face visible in the edge of the penlight's beam. Geedi wore no expression. Parson glanced up at Nadif.

"He's fucking with us, right?" Parson said. "We're hiding from al-Shabaab, and he wants us to babysit one of their Cub Scouts?"

Parson let his question hang in the air. From the blackness around him, he heard Gold speak up.

"The boy is a wounded prisoner now," Gold said. "If we have any ability to give him medical treatment, we're obligated."

Once again, Parson thought, she's the voice of my better nature. Sometimes I wish my better nature would shut the hell up.

Parson could think of several reasons to disagree with her: The protections of the Geneva Conventions applied to lawful combatants, not terrorists. And this was between Nadif and the little murderous son of a bitch he'd taken in. Right now, Parson thought, we should just blow out of here and take our chances in the bush.

But Parson knew their chances would be pretty slim. Sooner or later his group would encounter terrorists again, and the next al-Shabaab fighter they ran into probably wouldn't be unconscious. Or a kid.

And all his reasons to disagree with Gold were technical, hair-splitting excuses. Yes, Parson was on leave. As far as the military was concerned, he was on *vacation*. Instead of coming to Somalia, Parson could have hopped a space-A flight to Spain and spent this time by the sea at Rota. He knew a beach bar where they served garlic shrimp, and the owner loved American jazz. Instead of running from al-Shabaab, Parson could be sitting under the cabana, feeling breezes off the Gulf of Cádiz. Sipping Rioja and listening to Dave Brubeck. Watching the women go by, some with bikini tops, some without.

But no. He had come to a war zone to court mayhem. And, on leave or not, he was still a senior officer of the United States Air Force.

Guess I better act like one, Parson thought. Even if I don't want to.

"Damn it," he said. "Somebody grab the medical ruck."

When Hussein saw the *gaalos* come into the hut, he thought his life was over. The old couple, those *kafirs*, had betrayed him to Crusaders. They would all burn in hell for this. Hussein's eyes widened, and he struggled once more against the bonds that held him. Useless.

Just let them shoot me, he prayed. But if they torture me, let me resist like a man.

Through his gag, Hussein mumbled, "There is no god but God, and Mohammed is his Prophet." He wanted his profession of faith to serve as his final words.

But the *gaalos* did not kill him. At first, they did not even touch him. They stood around him and talked in their harsh language.

American words, he supposed. Their words reminded him of a knife against a whetstone, all sharp edges and hard corners. Yes, even their speech was unclean.

There were two white women, both with their heads shamelessly uncovered. They even wore their sleeves rolled up so that their arms were bare. What manner of harlotry was this? And why did the infidels bring women with them into a war zone? Could they not live without their whores for even a few days?

The group also included two white men, one a little older than the other. Hussein assumed the oldest was in charge. Both carried pistols. One of the weapons was an automatic like Hussein had seen many times. The other handgun looked strange, all silvery and old-fashioned looking, with a very wide muzzle. More than likely, the bullet that tore up his foot came from one of those guns. If not for the gag, Hussein would have spat at these Crusaders.

Neither of them pointed a weapon at Hussein. What were they waiting for? They talked among themselves and made no threatening moves.

The strangest member of the group was a young man who looked like he could have been Somali. The man was several years older than Hussein, though not as old as the al-Shabaab bosses like the Sheikh. He wore normal clothes—not the odd coveralls of the white men, but he spoke their ugly language.

Obviously this Somali man conspired with the *gaalos*. A *kafir*, perhaps, paid to join the forces of infidelity. Maybe someone who had even betrayed his God and become a Jew or a Christian. Surely he would burn in the hottest corner of hell.

The young man kneeled beside Hussein.

"My name is Geedi," the man said in Somali. "You are hurt and very sick. We will not harm you. We are going to help you."

Help me? Hussein wondered. How could this unbelieving, Crusader-loving enemy of God help me?

"Get away from me," Hussein tried to say. He could not force the words through his gag, and the effort to speak made him more tired and weak.

Behind the infidel Somali who called himself Geedi, one of the white men opened a backpack. From inside the pack he took a clear plastic bag that contained some kind of liquid.

They're going to poison me, Hussein thought. Or give me some kind of potion to convert me to their false religion.

"Infidels," Hussein tried to shout. "Help me, brothers."

Calling for help was pointless. The gag smothered his words, and even without the gag he could have hardly spoken above a whisper.

The older white man took out a needle and attached it to some kind of tube. Then he attached the tube to the bag of poison.

"You are very dehydrated," the one called Geedi said. "And your wound could get infected. We will give you the fluids you need. The needle will sting just a little."

"Liar," Hussein growled into his gag. What did *dehydrated* mean, anyway?

They could poison him, but they could not make him betray his religion. There is no god but God, Hussein recited in his mind, and Mohammed is his final prophet.

The older man came at him with the needle. Hussein jerked his arm away. The movement sent a jolt of pain from his foot that spread agony all through his body. The one called Geedi held down Hussein's arm.

"Stop this," Geedi said. "I told you we would not hurt you. If we wanted to kill you we could have done it ten times by now. Don't be stupid."

Hussein lay still. He hated this apostate Somali. But the apostate's latest words rang true. The infidels could have killed him quickly and easily. What were they doing?

The older man slid the needle into Hussein's right arm. The needle did not sting nearly as much as he expected. The liquid felt cool going into his vein. It did not hurt; it did not burn. Perhaps it wasn't poison, then. Maybe it was some infidel potion to make him change his religion.

I will not turn into a Jew, Hussein thought. They will not make me a Crusader. There is no god but God.

26.

Parson had little medical training, but he'd spent enough time around flight medics to know how to stick a needle into a vein. When the Lactated Ringer's solution started flowing, the boy terrorist seemed to relax.

"Do you think he's the one who hit our plane with the grenade?" Chartier asked. "I didn't get a good look at him at the time."

"Me neither," Parson said, "but he could be."

"Can we take that gag out of his mouth?" Gold asked. "He doesn't look like he has the strength to shout, and he's probably uncomfortable enough as it is."

Parson thought for a moment. Oh, what the hell, he mused. Removing the gag isn't any crazier than what we're already doing.

"Yeah," Parson said. "Geedi, just tell him that gag's going back in tighter than ever if he starts yelling."

"Yes, sir," Geedi said. He spoke a few words in Somali. The boy did not respond, but Geedi untied the gag anyway. For whatever reason, the boy did not scream or shout. He just lay still, breathing heavily, eyes darting around the room.

"Is it all right if I get some video of this?" Carolyn Stewart asked. "It would be great—"

Parson opened his mouth to tell her what she could do with that damned camera of hers. Before he spoke, Gold glanced his way, and he decided to hear Stewart out.

"It would be great to show you guys helping this kid who maybe tried to kill us," the actress said.

"All right," Parson said. "But keep Nadif and his wife out of the frame. And make it a close shot. Don't have anything in the background that could identify where we are."

Letting Stewart shoot video—just like taking her along to begin with—ran against Parson's better judgment. But this situation fell so far outside his norm, he wondered how much to trust his judgment. As a military aviator, everything in his training and mind-set tended toward operational security. Hearts and minds were somebody else's job.

Now he found himself in a weird gray area between the civilian and military worlds. Normal rules of engagement didn't necessarily apply. Parson had no standards to rely on except his own moral compass—with some headings provided by Gold. He just hoped he plotted the right course, because a moral compass, just like the compass in an airplane, was not always easy to read. Back in the days of open cockpits, silk scarves, and leather helmets, pilots learned to anticipate a compass's natural magnetic error: *lead to south, lag to north.* Errors in your moral compass were harder to catch.

Stewart dug out her video camera and began recording. She ad-libbed a narration in a low voice: "The World Relief Airlift crew, stranded after al-Shabaab terrorists damaged their airplane, is trying to remain hidden from terrorists. After making their way to a hiding place, they ran across this boy, apparently an al-Shabaab straggler. Wounded and dehydrated, he needs a doctor. There is no doctor among the aircrew, but they are giving him what help they can with their own emergency medical kit."

Not bad, Parson thought. In fact, it sounded pretty damned good. Parson usually had little use for media people. He'd run across embedded reporters in Iraq and Afghanistan, and a lot of them just reported on how cool it was to be an embedded reporter. However, this desperate situation placed Stewart so close to the story that she couldn't help but get it right. Parson figured she'd probably make a darn good film, in the unlikely event he got her out of here alive.

Stewart panned from the boy to Parson, and she focused on Parson's face for a moment. He nodded but he did not smile. Stewart stopped recording.

"Geedi," Gold said, "did our new friend say his name?"

"No ma'am," Geedi said. "I'll ask him."

Geedi spoke a short sentence in Somali. At first it appeared the boy was ignoring the question. He just stared up at the ceiling and breathed in and out.

"Hussein," he whispered finally.

Geedi followed up with another sentence. Hussein answered with one word. When Geedi replied to the answer, Hussein cut his eyes at the flight mechanic as if something surprised him.

"Looks like you hit a nerve," Parson said. "What are you guys talking about?"

"I asked him what tribe he's from," Geedi said. "He's of the Rahanweyn. So am I."

"Small world."

"I don't think he believes me."

Gold gazed down at Hussein. Her eyes seemed to stop on his foot and the bloody, dirty rag wrapped around it.

"We need to see about cleaning that wound," Gold said. "Tell him I'm going to take off that filthy bandage and that I'll try not to hurt him."

"Yes, ma'am," Geedi said.

He spoke a few more words in Somali. Hussein responded in a testy tone. Geedi answered with soft syllables. Hussein glared.

"He wants us to leave him alone," Geedi said. "He says he does not need anyone's help but Allah's."

"Sounds like one of our surly teenagers in France," Chartier said.

"Or America," Stewart said.

"Shall I tell him he's grounded?" Geedi asked.

Gold and Chartier smiled. Parson appreciated Geedi's brand of humor, but this was no laughing matter. And this was not just a surly teenager. As far as Parson was concerned, this little bastard was a radicalized killer. Okay, so you had to show him mercy because you had to live with yourself. But it was like showing mercy to a wild animal. You could feed him and bandage his wounds, and he'd still turn around and bite you.

"No," Parson said. "Just tell him Sophia's going to change that bandage so he maybe doesn't get gangrene. And tell him if he kicks her, I'll slap that hateful look right off his face."

"Don't tell him that," Gold said. "Just tell him to hold still."

Geedi spoke just two or three words in Somali. Hussein said nothing.

From the medical kit, Gold took a pair of shears. Nadif held the oil lamp over her shoulder as she cut away the bloodstained rag from Hussein's foot. The scene put Parson in mind of Civil War surgery: drummer boy wounded at Petersburg.

Gold put down the shears and took hold of Hussein's ankle with one hand. With the other hand, she began to peel away the clotted cloth. The boy's foot twitched, and he squeezed his eyes shut. A high-pitched whine came from behind his clenched teeth, but he did not cry.

"Tell him I'm sorry," Gold said. "I know this hurts, but this dirty rag has to come off."

Geedi translated, and again Hussein offered no response. He neither resisted nor cooperated; he just lay there with his bound hands clasped together. Gold pulled the rag the rest of the way off his foot. The boy opened his eyes wide and cried out.

The bloody bandage looked like the freshly skinned pelt of some small animal. The foot made for an even worse sight. The big toe and two others were blown off or torn off. The ball of Hussein's foot was mangled, too. Splintered bones stuck out from what looked like ground meat.

"Dear God," Stewart said. "I can't believe he walked on that."

"He won't walk on it again if it gets infected," Gold said.

"Did he step on a mine?" Geedi asked.

"No," Parson said. "If he'd stepped on a mine, he'd have lost the whole foot at the very least. I think he caught a stray bullet."

"A very big bullet," Geedi said.

"And maybe not stray," Chartier said. His revolver hung in its holster on his survival vest. Chartier did not touch or even look at the weapon as he spoke.

"You don't know it was your gun that did that," Parson said. "And if it was, you were defending us. Don't start feeling guilty."

"I do not feel guilty," Chartier said. "Just sad. This boy should be at home, working on his multiplication tables."

"This ain't Toulouse, Frenchie. It's fucking Somalia."

"C'est dommage."

Gold kneeled beside the medical ruck and unzipped it until the front flap was completely open. She rummaged through its pockets and pouches, apparently not finding what she wanted. Looked up at Parson, hands on her thighs.

"This kit has all kinds of good stuff," she said, "but I don't see anything to give him for pain."

"There was nothing except Advil," Parson said, "and I gave that to Nadif."

"He needs morphine, but we'll have to make do. Can we see if Nadif will get him some water and a couple of the pills?"

Parson shrugged. Geedi spoke to Nadif and his wife in their language. The wife disappeared into the shadows for a few moments, then came back with a clay cup of water in one hand and two caplets in the other. She kneeled beside Hussein and spoke to him softly. He turned his head toward the wall and did not answer. Geedi said a few words in Somali. The boy answered with something that sounded curt, never taking his eyes off the mud wall.

"He thinks we're trying to turn him into an infidel," Geedi said.

"With *Advil?*" Parson said. "He's starting to try my patience."

Geedi spoke again in Somali. This time Hussein turned his head and looked up at Geedi. They exchanged a few more words. Hussein sounded skeptical about whatever Geedi was telling him, but he opened his mouth. Nadif's wife placed the caplets on his tongue. Before she could offer him the water, he chewed the painkillers. Hussein's face twisted at the taste, and he did not resist when the woman placed the cup to his lips. He drank until he drained the cup.

Since the boy didn't know to swallow the pills with water, Parson wondered if he'd ever been given medicine of any kind.

"What did you tell him to get him to open his mouth?" Parson asked.

"I told him I'm a Muslim, too," Geedi said. "Why would I make him change his religion?"

That probably helped, Parson thought, but the boy has probably figured out by now we aren't going to hurt him. What would the boy have done if our situations were reversed? Not likely he'd be trying to talk us into taking something to ease suffering.

"Ask him if he's the one who chucked a grenade at our airplane," Parson said.

Geedi put the question to Hussein. The answer took more words than Parson expected.

"He says he did," Geedi said. "He wishes he had killed us all."

"He came damn close," Parson said. "What the hell gave him that idea?"

More conversation between Geedi and the boy. Geedi hesitated before speaking again in English, but then said, "He says he was told to stop the plane because a famous person might be on it. He wants to know if it was the famous person who shot him."

Carolyn Stewart lowered her head, placed her hand over her eyes. Turned away. Gold looked up and said nothing. She opened a packet of antiseptic wipes.

Nadif brought a dish of water and a sponge. As gently as she could, Gold moved Hussein's foot so that it rested over the dish. She nodded thanks to Nadif, soaked the sponge, and squeezed it so the water dribbled out of her fist and over the wound. The water trickled back into the dish, clouded with blood and soil. Hussein sucked in air between his teeth.

"He'll need surgery on this foot," Gold said.

"No doubt," Chartier said.

Parson had no idea where the nearest doctor was. And even if there was a doctor as close as Ras Kamboni, he might as well be on the moon, because this little bastard's friends could be anywhere. No way to get Hussein to real medical help, or to get real medical help to Hussein. Parson supposed that in Somalia, people died for that reason all the time.

Gold unfolded one of the antiseptic wipes from the packet she'd opened. The damp wipe smelled like rubbing alcohol.

"This is probably going to sting pretty badly," she said, "but we have to get that wound clean. Tell him I'll get this over with as quickly as I can."

Once again, Geedi spoke to Hussein. The boy said nothing; he just lay there with his eyes wide, cutting from Parson to Geedi to Gold. The look in those eyes made Parson think of a feral animal, half wild, but with a dim memory of human kindness, frightened and unsure whom to trust.

Gold dabbed the wipe over the torn flesh and splintered bones. Hussein's muscles spasmed as if electrocuted, and that keening sound came from between his lips again. He did not sob or scream, but the pain brought tears to his eyes. The boy turned his head so Parson couldn't see the water roll down his cheeks.

He sure has a lot of pride, Parson thought. Why does he care if we think he's tough?

Blood soaked into the wipe. Gold wadded the used wipe into a ball and unfolded a clean one. She dabbed the wound some more. From the way Hussein tensed up, Parson could tell it still hurt, but maybe not as bad as before.

Nadif said a few words in Somali, pointed to an AK-47 and one of those old Soviet-style ammo vests lying on the floor. The gear also included a long-bladed machete in a sheath.

"Those are the boy's weapons," Geedi translated.

"One hell of a juvenile delinquent," Parson said.

Nadif spoke to Geedi again, and he motioned toward the outside.

"He says the sun will be up soon," Geedi said. "He says if we want to keep taking care of the boy, we need to hide him in the cellar."

Parson wished he could just send Hussein on his way. But that was impossible for a couple reasons. One—the boy couldn't walk anymore; it was a wonder he'd traveled as far as he did. Two—he'd tip off al-Shabaab to the crew's whereabouts. The situation reminded Parson of the SEAL team a few years back that ran across three goatherds while conducting surveillance in Afghanistan. The team's rules of engagement and their sense of right and wrong would not let them kill the civilians. The SEALs had no choice but to release the Afghans, and the team paid an awful price for doing the right thing. Enemy forces, likely alerted by the civilians, attacked the four-man team. Three died, and one suffered serious injuries.

When Gold finished cleaning Hussein's wound, she took a tube of antiseptic cream from the medical ruck. She unscrewed the cap, which revealed the foil seal over the opening of the unused tube. Gold pierced the seal with the plastic point molded onto the top of the cap, and she squeezed a rope of goo onto a clean gauze bandage. Folded the gauze in half and rubbed the two halves together to saturate the cloth.

Gold covered the wound with the antiseptic-treated gauze. Hussein winced, but the gauze didn't seem to hurt him nearly as much as the alcohol wipes. Over the treated gauze, Gold wrapped a dry bandage, and she secured it with medical tape.

"I'm not much of a doctor," Gold said, "but this is better than what he had."

Nadif unfolded a blanket and spread it out beside the boy. The blanket was a lot wider than the rug Hussein was lying on. Nadif spoke a few short words to Geedi.

"He says we can take Hussein to the cellar on the blanket," Geedi said.

"Yeah," Parson said. "Let's do the vampire thing and get him out of here before the sun comes up. Frenchie, grab his weapon, will you?"

"*D'accord,*" Chartier said. He picked up the AK-47 and slung it over his shoulder. Hussein glared.

"At least the little dickhead brought us some firepower," Parson said. "How many rounds are in the magazine?"

Chartier detached the magazine, checked it, reinserted it.

"About twenty."

"Better than nothing," Parson said.

Chartier picked up the boy's ammo vest and checked for more magazines. He found none.

"All right, Geedi," Parson said, "tell him we're going to lift him on the blanket and take him where he can get some sleep. And if he gives us any trouble, we'll drop his ass on the ground and drag him by his hurt foot."

"Be nice, Michael," Gold said.

I *am* being nice, Parson thought. Lord knows, I'm being nice. That's why I haven't beaten this juvenile delinquent to a bloody pulp.

27.

Oddly, Hussein did not feel any different. He still felt his love for Allah, his willingness to fight, his belief in jihad. So perhaps these pills and potions were not turning him into a craven infidel. Was it possible the *gaalos* weren't lying, that they really meant to help him?

He did not resist as they rolled him onto a blanket. The *gaalos* lifted the blanket and carried him from the hut. At first he wondered if they were taking him outside to shoot him, but then he realized they wouldn't have bothered to bandage his foot if they were going to kill him. These were strange, strange people. He could no more predict their intentions than those of the lion that had stalked him but let him pass unharmed.

Even if they wished to help him, Hussein did not want their help. He needed no help from Crusaders. In fact, he wished they had already killed him. He might have arrived in paradise by now, attended by a harem of virgins, his pain and struggles over.

But no. He lay on the blanket, in agony, as the infidels moved him. The stars whirled in the blackness above, stars in such number that only Allah could count them. A brother in jihad had once told Hussein that the Americans and Russians dared to shoot rockets among the stars—an act of blasphemy so unimaginable that the Quran did not even address it. Hussein doubted the story, though. Nothing mortals built could go that far.

The *gaalos* put him down beside a wooden cellar door. They opened the door, and one of them descended into the hole in the ground.

"We will help you stand and get down the steps," the one called Geedi said. "Just keep your injured foot off the ground."

Hussein wished this *kafir* Somali would stop talking. The man claimed to be a Muslim, but how could that be? Perhaps he had been captured, a slave who had surrendered all his will. Or worse, he had made himself an infidel by choice. Either way, they had swayed him with their luxuries: He looked well fed. He had straight teeth. He wore a watch.

My soul is worth more than a watch and pretty, girlish teeth, Hussein thought. He did not even know how to read a watch. The thing looked like a woman's bracelet.

Geedi and the older infidel helped Hussein sit up on the ground. They took him by the arms and pulled him to a standing position. He kept his injured foot raised, and he put all his weight on his good foot.

"I hate you all," Hussein said.

"Very well," Geedi said. "Be careful going down the steps. Colonel Parson will help you through the door."

"Go to the devil."

Geedi and the older white man helped Hussein place his left foot on the top step. Hussein bent to grasp the sides of the cellar entrance with each hand. He let his hands and arms take his weight for a moment, and he moved his foot down two steps. The younger white man, standing inside the cellar, took him by the right arm. Geedi reached down and grabbed him by the left arm, and they lowered him down the rest of the steps. Hussein stood on the cellar floor and leaned on the stairway, balancing on his good leg.

The older man, the one called Colonel Parson, climbed down and turned on a tiny flashlight. The light revealed a dirt floor, and shelves of food lining the walls. One of the women tossed down the blanket they had used to carry Hussein, and Geedi spread it on the floor.

"Let us help you lie down," Geedi said.

"Go to the devil."

"You already said that."

While Geedi arranged the blanket, Hussein considered whether to cry out for help. But he made no sound. He hardly had the strength and breath for a scream, and he contented himself with the thought that he really had no choice. He had taken a painful wound in battle with the enemy; anyone would say this soldier of God had come into a weakened state honestly and after long, hard fighting.

In fact, the deepest part of him felt relieved to have the injury and exhaustion as a reason not to shout for his al-Shabaab brothers. Because, in truth, he did not know whether they would take care of him in his current state. He would slow them down and use up food and water. For a while, he would be no good to them. These infidels had at least bandaged his wound.

I will bide my time, Hussein decided. I am wily like a fox. I will take from the *gaalos* what they are foolish enough to give me. When I regain my strength and when I see my chance, I will kill them all.

Sooner or later, he reasoned, these infidels would put down his AK-47. He could let them believe he had lost the will for jihad, and then he would go for his weapon. Someday, al-Shabaab recruits would sing praises not only of Hussein's strength and courage, but also of his wits. The brothers would tell the story of how he fell into the hands of the enemy, and how he fooled the fools.

The one called Colonel Parson held the flashlight to show the spot where they meant for Hussein to lie down. Geedi and one of the women—the strange yellow-haired one who spoke in such smooth tones—helped him lower himself to the blanket. Hussein did not want this uncovered harlot touching him, but he did not fight her. She seemed to have a strange power over the others—or at least over the older man. Whenever the one called Parson spoke harshly in that awful sharp-edged language of theirs, Yellow Hair said something quiet that calmed him down. What manner of men took their orders from women? These *gaalos* were not just sinners; they were mad.

"Try to rest," the one called Geedi said. "You need to sleep."

Hussein made no reply, but he admitted to himself the truth of that statement. For a second time, Geedi had said something that was not a lie. Perhaps these devils spoke truth just often enough to made it hard to see their falsehoods.

That, Hussein decided, was a matter he could puzzle over later. For now he would try to sleep. With all the infidels standing and sitting around, he barely had enough room to stretch out his bad leg. He kept his left leg bent, with his arms folded across his chest. At first he thought the pain would keep him awake, but sleep came over him in a strange manner. The ache seemed to move an ever-widening distance from him. Hussein felt the pain like the fading barks of a dog running farther and farther away.

He found himself dreaming of the lion he'd seen earlier in the day. The cat stalked effortlessly from his waking thoughts to his unconscious mind. In his dream, Hussein walked on an uninjured foot, with all his toes intact. The lion came bounding to him through the grass, and Hussein was not afraid. Somehow he knew the great cat would not hurt him. The lion stopped five feet from him, the sun shining on its fur, its tail lifted and curled.

Hussein did not know what to make of this. The lion gave no sign of its intentions other than a reluctance to attack. Hussein came awake just long enough to realize he'd been dreaming. He'd always thought Allah sent dreams to tell of the future or to convey a clear message. Yet there was nothing clear about the lion—not the real one on the creek bank or the spectral one of his dream. The creature's presence, Hussein decided, would have whatever meaning he chose to give it.

Once everybody got settled back into the cellar, Parson took the next watch. He sat on the steps, holding the AK-47 and cursing his luck. Things had gone badly enough to begin with; Osama bin Laden Junior here represented a complication he couldn't believe. Parson had no idea what to do with this boy.

The sun began to rise. As it climbed, the cellar filled with subdued daylight. The light, filtered by the threadbare tarp over the entrance, streamed from cracks between the planks of the door. The lumber that lined the cellar walls started to creak, perhaps from the rising temperature. Though Parson had never suffered from claustrophobia, he had the vague feeling he'd been buried alive. As a hide site, the cellar had little to recommend it except that it was big enough for everybody, and it was better than standing around in the open.

Hussein appeared to sleep peacefully. His hands remained tied together; Gold had checked to make sure the bonds didn't cut circulation. Apart from the tied hands, he looked like an eighth-grader about to wake up and get dressed to catch the school bus. Hard to imagine this child could have killed people.

After a while, Parson noticed a faint buzz, barely audible. He wondered if the sound came from a drone overhead, perhaps the Predator he'd seen on his departure from Djibouti. An academic question; the thing could do him no good now.

Gunshots registered in the distance, so far away they sounded like the cracking of twigs. The reminder of firefights going on around him made Parson feel impotent. He knew nothing about the tactical situation, so he had no information on which to base a plan. As a senior officer, he was used to having all kinds of data at his fingertips: intel reports, drone feeds, radio and sat-phone calls from the field. A commander seldom possessed all the information he wanted, but he always had *something*. Maybe he could try calling Ongondo again, after everybody woke up.

Depending on what Ongondo might tell him, Parson seemed to have two options. He could stay in one place and wait for rescue. Or he could try to move and link up with Ongondo or some other friendlies.

The second plan seemed pretty impractical. Evading capture by yourself was hard enough; with a whole crew moving together it was probably impossible. And you needed to know which way to go.

The first plan sucked, too. Waiting for rescue could amount to waiting for capture. Survival depended on whether AMISON or al-Shabaab came this way first. Fifty-fifty odds, at best.

Did other options exist? The DC-3 had carried a spare tire. If they could get back to the airplane, could Geedi change the tire?

Now you're thinking crazy, Parson told himself. They probably couldn't reach the airplane without running into more bad guys. And by now the bad guys had probably stolen everything in the airplane, including the tire. Jacking the plane and changing the tire would take a lot of time in an exposed location. And the sons of bitches had blown holes in at least one of the fuel tanks—the aux tank. Parson would have only whatever fuel was left in the mains: flying time measured in minutes, not hours. Once he and his group got airborne, where would they go?

As an aviator, Parson wanted to get back to his element, the sky. That's where the bulk of his knowledge, training, and experience gave him the advantage. For the same reasons, a Navy SEAL might head for water when in trouble. An Army Ranger might go for steep mountains or thick jungle. Parson's natural refuge seemed completely out of reach.

In the pool of darkness at the foot of the steps, someone stirred. Parson looked down and saw Carolyn Stewart waking up. She rubbed her eyes, sat up with her arms around her knees, and glanced at Parson. By now, with her mussed hair, dirty clothes, and circles under her eyes, she hardly looked like a celebrity.

"Good morning," Stewart whispered.

Parson gave her an amiable nod. Figured he'd keep the truce going. He needed no more complications.

"Can't sleep?" he asked.

She shook her head. "I'm just so sorry about sending that tweet. I was trying to make things better by coming here. But it doesn't help to make stupid mistakes."

Parson shifted his legs to avoid getting too cramped. He stood the rifle on his thigh, resting it by the heel of its stock. After a few seconds, he said, "I wouldn't know. I've never made a mistake."

His attempt at humor seemed to affect the actress like a painkiller. The lines around her eyes softened, and her drawn expression gave way to a hint of a smile.

"Thank you," she said.

In reality, Parson wondered if he was making a much bigger mistake than Stewart's. By showing mercy to this boy terrorist, was he putting his crew in more danger for no good reason? Kindness was a beautiful thing, but toughness had its place. Parson had certainly seen the truth of that during his years in the military.

More movement interrupted Parson's thoughts. Geedi woke up, covered his mouth with his palm as he yawned, and rose up on one knee. Fingered the corners of his eyes to clear the sleep.

"Shall I take watch for a while?" he whispered. "You look tired, sir."

I *am* tired, Parson thought. Still, he wanted Geedi to save his strength.

"I'm good for now," Parson said. "I'll hand off the rifle to Frenchie here in a bit."

Though Parson could not bring himself to say it out loud, he knew why he wanted Geedi well rested. As much as he hated the thought, he'd have to send Geedi out again.

In the cellar, they were just too vulnerable. They couldn't keep a proper watch, they couldn't defend themselves, and they probably couldn't even make a radio call. Parson planned to give the radio a try when everybody woke up, but he doubted the signal would go through. And if the group stayed, things probably wouldn't end well for Nadif and his wife. Holing up here had always been a temporary solution.

Geedi could scout for a better hideaway, maybe talk to locals and get an idea where the al-Shabaab fighters had gone. Act as a spy, basically. Parson knew it wasn't fair to ask a flight mechanic to be an intel spook, but the situation denied him the luxury of fairness.

Such decisions, Parson believed, were the hardest part of leadership under fire. The old cliché said you shouldn't send somebody out to do something you wouldn't do yourself. But sometimes you had to send a guy out to do something you *couldn't* do yourself.

Parson also had a more immediate problem. He had to piss something awful, and he supposed everybody else did, too. He wished he'd thought to ask Nadif for a chamber pot or something.

"See if you can find an empty container," Parson whispered. "When Hussein wakes up, we'll use his blanket as a privacy screen and we'll rig us up a latrine."

"Good idea," Geedi said.

"A *very* good idea," Carolyn Stewart said.

Geedi searched the shelves and found a couple nearly empty glass jars, about the size of Mason jars back home except the glass was smoked nearly to black. He passed them to Parson, and Parson looked inside. Just some dirt and dried roots. He shook out the debris; the jars would serve his purpose.

Gold and Chartier woke up. With everyone awake except Hussein, Parson no longer worried about keeping his voice at a whisper.

"Good morning, guys," he said. "Something tells me this joint doesn't serve a champagne brunch."

"*Bonjour,*" Chartier said. "Were you on watch the whole time?"

"Yeah," Parson said, "but I couldn't sleep anyway. I'll give you the weapon now."

"*D'accord.*"

Chartier took the AK from Parson and checked its fire selector. Parson had left it on safe. Gold tugged at her sleeves, tucked her shirt.

"Good morning, Michael," Gold said. "Any plan for today?"

Parson sighed. "I got a plan," he said, "but I don't like it." He explained what he wanted Geedi to do, and why.

"Don't worry, sir," Geedi said. "I got this."

"You're a good dude, Geedi."

Hussein slept for another hour. By the time the boy woke up,

Parson was tapping his foot in impatience to urinate. He grabbed a corner of Hussein's blanket and motioned for Hussein to slide off it. Parson took the blanket and strung it across a corner of the cellar. When he finished, the blanket and jars made for a makeshift latrine only a little less primitive than the urinals in the cargo compartments of old C-130s.

Parson started to unzip his flight suit, then had a second thought: Better let Hussein go first. Otherwise, the little bastard might throw a full jar of urine on somebody.

"Tell him to go to the bathroom behind the blanket if he wants to," Parson told Geedi. "And when he's done, he better not do anything with the jar except put it down."

Geedi spoke in Somali to Hussein, and he helped Hussein get to his feet. The boy took a jar and limped behind the blanket. Parson heard the trickle of liquid spilling into the jar. He thought about pointing his pistol at the boy to discourage any mischief. But after Hussein finished, he just left the jar on a shelf, came out from behind the screen, and sat down.

Parson and everyone else took a turn behind the blanket. The end result was two foul-smelling jars, filled to the brim.

"I'll get rid of those," Geedi said, "and I might as well get started on another look around."

"Wait," Carolyn Stewart said.

Geedi looked at her with a puzzled expression. Parson wondered what the hell she wanted. Hadn't she already done more than enough to complicate things?

"Your watch," Stewart said, pointing to Geedi's wrist.

"Oh, I forgot," Geedi said. "Guess I wouldn't look much like a local, wearing a Bulova." He took off the watch and stuffed it into the pocket of the trousers he'd borrowed from Nadif.

"Ah, good catch, Carolyn," Parson said. "How did you think of that?"

"He's playing a role," Stewart said. "His costume needs to be right."

Fair enough, Parson thought. This lady had screwed up real bad, no doubt about that. But maybe she wasn't a total idiot.

Without another word, Geedi took the urine jars and placed them on the top step. He climbed up and pushed open the door a few inches. He reached up, took hold of the tarp that covered the door, and slid it out of the way.

Geedi peered outside in all directions. The light pouring down from the entrance made Parson squint.

Apparently satisfied that no enemy lurked close by, Geedi pushed the door all the way open. For a glorious moment, full daylight flooded the cellar. The flight mechanic took the jars and climbed outside.

"For God's sake, be careful," Parson said.

Geedi poured the urine onto the ground. Then he closed the door, and the cellar went dark again.

28.

While waiting for Geedi to come back, Parson tried to make a radio call. He climbed to the stop of the stairs with his nav/com radio, and he slid the antenna through a crack in the door. Plugged in the earpiece and inserted it into his ear. He turned the volume knob to click on the radio, and he turned the squelch control until he got a constant hiss. Pressed the transmit key.

"Spear Alpha," Parson called, "World Relief Airlift."

No sound but the sizzle of static.

"Spear Alpha," Parson repeated, "World Relief Airlift. Do you read?"

Within the static came a slight warble, and Parson tweaked the volume a little higher. The sizzling rose to a surf's roar, and the warbles became coherent enough to recognize as words. But the words were not in English, and definitely not from Ongondo. Just the tailings of a stray transmission that had somehow bounced through the sky and snagged Parson's antenna on the way to infinity.

Parson cursed under his breath and turned off the radio. Yanked the earpiece out of his ear, descended to the bottom of the stairs. Transmitting from a hole in the ground, he hadn't really expected to make contact with Ongondo. But he had thought it worth a try. Learning otherwise put him in a worse mood.

Even if the sat-phone battery hadn't died, help still might remain out of reach. Given the drawdown of American forces, there might be no rescue helicopter available from Camp Lemonnier in Djibouti. Parson did not remember seeing one there when he first left on this god-forsaken mission.

He felt completely isolated. Getting help would first require getting a message out, and even that seemed impossible now. Then he'd have to wait for a transport helicopter to come from God knows where. Maybe Nairobi. How long would that take?

Parson blamed himself for getting everyone stranded. A good pilot always has an out, he thought. You never put yourself in a situation where you have only one option. If fog socks in your destination, you fly to the alternate. If the weather really sucks, you file two alternates. You plan for reserve fuel. You carry spare parts and extra fuses. You don't get down to where Plan A has to work because there's no Plan B.

But in my eagerness to get supplies to the AMISOM troops, Parson thought, that's exactly what happened. Like arriving over the airfield with minimum fuel and finding the weather down to zero-zero.

He had nothing to rely on but his crew and whatever resources he could scrounge. If we're ever getting out of here, he realized, we're going to have to get creative. And damned lucky.

Parson began to worry about Geedi. He checked his watch; the flight mechanic had been gone nearly two hours. What the hell could Geedi be doing out there for so long?

Hussein sat up and stared at the dirt floor. Gold and Stewart sat close to him, and whenever he looked up, Gold tried to give him a nod or a smile. As far as Parson knew, she didn't speak Somali, so she couldn't communicate with the boy in any meaningful way. Hussein never smiled back at her, but neither did he glare. Chartier leaned against the shelves with the AK-47 cradled in his arms.

After a time, Gold moved over to Parson at the foot of the stairs. As she settled back to a sitting position, she leaned her head on his arm. Her hair smelled of shampoo, sweat, and smoke. She said nothing, but her touch took the edge off his anxiety. He'd hoped this trip would involve more quality time with her in Djibouti, but now he felt grateful for this brief moment—even in a hole in the ground in Somalia.

He placed his hand on the back of her neck, let his eyes close for a few seconds.

"You should get some sleep, *mon colonel*," Chartier said. "I have the watch now."

"I know, Frenchie," Parson said. "I don't know if I *can* sleep. Wish I could make contact with Ongondo or somebody before I try to rest."

"I understand," Chartier said. "A fighting man hates getting cut off from help. It happened to my grandfather more than once."

"Your grandfather?"

"*Oui.* He fought in Indochina."

Chartier explained how his granddad served with French forces in Southeast Asia during the war that raged from 1946 to 1954. The war led to the partition of North and South Vietnam, and that division set the stage for the American war a decade later. As the Frenchman began his story, Stewart took out her video camera and held it up with a question on her face. Chartier nodded.

"Thanks," Stewart said. "It's too dark for good pictures, but I might use the audio." The actress recorded as Chartier told of his grandfather's service.

"My *pépère* was a sergeant," Chartier said, "and they often left him in command of a *post kilométrique*, a kilometer post along a road. Just him and nine men in a bunker."

Surrounded by jungles or mountains that hid Viet Minh guerrillas, Chartier explained, the French soldiers would string barbed wire around their perimeter. Along the wire, they hung empty ration cans that would rattle to warn of an insurgent's approach. Sometimes the troops didn't have enough wire to encircle their position, so they'd resort to sharpened stalks of bamboo.

"These PK posts were often too spread out for any kind of mutual support," Chartier said. "When one got hit, the men were on their own. And that's what happened when my grandfather's post was attacked."

One night, Chartier said, Viet Minh "Death Volunteers" blew through the wire with Bangalore torpedoes. They charged into the perimeter screaming *Tiên-lên!* or *Forward!* The Frenchmen popped parachute flares to see the attackers, and the otherworldly glow revealed dozens of insurgents armed with rifles and grenades.

The elder Chartier opened up with an FM 24/29 light machine gun, while his men fired their MAS-49 semiauto rifles. The bodies of the first wave of attackers weighed down the barbed wire, and soon the Viet Minh could cross the barrier on the backs and stomachs of their fallen comrades.

"For some reason," Chartier said, "I still remember how my grandfather said the FM 24 had two triggers—one for full automatic and one for semi. He burned through several magazines on full auto."

Eventually, one of the Viet Minh got close enough to put a grenade through the bunker's embrasure. The blast killed three Frenchmen, disabled two others, and sent a shard of hot metal ripping into Sergeant Chartier's thigh. Despite wounds that caused severe blood loss, the sergeant kept firing along with his men. And they held their position at the lonely *post kilométrique*.

"My grandfather received the *Croix de Guerre des Théâtres d'Opérations Extérieures,*" Chartier said with obvious pride.

"Had no idea your granddad was such a fighter," Parson said.

"We prefer to talk about him rather than the distant cousin who collaborated with the Vichy government," Chartier said.

"Every family tree has a nut," Parson said.

"So your grandfather went home a hero," Stewart said.

"*Oui,* but not then. They sent him to a hospital in Hanoi, and—"

Before Chartier could finish his story, the thud of footsteps sounded from above. Parson and Gold moved away from the steps to make room for Chartier to point the AK up toward the door. Then Parson pulled his Beretta and aimed it in the same direction. Unless this was Geedi or Nadif coming, Parson knew he might be about to make a last stand much more hopeless than the one Frenchie had just described.

Two coughs sounded from above.

"Don't shoot," someone said from up top. Geedi's voice. "I'm back."

Geedi opened the door, and once again light flooded the cellar. Parson squinted and turned the muzzle of his pistol toward the floor. He kept a close eye on Hussein to make sure the boy didn't try to bolt for the exit. Hussein only shaded his eyes, and Parson realized he was probably in no shape to bolt for anything.

The flight mechanic descended the first two steps, then reached up and closed the door behind him. He paused on the steps for a moment to let his eyes adjust to the darkness. Hopped down the last steps to stand on the floor.

"Talk to me," Parson said.

"I found an old bunker," Geedi said. "It's about a mile from here, and nobody seems to be using it."

"A mile in what direction?"

"Ah, east. It's between here and Ras Kamboni."

"See any bad guys?"

"Yes, sir. A patrol of five dudes came down a dirt road west of here about half an hour ago. They all had AKs. They wore black smocks or just ratty civilian clothes, so I'm pretty sure they were al-Shabaab."

"Good eye, Geedi," Parson said. The flight mechanic had fallen back on his military training, and he'd apparently remembered the SALUTE acronym for reporting enemy movement: size of the unit, activity, location, unit identification, time and date, equipment observed.

"Did they see you?" Gold asked.

"They did, and I wandered around so they wouldn't see me coming back here. They didn't bother me, so they probably thought I was just a camel boy or something."

"That's good," Chartier said.

"Great work, Geedi," Parson said. "Sit down and try to get some sleep."

Geedi fished his Bulova out of his pocket, nodded to Carolyn Stewart, and placed the watch back on his wrist. Stewart gave a weak smile.

Parson still hated that he'd sent Geedi out on such a dangerous recon mission. But no one else could have pulled it off, and now Parson had a little more information: There was another hiding place nearby, and the enemy still lurked in the area.

Now that he knew about another refuge, the question was whether to use it. If al-Shabaab fighters were looking for him and his crew, the bunker might be a place they'd check. But maybe they'd already checked it.

Worst case, Parson thought, if they find us in the bunker, we can defend that position better than this death-trap cellar. And we won't get Nadif and his wife killed in the process. And if I'm above ground, he considered, maybe I can communicate.

Parson did not have to make a decision right now. In no case would he move in daylight, so he had the rest of the day to catch up on his sleep and think about it.

Part of Hussein felt relieved when Geedi came back. At first he'd hoped this *kafir* who consorted so easily with *gaalos* would get killed out there. Hussein had no idea why the man had left the cellar for so long, and after a while he'd assumed Geedi had encountered the al-Shabaab brothers and received the punishment deserved by all infidels.

But, Hussein realized, without Geedi there was no way to communicate with his captors. He would not believe their lies, of course, but hearing anything at all might give him clues.

"How do you feel?" Geedi asked in Somali. The *gaalos* looked on as if they could understand.

"Almost half my foot is blown off," Hussein said. "How do you think I feel?"

"I can imagine."

"No, you cannot."

Geedi stopped talking for a couple minutes, and Hussein felt glad.

He wished this sinner, this friend of Crusaders, would shut up and die. But Geedi did not shut up and die. After a few moments, he spoke again.

"You do not look like a bad sort," Geedi said. "How did you get mixed up with al-Shabaab?"

Bad sort? Who was this *kafir* to say something like that?

"I am a soldier of God, and you are His enemy," Hussein said.

"I already told you, I am a Muslim, too. All my life."

"You lie!" Hussein said. Here they went with their tricks and deceit again.

The one called Geedi did not seem insulted. He even smiled. The other infidels looked on. That irritated Hussein even more; this was none of their business.

"Hussein," Geedi said, "if not for the grace of Allah I could be in your place. I simply got lucky."

What foolishness was this? Crazy, vexing words from this lover of *gaalos*.

"You think yourself lucky?" Hussein asked. "You are going to hell. You will scream in pain forever."

The idiot smiled again. "No, Hussein, I will not," he said. "I have read the Quran. Someone has misled you. Our faith should not be twisted into a cult of blood."

Hussein wanted to kill this *kafir*, to drive a blade right through his neck. Bragging of his ability to read, Hussein thought, and trying to confuse me. Because of his wound, Hussein could not strike out. He could only seethe and listen to this blasphemy.

"My friends have shown you mercy," Geedi said, "partly because you are so young. I do not know what they will do with you, but I do know they will not hurt you unless you try to hurt them. This could be your last chance to do something with your life other than throw it away."

One of the women, Yellow Hair, said something in American or whatever awful language they spoke. Geedi and Yellow Hair talked for a long time, all the while looking at Hussein as if he were livestock, a goat tethered to a tree.

Near midday—the darkness of the cellar made it hard to tell—the old man Nadif brought bread and tea. Hussein did not want any of his wicked gifts, but by now he was starving. The steam rising from the teapot smelled like heaven itself, and the sight of the bread made his mouth water. He decided he would eat their food and get stronger, and he would kill them when he could.

"Are you better?" Nadif asked.

Hussein looked up at Nadif and did not answer. He started to tell the old man to go to the devil, but a strange thought kept him silent. If my father had not been killed, Hussein thought, he would be almost as old as Nadif. Would he look like this man? Hussein tried to imagine how his father would appear now.

"I am hungry," Hussein said finally.

"Then eat," Nadif said.

The old man's voice had an even, cool tone. He did not sound friendly, but he did not sound hateful the way Abdullahi often did.

Painfully, Hussein leaned forward while Nadif placed a plate of bread on the floor. Not only did his wound hurt; all his muscles felt sore from yesterday's struggle. Hussein snatched a round of bread from the top of the plate and tore it in half. From one of the halves, he tore off a smaller piece and stuffed it into his mouth. Chewed twice, swallowed. The lump of bread went down his throat like a stone.

"Slow down," Nadif said. "No one will take the food away from you."

Hussein ripped off another chunk of bread. This time he chewed it four times.

"Slow down," Nadif repeated. Folded his arms and looked down at Hussein.

Hussein gulped the food again. Yellow Hair poured the tea into cups brought by Nadif. She handed a cup to Hussein, and he took a sip. The hot liquid warmed his tongue and felt good sliding down his throat; he had never tasted anything better than this lightly sweetened tea. He put down the cup and took another bite of bread. This time, he chewed it enough that it did not hurt to swallow.

"The one called Geedi talks too much," Hussein said to Nadif.

Geedi did not seem to hear. He sat with the infidels and spoke in their language.

"The one called Geedi is a smart young man," Nadif said, "and the only difference between you and him is a long airplane ride when he was little."

"I am nothing like him. He is a *kafir*."

"Then why has Allah smiled on him so? He has a good job. He comes from a good family. Everyone he loves is still alive."

Nadif's voice broke as he uttered that last sentence. The thought gave Hussein pause as well. Nearly everyone he loved was dead, and while he was still so young. Why was this? Some punishment from Allah? Perhaps because he had not fought hard enough?

Certainly not, Hussein decided. He could not have fought any harder, and his parents had died before he was big enough to wage jihad. And Allah would not have taken someone else's life for Hussein's sins. That would not have been just, and Allah was infinite justice.

Why, then? Hussein took another sip of tea and tore off another piece of bread. He placed the bread in his mouth and chewed it several times, pondering this mystery. He decided the answer was not for him to know, at least not until he gained more understanding and could read.

Nadif stood over him as if he had more to say but could not find the words. Hussein wished he would leave.

"The bread is good," Hussein said, not so much in gratitude but in hope it would make the old man go away.

"You are welcome," Nadif said. After a few minutes he added, "Islam demands kindness to travelers. I have shown kindness to

them"—he gestured toward the infidels—"and they have shown kindness to you."

Hussein looked up at the old man and blinked. Did he really mean
to say the infidels had done the right thing by Islam?

This was all very confusing.

29.

Parson and the others passed the day in Nadif's cellar, trying to sleep. The cool earth offered some relief from the sun beating down up top. As evening neared, the fissures of light shining through the cracks in the door began to dim, and Parson knew he had a decision to make.

"Let's move to that bunker when it gets dark," he said. "We can't stay in this hole forever."

"*Ouais, c'est clair,*" Chartier said.

"What about Hussein?" Gold asked. The boy looked up when he heard his name.

"What about him?" Parson asked.

"Do we take him with us?"

"Hell, no. It'll be dangerous enough as it is. We can't drag a wounded kid with us."

"If he stays here, Nadif and his wife are still in danger," Gold said.

Parson pressed his thumb and forefinger to the bridge of his nose. She had a point. A long time ago in Afghanistan, the family who had helped them lost their lives. He didn't care to repeat that horror, but he had no easy options.

"Yeah, I know," Parson said. "But what if he starts screaming and gives us away?"

"He hasn't done that yet," Gold said.

"Even if he never does, what would we do with him?"

"Let him get rescued along with us."

"Rescued?" Parson said. "The little son of a bitch tried to kill us."

"I know it, Michael. But the little son of a bitch is a boy. In his own way, he's as much a victim of al-Shabaab as anyone."

"He's an orphan," Geedi said. "That's probably why they got him in the first place."

"You guys are killing me," Parson said. "We can't save everybody in Somalia. We're gonna need a lot of luck just to save ourselves."

Nobody said anything for a few minutes. Hussein kept glancing around at everybody, and he looked more curious than scared. Parson went through the what-ifs: What if we leave him behind and he gets Nadif and his wife killed? What if we leave him behind and he just wanders off? Does he come back with his friends and take us out? What if he yells for help while we're moving him to the bunker?

The safe option, Parson realized, would be to shoot him right now, and that was out of the question.

In the back of Parson's mind, he knew what he'd do before he let himself say it out loud. What was that old mob saying? Keep your friends close and your enemies closer. This enemy, he'd have to keep close.

"All right," Parson said finally, "we'll bring him with us. Geedi, tell him he's going for a little excursion tonight. And he better not make any trouble."

Geedi spoke in Somali, and Hussein looked angry. Parson needed no translation for his response; clearly the boy was saying he wasn't going anywhere.

"He says—"

"I know," Parson said. "Tell him it's a statement, not a question."

The conversation in Somali quickly turned into an argument. Parson rolled his eyes.

"This doesn't require any more conversation," Parson said. "He's going with us or he dies. Simple as that. And he goes gagged and with his hands tied. All this is against my better judgment; tell him he's damned lucky he didn't get caught by somebody with better sense."

Gold gave that half smile of hers. She sees right through me, Parson realized. Now that she'd talked him into taking Hussein, he was as committed to the course of action as she was.

"We can't carry him that far the same way we got him here," Chartier said.

Frenchie was right. They'd brought him from the hut to the cellar by simply lifting him on a blanket. Too cumbersome for carrying someone more than a few yards.

"We'll improvise a stretcher," Parson said. "We can take a couple of poles and roll them into the sides of the blanket. Then two of us can just lift the poles."

Carolyn Stewart looked around the cellar. "I don't see anything like a pole," she said.

"Me neither," Parson said. "Geedi, if you don't mind going up top again, can you see if you can find a couple of fairly straight sticks?"

"No problem, sir," Geedi said. "I'm sure I can find tree branches or something."

Hussein started speaking again. Geedi ignored him.

"Tell that kid I'll bitch-slap him if he doesn't shut up," Parson said.

Geedi said nothing. Gold gave another half smile. Yeah, Parson thought, they both know I don't mean it. Just blowing off steam.

Sometimes it was hard to be a good guy. Good guys didn't always act angelic. Sometimes they got pissed off. And being a good guy was what got him here in the first place.

The crew began to gather up their backpacks and other belongings. Hussein watched everything with interest but said nothing. Evidently, now that he'd been bandaged and fed, pain no longer kept him from taking stock of his situation. Parson could relate; from his own experience he knew you came out of severe pain as if returning from a foreign land.

But with Osama Junior feeling better, would he make a nuisance of himself, or worse? No way to know. For now, he appeared docile enough.

In the last moments of daylight, Geedi headed up the stairs to look for sticks or poles to frame the stretcher. Parson watched him swing open the door to reveal a sky already dim enough to reveal the brightest stars.

"Good man," Parson said. "If you see Nadif, tell him we're out of here, and we appreciate his help."

"Yes, sir."

Geedi eased the door closed, and darkness again cloaked the cellar.

"Every time that door shuts, I feel like I'm in an Edgar Allan Poe story," Carolyn Stewart said.

"I know what you mean," Gold said.

Parson had a vague memory of reading Poe in school. Stuff about ravens and pits and pendulums and people getting bricked up behind walls. A hell of a note, Parson thought, that some weirdo writer in the nineteenth century—in his most tortured, drunken imagination—couldn't think of anything as bad as the real things people did in the twenty-first century. Progress.

By the time Geedi came back, night had fallen and the moon was beginning to rise. Bronze moonlight filled the cellar when the door came open. Parson wasn't sure if that was good or bad. It meant he could see to travel without resorting to his flashlight, which could draw the wrong kind of attention. But if we can see in the night, he thought, so can the bad guys.

"Are we set to go?" Geedi whispered.

Parson climbed the steps, the medical ruck over his shoulder and his Beretta holstered in his survival vest. Geedi held two long branches with all the twigs hacked away. The poles weren't entirely straight, but they'd do. Nadif stood nearby, holding a cloth-covered bundle.

"Just about," Parson said.

"I'll be right back," Geedi said.

Geedi turned and strode toward Nadif's hut. He went in wearing the clothes he'd borrowed from Nadif. He came out a few minutes later wearing his flight suit.

"We need to get Hussein ready," Parson said. He placed the medical ruck on the ground. "Come on down and remind him we're going to gag him and tie his hands. Tell him we won't hurt him as long as he cooperates."

Geedi dropped the sticks and followed Parson down to the cellar floor, and Parson clicked on his penlight. Hussein sat on his makeshift bedroll and looked up. Parson reached down and pulled on the blanket.

"Get off the blanket, dumbass," Parson said.

Geedi said something in Somali. Hussein rolled to one side and let Parson take the blanket. Parson handed the blanket to Gold, then unzipped a flight suit pocket and removed his handkerchief. He unfolded the handkerchief, took it by two corners, and twisted it into a gag.

The effort triggered a memory of the last time Parson had gagged someone. In that case, it had been an elderly mullah so extreme in his beliefs that even some radicals opposed him. Gold and Parson dragged the mullah through an Afghan winter storm, suffering frostbite and other torments to keep their prisoner in custody. Parson assumed the old terrorist still languished behind bars at Gitmo or somewhere, but that was just a guess. Once he'd handed over the prisoner to proper authorities, the matter went above his clearance and pay grade.

"Tell him to open his mouth," Parson told Geedi. He recalled asking Gold to say the same thing to the mullah all those years ago.

Geedi spoke in Somali, and Hussein balked, just like the old man had done.

"I don't have time for this," Parson said. "Tell him his choice is getting gagged or getting knocked upside the head and then gagged."

"Michael," Gold said. Once again, a voice in the dark urging compassion.

"I know, I know," Parson said. "I won't really hurt him. You know, Sophia, we gotta stop meeting like this."

Gold laughed softly. Apparently the parallels of the situation struck her, too. Though Parson knew she had a sense of humor, he had rarely heard her laugh out loud.

Parson wondered how far those parallels would continue. The old man was a dead-ender, too long radicalized to change his ways. Given Hussein's youth, could he turn his life around? Probably not, Parson figured. A person becoming a terrorist was like a dog getting rabies. Barring a miracle, the only cure was a bullet.

After a little more conversation in Somali, Hussein relented and let Parson approach with the gag. Just in case, Chartier held the AK-47 on the boy as Parson clicked on the penlight and handed it to Geedi. While Geedi held the light, Parson stuffed the gag into the boy's mouth and tied the ends of the handkerchief behind Hussein's head. He took care not to tie the knot too tightly.

"I'll leave his hands free," Parson said, "so he can pull himself up the steps if he has to. We'll help him out of here, and I'll tie his hands up top."

When Parson finished, Hussein cut his eyes at him. The look conveyed pure hate, and it gave Parson second thoughts about whether letting the boy live was a good idea. How many more innocent people would Hussein kill? Would he grow up to drive a truck bomb into the Mall of America?

Doesn't matter, Parson realized. We don't kill prisoners, and we sure as hell don't kill kid prisoners. End of story.

"Ask him if he wants me to lift him out of the cellar," Parson said.

Geedi spoke in Somali, and Hussein glared at Parson again and shook his head. To Parson, it seemed Hussein's entire vocabulary consisted of frowns and glares.

Hussein placed his hands on the cellar stairs at shoulder height. He pulled himself up and placed his uninjured foot on the bottom step. Then he reached higher with his hands, and he pulled himself up one more step. By repeating the effort four times, he reached the top. Hussein twisted himself out of the cellar opening and onto the ground, and Parson could hear Nadif talking to the boy in Somali.

"Everybody put your body armor back on," Parson said.

Chartier groaned, reached for the armor vests, and passed them out. Parson removed his survival vest, slipped his arms through his own body armor, and closed the fasteners. Just feeling the weight of the armor tired him. He put his survival vest back on over the armor.

Chartier went up the steps next, his revolver in his survival vest and Hussein's AK-47 over his shoulder. Gold and Geedi followed, leaving Parson and Carolyn Stewart alone at the bottom of the cellar. In the moonlight, Parson saw the actress pause before mounting the stairs, and he wondered what the hell she was waiting for. She opened her mouth to speak, and again she hesitated.

"Colonel," she said finally, "I know I helped put us in this situation. I'll . . . I'll never forgive myself."

Parson didn't know what to say. Yeah, this was her fault, at least partly. Maybe it was his fault, too. When Gold first asked him to come to Somalia and fly civilian relief missions, maybe he should have just said no. He could have praised her good intentions and then said it was too dangerous. On the other hand, nothing ever got done through intentions alone. He could help put her intentions into motion. Literally. And Carolyn Stewart had come here to help by telling the story.

"You'll have to forgive yourself sooner or later," Parson said. "Everyone else has."

Not necessarily true, Parson thought, but that's what Sophia would have said. And it was the quickest way to move on and get Stewart out of the cellar.

"Thank you, Colonel Parson." The actress put her hand on his arm as she took the stairs.

"It's just Michael," Parson said.

Stewart climbed the steps into the rectangle of starlit night above. Parson took one final look around his temporary refuge and climbed out last.

A bright sickle moon hung behind the acacia trees. Parson caught a whiff of some kind of food; evidently that's what Nadif's bundle contained. Nadif spoke in Somali and handed the bundle to Geedi, who stuffed it into his backpack.

"His wife has cooked us a bowl of *isku-dhex-karis*," Geedi said.

"Wow," Gold said. "What's that?"

"A mixture of vegetables and meat. He also gave us some bottles of water."

"Tell him thanks," Parson said.

"I did."

Parson held his hand out to Gold, and without a word, she gave him the blanket. It occurred to Parson that the two of them had worked together long enough that they could communicate without even talking. Their rapport reminded him of the way well-trained aircrew members clicked into a team; a glance or the wave of a pen could convey a request or an order.

With a flick of his wrist, Parson shook out the blanket. He spread it on the ground and reached for the poles Geedi had brought. Parson placed a pole at either edge of the blanket, then rolled the fabric around the poles to form a stretcher.

"Tell Hussein to lie down and hold his wrists together," Parson said.

Geedi spoke in Somali again, and Hussein sat on the blanket between the poles. The flight mechanic uttered another phrase, holding his hands together as if bound. Hussein glared and shook his head. Geedi spoke once more, and Hussein shook his head again. Parson rolled his eyes, and he unfastened the parachute cord bracelet from around his right wrist. He unbraided the cord, loops dangling from his fingers. Then he lifted the left pant leg of his flight suit enough to reveal the knife sheathed on his boot.

Parson pulled the boot knife and gave Hussein a hard look. Hussein placed one of his wrists atop the other. Parson cut a length of parachute cord and tied the boy's hands. As with the gag, he took care not to knot the cord too tightly. When Parson finished, Hussein looked down at the knife, which Parson had placed on the ground beside the stretcher, out of Hussein's reach. The boy seemed to stare at the knife with more curiosity than fear; Hussein had almost certainly never seen a knife like that one: a four-inch, double-edged blade made of Damascus steel, layers of pattern-welded alloy that created a sheen of wavy lines. The handle had been fashioned from the antler of a whitetail deer. Parson had carried it on his left boot his entire career.

"You like my knife?" Parson said. "My dad gave me that a long time ago." Parson picked up the knife and slid it back into its sheath. "He's not around anymore." Hussein looked at Parson almost as if he understood the English. "Guess your dad's not around anymore, either, huh?"

Parson did not share the rest of the knife's story—how in desperate circumstances he had jammed the tip of the blade under the mullah's fingernail. Parson might have done worse with the knife had Gold not stopped him; at the time, his friends lay dead and wounded around him because of that mullah and his like. A different time in a different war, when Parson was a different person.

A rip of gunfire echoed in the distance. The sound reminded Parson he was about to try one of the most difficult of combat maneuvers—a retreat under fire. The phrase did not apply fully, though. To begin with, the fighting seemed to swirl all around; Parson didn't know if he was retreating or advancing. He just wanted to get to a safer place. And he wasn't under direct fire—though that could change at any time.

"All right, guys," Parson said, "let's get moving."

Gold stepped over to the stretcher and bent to place her hands on the poles at one end. Parson took the other end, and together they lifted Hussein. The boy felt lighter than Parson had expected; Hussein lay still with his bound hands across his stomach.

"Lead the way, Geedi," Parson said, "and tell Nadif good luck and Godspeed."

"Yes, sir."

Geedi added several words in Somali, and Nadif nodded, his arms folded over his chest. Chartier handed the AK-47 to Geedi, and the Frenchman unholstered his Smith & Wesson. Geedi held the AK slanting across his chest like a pheasant hunter, and he led the way into the darkness.

30.

Hussein did not understand why the *gaalos* were taking him with them. They did not intend to kill him; that was clear enough. They could have done away with him easily by now.

Maybe they wanted him as a hostage. Hah! That would do them no good. Abdullahi or the Sheikh would no more bargain for him than for a rat. Whatever the strange purposes of these infidels, Hussein did not resist. He let himself be carried through the night like a pasha of old, riding on a throne borne by servants. If the *gaalos* wanted to keep him close, so be it. That closeness gave him options, possibilities. He might yet find a way to strike these infidels.

But another thing puzzled Hussein, something that Nadif had said to him when he crawled from the cellar.

"We pray five times a day, do we not?" the old man had said.

"Yes, so?" Hussein had said. He didn't really pray five times a day every day. Sometimes fighting prevented it, and sometimes he just forgot. But yes, when he was with other Muslims, which was most of the time, he prayed at least once or twice a day.

"And how does that prayer end?"

The way it always ends, you old fool, Hussein had thought. "With blessings on Ibrahim's offspring," he had said.

"Yes," Nadif had responded. "And Ibrahim's offspring include all the people of the book, not just Muslims but the Christians and the Jews, too. They call him Abraham. See how close the words are? Ibrahim, Abraham."

What sort of nonsense was this? Was it only the words of a *kafir*? Or was this a truth no one had ever told Hussein?

The people of what book? The Quran, of course. Hussein could not read it for himself. That was the problem with missing school. Hussein could know only what other people told him, so he had to judge the trustworthiness of anyone who told him anything. He had once heard an imam say the past before Mohammed introduced Islam was called *Jahiliyya*, the time of ignorance. Hussein wondered if he would be in his own time of ignorance until he learned to read.

The gag infuriated him; they had trussed him up like an animal, and he hated them for it. At first the gag nearly choked him, but now that it had become soaked with his saliva, it was less uncomfortable. Hussein ground his molars into the fabric, hoping perhaps to chew through it, spit out the gag, and shout so loud that the faithful could hear him in Mecca. No luck with that, however. The effort accomplished little other than making his jaw sore.

His foot throbbed, but not with the blinding pain of earlier. The bandaged foot hung over the end of the stretcher, and it bobbed in the air with each step taken by Yellow Hair and the one called Parson. Maybe the wound would heal now, and Hussein would lose no more than the toes already blown away. He had seen other people with serious injuries that began to rot. A bullet wound to a hand, for example, could worsen into the loss of an arm. Something to do with poisons getting into the blood. Hussein supposed the clean bandage the *gaalos* had put on him might spare him the loss of his entire foot. Maybe this was all part of Allah's plan: to let him take whatever benefit he could from these infidels, then kill them when he got the chance.

Or he might have to settle for merely escaping. For now, at least, Hussein was bound and unarmed. He resented the way the infidels handled his weapon, *his* rifle, with which he had already fought so bravely. At the moment, the one called Geedi carried it, up front as he led the way into a stand of trees. The other white man, called Shartee or something, held that tremendous pistol and walked behind Geedi.

Behind the stretcher walked the other woman, the one with the red-dish hair like Hussein had never seen before. She said little to the others, but every now and then she looked down at Hussein and gave a stupid smile. He wished she would stop it.

The moon, though narrowed to the crescent that symbolized Hussein's faith, gave off light bright enough to throw shadows. Somewhere in the forest, a night bird called. The infidels moved with caution, concerned with every sound. Well might you worry, Hussein thought. You do not belong here and we will kill you, one way or another.

More gunfire sputtered, way off. Hussein wished he knew what was happening with the battle, where his al-Shabaab brothers had gone. But of course, he had no idea.

Something made the infidels stop. They spoke in hushed tones, the scraping of their foreign words sounding even harsher when whispered. Yellow Hair and Parson set down the stretcher. Hussein raised himself on his elbows and tried to look around, but he could see nothing; they had placed him in the middle of a thicket of parched grass.

Obviously, the infidels had seen or heard something that worried them. Soldiers of God, perhaps?

Hussein tried to cry out, to call to his brothers in arms. Because of the gag, only a growl escaped his throat.

Parson fell on him as soon as he made that sound. He shoved Hussein flat on his back and clamped a hand over his mouth. Parson whispered something to the other *gaalos*. Hussein tried to struggle against the fingers digging into his cheek, the palm pressing down on his lips. He felt as if he would suffocate, and in a moment of animal panic, he had to force himself to breathe through his nose.

Hussein expected the end to come now. The sinners wanted him quiet; surely they would slit his throat. At any moment, the one called Parson would reach with his free hand to pull that marvelous boot knife that looked so much like the *tooray* that Hussein dreamed of owning. Parson would do what Hussein would do if their situations were reversed: He would place the tip of the knife at the hollow of his throat and thrust the blade upward.

How much would it hurt? No matter. The pain could not last long; Hussein had seen people bleed to death much faster than one would expect. These *gaalos* would not see him cry or lose his water. He would enter heaven a proud martyr.

Come on with it, then, he thought. What are you waiting for?

With his left hand a vise over Hussein's mouth, Parson reached for his Beretta with his right. He listened as intently as he could, and he hoped his years around loud airplanes hadn't robbed him of the ability to hear a twig snap. Geedi had seen movement up ahead and had given the raised-fist signal to stop. Movement didn't necessarily mean enemy, but Parson doubted the local villagers would traipse around in a forest at night with al-Shabaab in the vicinity.

By Parson's standards, calling this terrain a forest was a stretch. The trees did not grow thickly enough to meet most Americans' definition of a wooded area. But according to the VFR charts, a coastal forest grew in this area. At the moment, Parson wished for thicker cover.

He held his head up above the grass and scanned into the trees as best he could. Parson could make out only the silhouettes of Geedi and Chartier paces in front of him—Geedi poised beside a tree with the AK, and Frenchie crouching with both hands on his revolver. At the back end of the stretcher, Gold watched and waited. Unarmed, she could do little else. Carolyn Stewart kneeled behind Gold, probably panicked, but sensible enough, thank God, to stay quiet.

For whatever reason, Hussein lay still under Parson's grip. For a few seconds the boy had squirmed; the struggle reminded Parson of catching a big bass and having to hold the damned thing down to keep it from flopping all over the boat. Then suddenly Hussein had relaxed, and Parson thought he knew why. The kid probably believed he was about to be killed. No problem, Parson thought. Let him think that for a few more minutes.

Parson put his thumb against the safety of his pistol. He wanted the weapon ready to fire, but he didn't want to make a loud click. With only the slightest pressure from his thumb, he eased the safety lever toward the firing position. His lungs burned; he realized he was holding his breath. Parson let out the stale air just as the safety lever seated. If the mechanism made a click, he did not hear it. A single cumulus cloud, jaundiced by the yellow light of the moon, drifted overhead.

And the woods erupted with gunfire.

From maybe fifty yards away, an automatic weapon spewed rounds in the general direction of Parson and his crew. Muzzle flashes blinked like a rapid-fire strobe light. Bark, wood chips, and other debris filled the air; Parson felt shards of something sting his face.

Geedi returned fire with the AK.

A sledgehammer blow struck Parson in the side. Slammed the very air from his lungs. He'd felt that force before, and he recognized it immediately: a high-velocity round striking body armor.

He fell flat to the ground, on his back. Now Parson saw nothing through the grass. He struggled to fill his lungs again, gripped the Beretta with both hands, and rolled to the right. Ignored the pain in his side. Out of the grass now, he could see two sets of enemy muzzle flashes. He took aim at one and began firing his pistol.

Above the roar of automatic weapons, Parson could discern no report at all from his nine millimeter, though he felt the recoil of each shot. He did, however, hear the deep slam of Chartier's magnum.

Somebody cried out; Parson couldn't tell who.

The firing stopped. Was it over?

From up ahead came a long moan. Then voices in Somali. Clicks and the sound of a bolt snapping closed. Someone was reloading.

The shooter let out a war cry before he resumed firing: "Aaaaggh . . ." Then the sound of the shooter's weapon drowned out his scream.

Now Parson could see the muzzle flashes again. The flashes swept around like a child playing with a sparkler; the bastard was spraying all over the forest. Or maybe he was wounded and staggering. Parson aimed at the source of the flashes and pulled the trigger. He fired once, twice—and then he felt the slide lock open. Empty.

The woods fell silent.

Parson took in a long breath, resisted the temptation to run forward to check on Geedi and Frenchie. He listened closely again, and he heard nothing but faint rustles, perhaps the sound of hot brass cooling on the ground.

"Everybody all right?" Parson called.

"I'm good," Geedi said.

"I'm fine," Gold said.

"Me, too," Stewart said.

Hussein sat up and made a grunting sound through his gag.

"Watch him," Parson said to Gold.

"Will do."

Parson felt for a spare magazine in his survival vest. He ejected the empty mag from his Beretta, let it fall at his feet, and slapped in the fresh one. Thumbed the slide release to close the weapon. That left the Beretta in a cocked, ready-to-fire condition, and Parson kept it that way. He did not waste time looking on the ground for the spent magazine.

"Frenchie, what about you?" Parson asked.

"I am hit in the arm," Chartier said. "I don't think the bone is broken."

"Damn it, Frenchie," Parson said. "I'm sorry."

The darkened figure of Geedi rose from where he'd taken cover by a tree. "The bunker is close," Geedi said.

"Frenchie," Parson said, "You okay to walk?"

"Oui."

"Then let's move. We'll look at that arm once we get inside."

"Absolument," Chartier said.

"Carolyn," Parson said, "can you get up here and help carry Hussein?" Parson couldn't manage the stretcher and hold his pistol at the ready at the same time. And he felt as if an elephant had stomped him in the side.

"Sure," the actress said.

Gold and Stewart lifted the stretcher, and Geedi crept forward. Chartier followed close behind, and Parson noted that the Frenchman held his revolver with both hands. Maybe the wound isn't too bad, Parson thought, if Frenchie's still using the injured arm.

Geedi stopped and looked down at something. Parson kept scanning and listening for threats as he made his way to where Geedi had halted. He saw no movement other than his own people, and he heard nothing but their own footsteps.

A body lay at the flight mechanic's feet. The dim light made it difficult to see details, but the dead man certainly looked like al-Shabaab. He wore camo pants and a dark tunic, and he'd carried an RPK light machine gun. The weapon rested on the ground beside the body, sling tangled around the right arm. The man's bloodied left hand draped over the banana-shaped magazine. Given the firepower the terrorist had brought to bear, Parson counted himself lucky not to have lost anyone.

Chartier joined Parson and Geedi as they examined the corpse. The man appeared to have taken at least two hits, center mass.

"Good shooting," Parson said.

"I just aimed at the flashes," Geedi said.

"Me, too, but I don't know if I hit anything."

"There were at least two of them," Chartier said.

"I know," Parson said. He saw no other body, and in the pale light he could see no evidence that anyone had crawled or stumbled away. The other shooter, Parson realized, could be lying dead within fifty yards, or he could be dragging himself back to his buddies to tell them what he'd seen.

Gold and Stewart moved closer with the stretcher and Hussein, and Hussein raised himself enough to look down at the dead al-

Shabaab fighter. "Yeah, that could have been you," Parson whispered. He leaned over and picked up the RPK. Felt warm liquid on the rifle's receiver. He checked the body for extra ammo and found none.

"We should get to cover," Gold said.

"My thoughts exactly," Parson said. "Geedi, lead on."

Geedi began moving through the moon shadows. Parson and the others followed. Parson slung the RPK over his shoulder and put both hands on his pistol, the muzzle angled toward the ground. His right hand felt sticky from the blood, and he realized he'd probably gotten some on his Beretta. Though the RPK offered a hell of a lot more firepower than the handgun, Parson preferred his own weapon at the moment. He couldn't take the time now to familiarize himself with new equipment, and for all he knew, the RPK's magazine was empty. Nobody spoke, but Chartier walked closely enough for Parson to hear his breathing, and it sounded like the forced respiration of someone in pain.

Parson's breathing came with pain, too, after that hard slam to his body armor. He judged his ribs were just bruised and not broken; he'd taken enough blows to know the difference.

After what felt like miles, though it must have been only dozens of yards, Geedi stopped. Parson saw nothing that looked like a bunker, only an abrupt rise of the ground in front of him.

"Right here," Geedi whispered. "I'll need to use my flashlight for a second. Can somebody stand on either side of me to help block the light?"

Parson moved to Geedi's left side, and Chartier stood on the right. Geedi stuck his hand into a flight suit pocket and brought out a mini flashlight. He covered the bulb end with his palm and clicked on the light. The flashlight lit up the flight mechanic's closed fist with an ochre glow, emitting just enough light to reveal vines growing across the metal door of a bunker. The bunker's roof, long covered by earth, hosted small trees and scrub brush.

"Hold on," Parson said. He decocked and holstered his pistol, and he reached down to unsheathe his boot knife. Pulled at the vines with one hand and slashed them away with the other. After a couple minutes, he had cleared the vegetation enough for Geedi to open the metal hasp over the door.

"Lucky this wasn't padlocked," Geedi said.

Geedi passed the flashlight to Parson and pulled on the doorknob, but the door came open only a couple inches. The flight mechanic fingered the micro-light clipped to the zipper tab of his flight suit. Using the micro-light's green glow, Geedi examined the door more closely. Then, with ungloved hands, he gripped the edge of the door and pulled harder. Watching Geedi's unprotected fingers, Parson worried about spiders and scorpions, but he let Geedi continue. Getting everyone into some sort of cover ranked higher in importance than anything else.

While Geedi worked, Parson dug with one hand into his survival vest, looking for his GPS. He intended to mark the location of the bunker, just in case he had to leave and come back. When he found the GPS receiver, something felt wrong. As he pulled out the receiver, it made rattling noises he'd never heard before. He held it up in the moonlight and saw that a bullet had smashed through it—the same bullet that had knocked the breath from him.

"Shit," Parson whispered.

"What?" Gold asked.

"They shot my fucking GPS."

"Might have saved your life."

Parson doubted that. The heavy vest alone probably would have kept him among the living. But he couldn't deny that the GPS unit had absorbed some of the round's energy—maybe enough to spare him cracked ribs. Certainly enough to destroy the damned GPS. He stuck the useless instrument back in his vest pocket. Now he'd have to navigate old-school, with nothing but a compass and a guess. He didn't even have a topo chart now, because his land-nav charts existed only in digital form on the GPS SD card. Parson knew he should be glad the

bullet hadn't killed him, but he couldn't get past the frustration of losing such a valuable tool. It had taken days of phone calls and e-mails
just to get an SD card for Somalia, because who wanted to hike in
fucking Somalia? Parson muttered curses under his breath while Geedi
yanked at the door.

After two hard tugs, the door squeaked halfway open, barely wide
enough for the stretcher. Geedi took his flashlight back from Parson
and ducked inside.

31.

The bunker reminded Hussein of that children's tale his mother told him—about the mouse who led the prince through a hole in the ground to hide with the King of the Jinns. As soon as the *gaalos* shoved the stretcher through the rusty, half-opened door, Hussein's nostrils filled with the odors of dirt and decay. The place gave the impression of a giant grave, and when the *gaalos* closed the door and turned on their flashlights, the light did nothing to dispel that impression.

Surely if the King of the Jinns didn't have his own lair, he could have made do with this one. On the floor, Hussein noticed a scattering of bones, chewed by rats and bleached by time. No skull, only assorted ribs and a spine. Hussein could not tell if the skeleton had framed the flesh of man, goat, or dog, and he did not want to know.

In a corner lay the discarded yellow-haired head of a doll, its body nowhere in sight. How in the name of heaven had such a thing found its way into a place used by the army? Maybe children played here at one time, Hussein supposed, but he could not understand why any child, parented or orphaned, would come to this spot. If bandits or hyenas didn't get you, the jinns certainly would.

On the wall, a fading poster bore a face Hussein knew—not from any schooling but from his father's stories. The old government poster depicted a man nicknamed *Afweyne*, or "Big Mouth." The dictator Siad Barre, ousted long before Hussein was born. Evil spirits of many kinds seemed to haunt this place.

"A'adu bilahi mini sheydani rajiim," Hussein prayed. Oh, Allah, I seek protection from *Shaytan.*

Hussein feared no man, but he feared enemies who had no body he could pierce with a blade or a bullet. Was it bravery or ignorance that let these infidels trespass in the haunts of the spirit world? Hussein hated them for bringing him here. What was wrong with these people?

They went about their business as if jinns did not exist. First, they cut off the sleeve of the one called Shartee and took care of his wound. From what Hussein could see, it wasn't serious. The bullet seemed to have left a deep graze wound. Blood had soaked Shartee's sleeve, now lying cut and torn on the floor, but Hussein had seen people bleed like stuck goats from small wounds before. The *gaalos* put an odd-looking bandage over the wound—the bandage somehow stuck together without being tied.

Strangely, Hussein felt almost glad Shartee wasn't hurt badly. Shartee had a kind face for a *gaalo*, and he had never given Hussein a mean look.

"What is happening?" Hussein asked the one called Geedi.

"In a minute," Geedi said.

Geedi—and all the others, for that matter—seemed very interested in what their leader, Parson, was doing. Parson took a radio of some sort from his vest of many pockets. He turned it on and called somebody. At first, all the infidels seemed happy that he had made contact with whoever was on the other end of that radio beam. But then they didn't seem to like what they heard.

Hussein, of course, could understand none of the words. He didn't know if they were calling for help, or calling for instructions about what to do with him. He would have to ask Geedi—and trust that Geedi would tell the truth. Not understanding the conversations felt a lot like not being able to read: Hussein could rely only on the word of someone else. A weakness he knew he must remedy someday.

The one called Parson turned off the radio and spoke to the others. He gestured with his hands and talked a long time, like he was making a plan. Whatever the plan, Geedi seemed involved; Parson and Geedi talked to each other for several minutes. They included Shartee in the conversation, but he said little. Some of the time, the infidels appeared to argue. They looked at Hussein a lot while they were arguing. From time to time, Parson closed his eyes hard and held his side as if something hurt.

All the while, Yellow Hair stood guard at the door with Hussein's AK-47. Hussein wondered if the woman actually knew how to shoot. He doubted it, but one never knew about these infidels and their strange ways.

The main thing Hussein noticed was the way Geedi got treated. This boss Parson spoke to him in the tones one might use with a brother, not the way a commander would speak to an underling. And not the way Abdullahi had always spoken to Hussein. At the end of the conversation, Parson even patted Geedi on the back and smiled. Assuming these *gaalos* told the truth about anything, Geedi had once been a Somali boy like Hussein. How did he reach a place where these people treated him as an equal?

After a while, Geedi opened his backpack and took out the bundle of food the old man had given them. He unwrapped cloth from around a clay pot, and when Geedi removed the pot's lid, Hussein smelled the *isku-dhex-karis*. The food was still a little warm; it gave off tendrils of steam. To Hussein's surprise, Geedi came over and untied his hands. As Geedi worked, Hussein eyed the strange coveralls the man wore. Zippers and pockets everywhere.

"Why do you wear these coveralls?" Hussein asked.

"It is my flight suit, Hussein. The pockets are very useful."

Geedi unzipped one of the pockets and took out a small packet. He tore open the packet and removed a folded, wet piece of paper. Geedi handed the wet paper to Hussein and said, "Wash your hands with this, and then we will eat."

Hussein rubbed the wet paper over his fingers. The paper was wet with some kind of medicine; it stung all the little cuts and scrapes. While Hussein cleaned his hands, Geedi took a plastic water bottle from his backpack. He had a short conversation in American with Parson, and Parson took a small bottle of pills from his vest of many pockets. Parson gave Geedi one of the pills. Geedi unscrewed the cap on the water bottle, dropped in the pill, put the cap back on the bottle, and shook it. After a time, he handed the bottle to Hussein.

"Drink," he said. "I know you must be thirsty."

"Do you think I am a fool?" Hussein said. "I saw you put poison in the water."

Geedi sighed. "It is not poison, Hussein. It is a pill to kill germs in the water."

"You are lying."

Geedi rolled his eyes and unscrewed the cap. He took a long drink from the bottle, then held the bottle out toward Hussein.

"Now do you believe me?"

Hussein did not answer, but he snatched the bottle from Geedi and took a drink. The water tasted strange, almost like undrinkable seawater. Hussein swallowed, then looked at the bottle and frowned.

"What is that awful taste?" Hussein asked.

"Water purification tablets always taste bad," Geedi said, "but at least you will not vomit your guts out and die of dysentery."

Hussein had seen people do exactly that, but he said nothing. He took another drink. The water gave no pleasure, but it quenched his thirst. Geedi pushed the pot of *isku-dhex-karis* toward him.

"Eat," Geedi said.

"You want me to eat first?"

"Someone has to go first, Hussein."

Hussein reached into the pot with four fingers and took some of the potatoes and camel meat. He stuffed the food into his mouth, wiped his hand on his shirt. Chewed slowly, eyeing Geedi. As he ate, gunfire spattered in the distance. With each volley, the *gaalos* looked around and talked among themselves.

"Why have you not killed me?" Hussein asked, his mouth full. "I would kill you if I got the chance."

"That is not our way."

"Your ways make no sense."

"Lucky for you."

Geedi dipped his fingers into the pot and began to eat with Hussein. The rest of the infidels went about their business. Parson looked over the RPK. He examined the magazine and looked disappointed. He probably found that it had few bullets left. Good, as far as Hussein was concerned.

"I wish you had not brought me here," Hussein said. "I hate this place."

"Why?"

"It is spooky. I think jinns live here. The King of the Jinns could live here; it feels like it is underground."

"We brought you here because it is safer," Geedi said. "What if your friends had found us in that cellar and dropped in a grenade?"

"Then they would have won victory over infidels."

"And they would have killed you, too, Hussein. Do you think they would have taken the time to get you out first, in your crippled condition?"

Hussein did not answer. He just took another bite of the camel meat.

"My mother told me a story about the King of the Jinns," Geedi said.

"About the mouse and the prince?"

"I do not remember a mouse, but there was something about a prince who needed a place to hide."

"Yes, yes," Hussein said. "That is the story."

"Well, we needed a place to hide, too."

"You say your family comes from the Rahanweyn?"

"They do," Geedi said. "I told you that you and I are from the same tribe, and you did not believe me."

Hussein made no reply. He began to think that on this matter, Geedi had actually told the truth, just like he'd told the truth about the pill in the water. If Geedi's mother knew the same childhood stories that Hussein had heard, maybe they really were from the same tribe.

If I ever get my chance to kill them, Hussein thought, perhaps I will let Geedi live because he spoke to me in honesty and is a fellow Rahanweyn. Could we even be distantly related? It is possible, Hussein considered.

He took another drink of the purified water. This time it tasted as if someone had sprinkled ashes into the bottle, but he forced himself to swallow. He wiped his mouth with the back of his hand and said, "Who did your boss talk to on the radio?"

"A friend."

"What did they talk about?"

"Getting home."

"How are you going to do that?" Hussein asked.

"We are not sure, exactly."

"What are you going to do with me?"

"We do not know that, either," Geedi said.

"You do not know much, do you?"

Hussein intended that remark as an insult, but Geedi did not seem to take it that way. He only chuckled and said, "Not as much as we would like."

Geedi and Hussein took a few more handfuls of the food, and then Geedi took the pot and gave it to the infidels. While they ate, Geedi came back and sat next to Hussein. Hussein noticed an object clipped to the zipper tab of Geedi's flying suit. The object was the size of a small coin, but shaped with angles. Parson wore one, too.

"What is this thing you wear on your zipper?" Hussein asked.

"A tiny light," Geedi said. He fingered the object, squeezed it, and it shone a beam of green light. "It is made for key chains, but we fliers wear them like this, on our flying suits. You never know when you might need to see in the dark."

"Why is the light green?"

"That color works best with night-vision goggles."

"You have those, too?"

"Not with us tonight, but our military has them."

"And you are a pilot?"

"No. I am a flying mechanic."

"You infidels have fine knives and gadgets, but strange ways."

"I will not argue with you on that, Hussein."

Hussein could not remember the last time he'd had a friendly conversation like this. This flying mechanic was not such a bad fellow. Yes, when the time came—if it came—Hussein would kill the others but, if possible, he would let Geedi live.

32.

After everyone finished eating, Parson ordered the flashlights turned off. Chartier picked up the AK-47 and took watch by the bunker door. The Frenchman moved his bandaged arm stiffly, though he insisted he could still shoot. Parson lay in the darkness, listening to the breathing of his crew members and to the occasional crackle and thud of weaponry—sometimes barely audible, sometimes closer than he would have liked. He tried to sleep, but his mind raced with problems and possibilities.

In leaving the cellar and coming to the bunker, he had accomplished his main goal: getting enough radio reception to reach Lieutenant Colonel Ongondo. But Ongondo had offered little in the way of good news. In Parson's mind, he replayed the conversation with Ongondo:

"It's good to hear your voice, Spear Alpha," Parson had said.

"And yours as well. I had almost given up on you."

"Spear Alpha, be advised we are close to our previously reported position." Parson spoke in vague terms because his civilian nav/com radio did not encrypt transmissions. If al-Shabaab had enough initiative to tune in the aviation emergency frequency and find a good English speaker, they could listen in.

"Understood," Ongondo had said. "My unit is still in contact with the enemy. We hope to receive some support from your kindred, if you know what I mean."

At first, Parson did not know what that meant. Support from the

American military? Unlikely, given the drawdown at Djibouti. If the Pentagon learned American aid workers were in trouble, the brass might send help, but that help couldn't arrive this quickly. To task a Delta Force team or a SEAL unit and get them here on a C-130 would take a few days of planning. Even if SEALs or Air Force pararescuemen were on alert as close as Mogadishu, they'd need Parson's exact location—which he'd never transmitted.

Then Parson realized that by "kindred," Ongondo probably meant aviators—just not American aviators. An air strike by AFRICOM forces? Entirely possible. Parson remembered that Ugandan L-39 Albatros attack jet on the ramp at Mogadishu. So, after the air strike, maybe somebody could come in with a helo?

"Ah, Spear Alpha," Parson had radioed, "do you think we can get a ride?"

"Unknown at this time."

Unknown? That meant no. Negative. Not happening.

That was when Parson realized he and his crew needed a hell of a lot of luck—and they'd have to make that luck for themselves. He'd tallied up what he knew—what *little* he knew: An air strike might happen. But a rescue chopper wasn't coming. He and his team would have to effect their own rescue by trying the same bold move Parson had considered briefly back at Nadif's cellar. He'd considered it *briefly* because it was so crazy.

Funny how crazy starts to make sense, Parson thought, when you're running out of options. If the air strike scattered al-Shabaab forces, maybe that would give Geedi time to make the DC-3 flyable.

Geedi would have to change a tire, and he'd probably have to patch or plug bullet holes in fuel tanks. The aircraft had carried all the necessary parts and tools—unless those terrorist bastards had stripped the plane. They might have stolen anything remotely useful, and they might have smashed instrument panels and shot up the engines, just for fun.

Or maybe the running firefights with AMISOM had kept al-Shabaab too busy to mess with the DC-3. No way for Parson to know except to go take a look, as soon as he could try it without getting shot.

Then there was the question of fuel. He'd have only what was left in the main tanks. Not enough to reach Mogadishu. Where could he fly?

He was close to Kenya. Maybe the old bird had just enough gas to hop over the border and get to the little airport at Kiunga. That would at least get Parson's group out of the combat zone. Hell, he didn't even need an airport. He could just limp the DC-3 over the border and set her down on any flat patch of dirt or grass.

Yes, it was crazy. But he could think of no other option except to wait around like some damsel in distress. That ran against everything in his nature and was probably no safer than trying to fly out.

From his military courses, Parson knew many tales of leaders who escaped bad situations by pulling off bold moves. He recalled a War College discussion about how Joseph Hooker tried to trap Robert E. Lee at Fredericksburg. With a force nearly twice the size of Lee's, Hooker planned to use part of his men to pin down Lee's army, while sending another element to smash Lee from the rear.

Lee responded with maneuvers so audacious they bordered on attempted suicide. He divided his already outnumbered army—sending most of them to surprise Hooker head-on. Then Lee divided the troops *again*, to circle around and hit the Federals at a place called Chancellorsville.

The Confederate counterattack came with such surprise that it caught some of the Union troops eating their evening meal, their weapons stacked. The first sign of trouble for the Federals came when deer and rabbits bounced out of the underbrush. The animals were driven by enemy soldiers advancing through brambles supposedly too thick for marching. What started as Hooker's confident plan to stop Lee once and for all turned into a near rout for the Union.

Parson didn't sympathize with Lee's cause, but he admired the general's military prowess. And he took from the story this lesson: When you get trapped, when you find yourself in a bad way, do what the other side least expects you to do.

We've already been shot out of our airplane, Parson reasoned. They sure as hell don't expect us to try to fly out.

At midnight, Parson was still awake when Chartier came to get him and hand off the watch duties. He sat up as soon as Chartier stepped toward him.

"You're already up?" Chartier whispered.

"Never got to sleep," Parson said.

"Then rest a while longer."

"Nah, I got it, Frenchie. Too keyed up to sleep anyway."

"As you wish, sir."

Chartier passed the AK-47 to Parson and lay down on the floor. With the rifle, Parson sat on an overturned bucket they'd found in the bunker. With this makeshift stool, he perched by the half-open door, peering into the darkness and listening for any sound. The RPK they'd taken from the dead al-Shabaab fighter rested against the wall near the door. The weapon would do little good; when Parson had checked its magazine, he'd found only five rounds left. The magazine in the AK-47 was getting low, too; it had only ten rounds. If another firefight took place, the ammunition might last only seconds.

Parson sat listening to the breeze, the breath of the landscape, and he let his mind work on details. Hussein was one of the loose ends. What to do with him? Just let him go? Try to turn him over to AMISOM?

The group had discussed all the options, and Parson didn't like any of them. If they let Hussein go, he'd probably return to al-Shabaab—and, worse yet, identify Nadif and his wife. Turning Hussein over to AMISOM required making contact with Ongondo's men before taking off in the DC-3. That called for two miracles. Just getting the plane started and airborne would probably prove impossible. There would be no time to find AMISOM forces first.

The night remained clear except for the occasional cumulus cloud. Where Parson sat, far from any urban area, no light pollution competed with the stars, and silver dust blazed overhead. In better circumstances, he might have enjoyed gazing into the heavens with night-vision goggles to bring thousands more stars into view. Or perhaps with a telescope, which could magnify some of the silver dots into elliptical galaxies, deep-sky coins.

Trained as a navigator before becoming a pilot, Parson could set courses by stars. He considered himself part of an ancient guild going back to the days of Magellan, a guild whose members bore a special kinship with the cosmos. Tonight, however, the stars gave him no answers. They presented a beautiful backdrop, but he could not choose one of them, sight it with a sextant, and determine which way to go. With a busted GPS, he couldn't navigate by manmade stars, either.

Behind him in the bunker, someone exhaled. Not the regular breathing of a sleeper, but the sigh of a person frustrated by insomnia. Parson could sympathize. He heard the shuffling sounds of someone getting up, then footsteps. Carolyn Stewart emerged from the gloom. She stood next to him for a moment, then sat cross-legged beside him.

In the light of the moon and stars, Stewart appeared nothing like the actress who'd graced the cover of magazines. Fatigue sagged the skin under her eyes, and her red hair looked matted and dirty. In such a state, without makeup, she might have been mistaken for an anonymous, exhausted relief worker.

"Can't sleep?" Parson whispered.

Stewart shook her head.

"Me neither," Parson said.

"I've been thinking about Hussein."

"Me, too."

"And what are you thinking, Colonel Parson?"

"Call me Michael. I'm thinking he's a pain in my ass."

Stewart smiled for a second, bringing back for a moment a hint of celebrity, but then her face resumed the worry of an unknown relief worker.

"Well," she said, "I have an idea. That is, if you want to hear an idea from me."

So, she still feels guilty, Parson thought. Not necessarily a bad thing. Parson disagreed with the notion that everyone should feel good about themselves all the time. A little pang of guilt could remind you of a lesson learned. Once, as a young navigator, he'd taken off on a high-profile training mission—the Red Flag air combat exercise at Nellis Air Force Base, Nevada. The crew included an observer who happened to wear three stars on his uniform.

Before takeoff, Parson did the usual oxygen check: He put on his helmet, clipped on his mask, and tested his oxygen regulator for proper flow. In the normal position, the blinker blinked white every time he inhaled. But he left the regulator in the emergency position, which let oxygen continue to flow whether he inhaled or not.

Parson took off his oxygen mask so he could use the helmet's boom mike, not realizing he was depleting the aircraft's oxygen system. Nobody noticed the quantity needle dropping until the LOW OXYGEN light illuminated. By then, the C-130 was airborne and the mock fight was on, the Herk zipping through mountain passes to avoid getting locked up by a fighter jet.

The crew had to break off the fight and go back and land to service the oxygen system, all because Parson screwed up. The general was pissed. For a couple days, Parson felt like turning in his wings.

But Parson's aircraft commander was a pretty good dude. The guy told him, "Everybody does that one time, nav. Don't worry about it."

Not everybody did it with a general on board, however, and Parson *did* worry about it. But he never, ever made that mistake again.

Since Stewart seemed properly remorseful, Parson decided to emulate his supportive aircraft commander.

"Of course I want to hear your idea," he whispered. "I'll take all the help I can get."

"Thank you, Michael," Stewart said. "What if we see if Hussein wants to come with us?"

Okay, Parson thought, maybe I don't want to hear this idea after all.

"Why would he do that?" Parson asked. "Why would *we* do that?"

"He has nowhere to turn here. If he stays in Somalia, he'll go back to al-Shabaab, and he'll die violently and soon. And he might be smart enough to realize that."

"We can't save everybody in Somalia."

"Yes, but we can save *him*, if he wants to be saved."

"That's a big *if*, and what if we do save him? That is, if we actually make it out of here. The Kenyans will just love us when we show up with an illegal alien terrorist."

"I'll take responsibility for him," Stewart said.

"How are you gonna do that?"

"He's a minor. My organization will take him in."

"Ah, yeah," Parson said. "Good luck with that."

"We've taken in children before."

Yeah, but not children who are killers, Parson thought. And there was still the issue of dealing with the Kenyans: *Hi, folks. We got a passenger without a passport. And he has a history of violent crimes.*

Parson reminded Stewart of that little problem. As if to emphasize his point, four distant gunshots echoed while he spoke.

"We can say he stowed away in the airplane," Stewart answered.

"Forget it. I'm not losing my pilot's license and my Air Force commission over this kid."

"We can say he's a refugee. We can say we had reason to fear for his life if we left him. And it would be the truth."

Parson thought about that for a minute. He didn't know what laws and air transport regulations applied to refugees in this situation. If this had been an Air Force mission, the decision would have been easy:

We don't do anything like this without approval from Air Mobility Command or some other adult supervision.

But, Parson reminded himself, this is a civilian mission. He'd been operating in a gray area since he started the engines on that DC-3.

None of this mattered, he realized, if Hussein didn't want their help. Flying out a willing refugee pushed legality hard enough; kidnapping a minor went way over the line.

"I'll ask Geedi to find out what the boy is thinking," Parson said. "He'll probably tell us to go to hell, and that will be the end of it."

"That's all I can ask," Stewart said. "But if he wants to get out and you decide to let him on the plane, I'll take it from there. Whatever the costs, whatever the repercussions, I'll handle it."

Parson nodded, looking not at Stewart but out at the night. In another hour, it would be Geedi's watch. Parson could talk to him then and tell him to have a sit-down with Hussein in the morning.

"Thanks, Michael," the actress whispered. "You know, I can't tell you how much I admire what you and Sophia are doing. You two make quite a pair."

With that, Stewart got up and went back to her place on the bare floor. Parson shifted the AK across his knees and thought about Hussein. Did the boy stand any chance of redemption?

Probably not, but you never knew about these things. In Parson's sleep-deprived state, his mind made unlikely connections. Thoughts of Hussein reminded him of a time he'd gone grouse hunting in the hills of West Virginia. Way back in a hollow, he came across an abandoned farmhouse. The porch sagged, and kudzu climbed the clapboard walls.

Parson and his dog, a little English setter named Lucy, had worked hard that day. They'd climbed many a steep, wooded grade, and they'd bagged only one bird. For every mile Parson had walked, Lucy had run three. She stood beside him panting, tongue dripping, tail wagging. Clearly, she needed to drink, but Parson had already given her the last of his water. And in the afternoon of hunting, they had not come across a stream.

However, a few yards from the house, Parson noticed a well. A dented, galvanized bucket hung from a pulley. Kudzu vines encircled the bucket's chain and the stones that surrounded the well shaft. Parson broke open his Browning double-barrel, placed it on the ground, and drew his boot knife. The sharp Damascus blade made quick work of the vines, and soon he disentangled the bucket and chain.

Rust had frozen the pulley, but Parson freed it and began lowering the bucket. As the chain snaked through his hands, his leather and Nomex flight gloves—which doubled as good shooting gloves—became caked with rust. From the darkness far below, he heard a faint splash.

Hand over hand, he pulled the chain back up. Set the water down for Lucy, who had become so thirsty she lapped for five minutes.

Parson wondered if Hussein's mind was like that disused well. If you lowered the bucket far enough, would clean water yet come up?

33.

A rattle of gunfire pulled Hussein from a deep sleep. At first he could not remember where he was; he looked around in confusion at the inside of the old bunker. The sight of the *gaalos* snapped him back to reality. The report of the rifles brought all of them to their feet. The shots sounded closer than they had last night, though still a good distance away—maybe as far as Hussein could sprint in one go without getting winded. Then he felt the ache of his wound, and he remembered he could not sprint anymore.

Yellow Hair was holding his AK-47 again; she seemed to be the main one on watch. It still irked him to see an infidel—and especially a woman infidel—holding his most prized possession. She might yet pay for that insolence.

Though Hussein did not like waking to captivity, anything was better than his dreams of last night. In his sleep, he had gone back to the day the Sheikh had made him and other boys stone the adulterer. Hussein saw the condemned man buried to his waist, wailing in agony, one of his eyes dangling from its socket as the rocks rained down. Tears and blood streamed across torn cheeks.

However, in the nightmare the man did not simply die—he turned into a vengeful ghoul. This was no jinn, but something worse. The living corpse grew to twice, three times the normal size of a man, and it pulled itself from the ground. Dripping blood and showing his broken teeth, the ghoul came after Hussein. Of all the boys who had stoned the man, why Hussein? Why not one of the other boys? Why not the Sheikh? Perhaps because Hussein had hurled the first stone that hurt him.

Hussein tried to flee, but he could not move fast enough. He had always taken pride in his fleetness of foot. No one could catch him; no other boy could outrun him. Yet he could not get away from this bleeding fiend; Hussein's arms and legs moved as if trying to run through a pit of mud, and his injured foot kept making him fall down.

The ghoul said nothing to him. Through its broken mouth it could not speak. It made only the gurgling sounds of the dying as it placed its broken fingers around Hussein's throat. Somewhere off to the side, Hussein heard another sound: the laughter of the Sheikh and Abdullahi.

Wakefulness came with a flood of relief; the bloody fiend was not real. Still, Hussein feared he would have that same dream again. He had seen things he could never unsee.

The bunker door stood half open, and the first hint of dawn grayed the sky. The infidels were gathering their belongings. Were they going to move again?

What they were not doing was preparing any kind of food. They seemed to have nothing to break their fast, and Hussein found that disappointing. Familiar fingers of hunger pulled at his stomach, and he'd assumed the infidels would feed him again. No matter; he had spent most of his days hungry.

When Hussein sat up, the one called Geedi came over to him. Geedi brought a half-filled water bottle.

"Good morning," Geedi said in a soft voice. "Do you want a drink of water?"

Hussein held out his hand and took the bottle. He tipped the opening to his lips and took a drink. The water had that same awful taste that supposedly kept you from getting sick. He swallowed and wiped his mouth on his shirtsleeve.

"Are we going somewhere?" Hussein asked.

"That is exactly what I want to talk to you about," Geedi said. "We are going to try to fix our airplane and get out of here. That woman over there," Geedi added, pointing, "is a famous person in our country. She wants to help you."

Hussein's mouth dropped open. He looked at the infidel woman with her hair the color of a rusting shipwreck. This was the famous person the Sheikh had wanted? This red-haired mouse who sat in the corner and said nothing?

"To help me what?" Hussein asked.

"To help give you a new life. A life without all this killing and dying."

"Why would she do this?"

"She is sorry that you were hurt looking for her. But it is more than that. She tries to help people in poor countries."

Hussein stared at Geedi and blinked. He might have expected all manner of vile deeds from these *gaalos*. If they had torn up a Quran in front of him, that would not have surprised him. If they had tortured him to death, that would not have surprised him. If they had tried to make him renounce his faith, that would not have surprised him.

But *this*? He had believed he remained always one step ahead of them, in thought if not in deed. He had anticipated every possibility, and he was still waiting for them to make a mistake and give him his chance to kill them—except Geedi, perhaps. But he had not for one moment anticipated that they would make an offer like this.

"To give me a new life where?"

"We do not know," Geedi said. "Not necessarily in America, but possibly. Maybe Europe. Maybe somewhere else in Africa. Anyplace other than Somalia."

"How can she do this?"

"She is on the board of directors for a refugee organization."

"A board? What is a board of directors? What is a ref— What is this word?"

"Refugee."

"What is that?"

"It is you, perhaps."

"It is an insult word?"

"No, Hussein. It is someone who needs a new life. I would say you qualify."

Hussein opened his mouth to reply, then stopped himself. He might not possess the gift of reading, but he was no fool. He knew when to stop talking. His first impulse was to tell them all to go to *Shaytan*, to go to the devil. But this thing—this miracle from Allah—presented opportunities. He could tell them yes and they might trust him, let their guard down. Perhaps give him a chance to get a weapon and let them all meet *Shaytan* face-to-face. Except for Geedi.

Or, maybe . . . No, this was too much to consider all at once. Hussein could hardly get his mind around the possibilities. Surely this was a time to keep one's thoughts to oneself.

"Let me think about it," Hussein said.

"You may not have long to think."

"Why? Are you leaving today?"

"Perhaps. We do not know."

"Wait—you cannot. I destroyed your airplane. I kept you from taking to the sky. You can go nowhere. Because of *me*." Hussein slapped his chest with his right hand.

"You did a pretty good job, Hussein. I will admit that. You damage airplanes, and I fix them. Perhaps we will see who is better, huh?" Geedi gave Hussein a playful slap on the arm.

Hussein smiled, and he almost laughed. Then he forced the smile from his face. He must not get too friendly with these *gaalos*. Not even Geedi. He intended to spare Geedi because Geedi treated him with respect. But when the time came, the situation might force him to kill this flying mechanic along with the others.

"I will think about it."

"Very well. Think quickly, little brother."

Brother? Had Geedi really said that? This was all very confusing.

Hussein tried to let his thoughts settle down—much the way a flock of pigeons might settle down after a cat has run through them and forced them into the air. Just keep quiet and think, Hussein told himself. Talk about simpler things.

"Do you have any food?" Hussein asked.

"We ate everything Nadif gave us last night. I can see if anyone has a little something left, but I doubt it."

Geedi turned and began talking to the infidels again. While they spoke, more gunfire clattered from afar, and it set off more talking among the infidels. The one called Parson pointed in the direction of the firefight, and he and Geedi and Shartee spoke for long moments in that sharp-edged language of theirs.

Hussein did not know what to make of what Geedi had said about a new life. A part of him resented having to make such a big decision with so little time to think. If he had not gotten wounded, if this temporary weakness had not placed him at the mercy of these *gaalos*, he would never have faced such a choice. But fate had put him in a position where he could strike a mighty blow for Allah—or he could travel in directions unforeseen. Even though he was only fourteen, Hussein knew moments like this came rarely. The doors of fate could snap open and shut very quickly.

The conversation among the infidels ended, and Geedi began searching through his backpack. He pawed through the main compartment and did not find what he was looking for. He unzipped little pockets on the outside and looked into them as well. Finally, he pulled something out of one of the pockets and brought it to Hussein. Something small, in a paper wrapper with writing all over it.

"I found some food after all," Geedi said.

Hussein tore open the wrapper. Praise be to Allah, it was a chocolate bar. He bit off a third of it and began to chew. Saliva flooded his mouth at the first taste of this food of angels.

He had eaten chocolate only two or three times in his life, and this tasted a little different. Maybe not quite as sweet, though certainly very good. But very thick. Hard to chew. A gooey substance stuck to

Hussein's molars, though that was a good thing. It kept him from wolfing the bar, made the treat last longer. Hussein swallowed that first bite, wiped his mouth, and paused before taking another.

"This is different," Hussein said. "My teeth do not grind it so easily."

Geedi laughed. "It is a protein bar, Hussein. Maybe you had a Hershey bar before, but yes, this is different."

"What is this 'protein bar'?"

"Ah," Geedi said. He looked up at the ceiling as if trying to find words. "It has more food value than a normal chocolate bar. It is not just candy. I keep them with me when I work, for energy."

Hussein took another bite, again attacking the thick substance with his back teeth.

"This helps you work harder?" Hussein asked, his mouth still full.

"Perhaps. Sometimes I eat them after I work out."

"What do you mean, 'work out'?"

"I lift weights, do push-ups, run."

"Why do you do this?"

"To make myself stronger, little brother. My imam says a healthy body is a gift from Allah. One must take care of it."

"Your imam tells you this?" Hussein asked.

"Yes, he does."

"Where is your imam?"

"In a city called Minneapolis."

"You live in that city?"

"I do, when I am not flying," Geedi answered. "I have since I was little."

Hussein stopped chewing and regarded Geedi.

"What is this place like?"

"It is very cold, Hussein. Cold like you have never known. But most people have more than enough to eat. Most people do not worry about getting shot."

Hussein tried to picture a cold city. He had seen magazine photos of white people in heavy coats, sometimes with white, frozen rain on the ground. He tried to picture a market with so much food. How did they keep people from stampeding to take the food before it ran out? Perhaps because it never ran out? Hussein had so many questions he hardly knew where to begin. But with the searing images of last night's dream still in his head, he found a starting point.

"Your imam," Hussein said. "What else does he tell you?"

Geedi pressed his lips together in thought. "Well," he said, "he tells us to avoid the temptations of alcohol and drugs. He tells us not to miss prayers. And, Hussein, he tells to avoid false teachings by those who use the faith for their own purposes."

"Has he ever made you do something you did not want to do?"

From the darkened expression on Geedi's face, Hussein could see that the flying mechanic did not understand the question.

"Like what, Hussein?"

"Like . . ." Hussein paused. "Nothing," he said. "Never mind."

Hussein turned his eyes downward. He looked at his bandaged foot. The foot hurt with a strange kind of pain, almost as if the missing toes were still there. If Hussein had not known better, he would have thought he still had his big toe and that he had just stubbed it hard on a rock.

"We will change those bandages again before you have to move," Geedi said.

Hussein looked up. "How do you know I will go with you at all?" he asked.

"I suppose I do not," Geedi said. "But you do not have long to decide. Perhaps you will know what to do when the time comes. I hope you choose well, Hussein. You will never get a chance like this again."

No, I will not, Hussein thought. For that reason, he wanted to keep all his options open for as long as possible.

"Take me with you," Hussein said.

34.

The heat woke Parson. Following a restless night, he had drifted into sleep after that first burst of gunfire at dawn. Now the air warmed around him as the sun rose, as if the landscape ran a fever.

He sat up, rubbed his eyes, and tugged at the sleeves of his grimy flight suit. Then he just listened—for the sound of gunfire, of aircraft, of explosions.

Nothing. Parson heard only the exhalation of the wind and the squawk of a seabird.

Everyone was awake. Frenchie had the watch. He sat by the door on the overturned bucket, holding the AK-47 like a dove hunter sitting on a field stool with a shotgun. His Smith & Wesson revolver rested in a holster on his survival vest. Geedi kneeled beside Hussein, chattering in Somali. Gold was looking through the medical ruck; Parson supposed she meant to change Hussein's or Chartier's bandage. Carolyn Stewart stood near the back of the bunker, brushing her teeth with a toothbrush she must have kept in her pack for emergencies— though she'd probably never imagined an emergency like this. She spat white foam and wiped her mouth with a handkerchief.

Parson wondered if Hussein had decided to take her offer of help, but he didn't have to wait long for an answer. When Geedi saw Parson awake, the flight mechanic came over.

"Good morning, sir," Geedi said, keeping his voice low. "He says he wants to go with us."

That surprised Parson. He'd expected—hoped, even—that the boy would say he wanted nothing from the evil infidels. That would have made Parson's life a little simpler. He glanced at Hussein. At the moment, Osama Junior didn't look like a dangerous terrorist; he looked like a clueless, homeless kid. But Parson knew appearances could deceive.

"All right," Parson said, "we'll take him with us, then. Once we land—assuming we ever get airborne—he's Carolyn's problem. Don't let your guard down. I still don't trust that little fucker."

"Yes, sir."

"Do *you* trust him?" Parson asked.

Geedi sucked in air between his front teeth the way Parson had seen other Somalis do when they were thinking.

"He's a wild card," Geedi said. "Who knows what trauma he's seen? He just said something to me about somebody making him do things he didn't want to do. I can only imagine what that might have been. Maybe he's decided he wants to get away from all that."

"Hmm," Parson said. "Well, anyway, now that he's said he wants help, it's hard not to give it to him. But watch him."

"I will."

Parson's career had required him to make a lot of tough calls, some quickly and under fire—but he'd never anticipated a dilemma quite like this. He hoped this decision didn't turn out to be one of his worst.

Despite having eaten his fill last night, Parson felt hungry now. His crew had no more food, so he told himself to suck it up and press on. He stood up, found a bottle with about two inches of water left in it. He picked up the bottle and sloshed the liquid inside.

"Anybody thirsty?" he asked.

When no one answered, he turned up the bottle and poured its contents into his mouth. Swished the water around and swallowed it. Picked up his survival vest, which he had taken off during the night, and found the nav/com radio. The earpiece was still plugged into the set. Parson carried the radio to the half-open door for better reception, and he slipped the survival vest over his body armor.

"See or hear anything?" Parson asked Chartier.

"Just a few random shots about an hour ago," Chartier said. "Since then, *rien*. Nothing."

Maybe that was good news, and Parson knew only one way to find out. He placed the earpiece in his ear, turned on the radio, rolled the squelch control until the hiss stopped. Pressed the transmit button.

"Spear Alpha," he called, "World Relief Airlift."

No answer.

"Spear Alpha, World Relief Airlift," Parson repeated. "You up?"

After a long pause, Ongondo answered. "Spear Alpha here," he said. "Very glad to see you made it through the night."

"Same to you, friend. Hey, it's pretty quiet at our location. Do you think it's safe for us to . . . Ah, do you think we should proceed now as briefed?"

What Parson wanted to ask was whether it was safe to move in the open. But he didn't want to say it out loud on a nonsecure frequency. Instead, he had to hint at what he wanted to do and hope Ongondo understood. A bit like being a teenager, Parson thought, and trying to ask a girl out on a first date without being too direct. Stakes a little higher this time, though. Parson would have given six months' pay for a proper military radio, so they could use encryption and stop talking in circles.

"Negative," Ongondo said. "Negative. We have some eyes to help us. You need to wait for showtime."

Eyes to help you? Parson wondered. Ah, maybe eyes from that drone I thought I heard back at Nadif's. Surveillance for an air strike?

For the moment, it didn't really matter. Ongondo clearly wanted him to stay put for now.

"Copy that, Spear Alpha," Parson said. "World Relief Airlift out."

Parson turned off the radio and removed the earpiece. Chartier, who had heard only half the conversation, asked, "What did he say?"

"I think he's still expecting an air strike," Parson said. "But when I asked if we could go to the airplane now, he said negative."

"If he does not want us moving, it probably means the bad guys are moving."

"Yeah," Parson said. "I think he might be getting data from that Predator we saw the other day."

"The aircraft will find them. I would like to show these terrorists a thing or two in my Mirage."

"I bet you would. Put a hurting on those bastards."

"*Ça, c'est sûr.*"

With little to do but bide his time, Parson sat by the door with Chartier and looked out into the trees. A discarded plastic bag tumbled with the breeze until it lifted into the air and caught on a low, stunted branch. The occasional gust whipped grit into the air, and the airborne dirt made Parson squint. So did the sweat running into his eyes as a result of the rising temperature. No animal life moved within the woods, not even a wayward bird.

"I feel like a critter waiting to get sprung from a trap," Parson told Chartier.

"*Moi aussi,*" Chartier said. "Me, too. I wonder if my *pépère* felt this way at Dien Bien Phu."

"Your granddad was there, too?"

"Oh, yes. And if things had turned out a little differently, I might never have known him."

Parson had read of the French defeat at Dien Bien Phu, which effectively ended their hold on Indochina—and helped lead to the American entanglement in Vietnam. The French tried to establish a strongpoint near the border with Laos, to cut off Viet Minh supply lines. The Viet Minh would have none of that; they brought up artillery and placed Dien Bien Phu under siege.

"From March until May of 1954," Chartier said, "that valley was a cauldron. Things got so bad that they asked for volunteers to parachute into the battle to replace soldiers who had died." Some of those volunteers, Chartier explained, had never jumped from an airplane before. Including his grandfather.

"Damn," Parson said. "He must have been scared to death."

"He said the jump was the least of his worries, because if he went splat, he would have died much easier than at the hands of the Viet Minh."

"But he made it, obviously, if he lived to tell you this."

"Oui, heureusement," Chartier said. "He jumped from a C-119 Flying Boxcar, and he said when the chute opened it jerked him so hard he bit his tongue."

As Frenchie told the story, things got worse from there. His grandfather could hear the explosions of artillery as he floated down under his canopy. Once on the ground, he learned that the tactical situation for the French was so hopeless that the French artillery commander had committed suicide with a hand grenade.

"The situation was awful," Frenchie explained, "but my *pépère* became one of the lucky few. When the garrison fell, he escaped to Laos."

"Man," Parson said, "I bet he had some stories."

"Would you believe that after he managed to evade the Communists, a tiger almost got him?"

"Wow. He shot the tiger?"

"No, he did not. He said he did not wish to harm such a beautiful creature, so he fired a bullet at the ground in front of its paws. The cat turned and ran away. He thought showing the tiger mercy gave him luck. Troops of the Kingdom of Laos found him nearly starved to death and eventually took him to the capital, Vientiane. A French plane flew him out and brought him home."

"Is your granddad still around?"

"No, sadly. We lost him in 2002."

"He must have been a badass."

"A what?"

"Tough guy."

"Oh, yes. Though in his later years he liked nothing better than tending his vineyard."

Though Parson didn't say it, he hoped some of the elder Chartier's luck had been passed down. Parson and his crew were about to attempt an escape with similar long odds. Chartier, in his bloody flight suit with one sleeve cut off, looked himself like an escapee from Dien Bien Phu.

"How's that arm, by the way?" Parson asked.

"Sore, but I can still use it."

A smattering of bloodstains marred the pressure bandage around Chartier's arm. The blood had, of course, seeped from the wound, but the bleeding had stopped.

"Can you fly?"

"*Oui.*"

Well, at least I still got a copilot, Parson thought. Thank God for that.

"Ah, sir," Geedi said. "What if we get to the airplane and they've torn it up so bad we can't fix it?"

"We'll just have to make our way to AMISOM, to the friendlies," Parson said.

Not much of a Plan B, Parson realized, but it beat the hell out of waiting to get slaughtered by al-Shabaab. He considered trying to get more rest, but he knew he'd never get back to sleep. If an air strike— or whatever the hell Ongondo was talking about—was going to happen, it could happen at any moment. Parson decided he'd better make sure everyone was prepared to move.

"Sophia," Parson said, "can you get Hussein ready to travel?"

"Sure," Gold said. She picked up the medical ruck and placed it beside Hussein's feet. She held up a roll of gauze to show the boy she intended to change his bandages. Hussein tipped his chin in assent.

Stewart was rummaging through her backpack. Through the open zipper of the pack, Parson noticed her video camera. He felt charitable toward her now that she'd offered to take responsibility for Hussein.

"You were shooting a documentary, right?" Parson said.

"Uh, yes," the actress said. "But that's not important right now."

"Well, we might have to move fast pretty soon, so you might as well shoot some scenes while you can. What do you media people call that? B roll?"

Stewart laughed. "B roll is an old-school term, but yes." Then she turned serious. "Are you sure? I don't want to cause any more problems than I already have."

"It's okay, Carolyn," Parson said. "I think we're going to get out of here today or tomorrow or not at all. Either way, whatever's in your camera won't hurt us now."

"Thank you, Michael. This means a lot."

"Just make sure you get my good side."

"I promise," Stewart said, smiling. She lifted the camera and fiddled with its settings. Looked around for a moment. Then she spoke under her breath, perhaps more talking to herself than anyone else: "Not much light in here, but at least it will look authentic."

Stewart began recording. She took video of Gold working on Hussein's bandage. After a few moments, she panned toward the door for a shot of Chartier on watch with the AK-47. The Frenchman waved with his wounded arm and winced. Stewart recorded Parson arranging the poles and blanket to remake Hussein's stretcher. Then she panned back to Hussein, and she spoke while she shot the video.

"This is a young al-Shabaab fighter named Hussein," Stewart intoned. "We have learned few details about his background, but it is likely he has known little but mayhem in his few years. Despite his youth, he seems experienced in the ways of violence. Hussein took part in the attack that grounded our airplane, and he continued to pursue us despite a crippling wound to his foot. We found him wounded, bleeding, dehydrated, and intent on our destruction. But we hope this marks a new beginning for Hussein."

For the second time, Parson listened to Stewart's ad-libbed narration and thought: Not bad. This wasn't Hollywood fluff; this was somebody getting into the shit and telling the story. Parson had heard of reporters and documentary filmmakers in war zones who got close enough to the action to take a bullet. Yeah, a lot of them were ass clowns. But maybe a few of them actually did some good.

A noise interrupted Parson's thoughts and Stewart's work. She stopped talking, but kept recording.

Parson heard it, too. The sound of a jet. No, more than one. Maybe two pairs. Coming in low and fast.

35.

Parson darted to the bunker door. Chartier was on his feet, looking up. The branches of the nearest tree obscured the sky, but through the leaves, Parson saw objects slicing through the scattered cumulus. When they flew beyond the tree into clear view, Parson recognized two sharp-nosed attack jets. Both aircraft featured two-seat tandem cockpits and short, stubby wings. The wings' low aspect ratio gave the jets the appearance of machines built for speed, and the roar of the engines rumbled down in waves.

"L-39 Albatros," Chartier said. His tone suggested he was not impressed; the L-39s were no match for his Mirage.

But Parson was impressed as hell; the L-39s were good enough to rip the shit out of a bunch of bad guys.

"Rock and roll, baby," Parson said.

Behind the first pair of jets, another pair followed—the formation comprised two sets of lead and wingman. The lead jet of the first pair peeled off and began a steep descent. As the aircraft drew nearer, Parson thought he recognized the tail markings—including a flag with black, orange, and red stripes.

"I think they're Ugandan," Parson said. "I saw one of those jets at Mogadishu."

Presumably, aircraft of the Uganda People's Defence Force, detailed to AMISOM. Parson didn't care where the damned planes came from, as long as the pilots and back-seaters could shoot.

"Saddle up, people," Parson called. "Get ready to move."

He wanted to head out the door and sprint for the DC-3 right now. But he quashed that impulse. Better see if Ongondo has a sit-rep first, Parson realized.

Once more, he pulled the nav/com radio from his survival vest and turned it on. Didn't bother with the earpiece this time. Pressed the talk button.

"Spear Alpha," Parson transmitted, "World Relief Airlift. Talk to me, buddy."

The radio hissed for a few seconds. Then Ongondo's voice came on the frequency.

"World Relief Airlift," Ongondo said. "It's showtime." Rifle fire popped in the background as he spoke.

Then we don't need to talk in riddles anymore, Parson thought. He pressed his transmit switch again and said, "Copy that, Spear Alpha. We're going to try to get to the LZ and see if we can fix the plane. Where are the bad guys?"

"Surveillance feed shows them west and north of your aircraft and moving. Spear Alpha's in contact—gotta run."

"Surveillance feed" probably meant a downlink from a drone. So Parson's hunch had been correct. And "in contact" meant in contact *with the enemy*. Ongondo had no time to talk. Parson had to make a quick decision with little to go on. He did not ponder long.

"Let's go," Parson said. "Follow me."

"D'accord," Chartier said.

Parson picked up the RPK machine gun and checked its fire selector. Clicked the selector to semiauto. He wanted to be ready to shoot instantly, but he didn't want to waste what little ammo he had in one full-auto rip. With the weapon poised, he moved out of the bunker. Kept his Beretta holstered.

Chartier followed close behind, armed with the AK-47. Geedi and Stewart brought Hussein on the stretcher. Gold came out of the bunker last, carrying the medical ruck over her shoulder. Chartier handed off the AK to Gold, then drew his Smith & Wesson Magnum. That made sense to Parson; given Frenchie's wounded arm, it was better to let Gold handle the long gun for now.

"Should we tie the boy's hands again?" Chartier asked.

"Don't worry about it," Parson said. He wished he'd done that earlier, but he didn't want to stop now. Though he'd warned everybody to keep an eye on Hussein, he figured the kid couldn't do much at this point, anyway. Hussein's wound weakened him and kept him from running. And with an air strike going on, his terrorist friends weren't coming for him anytime soon.

While leading the team out of the bunker, Parson lost sight of the jets. But their Ivchenko turbines thundered a crescendo that split the morning. When Parson spotted them again, one streaked just above the tree line, pure kinetic menace. Now Parson could make out the weapons mounted on pylons under the wings, bombs bristling with tailfins.

One of the bombs detached from its pylon and cut a diagonal path away from the Albatros. The bomb dropped below the trees . . . and for a moment Parson thought it was a dud.

He felt the explosion before he heard it. The blast creased the air; the pressure wave felt as if a professional fighter had smacked him square in the breastbone with a palm strike. A beat later, a mass of smoke and fire, a miasma of orange and black, boiled above the trees.

Under any other circumstances, Parson would have taken cover during a bombing raid like this. But now he counted on the air strike to make the bad guys keep their heads down while he moved. Parson headed toward the LZ at a brisk walk. He wanted to go faster, but he didn't want to outpace Geedi and Stewart as they carried Hussein. Parson moved in a crouch, his index finger across the trigger guard of the RPK.

The jet that had dropped the bomb pulled up and away in an escape maneuver. Clawing for altitude, the Albatros screamed toward the sun. As Parson ducked through the forest, the flight path of the small attack plane reminded him of the fierce little Mississippi kites that terrorized joggers at Altus Air Force Base, Oklahoma. If you got too close to their nesting trees, the miniature birds of prey would dive-bomb you to deliver a nasty peck.

It's not the size of the bird in the fight, Parson thought. It's the size of the fight in the bird.

The small jets above him had plenty of fight left. The aircraft that dropped the first weapon joined up with its wingman, and the second pair set up for a bomb run. Parson led in the direction of the DC-3—or whatever was left of it. That meant traveling west. The jets seemed to focus on a target even farther west, beyond Parson's airplane. He couldn't be sure, however. Though an expert navigator when equipped with the right tools, he lacked even a map. He'd have to rely purely on an innate sense of direction. He hoped he could get by without the precision of his handheld GPS, now smashed and useless. Even if he missed by hundreds of yards, maybe the sparse cover would make it easy to spot something as big as his airplane.

Parson could not guess whether he and his team would ever make it to the plane, let alone get airborne. But now that he'd set things into motion, he felt a small turn of satisfaction. It was like pressing a jet engine's start button and watching the sequence on the instruments: rotation, fuel flow, ignition, acceleration to a stable RPM. The unleashing of energy and the opening of possibilities.

Hussein gripped the poles that made up the frame of his stretcher. He bounced along so much he feared that Geedi and that little red mouse would drop him. At first he resented being carried like a crippled child, but now the sights and sounds assaulting his senses made him forget all else.

Quick little flying machines danced and roared in the sky above him. He had seen airplanes before, to be sure. But not like these, and never so close. And, by Allah, he had never seen an explosion like the one that had just made the earth shudder. Once, from a distance, he had seen a suicide bomber detonate himself, but that registered as a mere firecracker compared to the weapons unleashed by these machines. And the airplanes looked like they might loose another bomb at any moment.

Wonder, not fear, dominated Hussein's emotions. And one of the many things astounding him now was the infidels' evident lack of fear. They were heading *toward* this storm of fire wrought from above.

Whatever their sins, these *gaalos* were no cowards. Hussein knew courage; he knew he possessed it in abundance. But the infidels displayed a strange brand of courage. To see such a mass of flames and smoke and rush to it? Where did courage end and madness begin? Could they really believe they would escape?

This day may bring my death, Hussein thought, but it will bring amazements as well. He hoped he would live long enough to see what the day might offer.

One of the flying machines fell from the sky like a knife dropped point-first from a high place. For a moment Hussein thought the airplane would crash into the ground; perhaps its motor had stopped or its driver had died. But it pulled up and swooped across the treetops with a noise so loud it invaded Hussein's body and vibrated his bones. He wanted to put his hands over his ears, but he dared not let go of his stretcher.

An object fell from the flying machine, and the falling shape looked different from the first bomb. This time, a cylinder without fins flipped end over end until it vanished behind some trees. The weapon struck the earth about twice as far away as Hussein could throw a stone.

The cylinder split open and released a mountain of flame; the *gaalos* must have found a way to bottle *Shaytan*'s lakes of fire. Heat singed Hussein's skin. He let go of the stretcher and shielded his eyes. The smell of burning oil filled his nostrils. The fire sucked the very air from his lungs. When he looked up he saw ash and debris, some of it burning and trailing smoke, fluttering down like leaves from the trees of hell.

The infidels crouched low. Geedi and the red-haired woman put him down, and that little red mouse took hold of him and held him close as if to shield him. Hussein did not want her so close, but he did not resist. So much kept happening that his mind could not take it in fast enough. He had trouble deciding what, if anything, he should do.

Think, Hussein told himself. Watch and understand. You cannot use this situation if you do not keep your head. Choose what to do and then do it.

Just when he believed his eyes and ears had caught up with everything around him, a vision of horror rushed toward him. A figure—no, two figures—emerged from the black smoke and trees. They ran out of the fire and in Hussein's direction. But they did not escape the fire; they *were* the fire. Flames clothed them, wreathed them, as if they were jinns formed from fire itself.

But they were not jinns; they were men, overtaken by that hell bomb dropped by the airplane. They sprinted as if they might outrun the fire if they just pumped their legs fast enough. One, apparently blinded, ran full into a tree, collapsed, and lay twitching and smoking. The other came on fast, as if rushing to gather Hussein in his arms and deliver him to *Shaytan*. The air filled with the smell of cooking flesh.

Hussein's mind struggled to keep up. Just as he realized these were men, not demons, and probably al-Shabaab brothers, the infidels surprised him again. Yellow Hair and the one called Parson raised their weapons and fired quick shots. That woman could shoot after all; the burning ghoul fell to the ground.

They must have killed him out of mercy. Surely he would have died anyway within minutes or even seconds. Apparently these strange people could not bear to see the man suffer. *And he was their enemy.* Hussein thought he knew the ways of men, but clearly he had things yet to learn.

Red Mouse released Hussein from her shielding embrace. The heat from the fire made him sweat, and he felt his limbs grow damp. Geedi and Red Mouse lifted the stretcher again and began to carry him away from the fire. All the while, the red-haired woman kept speaking to him in words he could not understand. Despite the harsh sound of her native language, her tone sounded gentle, as if she were telling him not to be afraid. Foolish words, spoken from misplaced kindness. A mindless, knee-jerk form of kindness, in Hussein's estimation. But better than mindless cruelty; he had to give Red Mouse credit for that.

The infidels carried him out of the forest and to the edge of the grassland. They passed the village where the old couple had taken them in. Hussein saw no signs of life among the huts. Amid the fire-fights and the bombs from hell, anyone with any sense was surely taking cover. Rifle fire popped in the distance; Hussein could not tell who was shooting or where.

He'd expected the infidels to retrace their steps, to follow the dry creek bed in reverse direction back to their airplane. But that's not what happened; evidently the one called Parson was trying to save time and cut a corner directly to his damaged flying machine. They waded into the grass beyond the village. The rustling blades brushed at Hussein's elbows as Geedi and Red Mouse carried him into open country. The *gaalos* made no effort to hide; they plowed headlong through the grass, using only the chaos around them for cover.

With no trees to block the view, Hussein saw the full extent of that chaos. Smoke as black as a vulture's feathers churned into the air from three different spots, all in the general direction of where the sun goes to set. The fast airplanes—Hussein could now tell there were four of them—turned and climbed and zoomed in a pattern that made no sense to him. The smell of frying meat had faded, but now the landscape stank of burning oil.

Something on the ground exploded; Hussein had no idea what it was. One of the three columns of smoke grew larger. The smoke towered into the sky and bent with the breeze toward the ocean. Someone on a ship, Hussein imagined, would think all of Somalia was burning.

From somewhere between the fires, a rocket speared into the air. Gray smoke trailed behind the weapon as it cut a path toward one of the attack planes. The airplane turned hard and the rocket missed. Another of the flying machines rolled onto its side, curved around, and dropped nearly as low as the treetops. It dropped a hell bomb where the rocket had come up. Flames leapt from the ground as if Allah himself had pointed a finger that cut a long trench in the earth and brought forth fire.

An explosion sounded from behind Hussein, in the direction of the village. He turned his head and saw men with guns running through the trees. Some stopped to fire—at what, Hussein could not tell. Another blast boomed, and he recognized the sound: a mortar, one of those little bombs that you dropped into a tube. The battle seemed to swirl on every side with no shape at all. If he could have jumped from the stretcher to find al-Shabaab, he would not have known where to go.

This is hopeless, Hussein thought. Infidels or Muslims, sinners or righteous, we are all going to die.

36.

Parson had counted on an air strike. But he hadn't counted on fucking napalm. This wasn't the laser-guided, thread-the-needle close air support he'd seen in Iraq and Afghanistan. This was fury set afire, and he prayed the next shower of flaming jellied gasoline didn't fall on him and his people.

There was no turning back. Parson could only look for the DC-3 and hope to get into the sky before the bad guys recovered from the air strike and regrouped. Where was the damned airplane? He thought he remembered landing closer to the village. Maybe he should have backtracked up the creek bed, but now with gunfire behind him, turning around and starting over was not an option.

Of all things for that damned bullet to hit, Parson thought, why did it have to nail my GPS? Better to lose his radio or even his pistol than to lose his main tool for land navigation.

In the dry brush and sparse trees, flames ignited by the napalm began to spread. What had started as three distinct fires in the trees beyond the grassland now melded, and the grass at the tree line began to burn and send up gray smoke. The wind caught the smoke and carried it across the ground toward Parson and his crew.

Parson stopped and tried to scan his surroundings. Chartier and Gold came up behind him, and Geedi and Stewart put down Hussein's stretcher. The boy looked alarmed but not panicked. He observed with wide eyes, apparently trying to take everything in.

"I can't see shit now," Parson said. "Frenchie, do you think we've come too far?"

"I do not remember the grass field being this big," Chartier said.

Parson didn't, either. But when they'd come through the grass be-fore, they'd crawled along the ground, keeping as close to the dirt as possible while bullets sang overhead. Hardly a good way to get the lay of the land.

The last thing Parson had seen while standing up was the landing field itself: a clearing not as wide as this grassland, with woods and thickets to the west and sparser trees to the east and north. Maybe he'd passed a little too far to the right of his intended course—which would mean he'd erred to the north.

He gazed toward the south, trying to see if any of that landscape looked familiar. The gray smoke lifting from the grass fire obscured his vision—and raised another worry: The breeze was blowing from the west. What if that damned napalm started a wildfire that took off with the wind? Spreading in that direction, the fire might burn across the field where the DC-3 was parked. Wherever the hell that was.

A gazelle came bounding through the smoke, fleeing the fire. The animal ran toward the village. Carolyn Stewart took out her video camera and began shooting. Parson couldn't tell if she'd moved quickly enough to get footage of the gazelle, but then she panned across the grassy, smoking expanse. He didn't yell at her for taking the time to shoot. He needed to pause anyway, because he needed a moment to think.

He knew he had to correct course to the left or right, because noth-ing directly in front of him looked like the landing field. To the right, or to the north, he saw more thickets and trees. Yeah, he probably *had* come too far north. He sure as hell didn't want to go any farther that way; Ongondo had warned about enemy in that direction. To the left, or to the south, Parson saw little but drifting smoke. He pulled the lensatic compass from his vest and checked it—but with no map and defined course, he could confirm only that the bombs had fallen pretty much due west.

"Son of a bitch," Parson muttered. "I think we need to take a dog-leg to the south. Sophia, what's your gut telling you?" He closed the compass and tossed it to her. She caught it one-handed while holding the AK. Opened the compass and watched it spin and settle down.

As a former soldier, Gold had land nav skills herself, and Parson wanted a second opinion. But without a topographical chart, neither of them could do better than make an educated guess. Parson's SD card contained all the nav data he needed, but with his GPS receiver destroyed, the SD card was useless.

"I think you're right," Gold said. She closed the compass and gave it back to Parson. "Pretty rough dead reckoning, though."

"That's for damn sure," Parson said. He hoped *dead* wasn't the operative word.

Hussein raised himself up onto his knees so he could look around. He shaded his eyes with his hand, looked at Parson. The boy pointed to the south and said something in Somali.

"What's he saying?" Parson asked.

"He saw you two looking around," Geedi said. "He says the airplane is that way."

Parson considered that for a moment. He still didn't trust Osama Junior, but the boy had probably gotten a better look at the terrain than anyone else. And Hussein was confirming what Parson thought, anyway. Hell, maybe Hussein had actually decided to make himself useful.

"Tell him thanks," Parson said. "Let's get the fuck out of here."

Geedi and Stewart lifted the stretcher, and Parson led the way again, this time angling to the south. All the while, he kept a wary eye on the thickets to the north. He thought he saw men moving among the brush, but at a distance of a thousand yards he couldn't be sure. Though the L-39s had lit up bad guys to the west and back toward the village to the east, the planes had dropped nothing to the north. If there really were enemy in that direction, they were still very much alive.

As Parson slogged through the grass, a butterfly flitted in front of him. Its wings were mainly white, but the tips sported a burnt orange nearly the same color as the flames crackling in the distance. The insect flew in crazy dips and climbs, as if its flight augmentation computer had gone tango uniform. Eventually it decided on a course and zipped to the east aided by a tailwind. Parson wished he could take to the air that easily. Even if he *did* get the damaged DC-3 airborne, he'd be flying a craft almost as fragile as that butterfly.

The smoke grew thicker and stung his eyes. Oddly, the woodsy smell reminded him of pleasant things: campfires, cookouts, venison roasting on a spit. But that meant bad news. If he'd smelled petroleum, that would be napalm burning itself out. This was dry vegetation burning, so the fire was growing instead of dying.

Parson looked around and realized he could no longer see a horizon in any direction. In fact, he could see nothing beyond forty yards— only his crewmates, Hussein, and smoke swirling on all sides. Almost as if he'd flown—or, in this case, walked—into a cloud of smoke. Fliers would call it IMC: instrument meteorological conditions.

No choice but to fly on instruments. Parson cradled the RPK across his elbow, fished out the compass, and opened it again. He took a bearing to the southwest, about two-three-zero degrees. Nothing to do now except walk in that direction and hope for the best. And pray the fire didn't get close enough to force him in a direction he didn't want to go.

That would happen, too, if the smoke got any thicker. Breathing became more difficult by the minute, and Parson wondered how long it took to suffer permanent damage from smoke inhalation. He began to cough, and his crewmates started hacking, too. He recalled a story about a smoke jumper somewhere in Montana who had been fighting a wildfire when flames overtook him. The guy used his emergency shelter to keep from burning to death, but three days later he died from lung damage.

Parson realized the smoke presented another problem, too. If they managed to reach the airplane without getting shot or burned to death, and if they managed to get it fixed, and if both engines started, he might not be able to see to take off.

He shook his head and cursed under his breath. His brilliant escape plan had turned into a total, absolute, maximum-effort, high-performance, redline RPM goat fuck.

Through the smoke, Parson pressed on toward the southwest. The jet noise faded to a low and constant rumble; apparently the L-39s had paused their attack and started orbiting at a higher and safer altitude. Or maybe they'd gone Winchester: in fighter pilot parlance, that meant running out of ordnance.

Every few seconds, a fit of hacking seized Parson. After one especially wracking cough, he spat phlegm and wiped his mouth on the sleeve of his flight suit. His chest had hurt to begin with, still sore from the bullet that had whacked his body armor and destroyed his GPS. With each ragged breath, his armor grew heavier and his body more tired. He knew he and his friends could not last much longer in this smoke. In Afghanistan all those years ago, Parson had not been able to save his crewmates. Would he lose crew members again, this time amid fire instead of ice?

The thick grass tangled around his legs as he forged ahead. The effect put him in mind of wading through a fast stream; in fact, the entire scene seemed a perversion of a peaceful memory: Parson recalled fishing for trout in the Firehole River at Yellowstone National Park. He remembered the way the current surged against his knees while steam—like this damnable smoke—rose from nearby geysers. Instead of terrorists stalking him, bison grazed placidly along the riverbanks. Instead of an RPK machine gun loaded with 7.62 millimeter, he'd carried a bamboo rod loaded with five-weight fly line.

Surrounded by fires and threatened by the enemy, it seemed to Parson that the evil in this tormented country had risen to a whole new dimension. Somehow it had found a way to get inside his head, invade his best memories, and play them out in hellish interpretations.

Time to get out of this place, Parson thought. Or die trying.

He halted for a moment and turned to look at his crew. Gold and Chartier had tied handkerchiefs across their faces to filter some of the smoke. For a moment Parson considered stopping to let Geedi, Stewart, and Hussein do the same, but he decided the best thing he could do for them was to keep moving. Chartier coughed despite the handkerchief, and each time he did, the fabric puffed out in front of his nose and mouth.

"You guys all right?" Parson asked.

Chartier tried to answer, but coughs overwhelmed his words. Parson bulled through the grass faster, kicking at the vegetation. His inability to ease his friends' suffering did more than frustrate him; it *angered* him. An officer's most sacred duty was to those under his command.

In an airplane, he could have done something about the smoke. For an aviator, smoke and fire ranked among the worst of emergencies, but you had procedures: Order everybody on oxygen, open the safety valve and depressurize the airplane—which would suck out the smoke in an instant. Keep the plane on autopilot, spin a lower number into the altitude selector. Chop the throttles back to idle and let the autopilot take you down low enough to breathe without oxygen.

But here, on the ground, the best of his knowledge did not apply, and the best of his tools no longer worked. He had no option but to keep putting one boot in front of the other—through this damned burning grass. Parson found himself looking straight down as he struggled with the ensnaring blades and vines. That's why it came as a surprise when he tore his boot free one more time—and placed it on bare, dry earth.

Parson scanned around and realized he'd come to a shallow depression in the ground. He blinked, rubbed his watering eyes. When a gust thinned the smoke for a moment, he realized this wasn't just a depression but a wide, shallow spot in the creek bed. Sure enough, they had strayed north of the objective. But now they were back on track. His gut—and Hussein's sense of direction—had been right.

"Hey, guys," Parson said. "I think we're getting close."

"Dieu merci," Chartier said, coughing.

Geedi and Stewart brought Hussein to the edge of the creek bed. Stewart's eyes streamed, and they looked an unhealthy shade of red. Mucus ran from Hussein's nostrils, and he wiped his nose on his sleeve. Chartier tore the handkerchief from his face, spat into it, and stuffed it in a pocket.

"This rag isn't doing me any good," Chartier said.

Parson crossed the creek bed, climbed the opposite bank, and entered the grass once again. The smoke thinned further; apparently, Parson's heading had taken them away from the fire—at least for the moment. With visibility now perhaps a hundred yards, he could see trees in front of him. Not a forest, just three acacias appearing ghostly in the haze and smoke.

Rifle fire echoed from somewhere—four evenly placed shots on semiauto. Listening to the gunfire, Parson realized he no longer heard the jets. So they probably *had* gone Winchester—or bingo fuel. He drew a breath and it went down clean, the first clear air he'd inhaled in several minutes.

Peering through the smoke, Parson kept moving along that same two-three-zero course line. He glanced at the compass from time to time to keep his heading true, hoping he'd soon see something he recognized. This is why you trust your readings, Parson thought to himself, because memory is unreliable.

He recalled his stint as an adviser to the Afghan air force, and how he always preached proper use of current charts. Some of those guys wanted to navigate from memory. At night or in marginal weather, that was a good way to fly into a mountain.

The smoke cleared enough to reveal the sky overhead, clouds in white patches. One of the patches obscured the sun. After several seconds, the winds aloft pushed the clouds enough to expose a rind of sunfire. That's when Parson noticed a glint on the ground.

It was back to the east, not as far west as he'd expected. But he could not mistake the source of the reflection. Through another small stand of acacias, he recognized the aluminum sheen of the DC-3.

37.

When the infidels spotted their airplane, they rushed to it in such haste that they nearly dropped Hussein. He hung on tight to the stretcher, grateful finally to have better air to breathe. Geedi thanked him for helping show the way. Hussein's assistance had convinced the infidels he'd come over to their side once and for all.

But he had not.

Hussein had merely wanted to move things along. He still did not know how best to use this situation, what course to take. But he'd needed to escape that burning field. No good plan involved choking to death on smoke.

He recalled Geedi's words back at the bunker: "Perhaps you will know what to do when the time comes." Maybe a sign would present itself, some signal from Allah. Hussein knew he must remain alert to find his moment of opportunity.

Geedi and Red Mouse put him down behind the airplane's left wing, where his grenade had done most of its damage. Hussein saw the flattened tire and holes torn by shrapnel. In his mind's eye, however, the destruction had been worse; he thought he'd nearly blown the wing off. Now he felt a little disappointed to see that his deed—while certainly effective—had somehow grown in his imagination.

The one called Parson and the other white man, the one called Shartee, talked in excited tones. They walked around the airplane, pointing at the engines and other parts, examining everything closely. Parson still carried the machine gun taken from the al-Shabaab brother killed in that firefight near the bunker. Yellow Hair kept Hussein's AK-47; the sight of a woman holding his rifle gave unending offense.

Hussein sat up on the stretcher, supporting himself with his arm. A coughing attack came over him until he spat smoke-darkened mucus, and then the hacking eased. The injured foot throbbed. Hussein placed the wounded foot on the ground and tried putting weight on it. That worsened the pain, though not more than he could endure. And it told him what he wanted to know: If necessary, he could take a few quick steps on his own. Such a move might tear open the wound, but he could do it if he had to.

In the distance, across the grass field, a wall of smoke rose from the ground. The *gaalos* pointed and seemed to talk with some concern—and Hussein could see why. The fire was burning its way toward them. The smell of charred brush hung heavy in the air.

As the fire spread, so did the firefight. Gunfire chattered all around, though smoke obscured the shooters.

Parson handed the machine gun to the one called Shartee. While Shartee and Yellow Hair stood guard, Parson disappeared into the flying machine. Geedi climbed in after him and came back out with a metal box. When Geedi opened the box, Hussein saw it was filled with tools.

"What are you doing?" Hussein asked.

"I am going to try to give you a ride," Geedi said. "But I cannot talk now, little brother. I have much to do."

To Parson's tremendous relief and surprise, the condition of the DC-3 was not much worse than when he left it. Not that those al-Shabaab bastards hadn't tried. He sat in the left pilot's seat, sweating in the hotbox interior of the aircraft, and surveyed the damage to the instrument panel. Some asshole had smashed the altimeter, probably with the butt of a rifle. Shattered glass from the face of the instrument crunched on the floor beneath Parson's boots, and the bent needles indicated the impossible altitude of thirty-one thousand three hundred feet. The throttle levers were broken off, but when he pushed on the remaining stubs with the heel of his hand, they moved smoothly. Someone had stolen the tablet computer from Parson's flight bag, naturally, but he could live without that. No classified information on it, just charts and approach plates.

Whoever had come on board had clearly intended to render the plane unflyable, but must have gotten interrupted. Maybe the course of the battle had allowed no more time. Somebody swinging a rifle stock could have torn things up a lot worse in just a few more seconds, so the bastards evidently left in a hurry. Fortunately, they'd not stolen his headset. And the panel-mounted GPS screen was scratched but intact.

Parson felt lucky to have an airplane at all. He'd half expected to find that one of the al-Shabaab geniuses had opened a filler cap on a fuel tank and dropped in a match—thereby earning martyrdom and the Darwin Award.

As it was, Parson figured he could manage with what he had: He could still control his power settings, and he didn't need the altimeter for a quick VFR flight over the border into Kenya. Assuming, of course, Geedi could get the tire changed and fix whatever else needed fixing. And assuming both engines started. Before the fires got here. Or the bad guys.

After only a few minutes inside the sun-beaten aluminum, sweat made Parson's flight suit cling to his limbs, and his wrists bore red mackling from the heat. He rose from the pilot's seat to help Geedi move the spare tire and the jacks—which, thank God, remained strapped down in the back. So did the little motorized pump to provide hydraulic pressure for the jacks.

Parson released the tie-downs and rolled the tire to the door. Geedi and Carolyn Stewart took the tire and carried it to the left landing gear while Chartier and Gold stood watch. Parson wasn't sure how well Frenchie could shoot, given the arm wound, but the man sure as hell couldn't lift heavy equipment. Geedi climbed back on board, and he and Parson wrestled the jacks and pump out of the aircraft. Carolyn Stewart shot video as they struggled with the hardware.

"I don't know how well this will work," Geedi said, "but I guess we don't have any choice. Do we still have cargo chains?"

"I'll look," Parson said. "What do you want those for?"

"I want to chain the strut so it doesn't extend any farther. Then I won't have to jack the plane so high."

"Good thinking there, flight mech."

"Thanks, sir," Geedi said. "This operation's going to be dicey enough as it is."

Parson understood Geedi's concern. Normally, you jacked an airplane on a flat, hard surface of asphalt or concrete. Here, if the weight of the airplane pushed the jacks deep into the dirt, Geedi could never change the tire. Parson climbed back into the cargo compartment and checked the chain boxes. He found two ten-thousand-pound-test chains.

"How many chains you need, Geedi?" Parson shouted.

"Just one, sir."

The metal links clattered as Parson pulled them from the chain box. He jumped down from the doorway and brought the chain to Geedi.

"Perfect," Geedi said.

"At least the plane's light," Parson said. "No cargo and almost no fuel."

"Hey, no fuel," Geedi said. "Nice we got that going for us."

Light was a relative term, Parson realized. For a DC-3, that meant about eighteen thousand pounds.

Geedi positioned the jacks under the wings and went to work. He connected the hoses between the pump and the jacks, and he looped the chain over a trunnion bar on the side with the bad tire. He secured the chain around the landing gear, taking care not to block the lower axle clamp. Then he yanked the starter cord for the pump. The pump sputtered to life and chugged with a sound much like a lawnmower.

Over the noise of the pump motor, Parson heard rifle fire popping in the distance, and he resisted the temptation to tell Geedi to hurry the hell up. This kind of combat repair reminded him of stories he'd heard early in his career, when the Air Force still had people who'd served in Southeast Asia.

They told harrowing tales of fixing C-130s that had broken down on dirt strips in Vietnam or Laos—sometimes where the enemy owned the night, and fliers needed to get their mortar magnets off the ground before sunset. Crew chiefs and flight engineers came up with ways to field-repair their airplanes that Parson found truly ingenious: They learned that when a pneumatically operated engine valve failed, they could connect the valve to the anti-icing system—who needed anti-icing at low altitude in Vietnam?—and actuate the valve by flipping on the anti-ice. If an engine wouldn't start because a speed-sensitive switch failed, they got around the problem by wiring the pins in the switch's cannon plug. If a failed reverse-current relay left them with a screwed-up electrical system, no problem. They'd just rig a jumper wire and get the hell out of Dodge. And they thought up this stuff in combat and under fire.

The Air Force realized that when these guys retired, the military would lose all that hard-won knowledge. So they wrote down and institutionalized these last-ditch fixes and gave them an official-sounding name: Hostile Environment Procedures. Parson remembered crusty old instructors talking about what to do "when Charlie's in the wire."

Today it was al-Shabaab instead of Charlie, and there was not even a perimeter wire for defense. And Geedi, Parson, and Chartier would have to make up their own Hostile Environment Procedures for their antique airplane.

To make matters worse, the environment looked more hostile all the time. Flames danced in the grass and thickets, the closest only eight hundred yards away. The distance made it hard to judge the direction the blaze was moving, but if the wind kept blowing, the wildfire would soon reach the DC-3. And every time Parson began to hope the enemy had left the area, he heard another rip of gunfire.

"Frenchie," Parson said, "how many rounds you got in that RPK?"

Chartier ejected the weapon's magazine, checked it, smacked it back into place.

"*Trois,*" Chartier said.

"Three? That's *all?*"

"*Oui.* Remember, you fired a couple rounds into that poor devil who was burning to death."

Of course Parson remembered. Under the circumstances, a high price for mercy. But he did not regret it.

"What about the AK-47?" Parson asked.

Gold slid the AK off her shoulder and checked the magazine. "Seven rounds," she said.

"Well," Parson said, "let's hope we don't need them."

With so little ammo in the long guns, Parson and his crew had enough firepower to fight back a determined enemy for about four seconds. He still had a full fifteen-round mag for his Beretta, but that was a close-range weapon. The same held true for Frenchie's revolver, despite its massive caliber. Parson held out his handgun with the grip toward Gold.

"Here, Sophia," he said, "take my weapon. I gotta focus on the airplane from here on in." Gold set down the medical ruck near the DC-3's tail, took the pistol, and checked the red indicator on the extractor to see that the chamber held a round.

Note to self, Parson thought: Next time bring your own AR and plenty of rounds. Better yet, don't let there be a next time, at least not like this.

He decided to try to call Lieutenant Colonel Ongondo. The AMISOM officer would want to know Parson's team had made it to the airplane. Parson walked behind the airplane to get away from the noise of the hydraulic pump. He pulled the nav/com radio from his survival vest and switched it on. Adjusted the squelch control, pressed the transmit button.

"Spear Alpha," Parson said. "World Relief Airlift."

Parson waited several seconds for an answer. When Ongondo finally came on the frequency, he sounded out of breath. And, given the clarity of the signal, he also sounded close.

"World Relief Airlift," Ongondo said. "Go ahead."

"We've reached the LZ. Thanks for your help."

The radio hissed for a moment, then Ongondo responded: "That is good news, my friend. Be advised there is enemy movement to the north of your position."

Hell, Parson thought, I just can't catch a break.

"I was afraid of that," Parson said.

He started to ask whether the L-39s would hit the bad guys again, but he stopped himself. That wasn't a question to ask over an open channel. And he already knew the answer: He heard no jet noise now. Even if the planes had returned to their base to refuel and rearm for another sortie, they probably wouldn't get back in time to do him any good. Parson settled for a more general question.

"Spear Alpha," he called, "will we see you today?"

Long pause.

"Unknown," Ongondo said. "We are on the move."

"Copy that," Parson said. "World Relief Airlift out."

Just as Parson released his talk switch, he heard the popping and groaning of aluminum. The whole airplane shuddered as the jack pistons extended. Geedi moved away from the jack on the left side and went around to check the right side of the aircraft. The DC-3 shuddered and creaked. Parson looked at the flattened left tire. It hovered about an inch off the ground. . . .

And then it scuffed back to earth when the jack sank into the dirt.

■ ■ ■

Something upset the *gaalos*, or at least the men. Hussein was watching them work on the flying machine—he gathered that they wanted to lift it up to change the tire—and things went wrong. Geedi and the one called Parson kept talking and pointing at the metal objects they had attached to the airplane. That language of theirs sounded even more unpleasant when they spoke in urgent tones.

All the while, Red Mouse kept taking pictures, and Yellow Hair stood near Hussein. Her job, apparently, was to keep an eye on him. He wished Yellow Hair spoke his language. He wanted to know what was going on, but she could not communicate with him, and Geedi was too busy to talk.

Hussein had still not decided on a course of action. No opening had yet presented itself, anyway. He considered the possibilities. Yes, he knew some heroic Muslim brothers had flown airplanes into buildings in America. However, Hussein had no idea how to drive a car, let alone fly an airplane. If he had possessed more knowledge, he might have come up with a way to use this airplane to strike a blow for Allah, to use it as a weapon against infidels. But he had mixed feelings about these particular infidels. And Geedi—he was not even an infidel, but a Muslim of a different sort. Was there more to the faith than the older al-Shabaab men had told him? Hussein wanted glory, yes, as any good soldier of God. But he also wanted *knowledge.* Could this airplane take him to a place where he might gain knowledge, learn of new things?

Perhaps. Except right now it looked like this flying machine was taking no one anywhere.

I need a sign, Hussein thought. Allah, please give me a sign.

Geedi and the other men began searching the ground as if they had lost something. Hussein wondered what they could possibly be looking for, and curiosity so overcame him that he ventured to ask.

"Stones," Geedi answered. "Big, flat stones."

"What for, in the name of heaven?" Hussein asked.

"To put under the jacks."

After several minutes of searching, Geedi and the one called Parson found a couple rocks that seemed to meet their need. The one called Shartee found a wooden ammunition crate. Shartee climbed inside the flying machine and came out with a strange-looking ax. With the ax, using mainly his good arm, he whacked at the crate until he reduced it to boards.

Geedi and Parson removed the metal things—jacks, they were called—from the airplane. That task involved a lot of struggling and grunting and sweating. It reminded Hussein of when he had seen men try to start a car by pushing it. Then the fliers put the stones and boards under the jacks, and they connected the jacks to the airplane again. While they worked, the men coughed from time to time. Clearly the smoke had bothered them, too. But Hussein's lungs now felt strong and clear.

Once more, Geedi began the slow process of lifting up the flying machine. The machine made squeaking and popping noises as the jacks pushed on it.

The stones and boards must have done whatever the *gaalos* wanted them to do, because suddenly the men looked happy. Especially the one called Parson—and in Hussein's brief experience, that man *never* looked happy. Parson patted Geedi on the back and pointed to the flat tire, which had risen several inches off the ground.

Then the sound of explosions cut short the *gaalos'* celebration.

38.

The smoke-shrouded landscape yielded few clues about the source of the blasts. To Parson, they sounded like grenades, way the hell too close. The clatter of rifle fire followed. He thought he saw figures running through the smoke a few hundred yards to the west, but he couldn't be sure.

Gold gave Hussein a gentle push to get him to lie down. He kept trying to look around, heedless of the danger from shrapnel and stray bullets. Carolyn Stewart lay prone, still recording video. She panned the scene, then aimed her lens at Geedi, who cranked at bolts to remove the flattened tire. His elbows pumped as he worked the wrench as quickly as he could.

Parson wished he could order everybody aboard, sit down in the cockpit, and begin running checklists. That way, as soon as Geedi brought the jacks down, he could start engines and get moving. But the DC-3, jacked on uneven ground, was unsteady to begin with. Adding weight and moving around inside would invite disaster. So Parson tried to think of something his crew could do outside the plane to prepare for departure.

"Frenchie," he called, "can you do a walkaround while I pull the props through?"

"*Bien sûr,*" Chartier said.

Chartier slung the RPK over his shoulder, then began a preflight inspection on the DC-3. While the Frenchman examined the aircraft, Parson took hold of a blade on the right engine's Hamilton Standard propeller. He pulled the blade down until he could reach the next of the three blades, then grabbed another blade and pulled some more. He worked gently, mindful that the aircraft stood on spindly jacks, and he felt no unusual resistance that would indicate a hydraulic lock in the cylinders. When he finished with the right prop, he moved to the left side and repeated the effort. No lock there, either. So far, so good.

When Chartier finished his walkaround, he reported no damage to the flight controls. But he said he found a couple bullet holes in the left wing—and the bullets might have pierced a main fuel tank.

"Geedi," Parson said, "what do you think about these holes? Are we gonna lose fuel through them when the plane rolls into a bank?"

The aircraft might have already lost fuel through those holes, but Parson could do nothing about that. Right now he just wanted to conserve what little fuel he had left.

"I don't know, sir, but I'll plug them anyway."

"You got plugs?"

"Yes, sir."

"Good man."

In the Air Force, crews carried hostile environment kits that included wooden plugs for sealing bullet holes. A mechanic or flight engineer could jam a plug into a hole and saw off the excess. If the plug got wet with fuel, it expanded to seal tighter. Geedi had carried over that knowledge to his civilian job.

As Parson looked over the DC-3, a warning from Gold reminded him he had worse problems than fuel leaks.

"Michael," Gold said, "the fire's getting closer."

Parson stepped out from under the wing and looked to where Gold was pointing. Sure enough, the fire had jumped the dry creek bed and now advanced toward the landing field. The grass blackened and curled under orange feathers of flame.

"Geedi," Parson said, "we're running out of time."

■ ■ ■

Hussein began to worry. The smell of smoke grew stronger. Not nearly as strong as when the infidels carried him across the field, but strong enough to remind him with every breath that the fire was advancing. What if these *gaalos* could not make their airplane go? He didn't think the infidels would leave him to burn, but too many different things could go wrong. If worse came to worst, Hussein could move on his wounded foot; he'd already proven that to himself. But he doubted he could move quickly enough to outrun a racing wildfire. He wasn't fast like a cheetah anymore.

The infidels began to chatter as if something excited them. Their attention focused on Geedi, who had freed the bad tire from the grounded machine. Geedi said something to Yellow Hair, who adjusted the AK-47's sling to place it higher on her shoulder. The woman took a tool from Geedi and put it inside the airplane. Hussein followed her every movement.

For a moment, he thought she might put down the AK-47. If she'd done that, he could have reached the weapon in four or five steps. What if such an opportunity presented itself? Yellow Hair had a pistol, too, stuck under her belt. She might try to shoot him with the pistol, but perhaps she would miss. What would Allah have him do?

The one called Parson squatted down beside Geedi, and together they wrestled the bad tire out of the way. As they rolled the tire, Hussein noted the damage done to it by his grenade. The punctures and cuts in the rubber made him think of the flayed hide of a dead camel.

Parson and Geedi let the flattened tire fall over on the ground a short distance from the airplane. They moved to the new tire, raised it with much grunting and groaning, and rolled it into place underneath the wing. Parson stood back, and all the infidels watched Geedi work.

Everything seemed to depend on the Somali-turned-American. These *gaalos*, for all their knowledge and money and power, would very soon die of fire or gunshot without Geedi—who had much in common with Hussein. The thought gave Hussein even more satisfaction than the sight of what he had done to the infidels' tire.

Geedi reached for another of his tools.

Gunfire pounded from inside the smoke.

A black-clad figure, a brother from al-Shabaab, emerged from the gray cloud. The man pivoted to fire at something off to his side; Hussein could not see the target. The brass from three expended rounds flipped from the chamber of the brother's weapon. Then the man leveled his weapon at the airplane.

M ichael, look out!" Gold shouted. Taken by surprise, with the AK slung over her shoulder, she had quicker access to the Beretta in her waistband. In one fluid motion, she brought up the pistol and began firing.

Parson turned from the tire and strut to see a gunman shooting at the DC-3. Two rounds popped into the fuselage just at the wing root.

Chartier, standing with the RPK at the nose of the aircraft, fell to his knees. A gut-turn of fear twisted through Parson's stomach; had Frenchie been shot?

Frenchie brought the RPK to his shoulder. He had dropped, Parson realized, so he could see underneath the wing.

The RPK spat three rounds. The bolt locked open. Empty.

Forty yards from the airplane, the attacker fell and lay still. Chartier tossed away the long gun and drew his revolver. Gold held the Beretta with both hands.

"Geedi, you've done the best anybody could do," Parson said, "but we might have to run for it."

The flight mechanic never took his eyes off the wheel-and-tire assembly. He jammed a socket onto a socket wrench and spun the ratchet.

"Just a few more seconds, sir. I've almost got it."

More gunfire popped and sputtered. This time Parson could not see a gunman, but another round pinged into the aluminum hull.

Quick ratcheting sounds came from Geedi's wrench. He yanked the socket off a bolt and shouted, "Done! Let's get this thing off the jacks. Sir, can you help me?"

"Tell me what to do," Parson said.

"This isn't by the book, but we're going to bleed the pressure off these jacks all at once. You see this release valve?"

Geedi pointed to a tiny valve at the base of the jack.

"Yeah."

"Sir, you go to the jack on the other side. When I count down to one, turn the valve handle counterclockwise."

"You got it."

Parson scrabbled under the airplane and found the release valve on the right-side jack. He placed his hand on the valve's little T-handle.

"All right, sir," Geedi shouted. "Three, two, one."

Parson and Geedi twisted the valves simultaneously. Hydraulic fluid hissed through the hoses, and the airplane creaked and popped as it settled. Geedi ripped the chain away from the left strut. The steel links clanked into loops at his feet. Geedi turned his attention to disconnecting the jacks.

"When you get the jacks unbolted, just pull them out of the way and leave them," Parson said.

"Works for me," Geedi said.

More shots hammered nearby. Chartier's pistol answered. After the boom from the magnum came three quick shots from Gold firing the Beretta.

"Michael, here they come!" Gold called.

Hussein saw men emerge out of the smoke from all directions. Some wore the green camouflage of AMISOM; others, the black head-scarves of al-Shabaab. Yellow Hair fired the automatic pistol until it cked open and empty, while the one called Shartee thundered with his big revolver. Yellow Hair stuck the pistol in her waistband and swung Hussein's AK-47 off her shoulder.

Some of the men fired at one another. Two or three on both sides fell, closer to Hussein than the length of a soccer field. Hussein could not tell if any of the al-Shabaab brothers were shooting at the airplane on purpose. But some of their bullets, aimed or stray, smacked into its silver body.

Geedi ignored the firefight. He concentrated on nothing other than getting the jacks unhooked. The effort seemed to involve the spinning of many nuts and bolts. Yellow Hair fired the AK at an al-Shabaab fighter who disappeared back into the smoky trees to the west.

The rest of the brothers vanished, though the firefight did not end. Shooting continued, only a little farther from the airplane. The noise rose and fell as the battle ebbed and flowed in and out of the open field. Geedi pulled the jack out from under the left wing, then went to the jack under the right wing. There was much talking, pointing, and shouting among the infidels, as Parson jumped into the airplane. Through the plane's window, Hussein saw him sit down in the driver's seat. A few seconds later, humming noises came from the airplane, perhaps because Parson was turning things on. Shartee climbed aboard and sat down next to Parson in the other front seat.

Geedi dragged the jack out from under the right wing. He made no effort to salvage the jacks; he just left them in the weeds to the side of the flying machine. He took what looked like wooden pegs from a cloth bag, and he jammed the pegs into some of the bullet holes in the wings. Hussein could not imagine why Geedi would take the time to do such a thing now.

Hussein gave up thoughts of looking for an opening, waiting for a chance to do something. Things were happening too fast; events ran beyond his control. He could barely comprehend what was happening, let alone take action to control it.

"It is time to go, little brother," Geedi said. Yellow Hair handed Geedi the AK-47, then ran to get the bag of medicine.

Hussein's heart pounded as if it might burst through his breastbone. Should he let them take him with them, or run to his al-Shabaab brothers? He raised himself by his arms, prepared to move in one direction or another.

More gunfire came from behind the screen of smoke. More bullets pinged into the flying machine.

A voice called to him. A voice strangely familiar.

"Strike them, Hussein! Strike them, you fool!"

Abdullahi emerged from the smoke and fire. Geedi began to shoulder the AK. Abdullahi fired a burst.

Geedi went down.

Hussein scrambled over to the mechanic. Stumbling on his injured foot amounted to torture, but he ignored the pain. He saw no wounds to Geedi's head or chest. But bullets had struck both legs. Blood was already spreading under Geedi's knees and thighs.

"Get on the airplane, little brother," Geedi whispered through clenched teeth.

Hussein had no intention of getting on the airplane. Not at this moment.

He grabbed his AK-47, ripped it from Geedi's hands. Yanked the weapon to clear the sling from around Geedi's arm.

"This is mine," Hussein said.

Yellow Hair ran toward him, but not fast enough to stop him. Hussein was a hunter, a soldier of God. Now he felt no pain.

On his knees beside Geedi, Hussein clicked the rifle to full automatic. Brought the weapon to his shoulder. Closed his left eye. Lined up the front and rear sights—and emptied the last rounds into Abdullahi.

39.

In the cockpit of the DC-3, the stub of the right throttle scratched Parson's hand as he nudged it out of the idle position. The firefight raged nearby, and he ignored the thud and jar of grenades while he flicked on the battery switch and the right boost pump. Sweat dripped off the end of his nose and spattered on the control yoke.

Everybody should have boarded by now, but Parson heard commotion outside the airplane. He looked over at Chartier, sitting in the copilot seat.

"Frenchie," Parson said, "find out what the hell's going on."

"D'accord."

Chartier climbed out of the cockpit. Two seconds later, Parson heard him shout, "Geedi's been shot!"

Parson turned in his seat. "How bad?"

Looking aft into the cargo compartment, Parson saw Chartier in the door, using his good arm to grab Geedi by the collar. Pain contorted the flight mechanic's face. Geedi pressed his lips together tightly and squeezed his eyes shut as the Frenchman and Gold lifted him aboard. Blood stained his flight suit from the waist down.

"He's shot in the legs," Chartier called.

"Have we still got the medical ruck?" Parson asked.

"Yeah," Gold answered. She held Geedi underneath the knees and helped Chartier place him on the cargo compartment floor. Gold turned toward the door and caught the medical bag, apparently thrown from outside by Carolyn Stewart.

"Frenchie," Parson called, "make sure everybody's on board and shut the door. Stay back there and help stop that bleeding. I can start this beast by myself."

"Absolument."

Come on, baby, Parson thought. Come on, come on, come on, crank for me. He wanted to start both engines at once, like he'd done before. But with the batteries sitting unused and uncharged for days, he didn't trust them to have enough juice.

He flipped the right engine's mags to the BOTH position, shoved the mixture to AUTO RICH, and hit the starter.

Nothing.

"Don't pick now to be a bitch," Parson muttered. He released the starter switch, pressed it again.

Still nothing. The right prop did not budge. Another grenade exploded outside, this time close enough to fling shrapnel against the side of the airplane.

"Shit," Parson cried. He pounded the top of the main panel with his fist—and that gave him an idea. A grizzled crew chief had once told him that when an engine doesn't start, sometimes it's just corroded contacts in a starter switch. Especially if the switch is old.

The fix was simple: Air Force guys called it repair by "malletizing." Kick it. Shove it. Swat it with a mallet. Scare those electrons into going where they should.

Parson grabbed the switch between his thumb and forefinger. He cycled it rapidly between the on and off positions, then smacked the switch assembly with the heel of his hand. Pressed the switch with his thumb.

The right prop rotated, and the right engine's cylinders began to fire and cough. Wreathed in exhaust smoke, the Pratt sputtered to life. The prop blades whirred into a translucent disc. Parson shook his hand, wrist still stinging.

He watched the oil pressure come up, and he let the engine idle at six hundred RPM. Glanced back to see Stewart and Chartier lifting Hussein on board. Hussein chattered in Somali, and Geedi said something back. Geedi's blood spilled across the metal floor. Gold appeared to be holding pressure on one of Geedi's wounds with one hand and digging into the medical ruck with the other.

In a corner of Parson's consciousness, dread tried to invade his thoughts. He had seen men bleed to death from leg wounds: Sever the femoral artery and you got a serious problem. He forced himself into a temporary and artificial callousness, as if a check valve held back the worry. Gold would take care of Geedi; the best thing Parson could do was to get this pig in the air.

He repeated the start procedure for the left engine: boost pump, mixture, mags, starter. The left engine barked as soon as Parson hit the starter switch. The propeller spun up, and the Pratt hummed at idle.

In quick succession, Parson flipped on the generators, the inverters, and the avionics master switch. The radios hummed to life, but right now he had no intention of talking to anyone. He hadn't even bothered to put on his headset.

Parson twisted in his seat and looked aft. Gold, Chartier, and Stewart kneeled beside Geedi. Hussein sat on the cargo compartment floor, holding the opened medical ruck. Gold was wrapping a pressure bandage over a compress on Geedi's left leg. A bandage already covered the wound on his right leg.

"Hey, guys," Parson shouted over the engine noise, "hang on, 'cause we're going! How's it looking back there?"

"I got it," Gold called.

"All right, Frenchie," Parson yelled. "I'm gonna start taxiing. Come up here and make sure I haven't missed anything."

Chartier stood and ran forward. Ducked into the cockpit and slumped into the right seat. Winced in pain from his arm wound. Geedi's blood slicked his hands. He wiped his palms on the tops of his thighs before he touched anything. The Frenchman grabbed a checklist and put on his headset, and Parson donned his as well.

Parson held the yoke back to keep the tail down, and he shoved up the stubs of the throttles. The airplane began to roll. He placed his feet on the rudder pedals, ready to apply brakes if necessary. Behind him, the ancient hydraulic pressure regulator groaned as fluid coursed through it. Parson leaned forward in his seat and scanned outside.

Smoke drifted across the landing field, obscuring his view. The fire had reached the acacia trees at the far edge of the field, and flames leapt through the branches. Cinders flew with the breeze, and Parson knew the cinders would spread the wildfire even farther.

From the flow of smoke and cinders, he gauged the wind direction as he taxied. Tried to position the airplane to take off into the wind, which would shorten the takeoff roll. Parson wanted every advantage he could find. Getting off the ground two yards earlier could make the difference between clearing the burning trees or not.

"Gimme one notch of flaps for a short-field takeoff," Parson said. "How are we looking on that checklist?"

Chartier reached down and set the flap handle, then spun the trim tabs to neutral and shoved the prop controls to full low pitch. Touched the fuel selectors to double-check they were set to the main tanks. Before the Frenchman could say anything, two dark figures appeared among the smoke and blowing ash, directly in front of the airplane. Both held weapons, and both of them fired.

Two white holes exploded in the windscreen. Shards of glass pricked Parson's face. He felt thumps as other rounds slammed into the nose of the aircraft.

In that instant, Parson could do nothing. He could not move the DC-3 fast enough to keep those assholes from riddling the cockpit. He expected a burst on full auto to blast open the windscreen and tear him and Chartier apart.

However, a burst of fire came not from the front, but from the left side of the plane, practically under the wing. The gunmen in front of the aircraft crumpled. Parson turned to see Lieutenant Colonel Ongondo and two AMISOM soldiers firing into the smoke. Ongondo lifted his hand in greeting, then swept his arm forward as if to say, "Go!"

Parson held the brakes, shoved the throttles forward. The big radials screamed at full power, and the entire aircraft vibrated with pent-up energy. Chartier scanned the instruments.

"Power's good," the Frenchman said.

Parson released the brakes, and the DC-3 began to roll. The bodies of the two al-Shabaab triggermen passed under the nose and between the main wheels. Hard jolt when the tailwheel ran over the bodies. For an instant, billowing smoke dropped visibility to zero, but Parson let the airplane accelerate. The plane emerged from the thickest smoke, and through hazy, thinner smoke, Parson saw the burning trees getting bigger and bigger.

The airspeed needle came alive, and Chartier began calling the numbers.

"Thirty," Chartier said.

Parson held the throttle stubs to keep them from edging backward. Up ahead, a man ran to get out of the way of the airplane. Parson could not tell if the man was AMISOM or enemy.

"Fifty," Chartier said.

The DC-3 bucked and bounced over uneven ground.

Parson pushed forward on the yoke, and he let the tail rise off the ground. Now the plane felt like it was flying more than rolling.

"Seventy," Chartier said.

The acceleration felt a little sluggish. No doubt the rough ground made for a lousy takeoff surface. Parson hoped to get above ninety miles per hour before lifting off.

"Eighty," Chartier called.

The acacias, now fully wrapped in flame, rushed at Parson. Embers fell from the sky. This must be what it looks like, he thought, to make a short-field takeoff from hell.

Parson had only seconds to gather speed, to make enough air—filled with smoke and cinders—rush over the wings to generate lift. He wanted badly to hear Frenchie say "Ninety."

But he ran out of ground and time.

With no other option than to plow headlong into the flaming trees, Parson pulled back on the yoke.

"Fly for me, baby," he whispered. "Let's go, let's go, let's go."

Barely above a stall, the DC-3 staggered into the air. The burning terrain dropped away. Sparks and ash rising from the acacias showered the aircraft as it cleared the fire. Smoke and burning debris rushed through the bullet holes in the windscreen.

A tiny ember scorched Parson's hand, then flamed out and went dark. He let the airplane accelerate for a few seconds, then pitched for best angle of climb. Parson held the throttles at full power, engines straining for every foot of altitude. Bullets could still reach him here.

None did. Below, men ran among the smoke and fired at one another, but not up. The airplane climbed until the wildfire appeared as a gray quilt spread across a parched landscape. Parson turned onto a southerly heading, and the Indian Ocean rolled into view to his left, a glowing, brilliant blue.

"Hah-hah," Chartier shouted, "you did it, *mon colonel.*"

In the back, Gold and Stewart hooted and cheered.

"Gear up, Frenchie," Parson said.

Parson eased the power back to thirty-five inches of manifold pressure. Wiped sweat from his eyes with the sleeve of his flight suit. Glanced at the GPS screen to confirm what he already knew: The Kenyan border was already passing under his wings.

Though Hussein had never flown before, he made no effort to look out a window. He kept his eyes on Geedi, who lay on the metal floor, grasping the hand of Yellow Hair. Red Mouse took pictures with her camera, while tears streamed down her face.

Geedi wore the face of a man in great pain. Hussein had seen this face many times. He had caused it many times.

"You must not die, big brother," Hussein said. "You must not die."

Geedi took in a long breath. "I will die someday, Hussein," he said. "But I do not think it will be today."

"Why do you think this?"

"Sergeant Major Gold says the bullets did not hit my arteries. But one broke a bone."

"Who says this?"

Geedi cut his eyes at the woman holding his hand.

"You mean Yellow Hair," Hussein said.

"Yes, the woman with the yellow hair is Sergeant Major Sophia Gold."

"That is a hard name to say."

"You will learn to say other English words."

Hussein looked at Yellow Hair. How odd to respect a female—yet respect was exactly what he felt for this woman with the unpronounceable name. She had kept his friend from bleeding to death. Hussein turned and looked to the front of the airplane. There he saw the one called Parson and the one called Shartee working at the strange controls. Taking him into the unknown, into a new life. Hussein breathed in and out for a long while, trying to comprehend all that had happened—and all that he had done—in the last several minutes.

"Peace be upon you, big brother," Hussein said. "Peace be upon all of you."

Parson leveled off at what looked like about five thousand five hundred feet, though without an altimeter he couldn't be sure. The altimeter on Chartier's side wasn't working, either. Parson nudged the elevator tab to trim the pressure he was holding on the yoke, then turned toward Chartier.

"Let me get this straight," Parson said, "You're telling me Hussein shot a bad guy?"

"Oui, c'est ça."

Parson rested his hand across the prop and mixture levers, glanced back into the cargo compartment.

"Well, that's the damnedest thing I've ever heard," he said. "Little son of a bitch tries to kill us, and then he helps save us."

"I know," Chartier said. "But in a way, it is not surprising."

"Surprises the hell out of me."

"Think about it. He is a teenager. If a teenager has no parents, against whom will he rebel? Anybody telling him what to do. Al-Shabaab has been telling him what to do. And maybe he did not like what they told him to do."

Parson looked back at Hussein again. There was logic to what Frenchie said, but Parson figured things were a hell of a lot more complicated than that. God only knew what that boy had seen and done.

"Well, whatever. I'm just glad he didn't shoot one of us."

"He had a weapon and he made his choice."

"Yeah, I guess he did."

A quick scan of the fuel gauges reminded Parson he was flying on fumes. According to the airplane's panel-mounted GPS, the Kiunga airfield should be in sight off his eleven o'clock.

"Do you see the field, Frenchie?"

Chartier adjusted his sunglasses and leaned forward, peering through the windscreen.

"Ah, I think I have it. *Bon.*"

The Frenchman pointed to what looked like a long scratch in the dirt, maybe five miles out. Just as Parson spotted the airstrip, Gold appeared in the cockpit entrance and put a hand on his shoulder. Parson looked up at her and pulled his headset's boom mike away from his lips, so he could talk to her off interphone. Something about the light in her eyes told him what he most wanted to know: Geedi would make it.

"How's everybody doing back there?" he asked.

"As well as can be expected," Gold said. She raised her voice over the wind blast through the bullet holes. "We have the bleeding under control. Geedi's conscious, but he's in a lot of pain."

"Shit, I hate to hear that. We'll get him to a hospital in Kenya."

Gold pointed to the holes in the windscreen. "What happened here? Looks like our getaway was closer than I realized."

"You're damn right it was," Parson said. "There would have been a lot more holes than that, and a lot of holes in Frenchie and me, too, if Ongondo hadn't shown up."

"You saw Lieutenant Colonel Ongondo?" Gold asked.

"Only for a second. Couple of assholes opened up on us, and *WHAM*, Ongondo and his boys cut 'em down. Cleared a path for us."

Gold's eyes brimmed. A slight jolt of turbulence dislodged a droplet and sent it sliding down her cheek. "You know," she said, "Hussein cleared a path for us, too. If not for him, the terrorists would have finished off Geedi and maybe me, too."

"I heard," Parson said.

"Yes, and can you guess what he said to Geedi just now?"

Parson shook his head, raised his eyebrows.

"He said 'peace be upon you,'" Gold said. "That's not just 'have a nice day.' To a Muslim, that means something."

Parson looked out at the coastline, white breakers stretching to the horizon. "Frenchie," he said, "Can you take the plane for a minute?"

"Oui," Chartier said. "My aircraft." Chartier placed his hands on the right yoke.

Parson reached down to his left boot and unfastened the sheath for his boot knife. Passed the sheathed blade to Gold.

"Hussein was admiring my knife the other day," Parson said. "Give it to him."

"Michael?" Gold said. "Didn't your dad give you this?"

"Yeah," Parson said, "he did, when I enrolled in ROTC. He said it was to mark the day when I committed to help fight the good fight. Tell Hussein he's getting it now, for the same reason."

If Hussein kept Sophia alive, Parson considered, he deserves a hell of a lot more than a fancy knife. I could have just lost her. What if she'd been—?

The thought was more than Parson could handle right now, so he pulled his boom mike back into place and turned his attention to the instruments. Gold wiped her eyes, squeezed his shoulder, then disappeared into the cargo compartment.

"I got the airplane, Frenchie," Parson said. "Let's get this pig on the ground. Before Landing checklist."

Chartier picked up the checklist. He moved the cowl flaps into the trail position and placed his hand on the gear lever, waiting for Parson's call to lower the wheels. Parson hooked his fingers over the stubs of the throttles, and he eased the power back to start a gentle descent.

Carolyn Stewart appeared in the cockpit entrance where Gold had stood. She aimed her video camera out the windscreen. Parson decided to let her shoot all the way to touchdown; he'd just warn her to hold on tight with one hand. Not exactly by the book, but she'd get a good closing scene for her documentary.

"When I get this thing in the theaters," Stewart said, "I'll invite you guys to the premiere."

For just a moment, Parson imagined himself on the red carpet in his dress uniform with Gold on his arm, wearing that blue gown he liked. Then he scanned his panel again. The vertical speed indicator still worked, and it showed a descent of five hundred feet per minute through nice smooth air. The wind rushing through the holes in the glass ruffled Parson's sleeve and felt good on his face. As he set up his approach, he wondered about the future of his young Somali passenger. He counted it a minor miracle that the boy had lived long enough to get a second chance.

Cats and paratroopers had nine lives, Parson had always believed. Maybe the same held true for Hussein. How many of his nine lives had Hussein already used up? For that matter, how many lives had he taken? And how many lives had he just saved? Geedi's, certainly. Probably Gold's. Maybe everybody's. Parson did not long ponder Hussein's sins and good deeds. For whatever reason, a higher command had decided to give the boy a second chance.

I just provided the airlift support, Parson thought.

THE STORY BEHIND *THE HUNTERS*

In the late '90s, some of my squadron mates approached me with a civilian job opportunity. A charitable group wanted qualified C-130 flight crews. The organization planned to use donations to buy a small fleet of C-130 cargo planes and fly relief missions all over the world.

The group liked my résumé enough to ask me to come in for an interview . . . and the project never went beyond that stage. Perhaps the organization could not raise enough money to buy an airplane, or maybe there were other complications. For one reason or another, the good intentions never got off the ground, literally or figuratively.

But I've always thought: *That was a really cool idea. What could have made it work?*

What if they'd settled for a less expensive, less sophisticated airplane? What if they'd recruited unpaid volunteers to fly part-time? Could they have pulled it off with a rattletrap old DC-3?

In *The Hunters*, I send Parson and crew on that flight of imagination, bringing them in for a landing in Somalia. Their fates become intertwined with that of Hussein, a teenage al-Shabaab gunman who comes to face a split-second decision that will set the course for the rest of his life.

The reader has every right to ask: How likely a story is Hussein's?

Certainly, Hussein's decision would not be common for someone in his circumstances; once people become radicalized, it's hard to bring them back. But though Hussein is burdened by poverty, illiteracy, and the loss of his parents, he's blessed with natural intelligence. He thinks for himself.

Occasionally, news reports highlight the journey of a defector from a terrorist group such as ISIS. A common pattern often emerges: A young person seeks escape from bad circumstances and winds up with something even worse. But unlike most of his comrades in terror, he has the sense to question the group's propaganda, and finds himself repelled by pointless brutality.

In Hussein's case, an injury forces him to sit, listen, and observe instead of striking out. What he learns gives his intellect something to work with; he realizes he doesn't know what he doesn't know. He watches a crew of current and former military personnel work in a mutually supportive way, and his mind opens enough to see new possibilities for himself.

Parson's memories of military missions in Somalia are informed by real-world events. My own missions have often taken me to Djibouti, next door to Somalia in the Horn of Africa, and Djibouti provides the setting for some early scenes in *The Hunters*.

Two of those Djibouti missions stand out in my memory.

One day in 2003, my crewmates and I delivered cargo to the air base in Djibouti, then we departed for a return leg to our temporary home base in the Middle East. We lifted off in our C-130, headed out over the Gulf of Aden, and brought up the landing gear. At that moment, the biggest damned seagull in the world appeared in the windscreen.

I pointed and uttered one syllable: "Bird!"

The copilot ducked.

I don't know the seagull's airspeed, but ours was about one hundred and fifty knots. The gull smacked the glass with such force that it rattled the cockpit. The bird splattered all over the cockpit windows. Fortunately for us, the unfortunate gull hit a strong place on the windscreen near a metal post where two sections of glass came together. Somehow the windscreen remained intact, though smeared with blood and viscera.

Normally, when you hit a bird, you land immediately and inspect for damage. However, intel and tactics briefers had warned us of a terrorist threat in the area. Returning to Djibouti would have given the bad guys another chance to take a shot at us, so we flew on to home base. By the time we reached base, the remains of that bird had dried and frozen all over the glass. As we parked the aircraft, we saw the crew chief staring at the mess, arms folded, shaking his head as if to ask: *What have you idiots done to my airplane?* He and his team would be the ones to clean and inspect the plane before it could fly again.

On another trip to Djibouti, we found ourselves in a bit of a scramble. We needed to offload cargo and refuel quickly, then clear the limited ramp space for other aircraft.

Standard refuel procedures called for the installation of a locking pin to keep the nose gear from collapsing on the ground. Over the years, many a C-130 flight engineer had forgotten to remove the pin after refueling—which meant that when the C-130 got airborne, the nose gear wouldn't retract. When that happened, the crew had no choice but to return for landing, so the embarrassed engineer could remove the pin.

To guard against that mistake, I made a habit of placing the pin in a slot on the back of the copilot's seat. I would then hang my helmet bag on the pin. If I saw my helmet bag sitting on the floor instead of hanging from the back of the copilot's seat, I knew I had not removed the nose pin.

You really didn't want to forget the nose pin in Djibouti and have to turn back and land, for the same reason we didn't want to come back after the bird strike: unpleasant characters with AKs and shoulder-launched missiles.

However, on this busy day at Camp Lemonnier, with C-130s zooming in and out, helicopters clattering overhead, and sweat soaking my flight suit, I did something I had never done in thousands of hours of flying: As I strapped in, I failed to glance at the back of the copilot's seat to confirm that my helmet bag was hanging on the nose pin.

We began running the engine start checklist. Purely as a courtesy, not required by any regulation, my good friend Roland Shambaugh called on interphone: "Engineer, loadmaster. You got the nose pin?"

"Got it, load, but thanks—" I looked to my right. My helmet bag was on the floor.

"Uh, I mean thanks so much for asking, Shammy," I continued. "Ah, can you bring me that damned pin?"

"No problem, Tommy."

Sharp crew members look after one another, and that's what Hussein observes as he watches Parson, Gold, Chartier, and Geedi interact. He sees another way of living and working. In the final battle scene, he makes a split-second decision that sends his life in a new direction.

Of course, very few young terrorist recruits have the insight, courage, and opportunity to make such a choice. But I'd like to think Hussein represents the spark of good within humanity that allows for hope in a bloody and violent world.

ACKNOWLEDGMENTS

My wife, Kristen, loves to tell this story:

For many years, as I wrote short stories and worked to improve my craft, she'd read the manuscripts and make suggestions—to no avail. "You need to rewrite this scene so I can see it better," she might say. Or, "That dialogue doesn't work; this isn't how that character would talk."

I usually blew off her critique. I was the professional journalist and writer; I'd spent a decade with the Associated Press. She had a background in economics and math: What did *she* know about writing?

But Kristen had read books all her life. By osmosis, she had become a good editor. And when I began to write a nonfiction book about my Air National Guard unit, I knew I needed her critical eye. Because I was so close to the subject matter, I couldn't always judge what needed more explanation. Didn't everybody know that to fly an ILS you followed the CDI down to DH and looked for the MALSR?

While completing that book, *The Speed of Heat*, I accepted nearly all of Kristen's edits. The book got published to great reviews, so I also followed her suggestions when writing my first novel, *The Mullah's Storm*. Then came the day when my terrific literary agent, Michael Carlisle, called to say Putnam editor-in-chief Neil Nyren wanted to publish *The Mullah's Storm*.

Kristen's first reaction: "See what happens when you listen to me?"

I like that story because it illustrates how I couldn't do this by myself. This novel comes to you thanks to lots of support from Kristen, Michael, Neil, and many other friends and colleagues. One of my old college professors, Richard Elam, still uses his red pen on my manuscripts. A former commander, retired Brigadier General Wayne "Speedy" Lloyd, provides valuable advice on technical matters. Another squadron mate, retired Lieutenant Colonel Joe Myers, has been a longtime literary confidant.

The commander of my American Legion post, Navy veteran Ken Dalecki, turned a practiced eye to this novel. Ken has been a writer and editor for *The Kiplinger Washington Editors* and *Congressional Quarterly*, among other publishers. Novelist and editor Barbara Esstman has served as a great coach and adviser ever since I took one of her writing workshops years ago, and she critiqued this book as well.

Fellow Tar Heels Jodie Tighe and Liz Lee—along with Liz's French tutor, Agathe Dupré—kept me straight on French expressions as I wrote the dialogue for Captain Chartier. *Merci beaucoup* to Jodie, Liz, and Agathe. Millie Hast, a thriller writer in her own right, read an early draft and offered helpful suggestions. Bobby Siegfried provided help with proofreading. Author and professor John Casey helped me launch this new career when we met at the Sewanee Writers' Conference back in 2008.

My friends at Tony Scotti's Vehicle Dynamics Institute provide valuable resources when it comes to research. Their courses on protective/evasive driving and other security topics teach what counts when the rubber meets the road—literally.

Ultimately, the fine folks at Putnam and Berkley make it all possible. It's always a pleasure to work with Neil Nyren, as well as Putnam president Ivan Held and Berkley executive editor Thomas Colgan. I also owe a word of thanks to Alexis Welby, Michael Barson, Ashley Hewlett, Sara Minnich, Kate Stark, Chris Nelson, Alexis Sattler, and everyone at Penguin Random House.